The
Cthulhu
Heresy
and Other
Lovecraftian Sins

The Cthulhu Heresy
and Other Lovecraftian Sins

Peter Rawlik

WEIRD HOUSE

ISBN: 978-1-957121-78-9

"The Defense of Li Zhou" and "The Twilight of Stronti"
© 2024 by Peter Rawlik.
All other stories previously published as detailed on page 275.

Text © 2024 by Peter Rawlik
Cover Artwork © 2024 by Dan Sauer

Interior and cover design by César Puch

Edited by Curtis M. Lawson

Editor and Publisher, Joe Morey

Weird House Press
Central Point, OR 97502
www.weirdhousepress.com

Table Of Contents

The Cthulhu Heresy
Here be Monsters

The doctor tells me that I was found unconscious, floating amongst wreckage in the South Pacific near 47° 9' S and 126° 43' W. He says the wreckage has been positively identified as belonging to the *Dionysus*, and that all others, the nineteen other men that made up the rest of the crew are lost, that I alone have survived, and I must tell the tale. I have no reason to doubt him. I saw them die, all of them, but they did not die when the ship went down, they were dead before that, killed as much by their misplaced faith as by the thing that rose up out of the sea to shatter the *Dionysus* and scatter her across the sea.

May the Blessed Mother have mercy on them.

For the record, you may call me Dorian Morgan, not my real name but the one that is on all of my identification. Ostensibly, I am twenty-six years old, a graduate of Arkham College where I majored in Oceanography. For my Masters degree at Miskatonic, I studied the influence of various sampling techniques on water quality nutrient analysis. I am an employee of the Rowley Oceanographic Center and assigned to the Research Vessel *Dionysus* where I worked analyzing deep-sea water samples. Officially, the *Dionysus* was studying the aftereffects of the submarine nuclear testing that had been conducted in the early Nineteen Sixties, for which we have a permit from the Department of Defense.

Unofficially, secretly, we had come to pay homage to one of our Gods and witness His rebirth.

The People, the race men call Deep Ones has dwelt on the Earth for millions of years, and in that time, we have come to worship many Gods. The oldest of us still pay homage to our progenitors, who have long since passed from the world, they still live, dreaming what cool inhuman dreams their cool inhuman intelligences allow; that which is not dead can lie eternal, and in strange eons they may return to us. Others are content to worship the first of us: Father Dagon, Mother Hydra who still dwell deep in the abyssal oceans, where time is cold and slow, and the sounds of the world are little more than whispers in the dark grey light. If one is inclined the descent can be made and an audience sought. But you do so at your own risk. The deep abyss is a barren wasteland and while our ancestors are content to take sustenance from the dead things that drift down from the surface, they are not opposed to adding a little convenient fresh meat to their diet. The hybrids of the People, those whose ancestry is mixed with either human or other sources, have come to know another God. The Sleeping God dreams and some of us can hear echoes of those dreams. And from these dreams all of us know our place in the world, and our part in His great work. The Pure People cannot hear the call, they are too pure, too close to the progenitors, and are unable to violate their genetics. We hybrids, whether land-born or sea-born have heard the call for hundreds of years, and though we are weaker than the Pure, we can do things they cannot. We can break the seals, we can wake the Sleeping God, and we can make him free.

He is not an easy God to follow. He is indifferent, he cares nothing for sacrifices or worship, and he answers few prayers. Men have called him anti-anthropomorphic, for he cares nothing for the works of man. Their cities and roads, their art and their monuments to their dead, mean nothing to our Lord of the Green Abyss. And for this we embrace him as our savior, for it is he who would wipe out our pestilent land-dwelling cousins and leave us as rulers of the world. This he would do for his faithful servants; all we had to do was be patient. God was in his tomb waiting to be reborn, when the time was right.

IA Cthulhu!

Others had tried, and once in 1925, they had come close. The city of R'lyeh had risen, and a band of the faithful aboard the *Alert* had made their way to that remote island. They had done what was necessary and the seal had been broken, the Dreaming Lord had been released. But then another ship, the *Emma* had arrived, and after a fierce battle the interlopers slaughtered the faithful. The *Emma* was scuttled, and as it sunk beneath the waves the humans took command of the *Alert*, and later used it to attack our lord himself as he climbed back into the world. By all accounts Cthulhu retreated back into His tomb, to await another chance to be reborn.

That time came sooner than expected. The ages-old prophecy had for centuries been misinterpreted. Scholars who had read the prophecy and interpreted the word "great" as meaning many, and thus when the stars were right our lord would be free, but "great" should have been interpreted as large not many. The prophecy wasn't talking about a shift in stellar alignment, but rather a change in the sun itself, such as the increased solar activity that leads to more ultraviolet radiation, energy our Lord needs to be reborn. In the last couple of centuries, the sun enters into that phase every thirty-five years or so.

And so, it was in 1962 the United States military conducted Operation Fishbowl, a series of underwater nuclear tests that were designated Bluegill, Starfish, Starfish Prime, Bluegill Prime, Bluegill Double Prime, Checkmate, Bluegill Triple Prime, Miskatonic, and Kingfish. They hid the truth, saying such tests allowed them to refine the yield of these horrific weapons, while all the time we knew they were bombarding our Lord with radiation in a vain attempt to destroy Him, all they did was prevent His rising. And their warships kept us from coming to His aid, for another thirty-five years.

We used the time wisely, we were patient, and our memories are long. It took us years to create the Rowley Oceanographic Center, to hide behind double- and triple-blind corporate partners, to fool the Government into thinking that we were a legitimate, innocent organization. It took even more work to slowly build up our reputation as a serious and respected organization, rivaling the Cousteau Society and Greenpeace. We worked hard to avoid controversy, always supplying data and facts, but leaving the interpretation up to others. We focused on environmental disasters and gained a reputation as an impartial and level-headed group capable of serious scientific work. Most of our early work was in the New England area—Boston Harbor, Cape Cod, and Kingsport Head. We worked with the Army Corps of Engineers in Guantanamo Bay, and with the South Florida Water Management District in the Gulf of Mexico. We funded research projects, created scholarships, hired the best and the brightest. But all the time our goal was to gain access to the area where we knew our Lord lay dreaming. And in time the memories of men faded, and their warships withdrew. It took time but with relatively little effort we gained access to the area under the pretense of scientific research.

We came to this place in the South Pacific where the mate Gustaf Johansen said the *Emma* went down, and the *Alert* had been commandeered to interrupt the rebirth of our God, sending Him back to fitful slumber. There was no doubt in our minds that our Lord and his city were hidden somewhere below this vast desolate portion of the ocean. All we had to do was find Him. So, we came.

What fools we were.

We came, the twenty of us, the central cabal of the conspiracy that was the Rowley Oceanographic Center, as pilgrims summoned by our God to release Him from His slumber. So, we came to this remote and forgotten part of the world in an attempt to do that which so many others had failed to do. Too many times had His followers been thwarted, and the Sleeping God had failed to awaken. Too many times had His servants been slaughtered by lone but learned men, by teams bent on destroying our people, by the governments of men who rightly feared His coming. It had been seventy-five years since the *Alert* had briefly raised the Tomb-City, only to have it sink down again, but we would succeed where they and all others after had failed. There was nothing that could be done to stop us.

We were so naïve.

Had we only looked at the history, at the dozens of attempts that had been made to raise our Lord, we might have guessed at why they had all failed, why Great Cthulhu had not come up out of the ocean and laid waste to the cities of men. In retrospect it was so obvious, but all my friends had to die for me to see the truth.

In the cold waters of the South Pacific, I clung to the side of the Dionysus, all around me were my brothers, the faithful, the chosen ones, the high priests of Cthulhu. The *Dionysus* was abandoned, adrift; we would have no need of her anymore. With my free hand I clutched a twenty-pound weight. As one, we let go of the ship and let the weight drag us down beneath the surface into the cool, bright ocean. Down we went, plummeting faster than we could swim, schools of baitfish and predatory sharks fled as we rocketed past. I looked up and saw their graceful silhouettes as they swam across the face of the sun.

Deeper, and the light faded to a murky green dusk. A reef appeared, a submerged atoll of coral atop a seamount peak. Crabs and echinoderms, mollusks and exotic fish came out to stare at us and then were lost as we sank deeper and deeper. A hundred feet down and the sunlight vanished, but still we were aware of our surroundings. As I plummeted past a fleet of infant giant squid being pursued by a pair of gulper eels, I could see the first dim lights of the upper terraces of what I knew had to be the remnants of R'lyeh.

We have dreamed of R'lyeh, molded images of it in clay and stone. Such visions are mere shadows; the truth is beyond anything we could dream. Seen from above, the city is built in vast spiraling terraces that jut out from the base like mutant fungi. Channels and tunnels honeycomb the metropolis. Shoals of wondrous, unfamiliar creatures banked effortlessly in the current, their scales and eyes glittering back the pale light of the ubiquitous bioluminescent fish that crawled and swam around the towers. Squids with wings, fish with tentacles, and monstrous crabs with two sets of claws roamed through these waters, and I instinctively gave such things a wide berth.

The current suddenly quickened, and we found ourselves inexorably drawn down past the upper tiers and deeper into the subaqueous abyss below. Further and further down we went, following the faint trace glow that leaks from the lower tiers. Age and depth had taken its toll on the once magnificent towers, for they were covered with the parasitic and antiquated growths of a million years of algae and coral and mollusks. Blind crabs monstrous with thorny points and thick spiny hairs scuttled across grey colonies of unknown corals. Ancient anthropomorphic things floated past, with remoras and other parasites writhing hideously in their wakes. Once the pinnacle of the food chain, they had long ago ceased being predatory, their once sharp and gored stained teeth had elongated into brittle hair-like sieves, each breath, each movement of gill, each vast mouthful of water was a passive act of feeding.

Then, as quickly as the creatures had come into view they were gone. The strange current that carried us had suddenly accelerated and we plunged down. We were drawn deep, for how long I cannot say. The grey lights of the upper city rapidly grew dim and faded, and my sense of time warped and then failed me. I had a sense that my companions were still with me, but I could neither see nor feel them. Blind and deaf I retreated into the dark recesses of my own mind, for this descent was so much like my earliest fragmented memories of my life in the ocean.

I am sea-born, and my mother spawned me into the wild currents of the open sea. The first thing I remember is the ocean, and the ocean was everything. It surrounded me, supported me, carried me, it brought me food, it sang to me, it showed me the world, taught me how to survive, and how to live. How long I dwelt within the sea I cannot know. I know that once I was small, and then later I was larger, and then much larger. Once I feared the fish that swam swiftly through the shoals of the warm currents, and then the fear was gone, and then later those same fish feared me. I was beautiful then, graceful and I swam in the seas without a care in the world. There were others like me, the graceful swimmers, some were alone, and others were grouped together in schools of a dozen or more. If one of us was beautiful, a dozen of us swimming together were simply magnificent. I have these memories, but they are not continuous. It may be that in my youth, in the youth of my species, of the sea-born, we exist not as wholly sentient creatures, but rather as animals with occasional flashes of consciousness. It may be better this way. Should the butterfly remember her life as an earthbound caterpillar? Should a crab dwell on the fears it had when it was nothing but helpless plankton?

Without warning my memories retreated and I became less blind, able to once more sense those about me. I knew instantly we were in danger, the great towers had widened, grown fat as we neared their bases, and the space between them had grown thin. We clustered together, a school of minnows in the dark open abyssal ocean, and I knew the others, like me longed for a return to that state of unconsciousness that had shielded our minds when we were juveniles.

The thing that came out of the darkness was titanic in size, larger than the elder deep ones who dwelt in the old cities, though it shared their general shape and characteristics. It emitted light from a series of tentacles set about its mouth. It was a cousin of ours, an ancient hybrid Deep One, though in this case it wasn't humans that had contributed to its genetic code, but rather as the tentacles revealed, this creature's ancestry drew in part from the spawn of Cthulhu himself. As we dropped down, we watched a demigod rise up out of the darkness to greet us. So intent were we on studying the magnificent creature that we failed to comprehend that the thing was angling toward us. It focused on us with a single glassy black eye, and then in an instant a great transparent membrane rolled over that eye and its mouth opened wide revealing rows of razor-sharp teeth. It tore through us like a shark through a school of bluefish. Blood filled the water, and three of our companions were gone.

Panicked, our tight school broke up and we dashed apart, seeking shelter in the crags and angles of the tower walls. Still, we were adamant in our task, and those of us who could dove deeper into the city, searching for the door to the tomb of our God. We consoled ourselves in the knowledge that soon we would be masters of the world sitting at the right hand of God. I crept along the walls fascinated by both the diversity and amount of life found at such depths. Ancient currents carried fragments of bone and cartilage into drifts that piled up against the curved and bulbous walls. Vast colonies of barnacles covered the edifices and creaked open to extended vast feathery tentacles to harvest great quantities of the slowly falling debris and curled back into their calciferous pentagonal shells. Choked with debris and colonized by the strange invertebrate forces of abyssal decay, the byways of the city had become impassable, and I floated across vast deposits of detrital snow, searching for my elusive goal.

A mile above the bottom we gathered back together, and from our vantage point those of us who were left stared in horrified wonder at the great temple that occupied the center of the vast plaza that lay before us. There was no doubt, we had reached our goal, and this was the tomb of Cthulhu, in its entire hideous alien splendor. It was a vast lozenge shaped trapezohedron that jutted up out of the plaza. The resting place of our God was a great black crystal monolith, a thousand feet tall and half as wide. Unlike the city surrounding it, the surfaces of thing were clean, smooth, uncolonized by the myriad forms of sea life that had come to inhabit the city. There were no markings upon the titanic sarcophagus either, no writing, nor runes, nor any pictographs, or drawings. It needed nothing to declare what it was; we all knew what lay before us. And as we swam nearer to the cyclopean construct, the sight of it and its condition filled me with a growing sense of dread.

About the base of the construct were the accumulated remnants of thousands of years. Skulls and other bones littered the floor, as did bone daggers, stone axes, flint knives, the rusted remnants of guns and helmets. Nearby, a plane and a submarine hosted a nascent reef, and all about there were the scattered pieces of shell casings, and bomb components. The tomb had become a midden documenting the last two thousand years of history. Unable to stop ourselves we grew closer, and in doing so the truth of things began to unveil itself. The Great Seal that had kept the tomb closed was gone, and though it boggles the mind even now, the alien sarcophagus was open, only slightly, but open nonetheless. We peered into that vast darkened hold, reverent in our faith up to the last, but what we saw in there shattered the last of our resolve, and we fled from the sight of what lurked inside in blind and unbridled terror.

We flew up out of the ancient alien city, without caution or care and in doing so we drew the attention of the great monstrosity that had already devoured three of our number. It roared as we passed it and fell in behind us, pursuing our ragged and demoralized band with a vengeance. I gave it no heed. I was blinded by emotion, driven insane by the contents of the crypt of Cthulhu. So, when the beast caught up and swallowed two more of us, I barely even noticed.

When we reached the lower tiers, I watched through fear clouded eyes as the great monsters that lurked there scuttled away, fleeing from the creature that struck at us time and time again filling the sea with our blood and the stench of death. The descent, our sense of time dilated by wonder, had seemed to take only minutes, but the ascent, driven before a devouring predator, seemed to take hours. And as we reached the upper ocean our pursuit intensified. Blood and panic had scented the waters, and more mundane but equally deadly predators joined the titan that had chased us from below. Sharks, with cold dead eyes came at us from above, and those monstrous crabs swam up off the coral atoll to pick off any stragglers or scraps. In minutes we were surrounded, and though we ourselves were well armed, and killed more than a dozen sharks, the combination of exhaustion and despair left us vulnerable to attack. The sharks took six of us and I watched one of my friends succumb to a swarm of vampire octopi. Five of us broke the surface just yards from the *Dionysus*. We swam, we swam for our lives and when I reached the ship I turned and found myself alone.

I clambered up the ladder. The sea was quiet. My heart was like a drum pounding in my brain. Things moved so slowly. There was a great eruption of water, the air filled with the stench of death and blood. Two monstrous tentacles each as thick as telephone poles, smashed across the ship, and I felt the beams beneath the deck snap into pieces. The sky reeled, and something in my brain exploded. I saw the face of the creature bearing down on me, before I slipped into the cold sea and blessed, welcome unconsciousness. I dreamed of monsters marching across the sea floor on roiling tentacles spiked with chitinous claws.

I will escape this prison that masquerades as a hospital ward. I will return to my people. I will tell them the truth and they will reject the false God. We will return to the old ways, to the old Gods. Those that refuse will be slaughtered by the righteous, led by the one who has been to R'lyeh, seen the tomb of Cthulhu, and seen the truth.

Yes, I have seen the truth. Seen the great black crystalline tomb, and what lies inside. The tomb of our God was open, had been open, and Great Cthulhu was free to stalk the Earth and lay waste to the civilization of men. He had lied to us, for ages He had sent forth His dreams, promised us the world, but it was all lies, and in the end, just echoes of lies. He was free, had been free for decades! The thing, that terrible thing, that we saw in the tomb proved it. I understood so much in that instant. Understood what it meant to truly be anti-anthropocentric, why so many cultists had failed to free our Lord, why so many plans had been foiled by so few. I understood, and in that moment my mind, my wondrous mind, snapped.

When he rose seventy-five years ago, when Johansen piloted the *Alert* in a desperate attack, we assumed that great Cthulhu had retreated, climbed back inside His tomb, to wait for another more propitious time. We were wrong. The city of R'lyeh, the tomb of Cthulhu sunk back down into the ocean, but the thing that floated back inside wasn't the injured Cthulhu, but rather that terrible thing that had lain there for seventy-five years.

It took time for us to understand what we were seeing. It was a ship, a human ship, a schooner with two masts. It was old, covered with a thick layer of detritus that made identification nearly but not entirely impossible. But there, on the bow, the letters were clear. Four letters and the world as we knew it was destroyed.

After untold epochs, dead but dreaming beneath the ocean, He had risen, He had come up into the world of men, that fateful year of 1925, and He had done nothing. He left us, abandoned us, He cared nothing for the works of man, and therefore did nothing. Like an animal too long in a cage, He was finally free, and He left without a backward glance. He left to stalk between the stars, left the Earth behind, and the men who crawled upon its surface. He left us, His faithful servants, abandoned us with nothing to mark his passage save a derelict ship that had drifted into his former tomb. A ship that had gone down just hours before R'lyeh sunk back beneath the waves. A ship that lay there still, that marked the date of Cthulhu's release better than any monument ever could, a ship that after all these years still bore the name of *Emma*.

May Father Dagon forgive me.

THE CTHULHU HERESY
The Innsmouth Revelation

My name is Moses Fiske, I was born on February 17, 1982, in Madison, Wisconsin. My mother died in childbirth, and I was raised by my maternal grandparents. As for my father, my grandparents generally avoided the subject, but from what I could glean he was a crewman aboard an offshore drilling platform lost in the North Atlantic just days before my birth. I attended the University of Wisconsin-Madison from which I graduated with a degree in library science; it was a crowning achievement of my life, and also the day my grandparents lost their lives in a tragic car accident. In the settlement of the estate, it was revealed that my father, the last descendent of a once venerable shipping family, had left behind a substantial amount of property including a residence in New England. Overcome with grief and desperate to make a break from the city of my birth I leapt at the opportunity to begin again, and so I moved to the city that would become my home, Arkham, Massachusetts.

In addition to some money and a miscellany of papers, the property I inherited included a three-story office and warehouse complex on River Street. The building was in need of repair, but the structure, walls and roof were solid being made of steel reinforced concrete slabs. After six months of renovations, funded mostly by my inheritance, but also by a generous and somewhat ludicrous bank loan, I found myself the owner and resident of a small building consisting of a dozen stylish lofts overlooking the scenic Miskatonic River. Given its proximity to Miskatonic University it was not long until I had tenants; the first were students, sometimes three to a loft, but slowly these were replaced by a genteel and stylish set of professors and administrators from the University and also from Arkham State College. In 2007, tired of the difficulties of dealing directly with city code enforcement, I hired a property management firm which essentially divested me from the daily operations of the building.

The Innsmouth Revelation

Suddenly a man of leisure, one day I wandered down to the university library and volunteered my services. In 2008 the Head Librarian, Doctor Shea offered me a fulltime position as a junior curator in the Department of the Library of Miskatonic University. A year later my position was reclassified, and I was suddenly the curator in charge of digital archives, as which I have served ever since.

Officially called the Armitage Archive, after an influential former librarian, the vast majority of the digitized documents consist of personal recollections, holographic manuscripts, testimonies and final statements. So prevalent are these types of documents that the student body now jokingly refers to these archival holdings as The Confessional, and I as its curator have been nicknamed Father Fiske. It is a name I have come to embrace for it has bonded me to the students in ways that other faculty and staff cannot begin to appreciate. The archiving project is a vast undertaking and is funded in part by the non-profit Alexandria Project which seeks to digitally archive books and documents that have entered the public domain in attempts to preserve them for future generations. Labor intensive, I employ a small army of students from a wide range of fields beyond the core of library sciences, including computer programmers, data administrators, imagers, web designers, linguists, historians, and a surprising number of anthropologists, chemical engineers and forensic scientists. The archive and even the process of archiving serves to educate and train the students and has spawned no fewer than seventy masters and thirty doctoral degrees, as well as hundreds of papers including Price's A History of Publishing Practices in Colonial New England, Cannon's Annotated Poetry of Edward Pickman Derby, and Thelred's somewhat disturbing monograph on preserving and restoring bindings derived from primate leathers.

Given the size and reach of the archiving project, momentum is always critical. Thus, when one of the graduate students charged with validating the computerized scanning and characterization of a particular set of handwritten documents fell ill, a victim of the latest flu epidemic, I was forced to take action. Fearing the project would be delayed, I managed to redistribute much of his workload to other students but assumed some myself. Thus, I found myself reading and comparing the digitized text to the handwritten sheets commonly known as the Olmstead Apology.

Robert Martin Olmstead was a young man from Ohio who briefly visited New England in the late 1920s to research his family tree. Years later he apparently returned to the area and left the subject manuscript in a box in a dockside warehouse in Arkham. Published as fiction, in one of the more sensational periodicals of the time, the Olmstead Apology caused quite the uproar amongst the uneducated and superstitious masses, as well as the more genteel members of the city. The document is readily available, and I urge you to read it in its entirety, but in order to expedite your understanding I will summarize the tale. Olmstead discovers that he is descendent from the Marsh family of Innsmouth, who in the mid-nineteenth century made a horrendous bargain. In exchange for riches and eternal life the people of Innsmouth had given themselves over to a horrid race of batrachian humanoids from the deep called the Deep Ones. After decades of interbreeding with these monstrosities, the village became populated with a ravening half-human horde which in the dead of night pursued Olmstead, forcing him to flee. He reported his experiences to the federal government and then returned to Toledo. In response, government agents raided the village under the guise of quelling a vast smuggling operation and quarantined the population. All seemed to end well enough, but Olmstead began to have strange, disturbing dreams, his hair fell out and his skin became scaly. Slowly to his horror he began to resemble the hybrid fish things that had pursued him. In the end he embraces his heritage, swears to free his similarly afflicted cousin from the madhouse, and together join their brethren in the sea. There beneath the waves, he would worship the ancient gods of the Deep One's Father Dagon and Mother Hydra and worse. For the Deep One's also paid homage to Cthulhu, an alien monstrosity with the head of a cephalopod, imprisoned for eons in the deepest parts of the Pacific Ocean. One day, when the stars were right, Cthulhu would be free and not caring for the wants and desires of men, he would clear off the Earth, leaving it for his faithful servants to rule.

As literature, I found the writing of the Olmstead Apology to be mediocre and considered it to be either a psychotic delusion or a juvenile prank. I vaguely knew of Innsmouth and its reputation as something of a seaside slum and viewed the document as an obviously puerile attack on an oppressed minority. Were I in charge of acquisitions and such a document had come before me, I would probably have passed it over.

Regardless, I would not have given the story a second thought if it had not been for a small, attached note on official university paper.

> Henry,
> I am returning the Olmstead manuscript for your permanent inclusion in the archives. The legal challenge to our ownership has been withdrawn; apparently the threat of publicity has caused Mr. Fiske to change his position.
>
> Regards,
> Holden Hand, Esq.
> March 8, 1953

Suddenly, the Olmstead Apology was no longer a simple document to be cared for and archived, suddenly there was an implication of a direct link to my own family. Was it possible that the Fiske mentioned in the note was one of my own ancestors? And if so on what basis was his claim to the document made? And why even claim a right to ownership in the first place? Moreover, what type of publicity did Mr. Fiske fear enough to make him withdraw his challenge? These questions and others swam through my mind, and I spent several hours searching the net and requesting information from Miskatonic University's Law School and other departments before finally logging off and making the short walk home.

That night my dreams were fitful and obviously influenced by the weird imagery and flavor of the Olmstead Apology. Unable to sleep, I spent the wee hours puttering about my apartment before wandering to campus. My morning was unproductive, hampered by the lack of sleep and near constant interruptions by a bevy of students. It was not until well after lunch that I was able to devote any time to go through my email. To my delight an enterprising student clerk had found the actual papers filed in the lawsuit of Fiske versus Miskatonic University, while another student had assembled a brief history and genealogy of the Fiske family. Each had invoked their right for reimbursement under the University Commons Work Agreement and I sent each of them $10 which paid them for their work, but was not enough to invoke any exclusivity, meaning that if someone else was interested in the same subject, the students were allowed to reuse, expand and even resell the same research. That students could make a living doing such piecemeal work still amazes me.

According to the research, the Fiske Family of Arkham established themselves in the early part of the eighteenth century as shipwrights for the burgeoning fishing fleets being deployed out of Innsmouth and Kingsport, and then later in service to the revolutionary army. By 1800 The Fiske Shipyard occupied a full mile of Arkham's riverfront with offices in the very building I now called home and produced vessels of all sizes from small rowboats to ocean going steamships. By 1876 the firm was so successful that Erasmus Fiske joined the faculty of Miskatonic in order to teach the principles of naval engineering so that qualified staff could be hired to work the yard and offices. Sadly, the firm and family suffered greatly during the depression and by 1932 only the one austere building remained.

William Fiske, the Fiske who threatened to sue Miskatonic University for ownership of the Olmstead papers, was my grandfather. He was born in 1928 to Eleanor Fiske the last scion of the once proud family. Eleanor was not married when she gave birth, and this combined with her refusal to name the father caused quite a scandal at the time. It was only years later after the publication of the Olmstead Apology that she revealed the name of the father as Robert Martin Olmstead. To verify her claims she produced letters written to her and signed by Olmstead, the content and style of which bore an uncanny resemblance to the apology itself. Within a week of the revelation, Eleanor Fiske committed suicide by jumping into the sea and leaving young William alone with his grandfather.

This then was William Fiske's claim to the Olmstead papers, as Robert Olmstead's child, William had every right to claim his father's property, but this in itself did not explain why he felt the need to make such a claim. Not surprisingly, the source of such motivation, as with most things came from money. Arkham House, a local publisher had in 1939 announced that they had reached an agreement to publish the collected works of H. P. Lovecraft, the writer who had fictionalized the Olmstead papers as 'The Shadow Over Innsmouth" in the pulp digest Whispers. Lovecraft was a resident of Providence, who in his many letters described himself as sickly and reclusive, so much so that it came as no great shock when in 1937 it was announced that he had died. In truth no such thing had happened for no such person had ever existed. Seekers after the truth can find no death certificate, no residence, not even a birth certificate. H. P. Lovecraft was himself a fiction, a pseudonym created by an anonymous writer to hide his own identity. Some have suggested that it was Ward Phillips or Robert Blake, or even Halpin Chalmers. Others have suggested that H. P. Lovecraft was used by many people as a sort of a house name for Whispers. However, the most likely suspect, and the generally accepted is that Lovecraft was a pseudonym for eccentric master fantasist Randolph Phillips Carter, who was, from time to time, a lecturer at Miskatonic and had previously suffered scandal over such works as "The Attic Window" and "The Gnawing Worm". The most compelling evidence for this conclusion is the acknowledgement of Carter's love of word games, including anagrams and the notation that Howard Lovecraft can be rearranged to Ravdoowlf Cahter, or if one flips the v into an n it becomes Randoowlf Cahter. Given Carter's notorious New England accent this would be a fine phonetic approximation of his name. Regardless of whom the true author was, William Fiske was claiming that Robert, his father, had been the actual author, and that he was entitled to a share of the past, as well as any future royalties. The university, as executor of Lovecraft's "estate" was therefore liable for the wrongful literary actions of their "deceased" client.

Holden Hand, the University's legal counsel readily agreed to turn over ownership of the documents and rights to any royalties to William Fiske, as soon as Fiske signed an affidavit affirming that he was a descendent of Olmstead and placed it for public notice in the state register. Holden knew that such an act would link Fiske directly to the Marsh family and to Innsmouth. As of 1953 the country was in the grip of McCarthyism, and anyone linked to the village was assured a visit from the FBI. What Hand was suggesting was that Fiske withdrawal his complaint or risk being detained by the Federal Government simply for the fact that his father's family was from Innsmouth. Sadly, in a blow against decency, the ploy worked, and my grandfather simply walked away from the fight.

So now I knew, suddenly I was more than just a Fiske, but an Olmstead, and if the documents were to be believed an illegitimate Marsh as well. Not surprisingly, I had the over whelming urge to learn more about the decaying little village of Innsmouth. Like all of New England, regional history books abound, and I was soon up to my ears in T. E. Watkins' The Miskatonic Valley in the Twentieth Century and its chapter on scandalous Innsmouth. There was the obligatory section on the government raid and occupation, which remained in effect into 1935. The late thirties saw a rare earthquake spawn a tidal bore that devastated the central part of the village, as well as a catastrophic fire at the refinery. The Forties were ushered in with the Army corps of Engineers dredging the harbor and installing wartime fortifications and heavy guns above the harbor. The end of the war brought an influx of Italians, many of which were killed or injured when a freak squall struck in 1946. Following the crash of a jet on a local beach the Army occupied the town once more, not releasing control until an act of Congress ordered them out in 1962. In the mid-Seventies a small communications firm leased several buildings and suddenly the residents of Innsmouth found themselves at the center of the computer revolution. The boom continued through the Eighties and into the Nineties. When the sole owner of the Innsmouth Redevelopment Corporation drowned off the coast, the resulting scramble for control created a small building boom in Innsmouth which suddenly found itself with a casino hotel and a new fish processing and canning plant. The casino failed in 1993 when a hurricane blew out most of the windows, the shell was bought and renovated by a non-profit oceanographic institute. Always at odds with the institute, the fisherman's cooperative was dealt a catastrophic blow in 1998 when the cannery collapsed killing more than a hundred. Desperate to break from the past, and no longer rooted in commercial fishing, a large portion of the town successfully seceded and quietly incorporated under another more tourist-friendly name. The town of Innsmouth, or what remained of it, slowly vanished into the landscape of suburban overdevelopment.

Through it all, the shadow that hung over Innsmouth never withdrew. The strange gods that the town had adopted, Father Dagon, Mother Hydra and the eldritch Cthulhu, and the strange priesthood that served them, The Esoteric Order of Dagon, had cast a spell over the place. A natural curiosity filled me, and in time overwhelmed me. I spent a week pouring through the so-called black books. I read Von Junzt's Unaussprechlichen Kulten, the Comte d'Erlette's Cultes des Goules, De Vermis Mysteris, and the Johanssen Narrative. The next week I graduated to Wilbur Whateley's Diary, The Legrasse Reports and the strange Ponape Scripture. All of this was made easier for me as I had no need to suffer the cramped handwriting, black letter texts and strange unexplained references that had plagued scholars of the previous century. In the age of the digital archive my studies were made infinitely easier as they were supported by the scholarship of others which was readily available through various links. There were references and cross-references, annotations, and glosses, all linked in vast hypertext chains. Passages that once would have taken months to understand and place in context were instantly apparent to me. I understood much, the great cosmogony that encompassed Cthulhu, Dagon, Azathoth, Yig, Ubbo-Sathla and countless others became plain to me. I learned things about men, and things that were less than men, and things that were much more, about the universe and our place in it. The Necronomicon may be a shadow play of innuendo and metaphor, a cipher of many secrets, but it is clear on one thing. In the great scheme, man and his works are nothing, mean nothing, are naught but dust in comparison to the forces that strive and bend the universe. Our cities, our roads, our great works were hovels compared to that of R'lyeh, throne-tomb of Cthulhu. We have spread out over this world, walked upon its moon, sent probes to the Sun and to Mars, and even beyond the solar system. Our telescopes have peered and squinted at the things that flutter and flicker around other stars. All these things we have done, but they were nothing compared to the stirrings and dreams of the sleeping god Cthulhu.

It was during the course of my studies that I learned a most curious fact. Of all the digitally available documents, the one most commonly purchased was quite surprisingly The Codex Dagonesis, a book of rituals dedicated to Dagon and Hydra and confiscated from Innsmouth during the raid in 1928. Even more surprising was that the majority of purchases were coded as being paid for by the University's College of Divinity. With little effort I soon found that approximately a dozen students, all from Innsmouth had recently formed a faculty sponsored study group apparently devoted to comparisons between the tenets of Christianity and those of the Esoteric Order of Dagon. Moreover, the students traveled daily from Innsmouth to the University as a part of a scholarship program paid for by the order, which still existed, albeit in a highly diminished capacity. The commuter students rode a small bus that traveled back and forth from the University to Innsmouth's Federal Square, twice daily, early in the morning and then back with students for morning classes, and then a reversed trip in the late evening. Intrigued, I focused my attentions on the codex and spent a better part of a day delving into the strange religious beliefs of the cult. Devoted strictly to the rites of Dagon and Hydra the codex never once mentioned Cthulhu, and I assumed that the rites celebrating the third and greater god of the order were derived from another source, perhaps the R'lyeh Text. Strangely, a review of the purchasing practices of the study group revealed that they seemed uninterested in any other volumes.

That night what I had come to expect as inevitable, finally came to me, the dream of Cthulhu. I saw his tomb in R'lyeh, heard his whispering voice and marveled in his unearthly magnificence. I succumbed to his roaring call, awoke screaming in abject terror at his might, and fell to my knees in adoration. I swore devotion to my Lord Cthulhu, vowed to serve and strive for his release. When the stars were right, he would rise up and I and all of his other servants would inherit the Earth.

I sealed the pact with the only sacrifice worthy of his exalted being. Still in possession of a master key, I moved through the apartments and made my offerings to Cthulhu. One by one I gloried in the red offering and the devouring hunger. Like Cain I understood the needs of a true God and offered up eighteen fattened calves to quench his thirst.

Hours later, as the sun rose above the horizon, I boarded the blue and crimson van that ran from Miskatonic to Innsmouth. The driver, a man named Marshal, seemed quite surprised but I flashed him my faculty badge to and with an unintelligible grumble followed by the mechanical hiss of the doors sealing, we were on our way. In the darkness the drone of the engine lulled me into a state of extreme relaxation and in mere moments I fell once more into a deep and restless state sleep.

In my dream, I stood amongst the submerged terraces and towers that form the great city of Y'ha-nthlei. Around me the teeming masses of my brethren swarmed in vast silent shoals. I raised my hands and proffered my adoration to Father Dagon, and the crowd cheered in response. I fell to my knees and gave praise to Mother Hydra, and the masses roared in appreciation. I prostrated myself and groveled to the majesty that was great Cthulhu, and to this there was utter silence. I rose up from the seafloor and looked around me, but the city was empty, its citizens were gone, and I was left alone and confused.

I awoke with a start. My heart was pounding, my breath was ragged, and my hands were shaking. Panic filled my mind, for I was on the verge of understanding what had been told to me but didn't understand enough to make sense of it all. As the doors to the bus opened, I pushed past the gathered crowd of divinity students and out into the morning air. I stumbled down the streets, guided by Olmstead's decades old directions I found the moldering temple of the Esoteric Order and raced up the stairs and through the great fish-adorned doors.

As I ran through the hall, I saw the massive stone carved images that stared down at me with cold piscine eyes. The carved rock titans of Dagon and Hydra flanked a shattered base of stone where I knew a third and more revered statue should have stood. I fell to the floor before the altar and begged forgiveness from the one whose idol no longer stood in the hallowed halls. My cries rose up and filled the great room that once had been filled with devoted worshipers, but now was an empty shell.

From a vestibule suddenly appeared a priest, his eyes ablaze and his fists clenched around a golden jewel encrusted dagger in the shape of a shark. He came at me screaming blasphemies and as he closed the fetid smell of the ocean seeped out of his very body and filled the air. I grabbed his arm and then wrapped my other hand around his neck. He roared into my face, and I cringed at the glistening daggers of glass teeth as his mouth snapped at my neck. We grappled and for all of his strength the priest was no match for me, for beneath the muscle the priest's bones, those thin bones, snapped like twigs beneath my hands.

As he died, I slowly rationalized the things he had screamed, they had to be lies, my dreams, my dream of the Great Cthulhu, striving across the earth, clearing the world for his devoted followers, that was the truth. It had to be. It wasn't possible that I had been misled. Cthulhu was the truth, and the way, only through him were we, the children of Dagon and Hydra, to be saved. But in the end, I had no choice but to accept the truth that had been shouted at me in the croaking toad voice of the now dead priest of Dagon. Denial was futile. This was when I finally understood why the young students from Innsmouth had devoted themselves only to the Codex Dagonesis.

I will leave this manuscript with the body of the priest; no doubt it will end up in the Confessional were it will likely be added as a postscript to the papers of my great-grandfather. I will then proceed down to the docks and swim out to Devil Reef where I am sure that I shall be greeted by my brethren, and I shall beg their forgiveness for what I have done to them, and I shall beg the forgiveness of Father Dagon and Mother Hydra for forsaking the truth of their worship.

For it was the priest that told me the truth, Cthulhu dreams, and his dreams seep down into the minds of men. The dreams I had, of his magnificent conquest of the planet, of the clearing of the earth, of the dominance of his followers, they were just dreams, imaginings, my own interpretation of the brief images I glimpsed from the sleeping god. For the mad truth was that Cthulhu cares not for the works of men nor even his most devoted followers. Of his worshippers, of the mad artists, poets, and sculptors, of the lonesome madmen and cultists, of the Esoteric Order of Dagon, he gives no thought. All their devotions, all their prayers and machinations, all their sacrifices made no difference, were completely meaningless, had always been meaningless. How many thousands had been killed upon rough altars, amongst standing stones, in secret rites, in back alleys and even in stylish apartment complexes to satisfy the blood thirst of a god who was hardly even aware of the atrocities being committed in his name?

I had killed eighteen people, people I had known, people I lived with, who called me friend. I had killed in his name, and the being I had come to worship couldn't care less. He still sleeps, still dreams his uneasy dreams, and continues to wait for that day when he finally wakes to destroy all the living: man, deep ones and hybrids alike, regardless of their loyalty. The Earth will be cleared, and only he shall remain: Great Cthulhu, the feckless god.

Forgive me please Mother Hydra, to whom now shall I turn?

THE CTHULHU HERESY
Down Through Black Abysses

II ... to Cyclopean and many-columned Y'ha-nthlei, and in that lair of the Deep Ones we shall dwell amidst wonder and glory forever."

Are those the words my cousin wrote? Was he that naïve? Was I? It all seems so long ago, but in truth it has been only days, weeks at the most. They said I was a lunatic, all those years ago, and my father and grandfather shut me up in that Canton madhouse. But Uncle Douglas and Grandmother knew the truth and it cost both of them their lives. Only my cousin Robert was strong enough to discover the facts and embrace them. He engineered my escape and planned for both of us to go east to Innsmouth and then into the sea where our great-great grandmother Pth'thya-l'yi was waiting, calling us to the sub-aqueous metropolis of Y'ha-nthlei, calling us home.

We were fools.

I haven't much time to write this. I can hear them outside. I've taken refuge on the second floor of an abandoned warehouse that overlooks the Innsmouth waterfront. I write these words on pages I found in a long-forgotten desk. When I am done, I shall secure them into an abandoned mason jar and throw it into the harbor. It is perhaps the only way to tell my story and assure that it reaches the outside world. The world must know the truth, my cousin Robert must be stopped, before he too, reaches Innsmouth and undertakes the journey to Y'ha-nthlei.

Robert had a plan, but I, who had been locked away for years, could no longer wait. The voice of my ancestor was so loud, so insistent, so demanding. I stole his car, his money his supplies and I made my way to Innsmouth without him. I could have gone anywhere really. I could have slipped into Lake Eerie or the Ohio River, or any of a dozen waterways and then made my way to the Atlantic. Yet somehow all these options seemed wrong. I was drawn by something to the Manuxet. Some ancestral memory or impulse made it impossible to go anywhere else but the headwater of that dark river. Like some strange salmon I had no choice but to follow the path that my breeding had laid out for me, no matter how maddening, dangerous or ridiculous it seemed. I stopped only for fuel, rolling down the window only enough to slip the attendant the required payment, I collected no change. Never did I let my crude disguise of a hat and muffler slip. I relieved myself in the woods along deserted and desolate back roads, always with the motor running. I subsisted on the rations of dried foodstuffs and bottled drink that my dear cousin had assembled for the two of us. I followed the course Robert had laid out for us, passing through Erie and then wilds of western New York, before coming into Massachusetts and crossing the Round Mountains to pick up the Aylesbury Pike toward Arkham. I was careful to turn east and skirt Bolton before finally stopping the car at the headwaters of the Manuxet which steals water from the Miskatonic through a vast marshy land.

It was there, at the end of the land leg of my journey and the beginning of the waterborne that I let my guard down and was suddenly endangered. As I stood there in the stream, in a godforsaken marsh, in the morning hours, a man suddenly appeared in my field of vision. His uniform identified him as a soldier; one I supposed of those that Robert had told me had been deployed to occupy Innsmouth. He was alone, with a gun slung over his shoulder. That he surprised me goes without saying, but I think it was he who was the most startled, for he seemed surprised simply by my presence. I was naked, half submersed in the cold spring water of the creek, my gills flexing in the cold air, a strange-crested fin running down my back. Without a word he raised his rifle and took aim, I panicked and leapt through the air more out of reflex than conscious thought. In an instant I was on him, his throat was slit, and the claws of my right hand were warm with blood and gore. I left him there on the road to die; his hand clutching his throat his eyes wide in fear of the knowledge that he was close to dead, his mouth gasping for air and instead gurgling bubbles of blood.

Spurred on by the horror which I had inflicted on another man I slipped into the icy black waters and let them carry me downstream, toward the Manuxet, toward the harbor and the reef beyond, and deep beneath those fathomless waters lay my goal of Y'ha-nthlei! The stream twisted and turned, grew deep and then shallow. In places I could swim freely, my huge, unblinking eyes able to see even in the black-stained waters. Elsewhere I had to crawl across muddy shoals and rocky deposits. Each time I rose above the water I knew I put myself at risk and my actions during these exposures were swift and direct. Finally, I emerged from the stinking fen and the small stream consolidated with others which ran faster and deeper as a large creek. A little further downstream and the creek joined with others and the channel deepened to become the Manuxet River. So deep and dark were the waters that surrounded me that I no longer feared being observed. I relaxed and let the current carry me.

I rounded a bend and then suddenly there was a curious taste, metallic and electric at the same time, and my skin began to itch. I passed by a cavernous industrial pipe and could somehow sense the lingering accumulation of lye and other chemical wastes that still leached into the waters. Irritated I kicked my thick legs and sped away from the area as fast as I could. Another bend in the river and suddenly my speed was increasing without any effort on my part. There was an odd sound in the water like a thousand tiny drums being beaten. It took me a moment but only that to realize I was approaching the falls, the three-tiered water fall that were the heart of Innsmouth. Slowing my movement, I caught sight of a bridge pillar and latched on to it. Instinctively I had no fear of going over the falls, my body was resilient enough to resist the pressure of the deepest of seas, but consciously I was still just a man, one who needed to prepare himself for what was to come next.

I don't know what possessed me to rise to the surface and observe my surroundings, but I did, and I immediately regretted it. There were soldiers on the bridge above me, and the one further down the river, and along the roads that ran on both sides. In the bright morning sun, the shadows of the bridges were all in the wrong places and offered no protection. They saw me just after I broke the surface. Guns went from shoulders to hands and took a bead on my position. There was a rifle crack, and then another. Something whizzed past my head and smashed into the stones beside me exploding fragments into the river around me. One grazed my shoulder, cutting deep and sending a wave of burning pain through my arm. I didn't scream but instead reflexively sought the refuge of the deep water. They were yelling as I dove back under, and more rounds sped through the water around me.

Down Through Black Abysses

I was immediately caught up in the current and whisked downstream. I hit a rock, and then something that wasn't a rock, but rather a mesh of rope. There was a net across the river, and I was suddenly caught in it, but not yet tangled. More gunfire. Even through the water I could hear the rifles cracking. I suppose they were shooting at the bulge I made in the net. I crawled my way across the webbing, searching for a way through. Suddenly the lines tensed, and the net was being reeled in, with me in it. I was like a fish in a seine, but unlike a fish I knew how to escape from this trap and had the strength and tools to do so. I slashed at the ropes and felt them cut beneath my claws. I slashed again, and again, desperate to escape the closing trap. Then with another cut the ropes broke and I tumbled out of the enclosure. As I fell into the water, bullets whizzing past me, I hit a submerged rock worn smooth from ages of rushing water and sand, but my wounded arm throbbed from the impact. I rolled over the edge and down the falls. The pool below caught me and swirled my wounded body around before shooting me out and down over a second plunge. I barely had time to recover before I was caught in the speeding waters and shot down the river over a third drop. This time I was able to avoid any rocks and regain my bearings. I pushed off the hard bottom of the pool and sped down river.

In the lower part of the river, I could taste the freshwater of the Manuxet mixing with the brine of the harbor. I swam forward and with each stroke I could sense more of the open sea and less of the river. I cleared the river mouth and moved quickly through the harbor. The small bay tasted of diesel and rotted wood and dead fish and something else, something chemical that reminded me of gunpowder and dynamite. It only took a few strokes to propel myself across the harbor and out of the inlet. In the open ocean all the smells and tastes of the Manuxet faded, and soon all I was left with was the feeling of the sea as it passed through my gills, and the voice in my head calling me, urging me forward, louder than ever.

I swam east towards the rocks that marked Devil Reef. The sun was bright and flooded the surface layers of the sea with light. Around me small fish, cod and blues, swam gracefully in the clear green waters. A bull shark, presumably drawn by my blood, stalked me from a distance, circling, looking for a weakness it could exploit. When it finally decided to move off and leave me alone, I felt a wave of relief pass through me.

Not that I couldn't have taken the animal, he was no match for me, but I had no desire for conflict. I had had enough of conflict, of doctors, of nurses, of soldiers, and of boats that suddenly were coming for me. I could hear their engines and the men screaming orders. Soldiers were searching the waters for me. I slipped under the surface and dove deep, leaving the sunlit world of soldiers behind.

The water was thick with oxygen and my gills felt rich as it ran past them. I sped down with powerful kicks and not a backward glance. I had thought that the descent from the surface to Y'ha-nthlei would be a phantasmagorical transition from one world to another, but the only thing that happened as I fell into the deeper ocean was that the sun slowly died, and the darkness grew. I went deep, deep beneath the surface, down past where the fish danced in the last dim light from above. Beyond that there were still fish, but they were no longer joyous creatures of the shining sea, but rather dark brooding things with huge mouths that lumbered through the thick dark waters and menaced each other with long predatory investigations. As I fell, there began a kind of precipitation, not unlike snow in appearance, but entirely unlike it in composition. This strange pale fall was neither rain nor snow, but the accumulated particles from the upper levels which, for one reason or another, had lost their buoyancy and were now slowly falling through the abyss. It was a detrital rain, composed of plankton, algae, plants and even the carcasses and bones of fish. We all fell together, and I hoped that I was more than just another piece of decayed refuse raining down in the dark.

The great flat expanse of the ocean floor, covered with rock and silt was a desolate place, filled with batrachian beasts that could barely be called fish. Huge black shapes that were little more than mouths with fins hunted chimerical horrors that lay on the floor sifting nourishment from the rain of decay. Horned and hungry crabs picked through the carcass of an ancient whale, while great gelatinous worms bored through the bones with grinding teeth. I dared not pause but instead followed that siren call in my head and angled myself to fall below the surface and into the secret trench in the sea floor that seemed to crack the very world itself. I cut through the waters like I belonged there, like I had been made to dwell and sail in the dark and empty depths of the sea.

I was there, floating in an ocean that was both abyssal and subterranean, when I first caught site of the lights of the sub-aqueous metropolis of Y'ha-nthlei. My cousin described it as many-columned, but more appropriately it would be said to be many-arched, for great sets of arcs rose up from the center line and the outer edges bearing great tattered sails that billowed in the current. Terraced palaces covered in barnacles, corals, and twisting fronds of things that were only semi-vegetative surrounded the central row of arches and flapping tissues. Outside, beyond the fringes of the city, giant shadows moved about, ancient things, that I knew to be kin, descendants of our ancestors Father Dagon and Mother Hydra. These things were old even when my great-great-grandmother Pth'thya-l'yi was young, and I knew she had been born nearly three hundred millennia ago and had dwelt here in Y'ha-nthlei for the last eighty-thousand years. They were to be feared, these things of age, and avoided, for they were terrible and capricious.

A score of shadows rose up out of the city to greet me, and as they did the voice in my head, that whispering siren call that had haunted me for so many years finally ceased. Instead, my mind was filled with information, I was being spoken to, informed, and educated. These were the Daughters of Y'ha-dra, spawned by Pth'thya-l'yi through parthenogenesis. They were sisters, but more than that because they were genetically identical, not only to one another but to their parent as well, one of the primordial Deep Ones Y'ha. It was from her title "dra" meaning "virgin" that men had come to know her as Hydra. Only her daughters perpetuated that name, mostly amongst men, such as those in Innsmouth, they had cultivated as worshippers. Here in her city of Y'ha-nthlei she was known only as Y'ha, and I quickly learned that nthlei was the word for those bound to her service. I found this sudden influx of knowledge invigorating and was reminded of Greek place names which often were bound to a particular deity, such as Athens and Hermopolis.

Pth'thya-l'yi was amongst the Daughters, and she came to me and took me by the hand and led me down into Y'ha-nthlei. We floated down to a great open space at one end of the city. Around us, many other Deep Ones had gathered, all were female, though how I knew this I can't explain, but I knew it to be true. There in the floor of the city, located in the center of a slow descending grade, was a great reflecting pool, yards and yards apart, I thought it was glass, but as I stared at the glossy darkness, I could see liquid running across its surface. It was strange to see one fluid of a different color and density entrapped in that great circular pool while all about me the waters of the ocean itself flowed.

The Daughters, my ancestor included, intoned some ancient choral, and soon were joined in by those masses that lurked about the edges. It was a queer thrumming noise, generated from within the bodies of my companions, and filled the space around me with a fantastic, electric vibration. I realized immediately that I was participating in an initiation rite, one that had likely played out repeatedly over the vast epochs the city had existed. Thrilled that I was so quickly accepted, I allowed my limbs to be gripped by the Daughters and paraded above the black semi-translucent pool such that all gathered could see me. Any sense of modesty or shame had been lost, for there was no such concept amongst these things. The fear and humility involved with one's own body was discarded, left behind on the surface as the human construct and taboo that it was.

At some signal that I did not note, my retinue moved away from the pool, and I, not knowing what else to do, followed. We proceeded down the length of the city moving past the great arches wrapped in billowing material and down along a ridge where similar arches had either been destroyed or never completed. Beyond these, the structure of the city grew thin, though in the distance I could see another set of furled arches, which seemed even larger. I thought perhaps these massive spires were our destination, but instead we floated off to one side and skimming over the surface of the great barnacled city we ducked beneath a huge tubular outcropping that seemed to connect two different lobes of the metropolis. There in the shadow of this weird bridge I was ushered into a kind of cave or tunnel, which seemed not only artificial, for it was symmetrical, but also natural for the walls seemed to be composed of imperfect layers and veins. The chamber inside was vast and throbbed with a strange rhythmic vibration, the water was strangely warm and carried with it a peculiar scent that reminded me of blood and other bodily fluids. Across the floor a trail of globular cysts lay imbedded in semitransparent, gelatinous ooze that trailed off to the walls of the cavern which were lined with row upon row of telamons, sculpted male figures that functioned as columnar supports.

If only that had been true.

Pth'thya-l'yi pointed at the carvings and I heard the word nthlei. I saw that there was a vacancy amongst those grim statues of amphibious men, and toward it I was ushered. As we drew closer, I saw the details on those strange carvings. I saw the fine scales, the muscular arms, the veins that ran beneath, the blood that coursed there. I also saw the queer tendrils that seemed to hold them in place against the wall, the same tendrils that slowly unfurled from the wall and reached out from the vacancy and groped in my direction. In my mind I suddenly understood the true meaning of the word nthlei. As that terrible realization suddenly dawned on me and I recognized where I was and why. I recognized the horrific position I had been led to and was expected to voluntarily submit. I broke free from the gentle grip of my escort and fled toward the strange cleft that we had passed through. My captors seemed startled, and I somehow knew that in the eons that this ceremony had been carried out, that no one had ever rejected the honor. The Daughters of Y'ha-dra had been entombing their male brethren in this place for more than a hundred thousand years, and none had ever rebelled.

Until now. Until me.

They didn't know what to do. My reaction was unprecedented and so I was allowed to escape. Through the fathoms I sped, desperate to reach the surface and escape the fate I seemed destined to. I looked back only once, and that was enough to drive me to move faster, for what I saw, what I finally comprehended, what I finally understood about Y'ha-nthlei was enough to drive me over the edge. If I wasn't mad before, surely this revelation was enough to accomplish the task and set me firmly into the mantle of lunacy.

I broke the surface and discovered that the sun had set, and the moon now reigned in the sky. That dim light glistened off of the surface and illuminated the rocks of the Devil Reef. In the distance the village of Innsmouth glowed weakly, barely breaking the darkness that marked where the night was eclipsed by the land itself. Hours earlier I had had but one desire, to leave the world of the surface behind, now it beckoned to me and seemed my only salvation. With every effort I struggled against tide and time to lessen the distance between myself and that decayed refuge. I feared that in an instant the sisters would overtake me and drag me back down into the darkness, down through those black abysses.

That was hours ago. It had taken them time, but once the Daughters had recovered from their shock, they had no choice but to pursue me. Their voices called to me in my head, searching, pleading, and even commanding me to return. With each passing moment those voices are growing stronger, which I can only assume means that they are getting closer. My time is short. The trail I left from the harbor cannot have gone unnoticed. Either the soldiers or my ancestors will have found it by now. My discovery is inevitable.

The clues were there all the time in our dreams, and in the history of Innsmouth itself. How did I and my cousin not see the truth? For eighty-thousand years that which had been our great-great-grandmother had dwelled within Y'ha-nthlei. Were we to believe that for all that time that hidden metropolis had lain off the coast of Innsmouth and never before interacted with her neighbor? Why was it that only the men of Innsmouth were forced to take veiled brides? Why weren't the women forced into unholy matrimony with new and terrifying husbands?

I know why now. I know the secret of cyclopean and many arched Y'ha-nthlei. I know what lascivious purpose those rare, fertile male members of the Deep Ones and their hybrids are enslaved to. Stupendous and unheard-of splendors indeed! We shall dwell amidst wonder and glory forever, that was the promise. Yet that wonder is the thing called Y'ha-nthlei, an ancient and titanic thing, so huge that monstrous barnacles and corals and her own children have colonized her flesh, dwelling like parasites, like remoras and hagfish, like leeches on their own birth mother. And the glory for her rare sons is to be entombed in her own flesh, chained inside her birth canal to fertilize her eggs as they move through that terrible channel. My destiny is to live forever as a slave to the inhuman needs of an ancient and terrible goddess as she gives birth to thousand upon thousand perhaps millions of hideous spawn. This is the honor, the wonder, the glory promised me by Pth'thya-l'yi and her sisters. It is the promise made by Y'ha herself, who was once Y'ha-dra, but is now Y'ha-nthlei, the city-goddess Y'ha and her betrothed the nthlei, insignificant things that do not even warrant names. As I made that casual and cursed glance back toward her and saw from above that great black pool and realized that as I gazed into it, that huge single eye of cyclopean Y'ha-nthlei, so too did it gaze into me. I heard her speak as she watched me leave, heard her terrible and monstrous words as she called me, her own rebellious child, back to where she said I belonged. I heard her, and her very voice bellowing in my head drove me mad.

Down Through Black Abysses

They are in the streets. Are those the furtive, cautious steps of men in boots, or Deep Ones with claws? Are those the sounds of guns on shoulders, or scales rubbing against themselves in the cold night Innsmouth air? Does it matter?

In my head they call to me and tell me of their plans. Innsmouth is finished; it is too dangerous to stay. Y'ha-nthlei must move, she and those who are bound to her in unspeakable betrothal, and all of her children must migrate to deeper waters, where men with bombs cannot find them; a place where they can once more can lie and feed and breed in peace. They want me; they need me to come with them. She needs me. There is a place prepared, and it is a sin to leave it unoccupied.

They're at the door below, smashing through.

I have only moments before I am captured. Whether I have been caught by the Daughters of Y'ha-dra or the soldiers that occupy Innsmouth, I cannot yet tell.

I hope it is the soldiers; they at least might kill me.

THE CTHULHU HERESY

Notes for A Life of Nightmares: A Retrospective on the Work of Henry Anthony Wilcox

enry Anthony Wilcox (August 12, 1902 – March 31, 1931) was a sculptor of the Surrealist movement notable for his work in clay and later marble. Born and raised in Providence he was the son of Anthony Wilcox, a prominent businessman, and Margaret Phillips who had some success in her youth as a songstress on the stage in Boston and New York. As a child he attended the Thomas School where he showed aptitude in the visual arts and music. At the age of nine he was interviewed by faculty members of Brown and declared a precocious genius. This diagnosis only added to the attention surrounding the young man who would often relate strange stories and odd dreams. Dotted upon by his mother who called him "psychically hypersensitive", the rest of the household, including the cook, butler and maid thought of him as queer. Unsatisfied by the demeanor of his son Anthony Wilcox often would ridicule the boy and spent as little time at the family home on Waterman Street as possible.

In 1916 Wilcox fell victim to the Sleepy Sickness, also known as Encephalitis Lethargica, which manifested primarily through sleep inversion. As a consequence of his condition, Wilcox would often roam the house and streets of Providence throughout the night and into the early morning hours and became regularly known to the dairymen and fishermen who haunted those hours. It was during this period that he began developing an artistic style, filling sketchbooks with images of the people and things he saw on his nocturnal roaming. It was these people, his "night friends" as he called them, who found him on the morning of September 3, 1917, unconscious on the street, and carried him home.

When his condition failed to improve, he was transferred to a private hospital where he stayed until the early part of 1918. In March he began being seen by Doctor Christopher Eckhardt who subjected him to hydro-immersion therapy that, after six weeks of treatment, proved successful. Wilcox emerged from his catatonic state, and reports by those in attendance suggest that he came to consciousness screaming two distinct but unrecognizable words. He chanted these words over and over again for hours until he was sedated. Those words, found in the files of the Dr. Eckhardt were recorded as "Thulu fthan!" However, the notes of Doctor Loucks, the junior physician, record the words slightly differently and note a strange almost panicked lilt in Wilcox's words which suggested an interrogative form "Thulu fthan?"

In 1920, following several years of psychological therapy, Wilcox submitted himself to an examination by the local school board. These rigid and socially elevated gentlemen found that despite his lack of formal education over the last few years, Wilcox was in possession of sufficient knowledge on a variety of subjects such that his equivalency of a high school diploma must be fully acknowledged, and the board wrote him a letter to that effect. It was this letter, along with a collection of small figurines he had produced during his convalescence, that Wilcox submitted to the Rhode Island School of Design in hopes of admission. In the fall of 1920, he was granted probationary access to the college as a freshman in the Sculpture Program with Dr. Deschanes as his academic advisor.

These early figurines, six in total, four of which reside in the RISD Museum are collectively known as the Wilcox Submission, but each bear an individual title, which are assumed to be sourced from Wilcox himself though this cannot be ascertained and are a most bizarre set of clay moldings.

1. The She-Wolf. In the classical Roman style, an image of two infants being suckled by an anthropomorphic wolf. An allusion to the myth of Romulus and Remus, the deviation from traditional portrayals of the she-wolf Lupa is particularly disturbing in that the anthropomorphized figure is more akin to a jackal than a wolf and is replete with four sets of teats and reminiscent of more primitive Neolithic fertility idols.

2. The Star-Beetle. In the style of the Amarna Period of ancient Egypt, an image of a sphere representing the sun held by a stylized scarab. The sphere is marked with multiple concentric rings on its surface, the symbolism of which is not known. The beetle itself shows deviations from typical forms with fine protrubences in rays along the seams between the body parts.

3. The Crucifixion of the Wyrm. In imitation of traditional Celtic forms, a cross with two horizontal beams upon which a coiled dragon is entwined. The dragon has four limbs, all of which are severed and pinned with nails. The tail wraps around the base of the cross and then coils around it in a traditional knot pattern.

4. The Sea Mother. A whale or leviathan in the medieval style. Detail work on scales and the fount of water that curves from the front of the sculpture over to the rear are particularly fine. Claws of all four limbs are imbedded in a stylized ocean.

5. The Professor. A grotesque conical form reminiscent of a barnacle with four tentacles protruding from the apex. Two tentacles end in crab-like pincers. A third tentacle bears a complex tubular organ resembling a shell or fluted flower. The final tentacle ends in the head of a man wearing glasses. In the collection of Alice Keezar.

6. The Scion. A man in a modern suit done in the cubist style. While the body is done in large blocks, the face and hands are done with finer pieces and create an unnerving suggestion of corruption through disease or wasting. Whereabouts unknown.

Under Deschanes direction Wilcox immersed himself in the routine and mundane work of being formally trained, studying under a number of staff and senior students including Norman Isham, R.H. Knox, and Robert Eggleton. He was a regular at visiting lectures particularly those of Charlotte Perkins Gilman. During this period Wilcox's work was perfunctory, mediocre at best and consisted mostly of studies of human anatomy, still lifes and landscapes. There are, however, some notable pieces, mostly from the spring of 1921 when he gained access to the Cooper Home for Retired Mariners. These works included clay, marbles and bronzes of various human anatomies that had suffered trauma and were essentially twisted and broken forms. It was during this period that the Providence Art Club banned Wilcox from the premises, the trustees finding his work too disturbing to some of the more conservative members.

Banned from the club, Wilcox fell in with the like-minded painter Kenneth Hart, and the two were often seen wandering the city streets at unseemly hours. The work produced during the time Wilcox was under Hart's influence has come to be known as his Grave Period. This appellation was earned not only for their melodramatic style, but also for the pervasive subject matter. Generally, the most revered work in this stage of his career is A Madonna of the Cenotaphs, an exercise in the macabre held in the private collection of the Ward Family. However, a substantial number of critics cite The Black Stone, also held by the Ward Family, as a superior piece.

None of this work ingratiated Wilcox with Deschanes or the rest of the faculty, and the young man was given an academic warning. While the younger Wilcox scoffed at the censure, his father made it clear that the situation was untenable. In a conflict that reached the ears of several neighbors, young Wilcox was forcibly ejected from the family home with a single bag of belongings and a mother crying in the streets. Where he took up residence is not entirely clear, but it had long been suspected that he found a bed with Kenneth Hart in the seedier side of the city.

That arrangement soon changed, most likely through the intervention of Wilcox's mother who found and paid for lodgings for her son at the Fleur-de-Lys Studios on Thomas Street. The residence must have been to the artist's liking for he soon began to produce work of a more mainstream and marketable form. He seems to have put the period of grotesque and the weird behind him and developed a more refined and accessible style. This is designated his Aesthetic Period and is dominated by nudes and semi-nudes in classic forms including Hypnos, Janus, and Bellerephon on Pegasus. Outstanding amongst these is that of an enthroned sea god wearing an octopus as a cowl, entitled Oannes and is part of the RISD collection. This series endeared him to Professor Deschanes and earned him good standing with the rest of the faculty. Wilcox's Aesthetic Period spanned from 1922 to December 1924.

The Aesthetic Period was brought to closure in January 1925 by a resurgence of bizarre dreams that according to Wilcox's journal prevented any serious work. He described his condition as "Walking about in a muddled haze as if I was in that queer state between being asleep and awake where all sounds and other stimuli are magnified but the ability to respond is dramatically suppressed. Strange to see the world in such detail and yet not be able to react or respond in any significant manner. What a frustrating form of paralysis I find myself entrapped within! I must have relief soon or I shall simply explode out of this weird prison." Wilcox finally gained the relief he needed on the night of February 28th when after a nearly unprecedented New England earthquake the artist had retired and suffered from terrible dreams beyond that of which he was accustomed. He dreamt of a strange city, ancient and forbidden, with weird, cyclopean towers the angles of which were all wrong. Amidst this cyclopean architecture stalked a titanic creature that bore traits of a dragon, an octopus and something vaguely human. From this nightmare Wilcox awoke and in a feverish mania produced a rectangular bas-relief an inch thick and measuring five by six inches in area depicting the monster of the night before and surrounding it with strange hieroglyphics.

The piece, which is generally known as The Wilcox Bas Relief (Wilcox never titled it), created quite a stir at RISD, and Deschanes and other members of the faculty praised it as a culmination of technique and talent. Many were curious concerning the symbols surrounding the central subject and Wilcox denied any knowledge of their origin. Deschanes had a vague notion that they might have been Aramaic, and suggested that Wilcox show them to George Gammell Angell, a retired professor of Semitic Languages at Brown University.

Wilcox began meeting with Angell on March the First and did so daily for three weeks. During this time period Wilcox's art grew ever more bizarre focusing on the monstrosity he had created in the bas relief but extending into figurines, busts and even a larger piece, The Marine Abomination, weighing over three hundred pounds. In this three-week period Wilcox produced eighteen masterpieces, fusing cubism, futurism and primitivism into something wholly new that is best described as his Nightmare Period. However, despite the quality of his creations, working at such a feverish pace no doubt contributed to what happened next.

In the early morning hours of the Twenty-Third of March Wilcox suffered a severe psychological trauma and screamed out loud enough to wake several other residents. Kenneth Hart, who had been staying with Wilcox for some time found the artist ranting and feverish. When attempts to calm him failed a call was placed and in the wee hours Henry Anthony Wilcox was forcibly restrained and bundled off to his family home. Placed under the care of Dr. Frederick Tobey the boy languished in and out of consciousness until on the Second of April at around 3 p.m. every vestige of his curious illness suddenly ceased. Three days later he returned to his apartment with no memory of what had happened in his dreams or in the world over the last ten days. The weird nocturnal visions of the titanic monster had ceased and soon he stopped seeing Professor Angell. Sadly, with the loss of the visions so too was lost the ability to frantically create masterpieces.

This is not to say that his worked ceased, on the contrary, his work continued but seemed focused, if not obsessed with capturing the weird and esoteric minutiae of various anatomical features of his previously more perfunctory works. Hideous wings, multi-jointed claws and queer tri-lobed eyes regularly poured out of his workshop. These pieces of the fantastic were hailed by critics as fascinating productions from a morbid genius comparable to Goya or Munch. Wilcox however took no pleasure in his notoriety and became increasingly distant from his friends and family. When in 1926 police inquired concerning his relationship with Kenneth Hart, Wilcox seemed disinterested. Hart had moved to Boston and taken up with Richard Upton Pickman, but both had been unseen for weeks. Wilcox implied that his friend's disappearance, as well as that of Pickman, were not at all surprising, and rather predictable, but refused to explain further. He was however affected by the death of Professor Angell, and following a visit from the scholar's nephew produced a tableau of his former confidant standing amidst the ruins of an antediluvian metropolis of titanic proportions. In the collection of Brown University, the piece is entitled Perspective. Amongst critics it is viewed as a capstone to his Nightmare period.

In his final years Wilcox began studying a variety of philosophies including nihilism, anti-natalism, annihilationism, and the Buddhist concept of anatta. At one point he even investigated absurdism investigating the pantheon of the proto-Urartians and corresponding at length with the outrageous Dr. Emil Thoss of Miskatonic University. These studies created a profound shift in Wilcox's work, and he began to work in an entirely new direction that focused on a single motif, that of a tentacled wheel with a single spoke supporting a small cloudy blue ball. The first of these abstract works, Despair, was produced in 1928 has a diameter of five feet and is installed at the Morley Museum in Plunkettsburg.

In May of 1929 he joined the faculty of the Sanbourne Institute where he taught a course in contemporary art. The course was not a success, and both students and faculty filed complaints concerning Wilcox's behavior and attendance. Wilcox was dismissed after eight months when it was discovered that he had destroyed an acre of preserve land in creating a piece of his art. The installation was destroyed, and no photographs exist, but descriptions suggest that it was a larger iteration of Despair.

Although no records exist a similar piece entitled A Backward Glance exists in Mexico City on the grounds of the Diaz Foundation. Signed by Wilcox and dated in July 1930 the work rises thirty-two feet into the air and consists of steel cables entwined around each other to form vines or tentacles some of which reach inward toward the center. The central globe is hand blown blue and white glass supported by a single black steel wire. An in-depth investigation suggests that Wilcox designed the piece in less than eight hours and then with the aid of a team of twenty welders completed the full-scale installation in under forty-five days.

In January 1931 the Universidad Nacional Autonoma de Nicaragua in Managua announced that they would be undertaking an unprecedented project designed and lead by Wilcox. Over the next few weeks, a ten-acre plot was cleared, and a significant amount of steel, copper and lead were delivered to the site. From photographs it is clear that Wilcox was attempting to create two circles, one vertical and one horizontal with a central sphere supported with four spokes. The sphere was built from lead and stained glass mostly white and blue with some green. A progression of photographs makes it clear that at this scale the sphere is a representation of the planet Earth.

Work proceeded through February, and while notes suggest there were some engineering issues delays were minimal. The three arcs comprising the vertical circle were completed on the Second of March and hoisted into place on the Fourth. The Horizontal pieces were suspended on March Tenth and pinned the next day. Site work and safety inspections were completed on the Twentieth of March. Entitled Distant Vision, the installation was opened to select guests on the Twenty-Fifth of March and then to the general public two days later.

Notes for A Life of Nightmares

On the Thirtieth of March security was called concerning eighteen members of a local tribe who had occupied the site in order to carry out a religious rite invoking the Aztec deity Tlaloc. According to records the intruders were allowed by authorities to complete their rite after which they were forcibly dispersed. That afternoon the bodies of all eighteen individuals were found dead in a church. No signs of foul play were noted, and poison was suspected, but any chance of investigation was lost on the next day. On the Thirty-First of March 1931 at 10:00 in the morning a magnitude 6 earthquake struck the town. Between the quake itself and the ensuing fire more than two thousand people were lost and forty-five thousand were made homeless. Henry Wilcox's masterwork—Distant Vision—was swallowed up by the earth and lost forever. Only a few photographs remain. Henry Anthony Wilcox himself was never seen again and was assumed to be among the dead. A marker was placed in his memory on the university grounds.

The war sent Wilcox into obscurity, but in 1948 a review of the holdings of the RISD found several pieces by the artist in their archives. This sparked a resurgence of interest in his work and an effort to create a full catalog was made. While acknowledged to be woefully incomplete the pieces presented represent the first attempt at bringing the work of the artist to the attention of the public. It took four years and significant expense, but the RISD is proud to present the first retrospective of Providence native and true avant-garde genius Henry Anthony Wilcox.

The collection will open to the public on the Twelfth of August 1952, the fiftieth anniversary of the birth of the artist.

The Ghost Stones of Mthura

Common wisdom says that the light envelopes, the starships comprised of condensed photons, grant the Nug Soth access to Twenty-Eight Galaxies, but the science-wizards of that ancient race know a secret truth, that there is a twenty-ninth, an ancient gray cluster of dead stars. It's true name is lost to time, but those who study the skies refer to it as Q'yth, the Midden Stars, though those astronomers who turn their lenses toward that portion of the sky are few, and these are prone to inscribing sigils of protection in the air when that dread name is invoked.

It was to this place that Buo, the arch-hierophant of the Nug Soth, had charged the wizard Zkauba to travel. All the champions of Yaddith had been summoned home and beneath the gaze of Buo and his councilors the latest atrocity was revealed. The burrowing Dholes, which had for centuries made a habit of violating the brooding chambers, had in a concerted effort, undermined the very foundations of Ocsic, a city on the southern continent. Without warning, the entire metropolis had been swallowed up into an abyssal grave. With it were lost all the inhabitants, young and old, wizened and unbirthed, as well as the great archives of ancient knowledge and learning that were housed there amidst titanic statues and towering minarets dedicated to the memory of the magnificence of the Nug Soth.

It was with this disaster that Buo and his minions rallied the brave and the bold to a fever. For eons the Nug Soth had searched for a way to end the depredations of the Dholes, but to no avail. There was a reason for this, a secret reason, a secret that the wizard Zkauba had learned, but it had driven him mad, and forced his retreat into the recesses of his own brain. None of the other championed heroes suspected the truth, though Zkauba had reasoned that Buo, and his council also knew, and thus they accepted their assignments without question. They were

41

dispatched throughout the twenty-eight galaxies in their light envelopes on yet another mission to seek weapons and spells and sigils that might finally protect the Nug Soth from the hungers and machinations of the abhorrent Dholes. Into the sky they flew, their ships catching the solar winds and propelling them beyond the seven suns about which Yaddith orbited, until they reached the point beyond the gravitational sphere where they could engage the Yhnngrr Engines and slip beneath the ether upon which the galaxies themselves float.

It was to Q'yth that Zkauba had been assigned, and when that had been announced a low murmur had passed amongst the gathered masses. No others were assigned to travel to that haunted cluster of dying stars, for there was rumored to be only one world worth traveling to, a world where none dared go, though none would say why. Mthura was a world on the edge of the galaxy itself, a place rumored to be the last depository of the knowledge that snuffed out the stars of Q'yth. In the memory of all who still lived on Yaddith, none could recall any who had visited Mthura, and the archives themselves only hinted that a few necromancers had once dared to travel there, never to return.

None suspected when that terrible charge was accepted that it was not Zkauba who reached out for it, but rather something alien that had wormed its way inside his prosaic brain. How a man of Earth had been whisked across time and space and forced to occupy the body of Zkauba is another story, one that I have recorded before. Nor shall I waste time retelling how I learned the secret of the Nug Soth, solved the Riddle of Thaqqualah, and in the process drove Zkauba mad. The body of the Wizard-Scientist Zkauba had been usurped, and it was I, Randolph Carter, who had in his body responded to Buo's call, and it was I who accepted the charge to travel to Mthura, Randolph Carter, who had secretly proclaimed himself the Warlock of Yaddith!

There are other stories I could tell, of Stronti and Shaggai and even of Tond, but that is not what I wish to write of this day. This day, on these metallic amber pages, I shall record my journey to Mthura, what I learned there, and what happened next. It is I suppose my apology, my testament, perhaps my way of seeking absolution for what I have done. I came to Mthura searching for wisdom, for knowledge, I found only the dead, and worse.

My journey to Mthura was indirect, and I spent days circling the galaxy of Q'yth, studying it, playing the lenses and organs of the light envelope across its sickly visage. The stars of the Q'yth are ancient, primordial things and have long since decayed to the point where the only light they admit is pale, gray and slow. They are cold, collapsing things, so weak that they can no longer bind planets to themselves. Thus, the few worlds that remain wander in queer orbits through dying star fields, the dust of collapsed worlds, and the ashes of dead civilizations. Mthura's orbit is perpendicular to what remains of its ancient home galaxy, arcing deep into the void between star clusters. It was here that I found Mthura; just where the star charts on the seventeenth Tablet of Nhing said it would be, in the darkness of abyssal space, bathed in the sallow light of a dying galaxy.

Mthura was as gray and desolate as the galaxy it was once part of. It hung in the inky black of the night, a sickly thing with little atmosphere. There were no signs of life, nothing blue, or green, or red on the surface. Only a single tower rising from the surface and extending into space suggested that there once was or might still be anything sentient on Mthura. I spread the sails of my light envelope and tacked toward the tip of the tower. An iris portal spun open, beckoning me to enter. I complied, gliding in and settling the great tesseract onto the deck as the portal closed behind it and atmosphere filled the chamber.

As I waited, I equipped myself. I donned my armor, encasing all six limbs in protections that were both mystic and physical in nature. I checked my chainsword, and the crystals that powered and supplemented my defenses and wards. The ceramics felt cool against my rugose skin. If it was one thing that the Nug Soth knew, it was how to craft the weapons of war and the defenses against them. The pommel of the sword felt good in my upper right claw, as did the gauntlets that graced my other three limbs. Even the boots that wrapped around my feet and legs were not only comfortable but also capable of terrible feats, both offensive and defensive.

As the portal to my own ship opened, a great light in one of the chamber walls sputtered to life. A doorframe appeared and above it, written in ancient hieroglyphics in the language of the Progenitors, a single word. As with all such words there were meanings, and inflections and things implied but not spoken, still the meaning was clear and the easiest of all translations was the English *lychgate*, the entryway through which a corpse is carried into a cemetery. Though I will admit that there were certain inflections in the language that even Zkauba's memories and knowledge could not explain. I use the word "lich" for its old meaning of a corpse, but human language is insufficient here, there was a tone of distaste and of something malevolent and infectious. In one symbol, that might be described as little more than a stray punctuation mark, there was a suggestion of what men might refer to as the undead, but again language fails here. The symbol was similar to that used for the reanimated but was subtly different. Whatever was done in this place, on Mthura, it was not for the dead, it was not for the undead, but rather for something else entirely.

The lychgate opened and from it crept forth a wizened thing draped in robes. It wasn't any species I could identify, but Zkauba's memories suggested that it was a servitor, a construct made out of living tissue, to carry out specific tasks, the word Tethlaoth, bubbled to the surface of our shared brain. It slouched toward me, harshly breathing with each labored step. As it came closer the stench of the thing became overwhelming and I gagged as it lowered its cowl and revealed the confused mass of eyes and ears that it called a face.

When it finally spoke, it was all I could to keep from retching. "Tek thelli'tek the'melli az." When I didn't respond it spoke again, "Tek thelli'tek the'melli az." It took me a moment to process, it had been eons since anyone had heard this language spoken, but using Zkauba's memories and knowledge, I stumbled through the translation knowing that the sound "az" was related to memorials for the dead. "Give me the cenotaph."

It took a second or two for my mouth to stumble through the response, and I am sure my words were poor, but they did the job. "I have no cenotaph to give. I have come seeking knowledge." I made sure to use the same word he had used, but I had no idea what a cenotaph was.

The Tethlaoth whined in frustration. "The lychgate is for the acceptance of cenotaphs. Visitors are not allowed through the lychgate."

My mind raced the servitor before me seemed adamant. "I have come seeking assistance."

"The lychgate is for the acceptance of cenotaphs. Visitors are not allowed through the lychgate."

It wasn't a thing to be reasoned with. It may have looked like a living thing, but it wasn't, it was just a machine, and it responded only the way it had been taught. Visitors were not allowed through the lychgate. Something in my mind clicked, and in an instant, I knew how to circumvent the servitor. "I am not a visitor."

The servitor stretched its neck, and its eyes widened. "Are you a Mortician?" Once again, Mortician wasn't the proper term, but it embodied the concept, a concept that would take paragraphs to explain, and even now I am not sure that I fully understand it. I could have just as easily translated it as "management" or "controller".

I confirmed his statement, "I am the Mortician. Will you let me through the lychgate?"

The creature bowed, almost prostrated himself before me. I ignored him and marched toward the gate. The creature folded its cowl back over itself and fell into step behind me. The gate shimmered as we went through and in a single step, we weren't on the tip of the tower anymore, but on the surface of the planet itself. It was a cold world with little atmosphere. There was no sun, but the gray Q'yth galaxy that hung in the sky bathed the landscape in a weak gloom. Hard radiation permeated the thin air. If it weren't for my armor, I would have been dead in seconds.

All around me were stones. I was in a forest of graves. They were of all sizes and shapes, some towering pillars; others little bigger than my hand, but all of them were made from the same material, a kind of gray-green stone, and all of them carved with names written in the ancient language of the progenitors. I was standing in the middle of a world of graves; even the pathways upon which I was walking were paved with headstones.

"How many bodies are buried here?" I said aloud, not really expecting an answer.

"There are no bodies buried here." The voice of the Tethlaoth whispered through the receiver in my helmet. "There are over three vigitillion cenotaphs accumulated here." The slave-thing made a queer sound. "You should know this; you are the Mortician."

"Mortician?" The voice was weak and slow, but the source was clear, one of the stones was speaking. "Have you finally come for us Mortician?"

In an instant I knew where I was and what I was looking at. Even amongst the Nug Soth there were still tales of intrepid wanderers who had found and spoken to Ghost Stones. Where they came from and what they were was never revealed, but all the tales followed the same pattern: someone finds a stone which then proceeds to seduce the finder with promises of wealth, or power, or knowledge. A quest is undertaken, and the promise fulfilled, but always with a macabre twist ending that resulted in the death of the unfortunate finder.

And I was standing in a field, an entire world of them.

The Tethlaoth whined again. "You are not a Mortician; you do not belong here." It reared up and threw its cloak clear. Any semblance of pretense was over, and the full terror of the thing was revealed. It was an amorphous thing, in places transparent, and in others solid and fearsome. Tendrils of insubstantial mist spiraled through space towards me their tips full of claws and gnashing maws of curved and ferocious teeth. I spun the chain sword out of its sheath slicing through the nearest appendages. With my lower hands I formed the signs and sigils that would cast up a shield and block any further assaults.

Or so I had hoped. The Tethlaoth refused to cooperate. Instead of being stopped by the shield it phased out of this world and into the spaces between, rendering my shield useless. The creature impaled itself on my sword, allowing the circulating blades to tear into its flesh and send gore into the air and covering the nearby stones with chunks of alien flesh and the strange protoplasmic fluid that was held within. It squirmed down the blade screaming as it clawed toward me. I charged one of my gauntlets with energy drawn from the inbetween space itself and drove my fist into the creature's interior. It whimpered as I punched through to the other side of the soft fleshy matter. More gore exploded out as the creature shifted back into the inbetween, but the grasp I had on its guts kept it from escaping. It was pinned into the substance of our universe, like an insect on a mounting board.

It screamed at me, tried to claw at me, but where the mystical shield failed, the ceramic armor did its job. I punched up with another fist, this time into the head. My fingers, my claws dug around, followed the thick strands of protoplasm that it used as nerves. There was a bundle of something, of soft tissue with strands moving in and out of it. It wasn't really a brain, but it functioned as one and crushing it brought the struggle to an end. The creature died and crumbled into a lump of inanimate jelly and viscous slime. Then the world exploded.

Suddenly I was on the ground, my mind overwhelmed by the explosion of knowledge that suddenly filled my head. The Tethlaoth wasn't really a person, it didn't have memories, but it did have information. It knew what the cenotaphs, the ghost stones, were, and what Mthura was for as well. By crushing that small pseudo-brain, I released all that knowledge, and it rushed into my head like a wave of light.

Looking out at the viscera covered stones, I knew that they were more than just grave markers, they were ancient technology that preserved the memories and personality of a sentient being within a crystalline matrix that was nearly indestructible and powered by an ethereal link to the heart of a star. All around me, the shattered bits of servitor, ancient biotechnology, were seeping into the stones, slowly being absorbed.

Over the course of millennia, the use of cenotaphs spread. It crept from culture to culture, from world to world, from system to system, and became endemic throughout the galaxy. The cenotaphs were not alive, but nor were they dead, they were the Necrophiles, the Loved Dead. They were cherished and honored by those who knew them. They became treasures, advisors, leaders, and they ushered in a golden age of enlightenment for an entire galaxy.

That age was short lived.

Something stirred in the vast garden of stones. It shifted and creaked. I could hear stone grating against stone. Something electric was in the air, great sparks of blue lightning arced from stone to stone. Two technologies that were never meant to meet were suddenly meshing, integrating, learning how to accommodate one another. There was something shuddering out there in the labyrinth of stones, something going through the pain of being born, or reborn. A throat made of gravel screamed, cried out in agony.

Even with only choosing the wisest, the most learned, or the most talented, the number of minds that were converted into cenotaphs – Az - quickly outnumbered the living. In the process an empire was created where the living served the not dead. Great ethereal networks of energy and communications were fabricated. To power these webs of undead minds the stars themselves were enslaved. There were wars, the living against the dead and their allies. But as the living fell, the ranks and genius of the Az grew. How does one wage a war against an enemy that can recruit from the dead?

The screaming in the garden subsided. Stones were falling, falling into place, linking into a polycrystalline latticework. Tendrils of linked stone swirled into existence, as did bulwarks of great stela crashed together forming into cyclopean megaliths that shifted and groaned into a new kind of life. The stones were falling into place.

The Az fell from power the same way they rose, slowly and at their own hands. There were plots—grave plots within plots, which set ancient Az against the younger. Prison worlds, Mthura, were created, where the lesser Az could be held. The wars were terrible and the death toll amongst the living caught in the middle was immense. Those living that could, found ways to flee in vast fleets of ships that braved the gulf between galaxies. Those that remained were too few and too sparsely populated to be of service to the Az for long. A whole galaxy was abandoned by the living, and left for the dead, for the Az, and thus Q'yth, the Midden, came into being.

"MORTICIAN!" The voice of the dead, of the Az, of the cenotaph roared across the surface of Mthura. "Mortician you should not have come for us." All around me the stones had formed into monstrous creatures, like homunculi or perhaps the Golems of the Hebrews. "We should not go quietly into the void. And the death of the Tethlaoth, the caretaker, supplies us with the means to oppose you." They were of myriad shapes, nightmares of claws and tentacles, of talons and tendrils, of thrashing limbs and gnashing teeth, but each part was not of flesh or bone, but rather of crystalline stone, of cenotaphs of infinite variety assembled into patchwork monsters. They stumbled toward me their stone feet and paws gathering up their brethren with each clumsy step.

There had to be Caretakers, constructs to take in new additions, and make sure the prison worlds were cared for. It wasn't thought necessary to provide any security, the Conquerors couldn't think of anyone who would want to come to Mthura. That had been unfathomable eons ago, and in time Q'yth grew older and colder and greyer. Eventually, the Conquerors themselves vanished from the dead galaxy, and all that was left behind were their relics, their cold and barren worlds, places like Mthura, and their Caretakers.

And the Morticians. The Caretakers didn't know much about the Morticians, neither did the Az, but both knew that when they came, it meant the end of their existence. They were creatures of age and power, whose sole purpose was to find the remaining Az and bring about their final dispensation.

And I had tried to pass myself off as a Mortician, the embodiment of everything that the Az feared, and had struggled to avoid while entire species had evolved, flourished, and died. I had masqueraded as the embodiment of mortality, was it any surprise that they had risen up in fear to oppose me?

I stumbled to my feet, my sword smashing through stone monsters forming just beyond my reach. Rock trolls fell beneath my blade, shattering into dust as the chain sword, enchanted with Elder magics, ground through their component cenotaphs. They weren't as indestructible as they had thought, or perhaps age or the conglomeration had made them vulnerable. Whatever the case, they fell before my weapons like winter wheat before the reaping scythe.

A small squadron of simian things took up a position before me, buying time for the others to complete their transformation. It was a transparent strategy but effective. Two of them rushed me, drawing the attention of my blades, while two more aimed for my midsection, where my gauntleted fist fended them off. The last went for my head, wrapping an arm around my helmet, and trying desperately to pull it free. They may have thought of me as a Mortician, but they still recognized that if my armor came off, I would be exposed to the near vacuum that Mthura called an atmosphere. With a free claw I traced a sigil of protection into the air and reinforced my armor and shields, repelling the stone simians. They flew back through the air and crashed against a selection of their brethren, shattering into pieces. But the pieces didn't fall, they adhered themselves to the other stones and became incorporated into new more complex constructs.

Behind me a dragon roared.

It was an eerie sound, not unlike the high-pitched tinkling of glass bottles magnified through some alien amplifier. The source was a titanic thing, I call it a dragon, but it was nothing like those of human myth. Like the body I wore, it drew characteristics from a variety of species. Three great serpentine heads were counter-balanced by two tails, that all sat atop a thick gold-scaled body carried by two elephantine legs. It was inspired I suppose by some terrifying primordial creature drawn from the memory of one of those interred here. Great perfunctory wings graced its back supported by massive ribs of vermillion. It was all for show of course, meant to terrify me, to distract me, as the legions of cenotaphs bound themselves into something more.

The beast reared up, why it bothered was unknown to me, for the thing was easily five times my size and could have simply trampled me.

Instead, one of its mouths opened and a weird arcing shaft of electric energy exploded out pounding me with tremendous force. I was thrown backwards, my armor and weapons all sounding alarms as their various systems failed. I limped to my feet, the armor was sluggish, the power cells nearly drained. I couldn't take another hit like that. By my estimation I couldn't take another hit at all. I was nearly powerless as I watched the second head rear up to strike. I diverted what little energies I had into the armor and dashed toward the tower entrance. The beast's bolt impacted just behind me, and the ensuing explosion catapulted me forward. I used the momentum to my advantage, twisting my body so that I glided into the shimmering lychgate that would take me back to the pinnacle of the reception tower. In the blink of an eye, I was miles above Mthura in the docking bay where my ship waited.

I limped forward and signaled the light envelope to prepare to leave. The entryway dilated open, and the engines powered up. Behind me the lychgate sparked and something made of stone tried to climb through. A clawed tentacle whipped out and searched to find something to grab hold of. When it failed, it hooked itself on to the frame itself, but the structure was insufficient, and collapsed under the added weight. Its mechanics broken, the gate became unstable, gouts of liquid proto-matter suddenly bulged out and then collapsed. The lychgate ate itself, consumed itself and then collapsed into a single spark of light. It was a torch, a beacon so bright that even through the filters of my helmet it hurt my eyes. It burned bright and hot, scorching everything within its reach, and that reach was expanding, growing as the very air itself caught flame. As I fled toward my ship my arms and armor felt that heat and were scorched by it. Even the skin of my light envelope blistered as the collapsed lychgate exploded outward and devoured the tower that once held it.

My ship moved through space, urged on by my panic and fear. I tuned my lenses back towards Mthura. Any pretense of being something else was cast aside. Mthura or more specifically the cenotaphs of Mthura, the fallen Az of the galaxy known as Q'yth were becoming something else. The golems, the creatures constructed from the Az, the Ghost Stones of Mthura, were being consolidated, absorbed, not unlike the process that had destroyed the lychgate. But here instead of being a sudden bright and burning light, there was only darkness, a palpable evil forming from matter and becoming something else.

As I left the system, fleeing not only Mthura but Q'yth as well, I saw the terrifying horrific thing that was growing there, spreading, and consuming the planet and the tower that stood there. The Az and all the energy nearby had coalesced into a single crystalline formation that floated where once Mthura had been. It was a terrifying thing to look at, with angles that were all wrong, that opened into obtuse spaces and acute dimensions beyond those understood by even the Nug Soth. It hurt even my mind to look at what was happening there, but I was compelled to. For I wanted to see, needed to see, as the Az made Mthura the center of a new network of great tendrils that reached out into the dying galaxy of Q'yth. Ethereal conduits were spun and grey star after grey star was linked into a new and terrifying web. As galaxies go, there wasn't much energy left in Q'yth, but the Az, or whatever they had become were determined to drain it dry, to turn grey stars black, and to draw sustenance from the very collapse of an entire galaxy.

The light ship sailed on, and eventually moved beyond where even the strongest of enhanced lenses could still focus on the place where Mthura once was. I shuddered and went about repairing my armor and weapons, hoping that I would never again have to see the ghost stones of Mthura or what they had become, or what they would someday become. Once they had been men, or things not unlike men, but they had become something else. Time and power and fear had set them on a course of metamorphosis, and I had been a catalyst, an impetus for their final transformation. They were no longer the Az; I could not call them that anymore. So, I gave them a new name, my right I suppose, after all it was I and I alone who witnessed the birth of the singular and crystalline thing that devoured the galaxy that spawned it.

I called it Q'yth-Az, which I suppose is as good a name as any for the monstrous thing that now stalks the stars, and the places between the stars, and haunts my memories with its hideous crystalline nature.

For Scott David Aniolowski

Arkham Arts Review: *Alienation*

An Interview with Director James Romberg

Eight years ago, media producer James Romberg became a sensation with his docudrama *Innsmouth*. This week he debuts his new work *Alienation*, an account of the life of the film actor Abraham Waite. Earlier this week Mr. Romberg chattered with our own Mick Moon.

MM: Mr. Romberg, *Innsmouth* was a sweeping historical piece, and a critical and commercial success, why follow it up with an examination of someone like Abraham Waite? It seems a radical departure from your previous work.

JR: *Innsmouth* and before that *Jermyn* were period pieces, and *Alienation* is a contemporary film, but it's still rooted in the same source, still asking the same questions. What does it mean to be different, to be fundamentally inhuman in a human world, both physically and psychologically? I could do this through fiction, but adapting history, telling the stories of these people who actually lived, I think it is much more powerful.

MM: But, in both previous films your protagonists moved from a human world into an inhuman one. In *Jermyn*, Arthur rejects his origins with tragic results, while Robert in *Innsmouth* eventually learns to accept and embrace his ancestry. Abraham Waite begins in an inhuman world and moves into the normal one, finding a place, or at least trying to. That seems to be a bold reversal of direction.

JR: Actually, it's a natural progression that mimics the time and attitudes that each film was set in. *Jermyn* is an Edwardian piece, with the central character representing the dominant society, which violently rejects any revelations concerning the past that might impact their particular worldview. *Innsmouth* is purposefully a Jazz Age piece, and the response of Robert Olmstead to revelations concerning his ancestry mirrors the societal changes that were occurring during that time period. Yes, he rejects what he discovers, and reports it to the government, and the actions taken are just as violent and drastic as those portrayed in *Jermyn*. However, in the aftermath Olmstead reconsiders, his initial rejection is replaced with not only acceptance, but also a sense of outré wonder and elation. I think of *Alienation* as a commentary on post-humanism. Abraham Waite begins his journey in Innsmouth, isolated from what some would call civilization. His journey from that isolation into the spotlight of first fame, and then infamy, highlights the changes in mainstream society and the way in which it now embraces the fringe elements it once tried to deny, even destroy.

MM: But Abraham Waite is still alive, and still working in film, correct?

JR: He is. Abe has been working in film since 1962 when he first appeared in Corman's *Echidna*. He made sixteen films with Corman including the remake of *Freaks* and the classic *Galaxy of Fear*. In 1982 he began working with Tobe Hooper appearing first in *Tsathaggua*, and then later as the antagonist in *Warlords of Yaddith*. The failure of Romero's *Night of the Reanimator*, both critically and financially, drove Abe to take a number of minor parts, mostly as an extra or part of the special effects team. This led to him working with Carpenter on *Who Goes There?* and a Saturn Award for Best Supporting Actor.

MM: This was very controversial at the time.

JR: Right. There were a lot of voices, ugly voices, raised in response to Abe's appearing on network television. A coalition of actors, mostly character actors who specialized in roles that required significant amounts of make-up and prosthetics, objected saying that Abe had an unfair advantage. In the meanwhile, many people with similar characteristics suggested that Abe was catering to stereotypes. Just as ethnic groups had formed to protest the negative portrayals of Africans and Asians on film, the movement that protested Abe and similar actors became very vocal. However, while the Black Face and Yellow Face Movements worked in concert with each other, the Green Face groups found no such support and were forced to escalate their activities in order to garner national attention to their cause. Unfortunately, one radical faction chose to resort to violence to make their point.

MM: You're talking about the accident that occurred on the set of Larson's series *Galactics*.

JR: There was nothing accidental about it. The Esoteric Order of Dagon purposefully interfered with a dangerous stunt which caused the death of six of their members. It was a reprehensible act, and psychologically scarred those cast and crew members who witnessed it.

MM: The grand jury found that the studio was not responsible for those deaths. Abraham Waite sued and won significant damages from the Order.

JR: Well, he may have won the legal battle, but, in many ways, he lost the war.

MM: Care to elaborate?

JR: The trial was a spectacle, and it brought to light a significant amount of history, including family history, that Waite would have preferred to remain out of the public eye. There was testimony about religious practices, inbreeding, genetics, even miscegenation. It was all very ugly. There was even a Congressional Committee chaired by Tipper Gore to review the legal status of residents of Innsmouth and Dunwich. Afterwards, the studio wrote Waite's character out of the series, over Larson's protests mind you, and Abe was essentially blacklisted from Hollywood.

MM: This led to his working in some questionable films.

JR: Yeah, for about ten years or so he worked with a lot of independent directors. He even did some soft-core, what was unfortunately called fish porn. Eventually, he got work with some decent directors like Raimi, Smith and del Toro. All of which eventually led to his performance in Jackson's *Eldritch*, for which he won the Academy Award.

MM: This did not sit well with Tantamount, the parent studio of *Galactics*.

JR: They weren't happy at all, particularly with the toy line, which featured an action figure based on Waite that was almost identical to the one being marketed for the *Galactics* line. Tantamount took Abe to court claiming that he was infringing on their copyright of the character's appearance, a patently absurd tactic, but bolstered by some creative interpretation of language in the licensing clause of his contract. Waite's lawyers countersued, noting that he had only agreed to the use of his face, not his entire body, which in the series had never been fully shown. Meanwhile after reading the position taken in Tantamount's filings, the SAG union authorized a strike in support of Waite.

MM: That work stoppage lasted for six months, and eventually led to the downfall of the studio head Howard Lowe. It also changed the way studios contracted with actors and licensed their products.

JR: It also created a whole new class of actors, so called Living Effects. The portrayal of the monstrous that had spawned the Greenface opposition and groups like the Esoteric Order of Dagon, suddenly had little to complain about. MADS, the Monstrous Anti-Defamation Society, was formed, and like the ASPCA, now has a presence on any studio film. Though to be honest, the days of exploitation films like *The Blob*, *The Creature from the Black Lagoon*, or *I Married a Monster from Outer Space*, are long dead. Sure, there may be a few direct to video releases, but these are relatively minor films.

MM: *Humanoids from the Deep* set box office records at the Kingsport Film Festival last year. Jeff Wilmarth called it "A tour de force of cinematic sleaze that will leave you begging for more."

JR: I've seen that film, and I understand why it was so popular, and why the critics liked it. But the truth is that it possesses the same kind of nostalgic charm that things like *Madman* and *Red Hook* have. When we look at these dramas that are recreating what many see as a simpler more innocent time, what we are really doing is looking at that period and remembering it with fondness, but at the same time, we recognize that many of those behaviors and events were the product of an ignorant and bigoted society, that in retrospect can be very amusing, and yes entertaining, and therefore profitable. But that doesn't make them significant works of art.

MM: For example?

JR: Scott's film *Extraterrestrial* was very profitable, and the critics adored it when it came out. But now twenty years later it is forgotten, the effects are sub-par, the storyline is mediocre, and the acting was just bland. In contrast, *EXtro* by Burton lost money on its initial release, but has now become a cult classic and a cash cow for Dyson Pictures.

MM: Shifting back to Abraham Waite, what's his current situation?

JR: He's doing very well; he lives in Kingsport where he spends most of his time fishing and painting. He doesn't act much, though he just did a cameo in Lynch's *Devil Reef*, and he's scheduled to appear in an upcoming episode of *Professor Wyche*. He will be at the premiere on Friday.

MM: Was he involved much with the making of *Alienation*?

JR: Not as much as I would have liked. What many people don't seem to understand is that Waite is a consummate professional. The film itself relies heavily on his memoir *Monstrous*, but where Abe was really helpful was in the actual film making. He's been an actor for more than forty years, but he has also studied film and camera work. He actually has a credit in the film as a camera man. Also, Abe worked extensively with Rex Topf, the actor who played Abe in the film, to make sure that Rex had mastered Waite's very distinctive walk and cadence. This wasn't easy for Rex, he has three fewer tentacles than Abe, which we added in through digital effects, but capturing the way Abe moves was difficult for him.

MM: You told me earlier that the home release version of the film will have a bonus track, would you like to explain?

JR: Oh, absolutely, in fact we just came from the studio this morning, where I and Abe were working on the Director's commentary. So, we will actually have Abraham Waite commenting about the film of his life.

MM: That is kind of surreal.

JR: Isn't it though?

MM: James, I want to thank you for joining us here at Arkham Arts Review.

JR: Always a pleasure

MM: *Alienation*, the new film by James Romberg about the life of actor Abraham Waite premieres at Miskatonic University's Wilmarth Centre for the Arts in Arkham on Friday April 30th. Tickets are available at the box office, or online.

Editor's Note: Following the premiere of *Alienation*, Director James Romberg, and his wife Ellen, were joined by Mr. Waite at a reception for the press. According to eyewitnesses the three were actively involved in answering questions, when Reverend Enoch Marsh, the nominal head of the Esoteric Order of Dagon in Innsmouth, approached the panelists. Well known for his radical views in favor of racial segregation, Reverend Marsh was supposed to be barred from the reception. How he gained access is unknown. Security staff failed in their attempts to block his approach, and once Marsh reached the table, he threw himself at Mr. Waite reportedly screaming "Cthulhu fthagn!" Dr. Marsh then detonated explosives hidden underneath his coat killing himself, three security guards and the entire panel.

In light of these events Witch Hill Studios has indefinitely postponed the film's release.

The Angels of Pestilence

Prologue: The Madness of Herbert West

Madness is a terrible thing, and even a worse thing to be accused of, particularly if one knows for a certainty that one is truly not mad. I suppose it is the nature of madness to deny being mad, but this was the situation in which my colleague Herbert West found himself. I did what I could to defend him, but the military tribunal would hear none of it, and threatened me with arrest as well, suggesting that I may have not been a simple bystander, but rather a co-conspirator in the rampage that left one of our colleagues dead.

While there was a logical, albeit fantastical, explanation for West's rampage, there were other activities, the existence of which we intended to keep secret from the authorities. It would not help our cause if our true motive in serving the Allied cause were discovered. Back in the United States our studies in the field of the reanimation of the dead had drawn the attention of the authorities on several occasions. Back before I began my relationship with him, West had been questioned in the disappearances of both a professor and a student, though he was never detained I suspected he knew more than he let on. Our life after university had been equally rife with the danger of discovery. We took what steps we could to protect our illicit research, though by its very nature there were risks. After eight years in Bolton, I am sure we had raised the suspicions of various members of the community. West would suggest that our decision to join the war effort was driven by his desire to gain easy access to fresh corpses on which to experiment, but I would suggest that self-preservation was also a motive.

One would think that our experiments on the battlefield, even amongst the carnage of war, would have been noticed. However, our commanding officers seemed disinclined to investigate even the most outrageous of events. One might ignore the treatment of prisoners of war, and even the events at the St. Bru Orphanage, but to ignore the death of our friend and colleague Major Sir Eric Moreland Clapham-Lee seemed beyond the pale. West called it luck, but I grew to suspect it has more to do with the scarcity of doctors willing to serve in such conditions. As long as we tended to the wounded, there may have been something of a willingness to overlook our extracurricular activities.

At least until what happened in the trenches at Hulluch—the mysterious plague and what followed. I will not dispute the fact that a good man died as a result of West's actions, but those actions likely saved the lives of dozens if not hundreds of others.

I still cannot say with total certainty that I would not have defied West and told the tribunal what had really happened. It perhaps would have revealed our illicit experiments but that was a chance I was willing to consider, and so I set it down here for the first time.

Part One: The Plague Doctors

It was the sixteenth of April, the third day since the Germans had stopped shelling, and even then, the lingering stench of moldy hay still lingered. It was a tell-tale sign that the enemy had used White Star, shells containing not only chlorine but phosgene as well. It was a deadly and sinister combination, for the victims of phosgene poisoning can show no signs or symptoms for up to twenty-four hours. Thus, as the soldiers around us began succumbing first to a shortness of breath, then a rapid drop in blood pressure coupled with violent coughing, and the production of a pink-tinged fluid. Death is by heart failure. West and I assumed that the cause was the lingering aftereffects of exposure to the gas. There were however some symptoms that were not consistent with that diagnosis. These included low fever, accompanied by large nodules in the armpits, and violent hallucinations that always ended in unintelligible screams. The trenches are a cesspit of filth and disease, and it is not uncommon for soldiers to be ravaged by various illnesses and infections, but the fact that all of our patients were exhibiting these queer symptoms was puzzling.

But not puzzling enough for us to cease our experiments, indeed if anything we found our exercises revitalized. Perhaps it was a sense of responsibility, a desire to save those we could that drove us to experiment on those that had succumbed to this wasting plague, but I doubt it. If anything, it was simply the opportunity. There were so many freshly dead it would have been a waste not to take advantage of the opportunity. It was after all why we had come to this foul and dreaded place.

The process of reanimation is not without certain risks, and we had over the years developed a process by which to evaluate our potential subjects. Key to this was a measure of their suitability - their potential for responding to our reagent in a favorable manner. Part of this was the manner in which the subject had died. Those who had suffered a transitory interruption of the functions that sustain life were the most responsive. These included individuals who had suffered electrical shocks, suffocation or drowning. Those who had suffered chemical interruptions including poisonings also tended to respond well. Those who had suffered physical damage were not always so fortunate. Relatively minor injuries, particularly those that could be readily repaired, also tended to respond well, but only if the resulting blood loss was ameliorated. Those suffering from disease were not always the best choices, particularly if the disease was accompanied by a fever that led to organ damage, particularly to the brain.

It was for this reason that West and I decided to autopsy one of our casualties and determine how the strange malady progressed through the body, before we decided to subject any of them to our reanimation process. We carried out the procedure in the wee hours of the morning, in an isolated spur of the trenches that we had carved out as our own. We had hidden the entrance behind a muddy tarp that for all but the most keen of observers would appear as simply another piece of the trench wall. Behind this we had a rather well stocked makeshift laboratory, complete with electric lights powered by a secreted line we had run from the command bunker.

We did the easy work first, the lower abdomen and the organs within. We removed the liver, pancreas, and kidneys and even sectioned the bowel. None of these showed any signs of significant damage, and West cursed as we moved on to cracking open the ribcage. Here we examined the heart and lungs. The heart, that thick and heavy ball of cardiac muscle seemed entirely unaffected. In contrast, the lungs seemed to have suffered a minor a serious trauma. They were full of the same pink fluid that the patient had been coughing up. The source of this was sloughing off of dead cells—those killed by contact with the phosgene gas—mingled with blood from the underlining capillaries. The likely cause of death was seemingly by drowning in a mixture of blood, mucus and their own dying lungs.

Despite this obvious diagnosis we were ever the professionals, and therefore continued our investigations of the rest of the body. Herbert biopsied the enlarged and blackened lymph nodes and studied them under the microscope, while I cracked the skull and examined the brain. I expected to find a swelling, the result of a brain fever, or perhaps an aneurysm brought about by the physical stress of fighting off the disease, but there was nothing. The brain was perfectly intact, in fact it was one of the healthiest human brains I had ever handled.

West on the other hand had had more success. Under the magnifying lenses of the microscope the black tissues of the lymph glands had revealed a malignancy that both he and I were quite familiar with. It was a kind of lymphoma, a cancer of the lymph nodes. It was in the early stages of development, but it was clearly cancer.

"It is not possible," suggested West.

"Why?" I countered, "We've seen cancer in young men before, it is unusual, but not impossible."

"In one man yes, but we have a dozen patients showing these same symptoms. Cancer isn't contagious."

"A side effect of exposure to the gas perhaps."

West nodded, "Possibly, but this is an advanced growth. A cancer at this stage, in all of these men–men who weren't even here, who didn't even know each other three weeks ago, how is that possible? The odds of that are ... "

"Astronomical?" I suggested.

"Astronomical," West agreed. "But it changes nothing. There is nothing here that would stop us from experimenting."

"So, the next patient who expires ... "

West pushed his glasses back on his nose and ran his clean hand through his pale hair. "Prepare the reagent." He paused, "and double check the restraints. I don't want a repeat of last time."

We didn't have to wait long. Corporal del Col of Etobicoke, Ontario expired less than an hour later, ten minutes after that West and I had him in our secret surgery prepping him for the procedure. This consisted of me strapping the body down while I made various observations on its condition, and West made notes. Detailed noes were essential to the scientific process. Even now, I can still remember the details of that night.

"Subject is twenty-three years old, male, Caucasian." I placed the left hand in a leather restraint and buckled it tight. Approximately five feet and eight inches tall, one hundred and seventy pounds." I repeated the process on the other side. His hands were already cold. "No evidence of physical malformation or trauma." I strapped the head down and to the side, exposing the base of the skull. "Cause of death appears to be phosgene gas poisoning, with complications from an unknown pathogen with swollen lymph nodes in the armpit."

"I'm recommending fifty grains of the reagent 16C in solution," opined West.

I mulled the calculations over in my head, considering weight, time and cause of death. "I concur."

West handed me the syringe; he hadn't even waited for me to check his numbers. I didn't bother to check to see that he had prepared the mixture correctly. I simply cleaned the base of the skull with a bit of alcohol, inserted the needle making sure to penetrate into the brainstem. There was resistance at first, there always is, but then the tip of the needle penetrated into the soft nerve tissue with a satisfying and reassuring pop. After that I carefully pushed on the plunger releasing the semi-phosphorescent green reagent into the brain of our subject. After that, it was up to the DMSO, the solvent carrier we used, to spread the reagent through the brain, the peripheral nervous system, and the rest of the body.

This was the period when we were most anxious.

"Fifteen seconds, no reaction."

When we counted the seconds and held our breath.

"Thirty seconds, no reaction."

Waiting and watching.

I checked the eyes.

"Forty-five seconds, pupils are fixed."

Hoping against hope.

"Sixty seconds, no reaction."

Hoping against reason.

"Seventy-five seconds, no reaction."

That something, anything would happen.

"Ninety seconds, no reaction."

But there was a reaction, a horrible reaction. The body began to shake and then violently convulse. The eyes opened wide, and the pupils dilated fully creating what can only be thought of as black pits of wide-eyed terror. The lips pulled back in a snarling rictus of agony, and from that straining veined throat issued forth the most bone-chilling scream.

"Sedative." Ordered West.

I grabbed the second syringe off the tray, but I was too slow. The muscles flexed and strained and then the rivets on both restraints popped and Corporal del Col was free. Still, I managed to jab the needle into his leg and push the plunger halfway before he flung himself away and out of the makeshift entryway.

We followed, our side arms out of their holsters and at our sides. We found del col kneeling in the mud weeping and raving madly.

"They're everywhere," he gasped. "I thought there was just the one, just the one that came to me, that tortured me, but I see the truth now. They're everywhere."

West lowered his pistol. "Corporal del Col," his voice was calm and rational, "you need to listen to me. I'm a doctor, Doctor Herbert West, you've been sick, very sick, but we found a cure, we've made you well again."

Del Col looked up from the mud, his eyes held nothing but fear. "You can't see them, can you? Why can't you see them?"

"See who?" asked West.

Corporal del Col gestured about wildly. "They are all around us! Watching us, waiting for an opportunity. Infecting us, tending to us, feeding off of us."

"Reanimation paranoia," I casually diagnosed. It was a common reaction. West hushed me with a wave of his hand.

"There's no one else here Corporal, no one but you and me and my colleague. No one is going to hurt you."

"That's not true," del Col roared. I can see them. I can see their soft pale bodies glistening in the moonlight like a slug. I can hear their legs so much like a spider's, how could anything made like that move so quietly? And those anterior tentacles, the ones with the spines dripping black fluid from their tips." He looked down at the syringe still imbedded within his leg, and then looked at me. "You! You did this to me. You're one of them, a *Medico della Peste*!"

It was then that he stood up and ran, not down the trench but straight at the nearest wall. Before either of us could do anything, he was up and over the fortification and out of our sight. West made to follow, but I grabbed him and pulled him back down. There was shouting from our lookouts, and then the same from the other side. I like to think that he made it some distance before the machine gunfire erupted and cut him down. I like to think that our return fire did some damage to the Germans on the far side of the no-man's land that stretched between us. But I doubt it.

"What was that he said before he ran?"

I looked at my colleague and remembered that he had no love of the humanities, and even less for history, even if it was the history of medicine. "*Medico della Peste*. It's Italian, from the Renaissance, it means Plague Doctor."

Herbert West nodded, acknowledging that he had heard me and then wandered back to our makeshift laboratory. I waited for a moment, and then realizing I had nothing better to do, followed my colleague into the darkness.

Part Two: The Natural Order

By the next day the number of patients exhibiting symptoms had more than doubled. In response, we set up a makeshift ward and began isolating the infected in an attempt to create some kind of quarantine. Of course, the ward was adjacent to the area we used for our experiments, which facilitated the transport from one to the other when the need arose.

And the need arose often, and we readily took advantage of it.

Not to say that we didn't try to save our fellow troops. We did our best. Over the course of three days, we lost four more men, all in the same manner. All followed the same progression that Corporal del Col had followed. First there was the slight fever. Then came the aching joints. Within a few hours the fever was up over one hundred and two degrees. Six hours in the lumps in the armpits appeared. After this came the shortness of breath and the coughing up of pink-tinged fluid. After this came the hallucinations, and the screaming.

After our experience with del Col, we began to listen to what our other patients were saying as they descended into the fever dream of madness. They weren't exactly the same, but the things they described were strikingly similar. All described something larger than a man that was slug like, but not a slug. It had legs like a spider or a crab, and out of its back grew sinewy appendages. No one else used the term "*medico della peste*" or "plague doctor".

Despite it all we still had a greater goal in mind, and the ends justified the means. We had already proven that the victims of the unknown plague could be reanimated and were even somewhat rational afterwards. All we needed to do was adjust the dosage and administer the sedative before they could escape and do any harm. And so, Sergeant Hoade made his way onto our table as our latest subject.

I will not bore you with the details. Not all reanimations are successes, and some are more unstable than others. Sergeant Hoade was successfully reanimated for ten seconds, during which he wept uncontrollably and recited lines from the Book of Revelations:

I looked, and beheld, a pale horse
And he who sat on it was called Death
And Hell followed after him.

This, he said before he smashed his own head in by pounding it against the table, even after he was given a sedative.

After we disposed of the body West, and I sat exhausted and frustrated. We pondered the possible source of the madness that had plagued our patients. I suggested that it might be a kind of *folie à plusieurs* an infectious madness, passed from one victim to another. But West was skeptical; surely not all those infected by the disease would succumb to the same madness. I countered that the fever might have made them susceptible–made their minds suggestible to the germ of the concept, like a kind of mass hypnosis or hysteria. This might explain the subtle cultural variations in the phrasing. Why one called them plague doctors and the other described them as one of the harbingers of the Apocalypse. And then there was the cancer. How could we possibly explain that?

We talked back and forth on this subject for several hours, through most of a flask of bourbon West had confiscated from one of our patients earlier in the day. By that time whatever we were saying was making little sense. We were at best slightly intoxicated and at worse staggering drunk. A situation that was reckless given our responsibilities and position, but we had left our ward in safe hands and needed some way to relax.

As I rose to bid my friend goodnight, I told him I was going to "Hay the hit." I immediately apologized and corrected myself. "I meant to say, 'Hit the hay', I'm putting the cart before the horse."

West smirked and waved me away, but before I took two steps, he called out to me. "What was that you said?"

"I'm going to hit the hay. Sleep, I'm off to get some, and so should you."

"No, no. About the cart and horse."

Oh, that. Putting the cart before the horse. It means doing things in the wrong order. You see I had a slip of the tongue and said, 'Hay the hit' originally."

West was suddenly very excited. He stood up and rushed over to me. "The cart before the horse." He turned around and then seemed almost jubilant. "That is exactly what we've done here. With this whole plague doctors thing."

"I'm not sure what you mean."

"We've been trying to find a way to explain these symptoms and how they lead to a common delusion, the plague doctors—for want of a better term. But what if the truth were much more frightening than a simple new plague. What if the hallucinations weren't caused by the disease at all, but the other way round?"

"The hallucinations cause the disease?" Now it was my turn to be skeptical.

"What if they weren't hallucinations?" West's eyes were growing wild. "What if the thing our patients are seeing is real? What if there is some kind of invisible organism that was making them sick, infecting them with an accelerated form of cancer for some reason, so that they grow sick and die. What if only when the neurochemistry of the brain is in a particular state—say that achieved prior to death, or after reanimation—only then can these things be seen."

I admit, my intoxicated state made all this sound very plausible, but someone had to be the voice of reason. "Invisible monsters handing out cancer, for what reason?"

West stared at me. "What reason does a germ need to infect a host? Or a fungus? What debate do lice have before they infest a child's hair?" He didn't wait for me to answer. "They don't need a reason; it is simply the natural order of things."

It was all too much for me to take in. I felt my head grow light and then dizzy. The world was spinning. I remember my knees giving way beneath me and then falling to the moist ground. After that there was nothing but the welcoming bliss of unconsciousness.

Part Three: The Pestilent Daimones

I awoke the next morning in the corner of one of the trenches, a blanket wrapped around me, and a small stove keeping me warm. My head ached from the previous night's revelry, and I suspected that the liquor we had imbibed might not have been made by a reputable distillery. I even considered that it might not have been made by a distillery at all. I stumbled through the man-made labyrinth of earth, following my nose for what passed for coffee and food in the living Hell we called home. All around me I saw the ravages of war, the toll it took on the men who had been commissioned by their governments to fight it. Most were little more than walking wounded, and if we had been at home, I would have prescribed a regiment of sulfa drugs to battle various infections, and a week of bed rest. But here, under these conditions, infected wounds were the norm, exhaustion was the standard, and hunger was a constant. Proper hygiene and sanitation were nearly impossible, and cases of the trots were endemic through our population. Only through vigorous standards of personal care did West and I and our colleagues avoid infection. This was a necessity. It would do no one any good if we doctors were to fall ill. The consequences might be catastrophic.

I arrived in our makeshift ward to find that the number of patients had doubled overnight. Our colleague, Doctor Giuseppe Ciano was directing several orderlies in the construction of a makeshift bedding system that used scraps of lumber and blankets to elevate the men off the cold and damp earth, and then pipe warm air underneath them. It was an ingenuous concept that also served to keep our feet dry and warm as we tended to the sick. Ciano was in every way the opposite of West. Where West was tall and pale, Ciano was dark and squat. West was for the most part calm and quiet, while Ciano was always boisterous and loud. West drew his practical knowledge from years of study, Ciano from experience. West had volunteered to serve to further his own purposes, while Ciano had defied his nation's neutrality and volunteered out of a sense of duty to his fellow man. West was a formal medical doctor, Ciano for better or worse was a veterinarian, specifically for large livestock. But I swear, when it came to pure skill, he was a better doctor than either West or myself, and he brought to the table a skill set that formally trained physicians lacked, the ability to improvise and make do with the equipment at hand, even under the most abhorrent of conditions. And of course, he had been serving this regiment as their physician for much longer than West and I had. For all intents and purposes, he was in charge, and we were just qualified visitors, of this there was no doubt.

As I walked in, I caught his attention, and that of West, who to me looked worse than I felt. I raised my hand up, showed them the small pot of coffee I had absconded with from the Mess and waved them over. They nodded in acknowledgement and within a few minutes both had joined me around the small stove that we used to heat the area. I produced some bread rolls from my pockets, and we set about having a rather poor breakfast.

"West has told me of your idea, my friend," commented Ciano as he slurped his coffee. "It is not … how do you say … original."

"My idea?" I glowered at West who was picking at his roll. He really had overdone the drink last night.

Ciano's head bounced up and down in excitement. "The island where I come from, there are still temples there, to the old Roman Gods, and some families that still keep the old traditions." He took a bite of roll. "When we have festivals some of the old believers–*benandanti*–a kind of good witch, would tell us stories about the gods and monsters that haunted the world."

West's eyes caught mine. He looked so tired.

"Anyway, there was one legend, about the *Pestilent Daimones*, that mirrors your idea of invisible monsters causing disease. They talked of five invisible monsters that served the god Phoebus Apollo. They included Morbus who brought fevers, Pestis who brought the black pestilence, Lues who brought the red pestilence, Macies who cursed men with the wasting, and Tabes who brought corruption. Of course, we know now that given the description of symptoms Petis was bubonic plague, Lues was smallpox, and Macies is consumption, or Tuberculosis. Tabes was the infection personified—gangrene and the like."

"And what disease did Morbus personify?" Asked West, his voice was weak.

"More difficult to identify, but perhaps Cholera or maybe Malaria. There is some thought that she might have been venereal syphilis, but that particular malady was unknown in ancient Europe, having originated in the Americas, like tomatoes and the potato."

I couldn't help myself from wondering, "What did these evil gods of disease look like?"

"Too men they appeared as emaciated old women, very pale, and carrying scythes. It is I suspect the source of the image of the Grim Reaper. But to the other Gods they were beauty personified, the myths say that Apollo would take them as his lovers." He took another bite of his roll and continued. "But make no mistake, they were not considered evil. They were part of the divine order of things, like the Furies who meted out punishment for sin, so did these beings carry out the will of the gods. Would you call the Angels that destroyed Sodom and Gomorrah evil? No, they may act in a manner that we find frightening, but they are divine in nature, at least that is what the legends say."

"Angels of Pestilence," whispered West. I was about to respond but then he suddenly fell from his seat, his tin cup clattering against the side of the stove.

Ciano got to him first and looked back at me with eyes full of worry. "His pulse is weak, he's barely conscious."

I looked about the purgatorial plague ward from which none of our patients had recovered, the only way out of the repugnant place had been through death, and now I had no choice but to confine Herbert West, my friend and colleague as well, to wait through the hours of suffering as the disease plied its course towards his inevitable death.

Part Four: The Anastasis of Herbert West

When I could, I sat with my friend and tried to talk with him. He would not have it. He found the whole situation embarrassing, and denigrated my bedside manner, and the whole concept of a bedside manner. There was no point in mollycoddling patients he raged, it was better that they knew what to expect so that they could plan appropriately. He demanded that I leave him be, with some paper and a pencil. I complied with his orders, who was I to deny what would likely be his last request.

Ciano caught me as I walked amongst the beds. "So how long has he been addicted?"

I was confused. "What are you talking about?"

He nodded toward West. "I've seen it before, very common amongst medical men, particularly in the military." His statement didn't register. I still didn't understand. So, he may it clear. "Morphine I think, or maybe heroin."

I looked back at West and sighed. Ciano was right. How had I missed it I wondered, and how long had it been going on? More importantly I realized that I had completely misdiagnosed my friend. He wasn't a victim of the unknown epidemic. He might be in for a rough time as he went through withdrawal, but he was going to live. The same couldn't be said for his patients that would now have to go without while he recovered. I felt a pang of outrage rising up in my gullet, and decided to stay away, and let Ciano deal with the inevitable.

In the next few hours, I lost five more soldiers. Five more good men dead from a disease I had no clue how to cure. Five more subjects that without West I was in no position to experiment on. Which, in all fairness was not entirely an unwelcome situation. I had over the years expressed some reservations concerning West's studies and had on several occasions considered abandoning both my friend and the work. Was the opportunity finally presenting itself? I fell asleep—conflicted by the choices I might have to make but exhausted by the workload that never ceased. Death was all around me and slumber the only respite available.

It was all too brief. It was just before midnight when Ciano came for me. West had taken a turn and had wanted to see me. I cursed the man and stumbled to my feet and followed Ciano back to the Ward. The April air was cold, but the night sky was clear. If it wasn't for the thousands of troops just a few hundred yards away, it might almost be peaceful.

We found West sprawled out in his cot, his blue eyes open and lifeless, and a needle in his arm. I ran too him, but it was already too late, at least for any normal intervention.

"Help me get him up," I told Ciano.

"Why?"

"Just help me, damn it."

As we lifted him his hand dropped and from it a piece of paper fluttered to the ground. Ciano bent down to pick it up. "Do the names Galvani and Prévost mean anything to you?"

I grabbed the paper from his hand and looked it over. "Yes, yes they do." I took a quick look at West's arm. A trickle of blood ran down from the latest needle mark. There were two more marks, healed but no more than a day. "West you madman, come on Ciano we haven't a moment to lose!"

We dragged him down the trench and I exposed our laboratory to my sudden partner in crime.

"What is this place?" He asked.

"Our lab, get him on the table, strap him down. This isn't going to be pretty."

He did what I told him, but still had questions. "What are you going to do?"

I lit the oil lamp and stripped the light cord from the wall. "Luigi Galvani was one of your countrymen, he discovered that electricity was the energy behind muscular movement" I dragged the wires over to where West laid. "Jean-Louis Prévost is a neurologist at the University of Zurich, he demonstrated that the hearts of dogs could be restarted with another more powerful shock." I ripped the line out of the lamp. "West wasn't an addict, he purposefully overdosed, and then gave us the method for bringing him back." I made sure the two wires weren't touching. "I suggest you stay well clear; this is going to be dangerous." Then I flipped the switch.

It all happened so fast. West's body convulsed and then his backed arched, with only the leather straps holding him in place. I watched the electricity arc from the body and into the metal table. I was standing on a piece of wood, so I suppose that insulated me, but Ciano was standing in a puddle of water. I watched as blue traces of lightning travelled up his legs and created a kind of crown around his head. He was paralyzed and in agony, but I couldn't stop. I had to let it go just a few more seconds, just a few more.

Then I turned the switch off. Ciano moaned and crumpled to the ground, but I paid him no mind, I was more interested in West and whether or not we had done the impossible. My question was quickly answered as I heard a sudden gasping of breath, and he turned his head to the side and then opened his eyes.

"West can you hear me!" I shouted gripping his head and looking into his eyes.

Those eyes focused on mine, blinked once and then he spoke, "Yes, I think even the Germans can hear you."

I left out a whoop of joy. "He's alive!" I said looking over at Ciano as he clambered to his feet.

The Italian looked at his watch. "Of course, he's alive, it's after midnight."

I was puzzled. "What does that have to do with anything?"

Ciano shook his head. "You and West, and all the other Americans I've met, even lapsed Catholics know what day it is. It's Easter, Our Lord has risen."

I looked over at West, "Indeed he has."

Part Five: Seven Shots in the Dark

He hadn't been resuscitated for more than two minutes before West put his hand on my shoulder, "Give me your gun, would you?"

I didn't even think about it. I unbuckled my holster and handed it to him forthwith.

West took the Colt 1911, checked the cartridge and then looked me straight in the eye. "We were right. I can see one of them. It's about eight feet in length and four feet thick in the center. I can see why del Col described it as a slug, but I think it looks more like a lobster that has been cooked, the meat drawn out covered in butter and then placed back in the shell. The shell is black. There are six pairs of legs, also not unlike those of a lobster. In the front there are a single pair of manipulating appendages with crude three fingered claws. Toward the front there are two tentacles ending in three eyes each. I can't see a mouth or any other sensory organs. Across the back there is a single row of fleshy tentacles, each of which is tipped with a needle of black chitinous material. It isn't moving, but it is looking right at me."

He raised the gun slightly, surreptitiously. "I think it knows that I can see it." He pulled the trigger.

I inspected the wall beyond where he was pointing to explode into fragments, but instead something green and wet splattered against the earth. I could see fragments of a strange kind of flesh dripping down. I turned to West, but he took off out the entryway.

"It's wounded," he called back to us, and then a moment later, "I think its heading toward the ward! Damn its fast, it scuttles up the wall like a damned cockroach!" There was another shot.

As soon as we could Ciano and I were out of the lab and chasing after our enraged colleague. We found him just around the corner kneeling before something I couldn't see, but there was something there. Something had sunken into the mud, torn into the wall of the trench. The mud was caked over something, something very large, a thing that shuddered when West kicked it. Then he stamped down hard with the heel of his boot, and I heard something crack and then something soft squish.

West pulled his foot back. "With any luck the others won't have been alerted." Then began deliberately stalking down the trench, gun held upright.

We followed behind him, just a few paces. We couldn't see what he could see, so it made no sense for us to be up in front with him. Even so, Ciano had drawn his own gun and was holding it with both hands, pointing it toward the ground.

When West rounded the corner, he immediately stepped back and put his back to the wall. "There are three more in the ward."

I looked at West. "We need a plan."

West shook his head. "You can't see them, I can." And then he turned the corner and opened fire.

I followed of course, but I didn't see much of what happened. My Colt 1911 has seven shots, West had already used two on his first monster. He used two more before I made it into the ward and fired two more as I watched. The patients, the ones who could move rolled to the ground.

West stalked through the place like he was invincible, the gun held out before him like it was leading the way.

"Stand still you monstrous thing." The gun arced around at the end of his hand following something no one else could see. He fired once but when he pulled the trigger the second time there was nothing but a click. He dropped the gun and reached down to tack another from one of the cowering soldiers.

Ciano fell to the ground. Someone, an officer, passed beside me, and then rushed toward West. As he came up with the pistol the butt of a rifle came down on his head. West tumbled to the ground with Major Collins standing over him.

A moment later some soldiers hauled him up and dragged him away. He was in what passed for the brig when I tended to his wound and made sure that they hadn't done any permanent damage.

West looked at me in confusion. He knew where he was, and he knew that he had been arrested but for what charge he didn't know. I had to tell him what had happened, that in his rush to kill the monsters he had fired wildly and hit Ciano, hit him in the left eye, killing him instantly.

West looked up at me with confusion in his eyes. "What are you talking about? What monsters?"

Epilogue: The Bliss of Human Memory

That was a week ago. Just twenty-four hours after West's assault on the invisible creatures all of those afflicted showed remarkable improvement and were fully recovered by the next day. I made no note of any possible curative that may have been responsible. A day after that, just hours before we were to go before the tribunal the shelling began in earnest. We should have expected it. The Hun had not launched an attack in weeks. All the armaments that had not been used in those intervening days suddenly rained down upon us in it seemed an endless barrage of shrapnel and poison gas. Whether or not the tribunal survived I cannot say but in the fog of war, West and I managed to escape and make our way away from the war-torn front.

It is I think, the Thirtieth of April, in the year Nineteen Hundred and Sixteen, and we are near Croisilles. We have taken refuge in an abandoned farmhouse, portions of it are blasted away, but it offers us some semblance of shelter, a few scraps of food, and one or two bottles of wine. West has spoken little since we fled. I suspect that he is suffering from what Doctor Charles Myers has recently diagnosed as shell shock. I hope with time and proper care he will fully recover his faculties and once again be the man I knew, the man I have been proud to work with all these years.

As for West's memory, of the plague that ravaged our battalion, of the monsters that he discovered, and of the steps he took to confront them, he still recalls nothing. I am careful not to probe too forcibly or bring up details that night upset him. West is not the most noble of personages, but I think for once he may have acted in a truly valiant manner. It would be terrible if he were to learn how heroic he had been and yet have no memory of it. Perhaps it is best that no one ever learn of his actions that day: That no account of the curious Angels of Pestilence ever be presented, not to our medical colleagues, not to a military tribunal, and particularly not to Doctor Herbert West.

The Best Laid Plans

When you tend bar, you soon learn that the later it gets, the weirder it gets, and I have had my share of weirdoes. There was that vampire romance writer a few years back–a writer of vampire romances, not a romance writer who was a vampire—and then the guy who claimed he was a special ops agent fighting monsters, and of course the old lady who drank absinthe and crocheted quotes from Nietzsche onto throw pillows. Then there was this guy, our latest creeper, just before we got shut down. He sat at the dark end of the bar, by himself. He was tall and thin, with exaggerated features, what people used to call gaunt—a real Ichabod Crane type, but with this weird pot belly. He was a quiet sort, nursing his third scotch as we approached last call. He hadn't said anything about himself, didn't really have to, the faded, crude tattoo of digits on his arm spoke volumes. I had been in the business, and in this town long enough to know when to talk to people and when to leave them alone. They all come around to talking, eventually. It's like a church confessional, with booze, and without the guilt.

I rang the bell, "LAST CALL," I said to no one in particular. The few other patrons I had filtered out the door. I wandered down to the dark end and poured Ichabod one on the house.

His eyes looked up from the glass and there was something haunting in them. "Do you think you'll make a good parent?" He gestured at my belly, which was just starting to be not noticeable.

There it is, I thought. *Its confession time*. "Don't we all?"

He kept his eyes locked on mine and shook his head slowly. "I don't know, at least not yet" he whimpered. Suddenly his eyes took on a serious look. "Did you know that some insects, termites and ants mostly, will reabsorb their eggs if they feel that conditions aren't favorable for their young?"

I shook my head, but before I could say anything he continued. "There are mammals that can hoard sperm and delay fertilization, others can delay implantation in the womb. If conditions get really bad, some animals will even eat their own young."

I had no idea where he was going with this. "We've all done things we aren't proud of. Things that were necessary," I gestured at his arm, "to survive."

He looked down at the tattoo and pulled his sleeve down, ashamed I thought. "I wish I could say that was the beginning of things, or the end of it, but it wasn't either. It was just another stop on an incomplete life filled with disappointment."

"Do you want to talk about it?" They always want to talk about it. It's why they are here—pretty face, a friendly voice, a sympathetic ear—for some it's worth any price.

He didn't even nod, he just started speaking, and I settled in for the long haul. I didn't expect him to say what he said next.

"My first memories are from 1933. There was a student, Jerzy Zynger, a Polish Jew who had come to Miskatonic University to study microbiology. It was Zynger who had opened the crates that had been sitting in the back of the museum undisturbed for a year. The Antarctic Expedition had not gone well, there had been casualties, and concerns about the samples they had brought back, concerns about contamination, about infection, and about invasive species. It had been thought best that the collected specimens should remain in storage."

"Zynger had other ideas. He cracked open one of the crates, then he cracked open some of the things inside. Inside there was something black and moist, with pseudopods and a rudimentary intelligence. It oozed out of its million-year-old spore and then launched itself at Zynger's face. Zynger tore at it with his fingers, but it just oozed around them. He kept his mouth shut and closed his eyes too, but it found its way in through his nose, and then into his brain. In a matter of minutes what had once been Jerzy Zynger ceased to exist, and I stood there in his place. I had all his memories, all his skills–but I was so much more, and I knew it. Not many people know what a shoggoth is, but I did, I knew. The idea had been programmed into my very genetic material by the very things that had made me. Shoggoths, monstrous, protoplasmic engines that lived to serve the ancient and alien things that had once ruled this world, and I, I was *not* one of them. I was something else, though closely related—the word was *ghorth*—a kind of planula, a creature whose sole purpose was to feed, and to grow the spores of true shoggoths, and when the time was right, to spawn—to spread those spores across the vastness of the planet. They had to be spread so that they could feed and grow, isolated from each other, so that they didn't follow their baser instincts and devour each other. Ghorth had some of the same characteristics as shoggoths, they were both metamorphic, though the ghorth to a much lesser extent. Where shoggoths could freely transform themselves into other shapes, the ghorth would only ever have the appearance of whatever lifeform it first bonded with. For all my days I would look like Jerzy Zynger."

"I fled Arkham that very night. By the next day I was bound for England, and within the month I was back in Poland. Zynger was from Bialystock, but I couldn't go back there, friends and family might recognize problems in my behavior. My impersonation was good, very good, but not perfect, there were things I had to change. I had to put on weight both to feed the spores, and to house them. This was easier to do in Warsaw, where I was just another face amongst the urban masses. I found work as a chemist, an easy occupation for one of my education and skills, and there were certain benefits to knowing who in the neighborhood was ill. On more than one occasion I tampered with the medications of my more sickly patients and eased them on their way. I fed on these bodies of course, careful to avoid the organs where my poisons might accumulate, and I stole from them as well. Warsaw was not a cheap place to live. But I made do, I had no real need for the creature comforts, or any plans for the future. By 1937 I could feel the spores growing inside me and knew that it was only a matter of time, a few years before they were seeds ready to be sowed. I paid no attention to the politics of men, what they did didn't matter to me. I was too young, too naïve. I couldn't imagine how the machinations of men could interfere with the grand destiny that had been programmed into me in eons past."

"But just because I couldn't imagine it, didn't mean it wasn't true. In 1939 the Germans invaded, and by that fall I had become one of many imprisoned in the Warsaw ghetto. I did what I could, what I had to, to survive, to maintain my brood. But in the end, it wasn't the lack of food that ended my gravid status. No, that was my capture and deportation to Treblinka. There amongst the human skeletons I was an oddity, a man who still had some fat and muscle on his bones. The other prisoners thought me weak for breaking down into tears. They thought I was crying out of despair over our imprisonment. I couldn't tell them the truth. Without a way to disperse them the spores couldn't hatch, and they reabsorbed back into the flesh of my system."

"Soon I succumbed to the same horrors that my fellow prisoners had suffered. In months, the bulk that I had spent years accumulating was gone, and the human façade that I resided in was little more than a shadow of itself. It wasn't I who organized the escape, but I certainly took advantage of it. I was stronger than my fellow prisoners, more supple too. I should have taken advantage of my abilities earlier, escaped the NAZIs and Germany long before it had become too late.

Would have, should have, could have. Instead, I slipped into the woods surrounding Treblinka and kept moving south, feeding on whatever I could. Humans have such strange food limitations. Some of this is driven by biology, but mostly it's driven by social taboos. Insects and vermin are forbidden, except in the most desperate of situations. But in war, surrounded by death, such creatures flourish, and I found the larder of war-torn Europe well stocked, as long as one was willing to broaden one's palate. I have read stories that some isolated communities had resorted to cannibalism, devouring weakened refugees and even wounded soldiers. I cannot deny that when the opportunity arose, I too did such things—soldiers, men, women, the old and infirm, but never children—never, ever children. I am not a monster."

"At the end of the war I made my way to France, and then with thousands of other Jewish refugees I boarded a ship and made my way to Havana. I was still Jerzy Zynger, but my forged papers had sliced twenty years off my age. I thought perhaps that I might be recognized but I suspected that most everyone I had ever known was dead—killed by the NAZIs. There were a few people at Miskatonic University who might recognize Zynger, my fellow students and perhaps a professor or two, but they were thousands of miles away, and I was no longer a microbiologist. I found work as a diamond cutter. Once more I set about nurturing the gravid cells that would one day burst from my body. All I needed was time, and when the time came, the freedom to move about, leaving my deadly spawn in my wake."

"I was more careful this time and made sure to align myself with Batista when he came back from Miami and took power. Cuba became a corrupt paradise, and I began making jewelry for the Americans who came to gamble at the *Tropicano* and the *Hotel Nacional*. I once had coffee with Luciano, and Kennedy bought a ring from me for some island girl he wanted to bang. I grew fat from the money spent on my art, and people thought me soft, and I knew that they whispered terrible things about my vices. Some thought me a homosexual; others suggested I was an SS officer hiding under an assumed name. A few thought I was both. A rare few accused me of gluttony. None suspected the life that was growing inside me, or that I was biding my time to destroy them all. I even set a date for the apocalypse, April 17^{h}, 1960—Easter. I thought it ironic, and whenever I thought of it, I chuckled to myself."

"The rebels poured out of the mountains in late 1958. Even then we didn't take them seriously. But then the general populace joined the fray and by January Batista had fled to Haiti. Foolishly, I stayed in place, I thought I could weather the storm in place, at least until my maid stopped showing up and the sound of gun fire echoed from down the street. I fled, a suitcase full of money at my side. I tried for the airport, but the roads were filled with people of similar mind, and the battlefront crept closer and closer. I took a side road trying to make it to the harbor, but the battle closed in around me. I cut through a field of tobacco, mowing down the stalks like a scythe. I only got so far before the plants jammed the axle and it snapped like a tree branch. I ran on foot, following farm trails over hills and through forests. I thought for sure I would make it. The docks were just over that crest I said to myself over and over again. I would find a boat—buy passage to Key West. I would be free, free to carry out my biological imperative."

"The ragged band of soldiers that waited on the quay had other ideas."

"I was arrested, and my suitcase full of money seized, it branded me an enemy of the people. I was charged, with what I was never sure, but it didn't matter. In January 1959 I was thrown in prison. I didn't see the sun or a human for eight weeks. I think the guards were surprised when they found me still alive, emaciated and dehydrated but still alive. They fed me and gave me fetid water, and then threw me in jail with the other political prisoners. I didn't see the sun for eighteen months. And somewhere along the line my spores, my precious spawn, died once more.

I settled in, accepted that what was done, and bided my time. They couldn't keep me in prison forever. There would be another opportunity, another cycle—twenty years meant nothing in the great scheme of things."

"I was wrong."

"They held me for the whole twenty years. They fed me—all of us really—nothing, they expected us to starve, to die from dehydration, to succumb to disease or old age. I lived on condensation, and palmetto bugs and rats. Occasionally another prisoner would die, and I would drag them to a secluded spot and devour them whole. In twenty years, I ate twelve men. Don't look at me like that, they were dead already. I wasn't going to waste the protein."

"It wasn't until April 1980 when the doors of my prison were opened and I along with hundreds of others were herded on to busses. I didn't know what was happening, and it felt much like the train cars to Treblinka. But then we were at Mariel and there was a fleet of ships and thousands of people. We crammed onto the deck of a trawler—the stink of humanity and rotting fish was overwhelming. In hours we were in Key West, and I was free to roam the Earth once more.

It took time. I worked at losing the accent that I had picked up in Cuba and lost the tan. I changed my name—Jerzy Zinger became Jerry Singer. I shaved more time off my birthdate. I broke ties with the Cuban community but settled back in with the relatively more reclusive Jewish society. I bought a boat and ran fishing charters out of Miami. By 1985 the fishing business was little more than a front. I was smuggling cocaine from Haiti on twice a week runs. In 1987 I almost got caught and had to sink my own boat before the Coast Guard caught up with me. There were charges, but nothing ever stuck. I bought another boat and six months later began catering to the movie industry. My boat, the High Seas, can be seen in *Nightmare Beach*, a cheap Italian slasher flick. Most of my money came from using the High Seas as a set in porn shoots, and yes, I filled in as an actor from time to time. Until one of the actresses noticed I was starting to put on some flab around the middle."

"I sold the boat in 1994 and bought a little place on a road out in the middle of nowhere. You won't find Speck on any maps of Florida, and that was the point. The cracker box home on the canal next to the swamp was all I needed. Between groceries, fish and whatever wandered out of the swamp I was well fed. By 1998 I was quite the specimen. I checked my weight at the local Winn-Dixie, and I was more than three hundred pounds, most of it spores. At night I dreamt of flying cross-country and leaving a trail of my children in my wake."

"I spent almost a year researching the best manner in which to travel. I would of course, start out of Miami, and then up to Atlanta. From there I Would visit Boston, and then New York before heading west to Chicago, and the Los Angeles beyond that. I debated heading south to Mexico, but instead decided to head across the Pacific to Tokyo and then Hong Kong. Then I would move on to Australia and Africa. It cost me a fortune. Citing my weight I had the travel agent book two seats. She thought my plans rather queer and suggested there were better and more direct flights that I could choose. Spending just a few hours or a day in each city made no sense to her. I threw money at the situation, and she shut her mouth and did what she was told."

"It was early Tuesday when I clambered into the van, I had bought for the sole purpose of taking me to the airport. It was used and burned oil, but it was clean, and it drove. It wasn't likely to draw any attention. I got to MIA at 8:30, more than an hour before my flight. I wandered through the parking lot without really paying attention to what was going on around me. I had no bags so I made my way down the vast hallways to my gate, found a pair of seats that would accommodate my girth, and the settled in to wait for my boarding call."

"There was a crowd of people gathered under the TV. It was tuned to CNN. The scene was of the New York skyline. One of the Twin Towers was burning. The scene shifted and they showed a commercial plane fly directly into the other tower and a mushroom of flame and smoke explode behind it. September 11th, 2000. I never even got to see my plane."

"I waddled back to the van. It was by sheer force of will that I was able to hold myself together for the drive home. It was only after I pulled into the driveway that I felt the mass inside me liquefy. I grabbed my belt and held my pants up as I fled the car a trail of jellified flesh leaking behind me. By the time I got inside the house a chain reaction had taken control. I collapsed in the foyer in a wave of thick protoplasm that washed around me like a broken water balloon."

"That was almost twenty years ago." He pushed back from the bar and ran a hand over his fat round belly. "It's not like before, it's a small batch, but it will still be enough. I still have a few months to gestate. But this time I'm prepared. The United States is the safest and freest country in the world. Six months from now I'll be boarding a plane and spreading my seed around the country. Nothing can stop me this time, not as long as the planes are flying, and the people are wandering about doing their day-to-day chores. I will spread like the infection that I am, and not even you knowing what is going to happen can stop it."

He drained his glass and smacked his lips. "I am going to miss this world." Then he wandered out the door and it closed with an ominous clunk.

I walked over and locked it behind him. For a moment I thought about what he had said and then shrugged. We get all sorts in the bar; one nut job was no worse than another. I went in the back and rolled out the mop and bucket. While I half-heartedly scrubbed the floor, I watched the late-night news. It was December 2019 and BBC America was talking about an outbreak of flu in Wuhan, China.

I turned the TV off and closed up for the night.

It's been a more than eighteen months, my daughter has been born, and I've been triple vaccinated. It took me a long time to find Jeremy Sang. He's lost weight, but it's him. He doesn't even live five blocks from the bar.

He might just be a crazy old man. There's nothing to prove that he isn't. He's been through a lot, and I do feel sorry for him—the best laid plans and all. The monster thing—the ghorth—just might be his way of coping. He could just be a lonely old man telling scary stories in a bar, for attention.

But I can't take that chance.

If he is what he says he is, then sooner or later, things might go right for him, and if he is some sort of monster then he will succeed in spreading his spawn over the world. I really hope he is the horror he said he was.

Otherwise, what I'm about to do would be insane, criminal even.

I hope he burns quickly; I hope two cans of gasoline are enough.

The Calliope Comes Back

I t was just before midnight when John Raymond, sitting on his front porch sharpening his knife, heard the calliope coming across the bridge.

It was the second time that day he had heard that damned steam organ. The first had been just before noon when the carnival had come strolling down the highway out of the east heading west. The stretch of Route 66 that runs through Kansas was only thirteen miles, mostly homesteads carved out of the wilderness and three clusters of buildings that people liked to pretend were towns. Galena was to the east on the border with Missouri, Baxter Springs to the southwest on the border with Oklahoma and sitting on the west side of the Spring River was Riverton, where Raymond lived with his wife and grandson. It was a sad stretch of road, one which no circus ever bothered to stop at. Some thought it was because the county was dry, but Raymond knew better, they were too poor even for a two-bit carnival.

That didn't stop them from coming through. Everything came through on the Mother Road, it bore all kinds. Some moving west, some moving east, some making an annual circuit, and travelling shows were no exception. The difference was that most people who travelled the Mother Road, whether tourists or transplants, had a destination, so did cargo, but for travelling shows the road was the destination, for many it was the only thing they could call home. For towns that sat on the road travelling shows were welcome distractions, even if they didn't stop.

Raymond hadn't caught the name of the show when it came through town that morning. It hadn't been much to look at. Back in the day, he had seen the big shows, the ones that came by carriage, and later by train and played the big cities—Barnum, Batty, Bailey and even Pepin. This one was small, a handful of jugglers, a few acrobats, a sad looking bear with mange, some old lions that seemed to be missing some teeth, and some horses dressed up in finery that plodded along broken with age. The calliope came behind the horses in an old Ford truck wheezing and whining that sickly-sweet cacophony that drew kids like flies to stink. Behind the music car were the clowns—tall ones, short ones, fat ones, thin ones, all dressed up in garish costumes with whiteface and tufts of red hair—variations on the Bozo character that had become so popular over the last decade. Raymond hadn't cared for them much, he had his reasons, and he kept his distance, but the kids—including his grandson Will—ate it up. Will and his friends had wormed their way through the impromptu crowd to watch the show march through town. They had laughed at the jugglers and acrobats and danced to the calliope and had been rewarded with fat red balloons that bounced and floated at the end of ribbon tethers. The clowns had handed them out with aplomb, handing each one to a child and then quickly pulling back in strangely elevated joy, clasping their hands together and smiling, throwing their heads back and laughing, celebrating amongst each other as if they had accomplished something extraordinary. It was almost frightening to watch grown men celebrating like that, even if they were in costume, even if it was their job. Raymond never took his eyes off the troupe of zannis dancing in the streets of his town, even as they pulled away heading west toward Oklahoma.

The parade had come and gone, and it had been little more than a memory when Joan had called dinner and Will had brought to the table the fat red balloon that he had gotten from the clown. It hung over the dinner table while they ate, drifting back and forth in the breeze of the ceiling fan. The damned thing annoyed Raymond, and he opened his mouth to say something, but his wife put a hand on his arm and smiled at him. That was her way of defusing things. They had been together a long time. She knew what upset him and knew how to calm him down. She also had a soft spot for their grandson Will, letting him do what he wanted even when it was more risk than Raymond liked.

"He's just a boy," she would say, as if that explained everything, as if that allowed anything.

After dinner, Raymond had read the paper and then watched some animated show featuring a beagle flying his doghouse in a comedic World War One air battle. Raymond found it disrespectful but was more impressed with the main plot which followed a young man waiting for the harvest god to come and reveal himself. It was a mindless entertainment, but Will seemed to like it. It was all he talked about as he fell asleep with that damned red balloon tied round his hand. Raymond wanted to take it right then and there, but his wife was watching from the hall.

"Let it play out," she said wisely. "It'll all be resolved by morning."

He had nodded solemnly. She was right. It would be resolved by morning, if not sooner. He went to the closet and took out the case that was in the back and took what was inside out to the front porch.

He had sat there for hours beneath the pale-yellow porch light, the knife in one hand the whetstone in the other. He listened to the frogs as they croaked by the river, to the crickets as they sang in the grass, and the owls as they called from the woods, all the while moving the curved blade across the stone, slowly taking the blade to razor sharpness. It was an old thing, it had belonged to his father, and his father before him, and hopefully one day it might belong to Will. It was a dangerous thing, curved and pointed on the fore edge, with large teeth cut into the other set in a handle of polished green and red wood. It wasn't a fillet knife, or a hunting knife, or a boning knife. It was a killing blade, designed to cut flesh, penetrate, and tear—to cause as much damage as possible. It had no other purpose. It was too complicated, too bulky, too unwieldy for any practical function. Even the sheath testified to that. It was all straps and buckles that wrapped around and made sure the blade and the teeth were protected. It was a task to extract it from its protective covering, which made it abundantly clear that if you were bringing this weapon out you intended to use it for the purpose it was designed.

It was just before midnight that the crickets grew silent, and the owls flew off, and the frogs went still. It was then that Raymond heard the music, that damned clown music, the calliope organ as it rolled across the bridge. It came with its lights on, with no pretense of trying to hide itself, not that it could, not with that music wheezing. It came off the bridge following Route 66 from Galena. Raymond could see it, the dull sheen of the painted truck in the moonlight, the driver all painted up in his whiteface, the musician who sat in the bed, surrounded by the organ pipes and the pneumatic engine that supported them. He was wearing black robes with his red hair done up like seven horns, wearing fat white gloves that matched the paint on his face, his hands flew across the keys maniacally, impossibly.

Behind the truck came the rest of the clowns, dancing–prancing in the moonlight to the music that heralded their coming. There were a half dozen and if they had seemed joyous and comedic during the day, now they were nothing less than malevolent representations of the chaos that lurked just beneath the veil of humanity. Each clown had in his hand a red piece of ribbon that led up into the sky tethering what floated there.

They bobbed there in the sky just twenty feet up, fat things in garish colors and patterns. Some were yellow, others pale blue, one was covered with images of Tom and Jerry, another by Woody Woodpecker, a third bore images of Bugs Bunny. They were bloated things, not unlike what one saw in the Macy's Thanksgiving Day Parade, they bobbed and jostled each other, tugged along by their handlers but these were not giant balloons of cartoon characters. They were children, they were children of Galena, bloated up by dark, forbidden rites for the entertainment and sustenance of things that wore whiteface and pretended to laugh, pretended to be men.

"Gramps, I don't feel so good," moaned Will as he came through the screen door, the red balloon in tow behind him.

He didn't look good. He seemed puffy, not just around his face but his hands too, and his feet, they all seemed engorged. He took a deep breath and wheezed as he exhaled. As he did the balloon shrank a little. Raymond could see a bolus of air travel down the ribbon from the balloon to his grandson's hand. Like a tire being fed by a pump, Will was slowly but surely being inflated.

The boy took a step forward, but his feet barely grazed the floor. He was floating, floating toward the procession of clowns, toward the calliope, toward the other children who floated helplessly along on silken streamers.

The calliope and the clowns behind it turned off Route 66 and on to Raymond's street. As the clowns came for him Will took another step and his feet floated off the porch.

John Raymond's arm moved in a single fluid arc; the blade cut the ribbon in silence. The balloon no longer tethered floated away into the sky, drifted away and was quickly lost in the dark night sky. Gas escaped from the ribbon left tied around Will's hand in a bleating sound that reminded Raymond of a dying goat. The boy fell out of the air and back onto the porch with an audible *thunk*.

The music stopped. The clowns stopped dancing. All attention turned toward John Raymond and his grandson Will. In silence the calliope and its escort creeped forward, their malevolent eyes watching John Raymond as he helped his grandson.

The old man knelt down and lifted Will to his feet. "Go inside," he told the boy, keeping his eyes on the approaching danger.

Even disorientated, the boy knew something was wrong. "Should I lock the door?"

Raymond shook his head, "It won't help." With one hand he hustled the boy behind him and into the house. Then he stepped down off the porch, following the steps and concrete walkway toward the street, toward the approaching caravan. Toward the horde of clearly angry clowns.

He stopped on the edge of the road, still on his property, where his advantage was the greatest. He raised the blade in challenge. "I see you Children of the Laughing God—Ghu-Faugh—the Farce of Darkness, the Cackler at the Verge, the Chortling Abyss. I see you and acknowledge your sniggering, your snuffling, your spluttering absurdity. Under the terms of the Decrees of Gloom and Murk, I request that you depart unblooded."

The organ player rose up from his seat craning his neck, trying to get a better look at Raymond. "Who are you to invoke the old laws?"

Raymond's eyes locked onto those of his interrogator's, "Under the terms I am not required to identify myself, invocation is enough."

The black robed creature leapt from the truck roaring, "DO NOT QUOTE THE OLD LAWS TO ME! ME AND MINE WERE THERE WHEN THEY WERE WRITTEN. THEY WERE NEVER INTENDED TO APPLY TO HUMANS!"

Raymond remained calm and still as the clown marched toward him in anger. This made the other lesser fools twitter in confusion and distress. They had been defied before, but never had the law been invoked, and never had anyone ever stood their ground in the face of the rage of their hierophant.

Raymond let the thing come within arm's length and then placed the blade between them. "You think me human? So long have you relied on your eyes, you have forgotten how to see Phrenzy Tallacht." The clown drew back as he spoke. Raymond just smiled. "Yes, I know your name you scion of the Hysterical Shriek." He waved the knife in an arc, "I know all your names you descendants of the Lord Haw. Did you think your tribe forgotten by those who came before, by those who came first?"

The one called Phrenzy Tallacht sneered and stared at the man that stood before him. He sniffed the air and exhaled, and his breath reeked like a charnel house. He closed one eye and tried to see using long dormant organelles that sat between the rods and cones of his optical organs. Eventually, he saw something, he saw the truth that stood before him, and he took a step back in fear.

"Q'Hrell," he said. "You look like Q'Hrell. Not possible, the Q'Hrell are all dead or dreaming, have been for eons. Since the Second Annunciation."

"And yet here I stand." He made a queer gesture and for a moment the glamour that hid his true form fell, but only for a moment, and that was enough.

Phrenzy wheezed and twisted backwards. His hand went out in a gesture of supplication. "Our apologies Elder, we did not recognize you for what you were. We beg your understanding. We shall leave, unblooded." He turned to depart.

Raymond shook his head, "Your apology is accepted Phrenzy Tallacht, your troupe may leave, but you owe compensation."

The old clown clenched his teeth and waved his hand to silence the sudden wailing that grew up behind him. "Compensation? We beg for your mercy Elder One."

"And you have it, the compensation is not for me, but for the old laws, they were properly invoked, and you flaunted them."

"Please Elder, we ... I ... did not know who and what you were." There was fear in the clown's voice. "Spare them at least," he glanced over his shoulder, "they are but pups."

"All the better for them to learn," he stepped off his land and onto common ground, "but I'm not punishing you for disrespecting me Phrenzy, I'm punishing you for allowing yourself to be put into the position of disrespecting me."

A look crawled across the ancient thing's whiteface; it was a look of confusion. "I'm sorry, I don't understand."

"Have your tribe and troupe forgotten the rules of your own kind? You threatened me with the old law, but you've forgotten them yourself.

You've forgotten the very edicts that were put into place to prevent you and I from being put into this position." Raymond took another step forward and watched Phrenzy's face for some glimmer of understanding, but it wasn't coming. "Your herald Phrenzy, your harbinger, your twenty-four-hour man, where is he?" Phrenzy's face went slack. "You don't have one, do you?"

"No Elder." He fell to his knees.

"No. We have rules and rituals in place to keep shit like this happening Phrenzy, and you fucking ignored them." He proffered the knife. "Your arm Phrenzy Tallacht."

"You want to cut off my arm?" There was that sound in his voice, the sound of fear.

Raymond shook his head again, "No Phrenzy Tallacht child of the Laughing God, I want you to cut off your arm."

An hour later the thing that called himself John Raymond cleaned his knife and wrapped it back into its very complicated sheath. Then he went back inside his home to speak with his wife.

"It's over then?" She said not looking up from her knitting.

"It is," he nodded. "How's Will?"

"Sound asleep." She paused for a moment. "You let them go?"

"They paid, but yes, I let them go."

"and the other children?"

Raymond frowned. "Not my issue, in both meanings of the word. The spawn of Ghu-Faugh took them along."

He wandered over and kissed her on the forehead, and then laid an envelope on the table beside her.

"What's this?" She asked picking up the envelope.

Raymond put the knife back into the closet where it belonged. "Passes for the circus when they pitch in Tulsa, I thought we could take Will this weekend."

"That won't be problematic?"

He looked out the screen door at the arm that lay in the road, it was decaying rapidly, dissolving into muck and ether. By morning it would be gone completely. "I don't think so, they wouldn't have given me the tickets if we weren't even."

His wife nodded, "Sunday then, we'll go Sunday, after church." She smiled at the thought. "It should be fun."

The Calliope Comes Back

Raymond thought for a moment and then nodded, "Sunday it is then." In the distance he heard the calliope music start up once more, but he had done his bit. It wasn't his problem anymore. He turned the porch light out and went to bed.

The Defense of Li Zhou

November 8, 2016
US Outpost #31A
Miskatonic University Antarctic Research Facility

It was Spring, but in Antarctica that meant that it was still below freezing, and the wind crept down from the interior mountains and across the valleys full of ice and frozen rock. It cut through the parka that young Li Zhou wore and made her bones ache. Even inside the command tent the cold seeped in, it was insidiously pervasive. It was so cold that even the equipment had to be insulated against it. More money had been spent on that, than had been used for the students. Most of their gear, including the parkas, had been repurposed from previous expeditions. Everyone wore the same burnt orange parka, even the man in charge, though his had the name MORGAN emblazoned across the shoulders in bright yellow letters.

Professor Armitage Morgan, Armitage to his colleagues, including his assistants, stood at the edge of the tent surveying his team. He was an imposing figure with iron-grey hair. He was fifty, but looked younger, except around the eyes, there he looked older. Li always thought that her mentor had weary eyes. Li had first begun working for Armitage when she was a sophomore, that was six years ago. She should have been putting the final touches on her thesis, instead she was at the bottom of the world making sure that Armitage's work, everything that he had planned for decades, was brought to completion.

Beneath Armitage's gaze the students were running through their final checklists, making sure their equipment was properly calibrated, communicating with the recorders, and ready to collect samples. The radiation sensors had already begun to register increases and that had sent the team into overdrive. Mason was opening the lids on the polymer traps; Corey and Fowler were calibrating the gamma particle sensors; and the others were following suit, adjusting various sensors, cameras and microphones in order to capture what Armitage expected to be one of the greatest light shows any human had ever seen.

The just finished Antarctic winter had been unusually harsh, and the polar stratospheric cloud cover had been substantially greater than in the previous decade. This meant that because of the vagaries of atmospheric chemistry the ozone levels would be the lowest they had been in decades. For a helioastronomer like Armitage it provided a chance to directly collect solar material, and with the recent spike in solar flares that material was bound to be very interesting. He had been planning this for decades and cultivating students for just as long. He had churned out research assistants with a wide variety of skill sets, his Dynamic Dozen. It was both an honor and a pejorative, bestowed by those upper classmen who knew that if you made it on to Armitage's team your internships were guaranteed, your access to resources and lab equipment was elevated, and your personal time was reduced to almost zero. If you were one of the twelve nothing else mattered, Armitage made sure of it.

The sound from the gamma particle counter suddenly went from a slow clicking to a screaming whirr that reminded Li of summer cicadas. The machines were springing into action, doing exactly what they had been designed to do. All the team had to do now was sit back and watch. The sky above them had turned purple, with streams of blue and crimson, a sign that high-energy particles were moving through the magnetosphere. It was all coming together, exactly as Armitage had planned.

Suddenly Fowler wasn't standing anymore. She had fallen over her equipment and then tumbled from it with an audible thud. She was crumpled down on the snow like a rag doll. Professor Armitage started to move but the ice caused him to lose his footing. One leg went forward the other sideways and he fell to the ice in an almost comic manner. Li pulled him to his feet and brushed the snow from him. It took a moment for him to regain his composure and he even laughed a little when she took his hands.

Then the screaming began.

Chambers was holding Fowler upright. There was blood leaking from her eyes. There were words amongst her screams, babble really, she was speaking in tongues, but over the wind and the chorus of the other victims, those exact words were just noise. Li could hear them, but they didn't make any sense. She did a quick head count; six students were down. Corey was out cold and bleeding from every visible orifice. Jefferson and Moustafa were doing their best to hold onto William Bishop who was bucking wildly and yelling about how he couldn't see. The other four, including Sally Jenkins, were all screaming, bleeding and seizing. Hernandez and Jeyakumar just stood there. They were in shock, unable to process the carnage that had suddenly welled up around them.

Li saw Armitage slip off one of his gloves, the arctic air was dry and frigid, and his hand flushed with color. With firmer footing he crossed the space between himself and the nearest student. With his gloved hand, he gripped Jenkins' chin and shoved two fingers of cloth between her lips and worked them between her teeth. With a calculated but swift motion, Armitage brought his bare fist across her chin and knocked the young woman out of his arms. She spun through across the ice, blood from her eyes flying and forming arcs of crimson across the crystal blue icescape. Jenkins hit the ice shoulder first with a disquieting crack that Li suspected meant that her collarbone had broken.

Armitage moved quickly to Jefferson's side and using the accumulated momentum administered a more forceful blow to the struggling Bishop. As the young man fell unconscious he tumbled to the ground, his legs splayed out indifferent directions. With Jefferson and Moustafa assisting, Armitage worked his way through the other victims, putting each one down as rapidly as possible and then using their own parkas to bind their arms. Li sat down at the radio and started calling for help. Even at best speed, the choppers would be an hour at minimum, the remaining students would have to pack up for an emergency evacuation.

Jenkins stirred and moaned. Li saw her open her eyes and she started to whisper. Li bent down to hear her. "The sun," she had asked, a hint of desperation in her voice. "What's wrong with the sun?" Li had looked up. The sun was fine, clear and bright on the horizon. But Jenkins insisted, her voice had risen to a scream, "The sun is black! WHY IS THE SUN BLACK?"

The Defense of Li Zhou

November 20, 2016
Peaslee Center for Anthropology
Miskatonic University
Arkham

Javier Hernandez paused to catch his breath and then started speaking again. He had to speak louder than he would have liked to, the projector had been running for more than an hour and the cooling fan had kicked into overdrive creating a dull whirring noise that flooded the room. "In astronomy there is a phenomenon called the red shift, when a stellar object is moving away from the Earth, the wavelength of the light from that object is stretched out by that movement. Human beings perceive longer wavelengths as reds. In this case the exact opposite happened, the light emitting from the coronal mass moving toward us was shifted toward the portion of the spectrum we perceive as blue. Now for most people, such a blue shift would have gone completely undetected. We simply don't have the precision or range to detect such a change in the spectrum. However, the six students who suffered seizures are a little different. Their eyes appear to have the ability to detect wavelengths beyond those in the normal range of human vision. Specifically, our tests suggest that they can see well into the ultra-violet. This is something that wouldn't normally have been detected by any routine medical tests and was likely not even noticed by any of the subjects in their day-to-day activity. Only a significant event would have made them cognizant of their condition. We're pretty sure that the 'black sun' that some of the victims talked about was the blue shift generated by the coronal mass ejection."

Hernandez coughed. "At first, we thought this condition was the result of a genetic mutation, something linked to the mother's X chromosome. We were wrong. Then we thought it might be something in the mitochondrial DNA. Wrong again." Hernandez changed slides. "Our colleagues at the Malkowski found this." The image was grainy and looked like a pixilated pie tin filled with grey yarn. "Tentatively, for reasons that will become apparent, we are calling this a gammaplast. This is heretofore an unknown organelle that has characteristics in common with both mitochondria and chloroplasts. Like mitochondria it contains a cluster of DNA. Human chromosomal DNA is linear with 46 chromosomes coding for about 50,000 genes, mitochondrial is circular and codes for 37 genes, the DNA we've found in the gammaplast is globular and the computers estimate that it codes for over one million genes."

The audience murmured but Hernandez skillfully kept his voice just louder than the sudden increase in noise. "We don't know what these chromosomes are for, or where the gammaplast came from in the first place. What we do know is that the gammaplast functions much like a chloroplast, but instead of light being converted to chemical energy, it uses gamma radiation. Since the coronal mass ejection, the Sun has been emitting significantly higher amounts of gamma radiation and the gammaplasts have been taking advantage of this."

Armitage interrupted. "Javier, if this gammaplast has never been found before, if it's that rare, what are the chances that six completely unrelated people would all have it?"

Hernandez nodded. "Astronomical. We're currently doing random samples at medical facilities around the country. Preliminary data suggests that about one tenth of one percent of the population is carrying. So, the chances of six out of thirteen unrelated people being carriers are astronomical. It defies the odds and puzzled us for quite some time. The solution was simple—obviously really—they aren't unrelated. Our genetic analysis suggests that they share a common male ancestor about four generations back, say about 1930 give or take a decade. We've been looking at family histories and all of our subjects can be traced back to western Massachusetts, specifically in the vicinity of Aylesbury or Dunwich."

December 5, 2016
Dyer Retirement Village
Foxfield

From the sidewalk Li could see the old man sitting on the stoop staring at Armitage with a look of sad resignation, his eyes were milky, and Li suspected that he was nearly blind, but knew that his father, even at his ridiculous age, was too proud ever to reveal any such weakness. "Knew yew would be coming home soon." The old man's voice was phlegmy and slow. "Whose yer friend?"

Armitage didn't even glance back. This is Li Zhou, my research assistant."

The old man glowered. "Welcome Miss Zhou," he said as he rose and turned to go into the house, he motioned for them to follow. "Come on in son, before the sun fries your brain. I'll make us some iced tea."

Armitage followed his father through the front door, and Li followed her boss. The door opened directly into a small living room. There was a couch, a small television, a coffee table and even a small side table by a threadbare recliner. These were covered with stacks and stacks of books. They littered the house like fallen leaves in autumn, accumulating in corners and beneath tables. Towers of tattered bindings and shaken spines, the condition wasn't that important, all leaned precariously against the walls. Li knew Armitage's father by reputation, he still lectured on occasion. He had outlived two wives, and when he did lecture, he talked about his colleagues that had been lost during the Second World War. Everyone spoke fondly of him. No one mentioned he was a hoarder, but all of the Dynamic Dozen had seen the man at the annual Arkham Book Festival.

Everybody knew about Professor Francis Morgan's collection. Most of the books had been inherited from Henry Armitage, old Professor Morgan's friend, and the father of his first wife. Armitage had been named after the man who had once been the Chief Librarian at Miskatonic University. In addition to being a librarian, Henry Armitage had also been an obsessive collector, refusing to part with even the most distressed of volumes, even when the university acquired multiple copies or updated editions. After the man had died, his collection had gone to Professor Morgan, and his daughter Naomi had come to help Francis make sense of the collection. She never left, and had become the old man's third wife, and a year later, Armitage Morgan's mother. A semi-retired art historian, Naomi Morgan spent most of her time working at the Cabot Museum cataloging new arrivals, and only came back to visit her husband on weekends.

Li looked at the detritus of the ages and could see the dividing line between the old collection and what Francis Morgan had added. There was a place in the stacks where the font on the little stickers on the spines changed. The earlier versions had been typed and then secured by tape. The newer ones had been put out using a printer, and directly onto stickers. They ended up in Morgan's hoard because the old man had a habit of invoking faculty privilege. He was allowed to pick through the books discarded from the library before the boxes were put out into the Quad Lawn for annual library sale. The discards were books that were damaged, surplus, or that had been made redundant either by a newer edition, or by digital scanning. Most of the boxes were full of useless textbooks, but that didn't matter, Professor Francis Morgan got to pick through it first.

As they moved from the front room into the kitchen Li was thankful that the kitchen and the small Formica table within had so far resisted the call to absorb a share of the library castoffs. The old man pointed at two steel and pleather chairs. Armitage took one while Li took the other. After a moment Francis Morgan joined them with a stack of plastic tumblers and a glass pitcher full of ice and lemons and tea. Armitage filled the three glasses while his father sat down. Li didn't know it, but this was something of a ritual that Armitage knew well. His father had somehow come to believe that all conflicts great or small could be resolved over a large glass of iced tea.

Armitage spoke softly, it was unusual for Li to see him as subordinate. "Dad there's a book I need, one that is missing from the library."

The elder Morgan snorted. "There are lots of books missing from the library son. Maybe yew should talk to the provost about where they all went."

"I'm talking about a specific report, the one that Dr. Houghton wrote ... " he paused trying to find a way to phrase a sensitive subject. "It was about physical deformities in Dunwich ... "

"I know what book yer talking about! Do yew think I'm daft?" Morgan's eyes went wide and red and spittle flew from his lips as he yelled. "Houghton only ever wrote one book! Did yew ever think that there's a reason that book is missing from yer precious digital collection? That there is things people don't need to or maybe shouldn't know?"

Armitage closed his eyes and dropped his head. "Do you have a copy dad? It's important."

"It's always important, yew only ever come home when you need something." Morgan suppressed a chuckle. "It was important back when yer grandfather and I went up Sentinel Hill, but nobody paid any attention back then. They only listened when the Horror nearly wiped Dunwich off the map. Then they couldn't get enough. Research grants rolled in for just about everything; geological core samples, archaeology of the surrounding megaliths, ethnographic studies, construction of family trees, oral histories ... Hell there's hours and hours of Dunwich gospel music and hill songs."

"Dad," he took a deep breath. "I'm not going to debate university library collection policy with you. It's out of both our hands, and you know that." He took a sip from his tea, and watched his father do the same.

The old man sighed, it was full of frustration and sadness. "There's a thin pamphlet bound in blue leather on the third shelf next to the fireplace. What yew wants in there."

Li rose and without a word strolled back into the living room. It took her a moment or two, but she found the blue book. The gold letters down the spine were barely legible - *Houghton*. She pulled the volume out and flipped it open to the title page.

Armitage came into the room, and the old man was hobbling right behind him, refusing to disengage from his semi-estranged son. "One of them has come back, hasn't they? And yew've got hold of em! I know it boy. You would have known it too if yew'd a read the *Necronomicon* like I'd told yew. I've seen the signs. The sky at night, the sky is all wrong." He wheezed from all the excitement.

The younger man ignored the ranting and looked at the open book in Li's hands. He confirmed the author and title.

A. Houghton

A Report on Physical Abnormalities in Neonates Born in Dunwich Massachusetts from 1925 to 1927.

He snapped the book shut and with long poignant strides went to the door. He looked back at the sad old man leaning up against the wall, wheezing in the shadows. He felt a pang of sorrow for his father. "Yew've got one of them don't yew boy?" His voice became frantic. "Does it grow? Ye'll need space if'n yer to make it grow."

Pity turned to frustration tinged with anger. "No dad, I don't have 'one of them', though I would be grateful if I did." Armitage tucked the file under his arm and walked toward the door. Li followed, hustling to keep up as Armitage stalked off.

He was mumbling as he went. Not talking to Li, still talking to his father. "Sara Jenkins killed herself yesterday. So as of today, I don't have 'one of them' as you so crudely put it." Armitage moved down the sidewalk without a backward glance. "I have five," he spat the words out, "and yes they grow." His pace became almost a run. "God help us they grow."

December 12, 2016
Malkowski Biogenetics Laboratory
Bolton

Dr. Jane Morton was trying to remain unemotional; her colleagues would say clinical. Armitage had warned her, but she had refused to listen. The documents he had provided suggested growth rates that Morton found unbelievable, at least until the change began.

The bones were the first to go, replaced by a hydrostatic skeleton, of all the hard tissues only the teeth remained, but they had become enlarged, elongated, like tusks. Thankfully, only the main mouth had teeth. The other mouths, the ones that had erupted out of the abdomen on muscular tentacles had no teeth, but rather a muscular feeding tube tipped with a small stinger. The arms and legs had suffered transformation as well, and now resembled inverted anemones, they functioned like massive hydraulic jacks, and Morton suspected that each titanic limb was horrifically powerful, for each of her patients now weighed more than a thousand pounds and were forced to walk on all fours.

There were other changes, subtle changes that weren't discernable to the naked eye, and had only been found during the autopsies of the one that had killed itself. In the arm pits there were clusters of thin wiry tendrils terminating in dense neurochemical transceivers the purpose of which was only made more mysterious by the similar clusters of transceivers located in two symmetrical sensory pits at the base of the spine. More chilling, and sadly more relevant to Dr. Morton's current condition, was the gland located near the tip of each of the abdominal tentacles. That organ secreted a neurotransmitter, similar to serotonin, that analysis suggested had both anesthetic and paralytic properties. Now Morton knew from personal experience that they were right.

She wished she had listened to Armitage, that she had been less skeptical, less emotional, more clinical, more like she was now. She had always been emotionally reactive; her ex-husband had called her hormonal. So, when she entered the containment cell she should have reacted when the thing that was once Karl Mason shifted toward her, and his restraints snapped. She should have reacted, but she didn't. Instead, she had calmly sat down against the wall and let the Edwards thing wash over her, taking the ten-pound bag of dry dog food from her hands and tearing into it. Against the wall she sat motionless and unafraid as his monstrous tongue eagerly lapped up the dry pellets.

Doctor Jane Morton sat serenely as the thing fed. There was something hypnotic in the rhythmic throb that enveloped her. There had been an instant of pain, but Morton was so quickly overcome with calm that she barely remembered the sensation. She understood so much now, she understood everything that Armitage had told her, and why he had behaved as he had. She understood the thing that had once been Mason. It had needs, just as any creature did. It needed others of its own kind, which she had denied it by isolating them from each other. It needed space to grow, it needed to reproduce, and most of all it needed to feed. Jane understood all this and understood that this was simply the way the way of the universe, and this was her purpose in it.

As Karl Mason wrapped his six abdominal tentacles around the body of Jane Morton, he plunged in sharp chitinous feeding needles. There was pain, but the neurochemical in her system kept her calm, compliant. "Go ahead," she said, "I understand."

December 15, 2016
Faculty Lounge
Miskatonic University
Arkham

"Professor Morgan?" Armitage stirred from the shallow daydream of better days and sat back in the cold metal chair. "I'm FBI Special Agent Troy Castro, I would like to ask you a few questions if I may, about the Malkowski Lab?"

Armitage bowed his head. "They're all dead, aren't they?"

"We think so. We've initiated an evacuation of the town. I've lost two teams. We've contained it within the footprint of the university annex, but our weapons don't seem to do anything but annoy them." Castro fumbled with the case file. "Doctor Morton filed a complaint against you. She even filled out paperwork to have your access terminated. Care to explain that?"

"I tried to warn her, showed her the report by Houghton, and the manuscript for Rice's account. I even showed her digital photos from Dee's translation of the Necronomicon, there were drawings, images that depicted the same sort of physical characteristics as her patients. Dee called them the Vugg or Vugg-Shoggog, and said they were the spawn of the demon-god Yog-Sothoth. It warned that their appetites were insatiable."

Castro stopped writing. "You're saying those things are the children of the devil?"

Armitage shook his head frantically. "No. No. Alhazred called them djinn, Dee called them demons and devils, the Comte D'Erlette classified them as elementals, all were just using the belief systems they had to explain things they didn't understand in terms that they could. The hard part now is sorting through all the trappings of various occult belief systems, separating fact from fiction and revealing the truth."

"And what is the truth?" There was a long pause in the conversation as Armitage tried to stop himself from shaking. "Professor Morgan?"

Armitage bowed his head and shook it slowly, as if in defeat. "I don't know! You want the truth? It's roaming the streets of Bolton in the form of five things that ate more than fifty people in a matter of minutes. The truth is out there. They're waiting for you, they're waiting for all of us, and they're hungry, ravenously hungry."

Castro leapt up from his chair and grabbed Armitage by the collar. "What are they Professor? I have eight agents dead, and I don't have time pussyfoot around."

Armitage was ranting. "A hundred years ago, there was a man, Noah Whateley, he found a way to open a crack and something leaked in. Whateley's daughter gave birth in 1913. Wilbur was a monster; he grew ... by fifteen he was nearly eight feet tall. He came to Arkham, to Miskatonic to steal the Necronomicon, an ancient book of magic, a guard dog tore his throat out. He wasn't human—he was more like those things out in Bolton. After he died, his body dissolved. My grandfather thought that was the end of it, but it wasn't, he had a brother, trapped in a makeshift cage. Without Wilbur to take care of him he broke free and started feeding on the population of Dunwich, people, cows, state troopers. My grandfather used some kind of magic to stop the creature, but the resulting explosion leveled the whole area for miles around, like someone had dropped a bomb on the place. The Whateleys were all dead that should have been the end of it!"

Castro lit a cigarette and ran his fingers through his thinning hair. "So why … how are they back?"

"Before Wilbur was killed there were incidents. Teenage girls would go missing. Sometimes after six months or so the girls would come back, sometimes they wouldn't. There were rumors, and suspicion always involved Wilbur, but there were never any official investigations, just more of the Whateley gold being spread round to shut people up. A local doctor by the name of Houghton wrote a report. He said that the girls had been purposefully hidden by their families while they were pregnant. They had been raped, presumably by Wilbur Whateley who then paid off the families with hush money." Armitage's voice began to shake. "It wasn't easy, but Houghton was able to examine some of the infants born to these girls. All of them, every single one, exhibited some kind of congenital deformity. Most of these were minor, and not entirely unknown. Tails, webbed feet, polydactyly, those kinds of things, easily fixed with minor surgery. But there were also others so horrendous that the nurses and midwives who were in attendance ran screaming in terror. Houghton tells the story of one such birth, a bleating thing with far too many limbs. The nurse fainted when it opened its mouth and called her name. By the time she regained consciousness the attending physician and the child were gone. They found the man in the basement coming out of the room where they housed the furnace. When they asked him about the child, he refused to say anything. He wouldn't even acknowledge that he was even involved with a delivery that day. The girl and her family denied everything as well." Armitage paused hoping Castro would take his meaning and that he wouldn't have to say the rest of it, but Castro needed things spelled out for him. "Don't you see? I think some of these children, these bastard children of Dunwich, survived, and not only survived but were made available for adoption. I think Wilbur Whateley's children grew up and had children of their own, grandchildren maybe even great-grandchildren by now. I think the gene lines—oh." He stopped and let loose a sad little laugh.

Castro was annoyed. "What's so funny?"

Armitage shrugged and cracked a twisted smile. "My grandmother, she was something of a racist. Couldn't stand all the Italians and Spanish and Portuguese that were always moving in and out of the area. She called them wops and dagoes. She used to tell me how they were only Europeans because they had been born in Europe, but what they really were was Arabs and Niggers. They weren't white folk at all, no matter where they said they came from. She also said we had to be careful about miscegenation, about them coming in and contaminating the blood lines."

"And this is relevant?"

"Only to me I suppose. She was so worried about white people breeding outside of their race. But the real threat wasn't from Blacks or Asians or even those from the Middle East. The real threat has been here all along, hidden in the contaminated genetics of good old white Anglo-Saxon protestants." He turned and spoke, "Li, I'm so sorry ... " but Li wasn't there.

His research assistant had been left behind when Malkowski had been evacuated. She was back there, trapped with the monsters they had brought back from Antarctica. He wanted to cry, but it was all too much. So, he giggled. It was just a little laugh, but it seemed to influence him. He laughed some more. The FBI agent Castro tried to tell him to stop, but he just kept laughing. It was a sad sort of laugh, full of irony and regret and tears. He laughed for hours. He was even laughing as he took the elevator to the roof of the Science Tower. Some of the students saw him climb over the edge. One girl even saw him fall. She said he seemed happy; he had been laughing.

December 16, 2016
Delapore Chemical Research Annex
Bolton

Li Zhou burst into the entry hall cleared the foyer in three bounding steps and hit the button to call the elevator as she slammed herself inside the frame and tried to hide. She tried to control her breathing. She was on the verge of panic. The soldiers that had been supposed to get her out were all dead, eaten alive by the monstrous thing that was roaming the streets of Bolton. Once there had been five of them, each about the size of a minivan, but they had all come together and built something monstrous, something colossal, something that gibbered and screeched from five human mouths. Something with elephantine appendages and tentacles that probed in front of it. She peered out from her hiding spot. A tentacle was probing into the building, a viscous dark fluid dripped from the fat, bulbous tip. Panicked, she ducked back into the elevator frame.

The elevator arrived with an electric chime. The doors slid open. Li went to move inside but discovered she wasn't alone. There was a man inside, twenty-something, Caucasian, five-feet, six-inches tall, maybe a hundred and sixty pounds. In those first few seconds Li Zhou was extremely happy to see Bobby Chambers, even if he was holding a very large shotgun and pointing it in her direction. Before she could say anything, Chambers stepped forward and pushed Zhou out of the way. He pulled the trigger and the ammunition exploded out of the barrel with a cloud of smoke. Zhou cast a backward glance. Arcs of electric blue energy enveloped the tentacle, corrupting the fat, black tube of flesh. It drew back in pain, retreating out of the building.

Chambers cleared the gun and in a practiced motion and slid two shells back in. As he did, he caught Li's eye. He smiled and held out his hand. "Going up?"

Li collapsed against the back wall of the elevator as its doors slid shut. "Tell me Bobby, how is it that all the weapons that the soldiers had were useless against that against that thing, and somehow you are able to drive it off with a fucking shotgun loaded with birdshot?"

He smiled and with a deadpan face said, "Ancient Chinese secret."

Li's jaw dropped. "Do you have any idea how racist that is? You couldn't just give me a straight answer?"

The door slid open, and Chambers stalked out with a swagger. "I was serious. I found a formula in one of the Seven Cryptical Books of Hsan."

"The what?"

Jeyakumar, the Indian astrophysicist turned in his chair, "The Seven Cryptical Books of Hsan, a grimoire, a Chinese book of spells and alchemical formula."

"I didn't know you were into all that weird stuff." Li looked around. "I thought all of those books were back in Arkham, in the restricted section of the library."

Chambers grinned wickedly. "They are, but the Delapore is hooked up to the University mainframe including the library digital archive. Everything in the restricted section has been scanned and put online. I used Armitage's codes to gain access. After that it was easy. I read Chinese. Moustafa handled the Arabic. Jeyakumar has a working knowledge of Sanskrit. That thing roaming the streets helped give us a bit of motivation." He pointed at a work bench full of chemical canisters, "Delapore Chemical gives us the raw materials to do a little bit of magic."

"Magic?" There was sarcasm in Li's voice. "Don't tell me you have a six-demon bag?"

"Magic, alchemy, science. It's all the same thing—knowledge." Jeyakumar shrugged, "and we're going to use that knowledge to put an end to that thing out there."

Chambers gathered up some more shells from the desk. "We have a plan Li." He pointed at a monitor that showed the interior of a warehouse. Li could see three people driving forklifts—Jefferson, Moustafa, and Hernandez. They were stacking crates, all of which were marked Flammable in very large print.

"You're going to burn it?" There was a touch of panic in her voice. "How exactly are you going to lure it in there?"

Chambers smiled a wicked smile. "That thing really hates being shot."

Li nodded knowingly. "You have another one of those guns?"

Chambers looked at it and then at her. "You know how to shoot?"

Li smiled. "I'm on the Trap and Skeet team, so yes I think I know how to shoot."

He pointed to a table in the distance, "There's another gun over there and a handful of shells we've added our special mixture to." He paused and looked at the third person in the room.

"Mr. Jeyakumar," he turned to his other classmate, "any objections to bringing Miss Zhou with us?"

"We don't have the time or the luxury to argue about it," he said getting up from his chair and grabbing some electronic components from the table. "We all have to die sometime; it might as well be today." He walked toward the elevator and Chambers and Zhou followed. "Let's go save the world."

December 17, 2016
Delapore Chemical Research Annex
Bolton

It was just after midnight when Li found herself in position with the Vugg just yards away. She was in the corporate reception area, crouching behind a couch. She could see the thing at the far end of the hallway. See was maybe the wrong word—she couldn't really see it—but rather she could see what it was doing to the world around it. Space and matter were warping around it, light waves were bending, refracting through the unreal space that surrounded a creature that was only partially real. Even the floors and walls seemed to bend to its distorting presence. It passed in front of a wall of portraits, bending the stern faces of those who had once overseen Delapore Chemical. It was weird how her mind worked, focusing on tiny details when the world was on the verge of destruction. The first portrait of a stoic white man with a bushy beard that was labelled Our Founder ballooned into a funhouse mirror version of himself, the image magnified and distorted by the approach of the thing. The next painting was of a darker man–Hispanic maybe, or maybe a light-skinned African American- the placard said Toussaint Delapore, but it too mutated under the approach of the bubble of unreality, shrinking in weird directions while bloating in others. The third portrait was of a woman with hair so light it might almost be called white. She seemed a severe woman with a slightly prognathic maxillary that reminded Li of a famous rock star. The placard identified her as Jane Grimm, Lady Jermyn, but only for a moment. As the sphere of unreality moved forward the portrait and the whole wall that it hung on caved in on itself, disappearing into a small dot of light that shown bright for a moment and then sputtered out into nothingness. This was why she knew she had to fight. This thing threatened the whole universe, she and her colleagues had to defeat it, or die trying.

She depressed the button on the walkie-talkie they had scavenged from the security office. "I'm in position, get ready to move." She half-hoped that there would be a witty response, something coded as if they were secret agents executing a plan, but there was only the agreed upon silence. She stood up from behind the couch, pointed the gun in at the thing and pulled the trigger, releasing the two shells full of esoteric chemical shot in the right general direction and then turned to run. She hit the double doors hard and screaming began running down the road toward the warehouse, reloading as she ran. Ten seconds later the doors exploded behind her as the creature emerged in pursuit. She spun around, still screaming, felt the shells slide into place, and fired again. Lightning arced across the body of the thing, but Li turned away before she saw too much. It screamed a horrible inhuman but still human sound that chilled her to the core.

Panicked, she dropped the gun and ran, she ran faster than she ever had before. She ran putting one foot in front of the other until they were a blur, and the pounding of her shoes on the asphalt was indistinguishable from the beating of her heart. She ran down the road they had agreed on. She ran without looking back, but somehow knew that the thing was still there, creeping up on her, the wave of madness that warped space in front of it licking at her heels. She could see the walls of the buildings beside her begin to melt and that made her run faster, run so hard that her lungs ached. She passed an alleyway and saw the doorway marked in yellow tape, she dove for it and slipped inside.

Behind her, and perpendicular to her and the creature's path a golf cart careened out of the dark alleyway at full speed. Ten yards away, and it screeched to a stop. Chambers hung from behind the wheel, took aim with his gun and pulled the trigger. Li closed her eyes. She didn't want to see the thing. Fear was welling up inside her, but she stuffed it back down. She wasn't done yet. There was a delivery truck waiting for her, fueled up and loaded with cannisters of solvents. She jumped into the driver's seat, strapped herself in, revved the engine and took off after Chambers and the unseen horror that followed him.

The truck careened down the road, it may have been similar in size to a snowcat, but in handled like a brick. She grazed some boxes on one side, over corrected and sideswiped some empty pallets on the other. In front of her she could see Chambers and his golf cart. He still had the gun but wasn't firing it anymore. As long as the thing followed him, he didn't need to. Li stood on the gas pedal, accelerating the truck to over fifty miles an hour. The engine screamed in protest, but Li ignored it. The creature had gained on Chambers, and just as it seemed it was about to catch up to him, the low gulf cart slid under the partially opened garage doors of warehouse and vanished from sight.

The creature skidded to a halt, or at least tried to. It was taller than the opening and it plowed into the dangling section, which warped and bent both from contact with unreality and the creature itself. Li screamed and braced herself, plowing into the back of where she thought the creature was. The garage door gave way, and the creature was forced inside exactly as planned, but the impact between the truck and the creature left the vehicle behind, the front-end caved in. It had spun sideways, wedging itself in the opening. The safety straps had done their job, Li was alive. She took a deep breath and felt a sharp pain in her side that she suspected was a broken rib. While she fumbled with the catch, she watched what was happening out the window.

It came in, crawling out of another dimension, dragging itself into the thing mankind called reality with a myriad of tentacles that seemed to be grasping and anchoring it into the very atmosphere itself. It was like an octopus pulling itself forward through a torrent of currents that threatened to tumble it out of existence and into somewhere else. It was only partially visible, a shimmer here, a pustule there, a fleshy polyp, a throbbing tentacle, but it was so much more than this. So much more, and it was massive, it forced its way into the warehouse, bending the frame of the door backwards, and lifting the ceiling. It seemed to rear up and swell causing bulges to appear in the walls themselves. There was no question, Li and her team had made it mad.

Chambers darted out from the golf cart, his shotgun leading the way. He fired once then again; small clouds of smoke engulfed the brave figure and the creature seemed to recoil in pain and fear. Then the fear ended and was replaced with what Li supposed was rage. A tentacle surged forward, and Chambers stumbled back. He tried to turn and run, but he tripped and fell to the floor, the shotgun skidded away down the concrete. Jeyakumar dove out from the side, tried to get the gun, but it was useless, he didn't have any shells. In an instant the two students were erased from the world, not even blood stains to mark where they had once existed.

Hernandez appeared on top of a stack of crates. Li imagined he could hear him screaming. He was lobbing bottles at the thing. They exploded on contact, bright flashes of light that blinded her. For a moment afterwards her vision was blurred, and by the time it was clear Hernandez was gone, and the creature had moved further into the building. Suddenly, just as Li released the catch and fell out of the truck door, a forklift flew by. Jefferson was in the driver's seat driving at full speed. He never hit the brakes and rammed the rear of the creature. The blades penetrated the partially visible flesh and from these twin wounds a viscous fluid boiled out. It was definitely a fluid, but it was lighter than air so instead of falling down to the floor it billowed out and enveloped the forklift. Li saw Jefferson reach out and try to pull himself out of the cloud, but it swallowed him up and she never saw him again.

Only Moustafa remained, and he was at the far end of the aisle. He was just standing there waiting. In the last few moments, he had seen several of his friends die, he must have been in shock, enraged, panicked even, but he just stood there waiting as the thing came ever closer. It flickered in and out of existence, as if it was trying to tune itself in to our world. With each step it became more and more real, more and more tangible, more and more horrific. And then it was there in all of its horrific glory. This time, Li couldn't turn away, the scientist inside her needed to see it, the human inside her needed to see it die. It was a terrible thing to visualize. It was large, larger than she thought, as if three elephants had been molded together by a mad promethean god. There were tentacles flailing and tendrils and something that reminded her of the claws of an arthropod, but the worst thing was the faces on top, three human faces but terribly huge and bloated and split, one piled on top of the other, like immense flatfish, one lying on another. She screamed at the sight of it, but she couldn't hear her own voice over the screams that came out of those three mouths as the creature closed in on Moustafa.

He looked her in the eye. She could see his hand tighten on the detonator. She could see his mouth open and move. She somehow knew that he had said run. She turned and sprinted away from the building. The creature roared, and then there was a muffled thwump and a shock wave that picked her up and carried her through the air. Then there was a second sound, which she assumed was the truck going up. Windows shattered and the very foundations of the buildings shook as if they were made of matchsticks.

The fire burned for hours but was contained to a rather small part of the facility. Despite the damage automatic fire suppression systems had kicked on in the surrounding buildings. Li didn't know that. She was blissfully unconscious, knocked out by the second blast, or perhaps by debris that had caught her in the back as the warehouse exploded and reduced itself to burning rubble.

September 9, 2017
Miskatonic University
Arkham

Li Zhou strode across the stage and took her place at the lectern. Professor Francis Morgan touched her on the shoulder and gave her a pondering look. She nodded. She was ready. She had been practicing for weeks. It wasn't the speaking that bothered her but the questions that would come after. He touched her once more and then hurried off the stage.

Li tried to steady her nerves and swallowed hard. "Professors, classmates, honored guests. There have been many rumors about what happened to Armitage Morgan's Antarctica Expedition, why Morgan killed himself, and the disaster in Bolton. Tonight, with some audiovisual support I'm going to tell you—show you—what happened to my mentor, and to my classmates, some of the most intelligent, generous and courageous people I have ever known." Out of habit she touched the scar that ran across her chin. It was a reminder that would stay with her for the rest of her life. Not that she needed one. She would never forget what had happened to her and her friends, and Armitage. But the audience, the University—the world—they needed to be told, they needed to know, and this time they needed to remember.

The Spaces Between

According to the composer Claude Debussy, "Music is the space between the notes." I never really understood that before, but I do now. I understand this and more, so much more. But I'm getting ahead of myself.

It was two weeks ago when I was called into the Assistant Director's office. "Mr. Andersson," I hated the way he said my name, "I'm sure you know who Miss de Hond is," he gestured at the woman who sat in the red leather wing-backed chair. Rumor had it that no other chair in Miskatonic University's Library was as comfortable. Rumor also said that every other piece of furniture on the seventh floor had been chosen to encourage students to study someplace else. The woman in front of me wore a light orange jacket over a designer t-shirt which highlighted some of the purple that was hidden in her unfashionably short brown hair. She smiled a little when I looked at her, and it was a wide infectious smile that I thought would precede a laugh. Instead, her left hand began to suddenly shake, and she used her right hand to force it back down on to the armrest.

Of course, I knew who she was; I knew as soon as she walked through the door, even without her six-inch heels, platinum blonde wig, or her form-fitting latex body suit. She was, or had been, Madame Dogma, or Mad Dog for short, a pop culture diva beloved by fans and critics. At least until she had abruptly quit the business two years ago, a victim of Redfield's Syndrome, a disease that had ravaged her family for generations. She had once been a student here, earning a Master's Degree studying voice and piano. Back then she had been a struggling musician just like every other student. One of the local bars had a video of her doing covers of old Depeche Mode songs.

I liked her music; I had a copy of her third album *Saturnine Canines*. I nodded and introduced myself, "Marty Andersson, Miss de Hond, a pleasure to meet you. I saw you perform at the Kingsport Jazz Festival back in 2005." She smiled and nodded, acknowledging the event.

Dr. Harrison harrumphed. "For the next week or so Miss de Hond will be doing research with us in the Smeltzer Collection. I've made sure that room 726 is reserved for her private use. You are to meet her in the mornings at the side entrance, escort her upstairs and then assist her with her studies, including fetching whatever documents, recordings or equipment she may want to look at or use. When she is finished, you will escort her back to Hartwell House, where Mr. Hobbs will assume control. Mr. Hobbs will also be responsible for transporting her from Hartwell House to the library in the morning." As he exhaled, I caught a hint of frustration in his tone. "Do you have any questions?"

I thought for a moment, "What about lunch, coffee breaks, and the like?"

She spoke up. "My condition makes me sensitive to some rather common ingredients. Mr. Hobbs will be preparing my meals and teas. If you would like, I could make sure he has enough for two." Her voice was melodic, soft, not at all what I expected from the woman who used to belt out techno versions of Janis Joplin songs.

"It would be an honor." I told the fallen diva. "When do you want to begin?"

"Now, if it's convenient."

And with that, I was suddenly in service to one of the most talked about singers of the new millennium.

. . .

The job of a library assistant is less tedious than it sounds. First of all, I wasn't actually a librarian. I had majored in Music History with the intention of studying the influence of turn-of-the-century French Impressionism on modern music. I was particularly intrigued by the works of the composer Claude Debussy, whom I thought of as the Father of Atonal Music. Sadly, there are few paying positions for undergraduate degrees in Music History, and as I plodded forward on my Master's Degree, I paid the rent by working as a library assistant. The holdings of the Smeltzer Collection of Music are immense, and the stacks on the seventh floor of the library are cavernous. Helping others navigate the monstrosity of books, manuscripts and ephemera was almost a full-time job. It paid the rent and had significant fringe benefits. I had in my time of helping others, been privileged to work on a number of exciting projects including a retrospective study on the works of the band Inhouse, and a validation of pages thought to be the original score to *Don Juan Triumphant*. There was also a rather odd and expensive examination of several unusual violins using the hospital's CT scanner. For my service in these studies and others like them I had been acknowledged in twenty-two papers and given credit as a junior co-author thrice.

It is not the job of a librarian to guide researchers in any particular direction, but as I have said, I was no librarian. An unfocused researcher could often flounder in the library, see his work become too complex, and then abandon it completely. I had found that if I could connect with a project, with a researcher, find out what they were really working on, I could more often than not focus them on exactly what they needed to look at. In doing this, I could bring some projects to closure—days, if not weeks, ahead of schedule, freeing up time for my own studies. To do so required patience and a touch of subtlety. I knew little about Miss de Hond and thus let her wander about the stacks somewhat haphazardly a little longer than I would have any other student or researcher.

After three days together I finally broached the issue over lunch. Miss de Hond was some subspecies of vegetarian, and I had by this time eaten a variety of things I hadn't actually known were food. Most notable of these were seaweed salad, hummus with roasted garlic, and a dried corn and kale salad. Of course, I had some clue as to what we were doing. Amongst other things, she had requested copies of all of the manuscripts of her great-great-grandfather Ambrose de Hond, who had once been a pianist at the Paris Opera House before his own bout of Redfield's Syndrome had forced him to retire. Unable to play professionally, he primarily composed for the piano and violin instead. In the last few years of his life, he wrote feverishly, composing dozens of concertos, cantatas, and piano sonatas.

Of these the most famous, or infamous, was Piano Sonata No. 6, also known as *The Resting Requiem* for its unusually high number of silent beats. It had over the years been adapted and recorded by a number of avant-garde artists including techno-performing artist Laurie Anderson, shock rock impresario Alice Cooper, and the acid rock songstress Erika Zann. Even the pop group The Undead had released a version as a B-side to their chart-topping cover of "Life at Last". I had over the last few days been allowed to sample these performances as Miss de Hond listened to them over and over again, meticulously comparing them to the original handwritten manuscripts of the composer.

"I want to do an album of my Great-Great-Grandfather Ambrose's compositions," said Bela de Hond. "Other people have performed and recorded them, but they used the scores that my Great-Grandfather Jerad published, and those appear to be highly edited. I suspect Jerad took a great deal of liberty when he decided to publish Ambrose's work." She shuffled through some papers and brought up two pages: one that had been published in 1928, the other being the original, handwritten at the turn of the century. "At first glance these look identical, but if you really look at the manuscript you can see evidence of tampering. Most of this is written in a woman's hand, probably my Great-Great-Grandmother's, but here, here and here," she pointed at several notes and rests, "these are subtly different, and look like they might even be in different ink. That same ink, the ink different than used in the rest of the page is also used to title and identify the instrument to be used. Here is the symbol for harpsichord, but that looks like Jerad's writing."

"So, you're saying that Jerad de Hond altered Ambrose de Hond's compositions. Why would he do that?"

"I'm not sure," her left hand was trembling again. "Some scholars consider Jerad a rather sloppy composer. It would explain a great deal." Her voice trailed off.

"You don't think that's the case though, do you?"

"No," she shook her head slowly and grimaced. "I think Jerad made these changes on purpose. I just don't know why."

"How is it that all his manuscripts are here at the library? It seems an odd happenstance."

She blushed, and I immediately regretted the question. "When my father committed suicide, he left us destitute. My mother couldn't afford to send me to college, let alone graduate school. She made a deal with the former Dean of the Music Department, the school got the entire de Hond family collection, manuscripts, books, musical instruments, more than a century of music, in some ways priceless. In return, I received a proper education." She sighed. "The fellowship that paid for my Master's Degree I earned on my own."

Leaning over her shoulder, I tried to ignore the perfume she was wearing (it reminded me of grapes and figs) and focus on the manuscript page. Typical of the time, it crammed tiny writing and notes on prepared pages that had long since become yellow and brittle with age. I let the notes play out in my head. There were an unusual number of rests, and the score itself reminded me of Debussy's weird anti-harmonies. Still, there was something odd about the whole thing. I could hear the notes in my head, but when I tried to imagine playing them, I couldn't do it. The fingering was all wrong, too fast in some places, too discordant in others. I couldn't imagine moving my hands like that.

As I finished reading the page my eye caught on a small line at the bottom. "What's that?"

Miss de Hond squinted. "A note from Ambrose in French, something about an abbey named Escaladieu."

Two things in my mind suddenly connected. I nearly leapt over to the other end of the table. "There were liner notes, on one of these CDs ... " I rummaged through the pile of jewel cases until I found the right one and then I reread what was written there. "It says here that Ambrose visited the Escaladieu Abbey in search of inspiration. That the monks there were accomplished musicians, but their music had been banned from church services, and they themselves had been excommunicated for heresy."

"Does it say why?"

I shook my head, "No, but if I were doing research on heretical sects, I can't think of a place I would rather be than Miskatonic University." We nearly ran down the stairs. It took longer to find the book we needed than it did to find out why the monks had been disowned.

Escaladieu Abbey: The name meant "Ladder of God." It had once been an order of Benedictine monks, but in the mid-Nineteenth Century, one of their members had suffered a revelation that led to a rather curious divergent theology. They noted that three-dimensional objects such as cubes and spheres cast two-dimensional shadows, such as squares and circles. Similarly, if a three-dimensional object was bisected by a plane, the resulting section would also be two-dimensional. From this they extrapolated that the objects in our three-dimensional world were actually the shadows or sections of four-dimensional objects. In the case of human beings, the four-dimensional object that created the three-dimensional mankind was God Himself. All of humanity, from the lowest peasant child to the Pope was simply a manifestation of this higher dimensional demiurge.

The heresy threatened not only the Church, but the secular order as well. Not only had the order been excommunicated, but the French Government had forcibly disbanded the brotherhood and banned both its teachings and music, which of course, made it wildly popular. Some even said that Edwin Abbott's 1884 satire *Flatland* had been written in response to the disbanding and suppression of the Escaladieu brotherhood. There was no proof of this, but it was an interesting speculation by critics nearly a century later.

As Miss du Hond and I finished absorbing this material I saw her hand begin to shake, but this time she didn't suppress the tremor. "This makes sense now," she exclaimed. "Jerome altered the manuscripts because he was afraid that the Church or the State might suppress them because they were based on things Ambrose had heard when he was at the Abbey." I looked at her askance, but she waved my doubt away. "In 1896 when Alfred Jarry premiered his play *Ubu Roi,* the crowd rioted afterwards, and Parisian authorities banned it from the stage. Some years later, a whole swath of European countries not only banned a similar play but tried to destroy all copies of the script. Is it so hard to imagine the same thing being done with Ambrose's music, and Jerome altering it to make it more palatable?"

Both her hands were shaking now, and she was holding them in front of her watching them break free from her control. I reached out and grabbed them, I'm not sure why, it seemed like the right thing to do. Later after the minor seizure had passed, she talked to me about her ordeal.

"My manager found me convulsing on the floor of my hotel room just after we finished our tour of Europe. Three days later I and my doctors were in front of the press, talking to them about Redfield's Syndrome; the lesion on my brain that would cause my hands to tremble and lead to occasional convulsions. It was the same condition that had afflicted the last four generations of my family. My career as a performing musician was over; all my future tour dates were cancelled. Everybody wanted to know what I was going to do next, but all I wanted to do was hide, to distance myself from other people. I asked my fans and the press to let me leave the spotlight."

"Of course, the paparazzi refused to listen, camping out around my townhouse in Manhattan, snapping pictures of me as I carried out the mundane chores of living a somewhat normal life. I lost thirty pounds, stopped wearing designer clothes and outrageous costumes, even cut my hair to help me blend in with the neighborhood moms. After a few months of watching one of the most boring people on the planet, even the most vicious of photographers walked away."

"These last few days, working with you, it's been a long time since anyone has talked to me, just talked you know, person to person. I've been in seclusion so long, I forgot what human contact—real human contact was like." She stood up and stared out the window. "One of the first things I lost after the first album, the thing I regretted the most, was being able to reach out and connect with people, to establish bonds. Once you reach a certain point in your career everything becomes so one sided, you can't trust people, can't really meet anyone new. If anyone does express an interest, you have to wonder what they really want. The last few days we've been working, talking, talking like real people. I really like that." She paused and looked tremendously sad. "This project was a last-ditch effort, I didn't want to end up like my dad or Ambrose."

I knew that her dad had been unable to come to terms with his loss of motor control and killed himself, but I knew nothing about what had happened to her Great-Great-Grandfather.

"What happened to Ambrose?"

"In the last year of his life, which now looks like it was after he had returned from the abbey, he was incredibly productive. He was creating new works on an almost weekly basis. So fervent was his composing that his wife, who transcribed his compositions, demanded that he take on an assistant. The process was simple, Ambrose would play to the best of his ability, while his assistant, a young man named Lowe, would transcribe the performance onto a page. Then Ambrose would dictate corrections. It was during the process of trying to revise *The Resting Requiem* that Ambrose's wife apparently went mad. She doused the lower floors of their home with lamp oil and casually set herself and the house ablaze. Had not Lowe thrown himself from the upper floor, clutching the pages of the requiem, he and it might have been lost forever. As it was, Ambrose suffered severe burns and languished in agony for two days, all the while still dictating corrections to his final composition."

I was overwhelmed with a sense of guilt, not for anything I had done, but for the entire culture. Her stardom and condition had conspired to exile her from the human race, and the only person she could reach out to was a library assistant. "Miss de Hond, I'm sorry … "

She shook her head and never let me finish that sentence. "Would you please stop calling me Miss de Hond? My name is Bela."

"Bela," after days of being formal her first name felt weird in my mouth, "we've made a lot of progress today. I think you need to sleep on things and start fresh in the morning." She didn't disagree.

. . .

It was Sunday night when the breakthrough occurred. We were working past closing, something my position allowed us to do. The guards had wandered through about midnight and I flashed them my identification and sent them on their way. I suppose it was fortunate in a way, nobody else was in the building to see what had happened; unfortunately, nobody else was there to confirm my version of events either.

Bela and I had been working on her project for more than a week. She had produced three variations on Ambrose de Hond's *The Resting Requiem* but was unsatisfied with them all. She had been using infrared light to accentuate the differences between inks on the original manuscripts, hoping to come closer to Ambrose de Hond's original intentions. It was meticulous work, for which I was less than suitable. I could read music, I could even play a little, but I was not in any way as proficient as she. Consequently, I spent a good deal of time wandering the stacks, reveling in the smell of old print and the lingering odor of rosin used on the bows of string instruments. The great hall was dark, which didn't bother me; I had been in the library after hours before. The place is cavernous and can be unnerving for some as small sounds tend to echo through the great spaces, but for me it is a wondrous place, and I tend to run my fingers over the spines of books and portfolios as I walk, feeling as well as seeing and smelling the vast amount of information stored within those walls. I did this while she played, and then wandered back in when she stopped. It was a pattern we had gotten used to.

This time when I came back, she wasn't sitting at the keys anymore. She was leaning against the wall, tremors running up her arms. I went to help her, but she barked at me. "Sit down at the keyboard."

"Bela I can play, but not nearly as well as you," I complained.

She crossed the room, took me by the arm and sat me down in front of the instrument. "I need you to be my hands. I can't … they won't stop trembling. You'll have to do it for me." She pointed at the page.

I took a deep breath, flexed my hands and then began to play. The first few lines were easy, I had after all been hearing variations on this piece for days, but in seconds I was in trouble. My hands were tripping over themselves, and I could hear Bela become exasperated.

She came up behind me and pushed my left hand out of the way. Her arms were still shaking. "Your fingering is all wrong." She snapped at me like a frustrated teacher. "You have to do it like this!"

Her trembling hand hit the keys in a way I had never seen or heard before, and from the speakers emerged a sound that was unlike anything we had produced in the last few days. It was a terrible, monstrous noise that spoke of cacophonous beauty. Bela stepped back and looked at me as dumbstruck as I looked at her.

"We've been looking at it all wrong." She was overexcited, her voice was cracking. "It was the hand tremors. They run in the family, I have them, so did my father and grandfather, and so did Ambrose, but he didn't see them as debilitating. To him they weren't a handicap; he composed with them in mind! Jerad didn't understand that, when he was preparing the works for publication, he hadn't any symptoms yet. When Jerad played the works, they didn't sound right, didn't make sense because he wasn't suffering from Redfield's Syndrome yet, they sounded wrong, so he fixed them, altered the notes and rests and instruments! He corrupted the text because he didn't and couldn't understand it!"

Both her hands were shaking; the tremors ran up her arms. I reached out to try and control them, but she pushed my hands away. "Let them be, I need them like this, to play. Please Martin, I have to … I have to capture this idea, before the tremors become a seizure and I can't play at all."

Forgive me; I did what I was told. I sat back and let her play.

This is when I learned the truth. When I learned how to hear music, how to feel it not only in the notes, but as Debussy had said, between the notes as well. She was mesmerizing, entrancing—almost hypnotic, and as I sat there watching her play, listening to her play, feeling her play *The Resting Requiem* I saw the truth. There in that room where she fervently took her tremoring hands to those keys, where she had played notes and keys and arrangements which I had never even heard before, a queer green light began to seep into the room. It came from nowhere and everywhere and seemed to highlight some kind of invisible structure. It had shape, this unseen thing that was suddenly outlined, but that shape didn't make sense. At times it reminded me of a four-dimensional hypercube, a pulsing tesseract, that seemed to come down on either side of Bela, but wasn't part of her, but only briefly. Most of the time it reminded me of something horrid, something that reached out with a tentacle-like protrusion from its face to swallow Bela. There was something elephantine about it, something crude and lumbering.

As Bela progressed through *The Resting Requiem,* her playing became faster and more fervent and the thing forming in the air around her grew clearer, more tangible. She could see it too, and while I grew fearful, she grew elated, throwing her head back and letting her purple tinged locks catch a spectral wind. She was a maenad, a primal and uncontrolled muse made real and terrifying. The space above and between my eyes began to hurt. That the thing's tentacular fingers seemed to surround Bela didn't seem to bother her, and as she moved the outline of that thing moved with her. It moved as if it had always been there. I stood up to do something, but what that was I can't say. That movement changed my perspective and then I could see it, the thing that was there, surrounding Bella, defining her by its boundaries. I understood then, understood it all. I think I screamed.

They say that I killed Bela de Hond. They say I became obsessed and that I killed her, and then disposed of the body in the river, before trying to kill myself. It's not true of course. She was there in the room, playing the keyboard, playing Ambrose de Hond's Resting Requiem, the one that had been inspired by the monks who believed that God was a fourth dimensional being and that we were all just manifestations of different portions of God, extrusions of some titanic and pan-dimensional physiognomy into our three-dimensional universe. She was playing it properly for the first time in over a century.

They were wrong. It's not true. I know now why Ambrose's wife destroyed herself and her husband. Bela's music, Ambrose's composition let me see it, if only just for an instant, but that was enough to understand!

Please you have to believe me, I'm not mad. I didn't kill her. It closed its hand.

That's why she vanished into nothingness.

It closed its hand, closed whatever its equivalent of fingers are, and Bela ceased to exist!

We are the emptiness between musical notes, the nothingness that gives something else shape. We aren't part of that thing that haunts the universe. We aren't the appendages of a fourth-dimensional God.

Don't you understand?

We are the void that helps define it, we are the spaces between, and nothing more.

The Guilt of Nikki Cotton

"Have you much guilt Miss Cotton?" Asked Boris Thomashefsky. "My people, we are raised on it. Fed it like mother's milk. We do terrible things to each other, but we feel guilt, wallow in it, so that makes it acceptable."

Nikki Cotton took a moment to mull the question over in her mind. Was she guilty? By her count she was more guilty than most. She had been born black to parents who were not only poor but also uneducated. They had made their livelihood scratching the Mississippi mud and hoping that something would grow in it. She never went to school, but she was still smarter than her brothers, and her parents, and that caused a considerable amount of conflict in the house, with Nikki on the losing end more often than she would like. She was guilty of hating her parents.

When she was fifteen her parents married her off to a preacher man almost twice her age, and she moved north to a little town called Refuge. Her husband was worse than her father, and she was forbidden to travel to see any of her kin. Even when she was with child, and then miscarried, she was left to suffer alone and frightened. Her husband's idea of comfort was to bellow scripture at her until she could no longer bear it and collapsed sobbing in anguish.

That's how she remembered him, bellowing scripture at the angry gray sky, the wind-driven rain whipping around him, two dozen of his flock kneeling before him. They were praying that the levee wouldn't break, that the great river wouldn't tear through its banks and whisk them away. They had been told to leave, but they had refused. They had their faith, and that would be enough to protect them. Lillian had slipped away when no one was looking. She was on the hill about a mile north when she heard a great crack and saw the steeple shudder and then sink out of view. She turned and ran further up the hill and never looked back. Was she responsible, was she guilty for all those deaths?

The Guilt of Nikki Cotton

They put her in a survivor's camp for single women someplace in Georgia. It was supposed to be a safe place, but it didn't take long for the men who ran it to give in to their baser instincts. She had been cornered one night; three men had backed her into a storeroom. If it hadn't been for Tessie, if that big, dumb cow of a woman hadn't of wandered in and then whooped some serious behind … well she didn't like to think about it. When they came to punish Tessie and her, she ran to the railroad and followed the tracks north, hopping trains when she could. She hadn't set out to come to New York, it just turned out that way, and Red Hook was as good as place as any other she had ever seen. Better even, nobody ever asked about your past in Red Hook, because everyone had one. No one asked her about whether Tessie had lived or died. This was a blessing, because she didn't know, and thinking about it made her feel terrible.

"Guilt Mr. Thomashefsky? I suppose I've had my fair share." She replied. "Regrets too, but when it comes to taking care of things, I know what needs doing and when, if that is what you mean."

He eyed her up and down. She was still a sliver of a girl, nineteen maybe twenty, light-skinned and soft-spoken. Attractive if you liked that sort of thing. He didn't, he preferred his women short and a little plump, like his wife and mistress. There was a time when all men liked women with some meat on the bone, but times were changing, and he knew the younger men, men like his protégé Max, were drifting toward thinner, less voluptuous girls.

From his look Nikki knew what he was thinking. "I can handle myself sir."

He nodded. "It's not you I worry about." He turned the handle on the door and ushered her into the room. "Nikki, I would like you to meet the Red Hook Theater Company." It was cavernous, and from the mirrors on the walls and the polished hardwood floors Nikki could tell it had once been a dance studio. Windows at the far end let in a soft September breeze, setting the dozens of thin white curtains that hung from the bare rafters in motion, like gossamer ghosts in a strange ballet. The curtains created a semblance of privacy, dividing the room's occupants from each other. They lay in beds, still like statues, some with their arms by their sides, others with arms outreached but still unmoving. At first, she thought they were dead, but she could see them breathing, slowly, deliberately, clinging to life as best they could.

She managed to open her mouth and leak a few words out, "What … what is wrong with them?"

The old man shook his head and spat something in a language she couldn't understand. "I don't know," he said, "nobody knows."

It took a few weeks, but Nikki learned that wasn't exactly true. The nurses who came daily, and the doctor that came weekly, had a name for what had happened to the thirty-three men and woman that lay in the room. They called it *Encephalitis lethargica* or the sleepy sickness. It had first been diagnosed decades ago and had spread slowly. Estimates suggested that worldwide there were more than five million victims, now housed in various wards like this one. Contrary to her first impression they weren't immobile, they did move, just incredibly slowly. More than once she had returned to her charges to discover one of them out of bed, or almost out of bed, standing there eerily like a mannequin. There was a suspicion that millions more had contracted the disease and then died before aid could be rendered, either through starvation or simply being unable to avoid the most minor of incidents. Not that it mattered. There was no cure, merely palliative care. Some suggested that the origin of the condition was psychic and that the ills of the modern world were too much for some minds and that events like the Great War drove some people to withdrawal from it. Others suggested an unknown bacterium or something called a virus, that the sleepy sickness could be transmitted like the influenza or chicken pox. There were wilder theories, one woman who claimed to be an adherent to a mystical order in Sussex England, wrote in her scandalous memoir that the epidemic was the result of a mystical accident, a summoning gone horribly wrong. Most called her mad, but when she was decapitated in a terrible automobile crash her critics went quiet, and she and her claims faded into obscurity.

Nikki didn't care. She was happy to have the job. She wasn't a qualified nurse, but she was smart and a quick study. Most of it was common sense. Keep the patients clean and dry. Keep them moving, even if they were in bed, they had to be rotated so they didn't develop bed sores. They had to be fed twice a day, a thin gruel that didn't have to be chewed. Keep them warm at night and cool during the day. Give them sun, but not too much.

There was of course one rule above all others: Never fall asleep. Towards this end Mr. Thomashefsky had delivered an urn of coffee twice a day, and staffing was done in staggered shifts of eight hours each, rather than entire crews changing every twelve hours. In this way two or three attendants were always fresh. At least that was the plan. Given the extra hours off, some of the girls picked up part-time positions meaning they were already tired when they came to work on the makeshift ward that sat above Thomashefsky's stage.

With the entire troupe incapacitated, Nikki would have thought the theater would be empty, but Thomashefsky had taken to loaning out his stage to others in the community, but only during the day. Thus, in the early mornings the theater would fill up with actors and musicians, and even patrons who would come to see a show that wasn't quite ready for Broadway or the road.

It was not common knowledge that the resident cast lay dormant inside the back rooms of the building. Mr. Thomashefsky and his assistant Max wanted to keep it that way. Visitors, family members only, were welcome, but had to use the performer's entrance, where they were discretely whisked to a nearby door that concealed stairs to the upper level. They came and went at all hours. Some came to just sit and stare, others brought the daily papers or a book and read out loud. Some brought records and danced clumsily with their slow, stiff relations. It was sadly beautiful, both tragic and comedic, and somehow, they all knew it, and in their own ways acknowledged it.

Thomashefsky had ordered the room decorated with pieces from the prop room. There were masks on the walls, paintings made to look like windows offered up impossible vistas of deserts and tropical islands and teeming cities. In the four corners stood white marble busts that the sly manager had bought from an estate sale in London. The sculptor was a man of some fame and talent who had for reasons unknown been committed to an asylum and there had later hung himself. The marble busts were life-sized and though they bore different expressions each had the same classic countenance and were identified by names in Greek letters. Nikki couldn't read Greek, but one of the nurses could, and she said that the statues were of the Oneiroi, the Dream Kings and were Hypnos, Morpheus, Icelus, and Phantasos. The four were, or so she was told, traditional patron gods of actors and playwrights. Nikki didn't care what their names were, or what they represented. She thought they were creepy. Their eyes were too large, almost bulging, and too far apart. They seemed to follow her wherever she went. They were unnerving, even more than the still lives she tended to during the day.

After two months working nights, Nikki developed a system that allowed her to accomplish the routine tasks set to her in a rather efficient manner. Rather than working on a single patient at a time, she would work on them in small batches of four. Getting them all out of bed, feeding them, washing them, drying them, dressing them, and then setting them in chairs, while she changed their bed linens. It was a systematic way of dealing with things that seemed obvious to her, but anathema to everyone else, until they saw how it was done. Even then the nurses in charged huffed and then stalked out of the room leaving her alone. It wasn't forbidden for her to be alone, but it was frowned upon. But even here in Red Hook, where goods form the Erie Canal were made ready for delivery to the entire world, and the streets were filled with the voices of hundreds of nations, a poor, black girl from the south still got the short end of the stick.

Nurses Carr and Nicholas would often leave her alone for extended periods of time. Sometimes they went downstairs to the alley, other times they crawled out the window onto the roof and sat on the green, metallic blister of a hatch that provided access from backstage to the roof. They smoked cigarettes or sipped from a metallic flask. Nikki knew there was a stash of moonshine in a storage closet just offstage. They left her alone particularly when there was a visitor, and regularly when Mr. Gorski came in. He was old, and heavy-set, and smelled like boiled cabbage. No one wanted to be in the room when he came in. Being alone made her feel bad, small, and even sad, but Nikki Cotton knew how to turn that to her advantage. When no one else was around she took to reading the books and papers and documents that had for one reason or another found their way into the makeshift ward.

It was newspapers she read first because they were most ephemeral, followed by books. She had loved the books that had been brought in. She had read the poetry of Yeats and Graves, adventures by Burroughs, mysteries by Christie, and tragedies by Fitzgerald, and of course, she had read the works of Langston Hughes who so captured the spirit of the age and made her look at New York, and the people who lived in it, with different eyes. The world was an amazing place, filled with a myriad of people, and only a few of them thought like her father or her husband. Somehow that made her feel better, not only about herself but the world too.

It was on Friday October 24th that the first hint of what was to come occurred. Dawn had just broken, and she was in the last hour of her shift, the older nurse was in the alleyway smoking, so she was alone when Mr. Gorski came in. He usually came on Mondays in the evening. He was a businessman of some sort and always dressed the part. It was his daughter Katerina he came to see, who had been twenty-two when she had been struck down, she was the youngest member of the troupe. He sat there that morning and just stared at her. For a while he held her hand, and then he kissed her on the cheek and left. Nikki didn't think much of it.

That was until he returned Monday night, and again on Tuesday morning. He looked sad, tired, almost broken down. Nikki brought him a cup of coffee and he took it with trembling hands. There were tears welling up in his eyes. She asked if there was anything she could do for him, but he just shook his head.

"Thank you for the coffee." He muttered. "The coffee at my office is always hot and sweet and mixed with cream, they call it a *Franziskaner*. I hate it. I like my coffee like this; warm, black and bitter. This is good. This is what men should drink." He had an accent, it wasn't German exactly, but it wasn't Hungarian either, it was something in between that she couldn't place, Polish maybe, or perhaps Prussian. He set the cup down and looked at his hands. "Soft. My hands have gone soft. I worked once you know, in the shipyards when I was a young man. I was poor, but I did things. Now I do nothing. Perhaps it was better to be poor. We shall see." He put his hat on and wandered out without saying another word.

He was there again late on Wednesday morning. Nikki wasn't even supposed to be there, but one of the nurses had sent word that she was sick, and Nikki was asked to cover for her, just for a couple of hours. Gorski had come in with the small crowd that had gathered to rehearse some play or another in the theater downstairs. He walked over to the side of his child's bed and sat down. He hadn't even taken off his coat. He was sitting there holding her hand and he was crying. Whatever he had been holding back had been finally let loose.

Nikki couldn't watch him suffer. "Mr. Gorski? Is there anything I can do?"

Startled he stood up so fast that he nearly knocked the chair over. "No, no," he muttered through his thick accent and tears. "There is nothing anyone can do." He was walking frantically through the ward. "Everything is lost." He stumbled along with Nikki in tow. "The house is gone, the bank is gone, and the money is gone. It's only a matter of time before they come for me ... " He was frantic, almost spinning, like he was delirious.

"Mr. Gorski?" Nikki reached out but he pulled away.

He had spun himself into the corner. "The market has collapsed. They will take everything. I will have nothing. Not even money for food. Let alone to pay for Katerina's care." He reached into his coat and from it withdrew a wicked blade. It was at least six inches long and glinted in the morning sun. There were symbols etched into the metal along the edge and they seemed to Nikki something terrible.

"Where did you get that?"

The old man looked at the gleaming knife. "Katerina gave it to me the day before she fell ill. She said it came from London with these damn marble busts." He looked at the hateful thing that sat staring at him from the corner. "Damn Thomashefsky he and his horrible theater have taken my daughter from me! After today I have nothing left, but my life. And Thomashefsky can have that too!"

And then the knife flashed in his hand and red ran cross the edge. The blade bit deep and fast and as he pulled it from his throat a great arc of crimson flew across the room. Blood splattered across Nikki's eyes, across the floating curtains, across the walls and across the face of the bust that sat behind him.

Nikki opened her mouth to scream but before she could, her terror turned to morbid fascination. Gorski had fallen to the floor, and from his convulsing body blood was flowing freely, but it was not working its way downward across his shirt, but rather it flew across the air and into the suddenly open mouth of the marble bust. Like some grotesque vampire the stone carving was feeding on the vital fluid that streamed from Gorski's neck.

The feeding was not the only eerie occurrence that caught Nikki's eye, for with each gobbet of blood the eyes, those bulbous, unnerving orbs, began to glow with a terrible darkness that spread out and sucked the very essence of light from the room, turning into a gloom-filled twilight where blood-stained curtains swayed in unfelt breezes and the bodies of her statue-like patients were no longer immobile but rather had risen and now stood upright. Their faces were like those of the busts, mouths and eyes wide open, wider than they possibly could be, as if they were flesh and blood mimics of the queer stone carvings. Carvings that had once been pure white, but now were pulsing with sickly scarlet veins.

It was then that the other nurse burst into the room, whether she had been drawn by the commotion, or had simply entered at a most unfortunate time didn't matter. "Miss Cotton!" She barked. "What have you done?" And then she surveyed the room and began to understand, but not enough. "The sleepers ... how did you? They're awake!"

They turned toward her in a fluid motion, as if some singular intelligence controlled their actions. They turned toward her and stepped forward, arms outstretched, hands grasping. They turned toward her and with eyes and mouths wide they spoke a single word that seemed to echo back and forth from inside their throats. It was a horrible thing to hear, these vacant-eyed revenants with their stretched open mouths intoning a single word over and over again without moving their lips. As they descended on the hapless nurse Nikki covered her ears for, she could not bear that impossible sound that moaned out from the horde. But she heard it anyway and shuddered as they fell upon the woman who stood at the other end of the room, the word "Awake" reverberating in her head, a word spoken by all in imitation of Nurse Carr's voice.

Nurse Carr vanished beneath the wave of human monstrosities. Nikki watched with morbid anticipation as to what would happen next. There was a scream, something short and final, and then a kind of wet snap. Suspecting the worst Nikki gasped involuntarily but then saw the mindless horde part and this allowed her an obscured view of the woman.

With fear and trepidation in her voice Nikki called out "Nurse Carr?"

The silhouetted shape responded to the sound of Nikki's voice. Not in recognition of its name, but rather as if an animal had been suddenly startled. She turned and joined the horde as they shuffled forward, their mouths stretched wide and a new word echoing from within. No longer was the word "Awake" drifting out of those hollow throated creatures, instead it was the word "Carr" the last word Nikki had spoken, and it echoed in what could only be described as a queer, lifeless imitation of her own voice.

The door was cut off by dozens of grasping hands and horrible hungry mouths that were slowly shambling toward her. In the corners the darkness emitting from the eyes of statues was growing. Left with no choice she threw open one of the many windows and through it climbed out onto the roof of the theater below. There was an access hatch that led down to the back stage. From there she could make the alleyway door and then the street. In the back of her mind there was the dim idea of getting help, but it was only an afterthought. Her primary goal was to simply escape, to run home beyond the reach of what appeared to be a most terrible infection.

She slammed the window behind her and then sprinted across the tarpaper to the metallic green blister that was her escape. The icy November wind cut through her thin cotton dress and set her shivering. She cast a glance over her shoulder expecting to see her pursuers coming after her, but the window was still closed. Through the glass she could see them turning, wandering back toward the door, toward the stairs, and beyond that the theater where the rehearsal was just starting.

She grabbed the lid of the hatch and tried to wrench it open, but it didn't move more than a fraction of an inch. As she pulled, she could feel the metallic rod that locked the hatch in place. For all she knew it could have been a lock, or a simple bolt, the end result was the same, she was trapped on the roof. Or was she?

The hinges for the hatch were on the outside. She didn't have a screwdriver, but there was plenty of debris on the roof: a can, a broken broom handle, shattered glass, and a box of rusty nails. She grabbed a nail and worked through the pins on the hinges, popping them out and then ripping open the hatch just enough so that she could squeeze through. She tore her skirt on the way down, and nearly lost her grip on one of the rungs, but she crawled down that tiny access tunnel and landed backstage, halfway between the exit and the door that led up to the ward, to terror.

She glanced at the door and caught glimpse of Nurse Nicholas passing through, she yelled her name, but the woman didn't respond. Nikki ran after her calling her name again, but as she reached the door she saw the woman on the stairs, and the mindless, vacant eyed things bringing her down.

This time Nikki saw the whole thing. It wasn't complicated at all, they just touched her and then there was a spark, like black lightning jumping between the infected and the victim. Nurse Nicholas seized for a moment, and then fell onto the stairs. She rose up in an instant, her own eyes vacant and her mouth growing slack and ever wider.

Nikki slammed the door shut, threw the lock and then lodged a chair under the handle. She knew it wouldn't last, but it would buy her some time, a few minutes maybe, but that was enough. She was only steps from the exit, and she took them in seconds. Her hand fell on the doorknob, she turned it, but she never pushed it open.

She could hear the voices of the men and women in the theater. She heard them reciting their lines, and it was as if she was suddenly back in Mississippi listening to her husband and his flock pray against the rain, knowing that it would do nothing to save them as she snuck off up the hill to safety. She heard actors and the laughter from the crowd that had come to watch, and she knew that she couldn't leave them behind. She couldn't let people die again.

Next to the door was the small red box with the roof on it, and the word Sterling embossed on it. There were words in white too, directions. The operation was simple, deceptively simple. All she had to do was open the door and pull the handle down. Which she did. There was a short pause and a sudden pop of electricity and then the alarm was sounding, and people were yelling, and she could hear them running.

She smiled for a moment, but then she heard something else. Something heavy thudded against the door, the one that led upstairs, and she knew that the horde had reached the lower floor. She went to run again, to flee down the alleyway and out into the street. She wanted to go home and hide. Then she heard the other voices, those horrible voices calling the last word she had ever spoken, and she knew they would never stop, that she had to stop them here before they got out, before they were free, before they spread.

She turned away from the exit and ran for the other door, a thousand thoughts running through her mind. She was trying to come up with a plan. It didn't take long, after all she had already used the threat of fire as a ruse to get everyone out, why not use the real thing to keep things contained.

She scoured the backstage for what she needed. A box of matches came from a desk drawer, and from the closet she grabbed three bottles of moonshine, which she carefully threw in a gunny sack. She glanced back at the door. Incredibly the chair was still holding.

In a flash she was up the ladder, the cloth bag over her shoulder. It was easier this time, climbing up in a controlled way rather than falling down. The rungs were cold in her hands, but the pin that held the hatch shut popped right out and she pushed the metal door up with one hand, letting it clatter to the side.

Retracing her steps across the roof, she barely noticed the cold, and slid open the window with ease. She lowered the bag inside and then climbed in after it. She made a minimum of noise but wasn't sure if that mattered. The busts were still there, their eyes glowing black. Mr. Gorski was dead, his skin looked like a pile of dried leaves. At the other end of the room, she could see some of her former patients trying to get down the stairs, but they were still blocked in by the horde that was trapped on the stairs.

The curtains were now swaying in the cold breeze, and she moved amongst them dousing them with liquor from the first jar. She was quiet and fast as possible, and as she moved forward, she kept a careful eye on the monsters that were once human and tried not to listen to them. Then with the curtains prepared she took the second bottle of moonshine and threw it at the door where the mindless hungry things were trying to get out.

As it shattered, she cried out "Over Here!"

As expected, they turned and in their terrible shuffling way came after her, their voices calling out her own words.

Over here

Over here

Over here

They walked slow and steady, oblivious to the glass and liquor beneath their feet. They were coming for her, arms outstretched, fingers grasping mouths opened wide. She was all that mattered to them. And they cried out begging for her to join them.

Over here

Over here

Over here

She backed away toward the window, her eyes darting back and forth trying to count the monsters that were coming for her. They all had names, and once she had taken care of them, but now they were something else, something that couldn't be let loose on the world. Once she was sure they were all in she took out the matches and lit the nearest piece of curtain on fire.

The flames danced up the alcohol-soaked cloth and caught the wind spreading around the room like a living thing. In moments the former dance studio was ablaze, towers of flame raced from the floor to the ceiling like some scene out of hell. It was inevitable really, and part of her plan, a flaming piece of cloth fell and hit the floor setting first the moonshine ablaze, and then the feet of the sleepers. Flames raced up their legs and caught on their nightgowns and pajamas.

They didn't care. Step after step they came forward, driven by some hideous alien intelligence. In the roar of the inferno, she could still hear them calling, still hear them moaning. Their flesh burned and bubbled in the heat, and they didn't care.

Over here

Over here

Over here

She had hoped that burning them would work, but she had suspected that it would be more complicated than that. Which is why she had held back on the third bottle of moonshine. The body of Mr. Gorski was still laying there, all the life sucked out of it at the base of the bust. She carefully went over and poured the illegal spirits over top of the marble head, letting it soak down the small column and run up against the spent shell of Mr. Gorski.

Then she lit another match and dropped it into the heap of clothes and dried skin. "I've always hated you," she screamed at the formerly inanimate head as flames ran up its pulsing white and crimson flesh. At some point it had ceased to truly be stone. Maybe the fire acted as a purifying agent, revealing the truth hidden in the matrix, for beneath the flames the once classical image became something else, something twisted and inhuman, something plastic and fleshy. Something with huge eyes and a ravenous, churning mouth. Something that wasn't of this world, but thankfully still could burn.

She ran for the window, but as she dove through something caught her leg. It was Katerina Gorski, and she was on fire. Her hair was burning, and her clothes were gone. The skin on her torso was black and ashy, her arms were on fire and the hand she grasped Nikki's leg with was little more than smoldering bone and blackened muscle. Her mouth was still open, and from that deep, empty hollow place an imitation of Nikki's voice echoed back, "I've always hated you."

She kicked at the burning hand as her own shoe caught fire, and screamed as the flesh beneath it began to sear. She kicked again and again, screaming until her voice was hoarse and her throat raw. She kicked and kicked and screamed but the creature wouldn't let her go. Terror gave way to fear, and despair. It blinded her.

It blinded her so much that she never saw the man running across the rooftop: The man, the fireman who with a single stroke from his axe severed the hand from the body and set her free. She fell to the roof and was scooped up by two powerful arms. She was lowered down the hatch into other hands that whisked her away. She was screaming the whole time, and the men who would letter testify said that it was the phrase "Let them burn!" that she kept repeating even after she was delivered into the arms of a waiting policeman.

He carried her away from the scene, and there were witnesses to his heroism as he patted her down with his bare hands, smothering the last of the remaining flames. When she realized what he was doing she yelled at him "Don't! Stop!" But he grabbed the last bit of smoldering debris from her shoe and tossed it aside.

What happened next is open to some debate, but all witnesses agreed that Miss Nikki Cotton then grabbed the officer's gun from his holster and pulled out of his grasp, pointing the gun at him. Some say he fell to the ground and shook a little, stunned by the sudden impact, others say he was fine. Both parties agree that he then reached out for her to take the gun away. Some say they heard him beg for his life—or at least start to: He only was able to say two words before she pulled the trigger sending a bullet into his brain.

They said she was mad, unfit for trial. They committed her to an asylum for the criminally insane. There she became little more than a frail shadow of herself, wandering the halls muttering those same two words over and over again. Thomashefsky came once to visit, but he could not get more than a few sentences from her.

She spoke in a whisper, "I couldn't take the chance. I couldn't let it out into the world. He could have chosen a thousand other words, but he didn't, he didn't, and I didn't have time to waste. I'm so sorry. Tell his family I'm so sorry."

The old man who in the fire had lost everything, held her no animosity toward the girl, but needed to understand what had happened. "What did he say Nikki? What did he say?"

"He said the same words I had said." She looked up at him with soulful eyes. "He said the same words, but I don't know if he used his voice or mine. I don't know, I just don't know!" And then she went back to wandering the halls, wondering whether she had saved the world, or killed an innocent man, and repeating the same phrase over and over again.

Don't! Stop!
Don't! Stop!
Don't! Stop!

The Twilight of Stronti

There are twenty-eight galaxies readily accessible to the queer metallic-light envelopes of the Nug Soth, and in each galaxy, there are innumerable stars and innumerable worlds, some dead and some teeming with life, a great deal of which could be considered sentient. Even more, there are those creatures that walk in the spaces in between worlds, unbound to any one planet or star or galaxy. These are unique entities, whose very presence warps the fabric of space and time, corrupts the laws of physics and drives lesser minds to madness. These Great Old Ones, singular beings bearing no relationship to each other save their immense power, are akin to gods, and even their casual visits to primitive cultures have been known to warp and contaminate the minds of those who have glimpsed them. Many of the older races have developed the proper technologies, wards and sigils to hide their home worlds from the curious sensory apparatus of these wandering titans. Others have invented ways to redirect or discourage the approaching juggernauts, though in this it might be said that some are like unto the size of small planets or moons, while others are no bigger than a man. Fewer still are no larger than an insect but possessed of such powers to make cities crumble before their shrieks. Legend says that there are even creatures that have no dimension whatsoever and are composed of pure mathematics or exist hidden in the recesses of spoken or even written language. They exist, and they walk through space serene and terrible, and thankful are the worlds that have avoided them. There are other races, other worlds that have not been so fortunate, which have fallen under the shadow of such creatures. Indeed, on Yaddith where the Nug Soth raised their metallic cities, there was buried deep within the heart of the planet the primordial prison of the thing known as Thaquallah, an amorphous and terrible creation of the enigmatic Q'Hrell. Its very nature meant that it could not be killed and so was forever imprisoned within an impenetrable moon-lens. Monstrously fecund, she had given birth to all matter of creatures some of which now formed the Yaddithian ecology. Preeminent of these spawn were the squamous and rugose Nug Soth, and their constant bane, the titanic vermiform Dholes, or as they were known before the Jh'sosti's Reformation of Language, the Bholes. It was these cyclopean burrowers, and their terrifying appetites that drove the Nug Soth to search for ways in which to bind their noxious cousins. The emissaries of Yaddith travelled the universe in search of answers, but to little avail. It was true that effective means of eradication had been discovered, but such methods did as much injury to the Nug Soth as to their intended targets. This in itself was a clue, part of the Riddle of Thaqqualah, a conundrum that the Wizard Zkauba had answered, and in doing so had been driven mad.

It was thus that I Randolph Carter, a human consciousness displaced both in time and space did come to dominate Zkauba's body and did travel the universe seeking answers. On the surface, my mission was to find a solution to the Dholes, but thanks to Zkauba I knew the truth–that there was no solution—and that the fates of both Nug Soth and Dholes were inexorably linked. Instead, I used my time to search for a way home, back to Earth, my Earth, of the Twentieth Century, for not only was I countless light years away from my home, I had also been cast back eons in time. All this had been accomplished through the Hyperborean artifact known as the Silver Key, an object that possessed immense power, to travel through time and space, and even transform Zkauba's semi-insectile body into that of my own human form. Yet all these abilities and more were lost to me, I had forgotten the incantation that activated the key and thus was only able to access the most rudimentary of the key's capabilities. Still, I was not without hope. The universe was large, its minds wondrous and diverse, somewhere in the accumulated knowledge of the universe there must exist some solution to my dilemma, some way home. So as Zkauba I wandered the universe, searching for an answer, searching for a way home.

It was to trans-galactic Stronti that I journeyed, a planet I had been to before, but only when Zkauba himself had been in control. Then, I had been only able to wonder in awe at the sights I glimpsed through his multiplex of eyes, but now I was in control, and the decadent science-philosophies of Stronti seemed as good as any other place to start. Stronti is called trans-galactic for it resides in no galaxy at all. It is extraneous to the accessible twenty-eight, falling within what is known as the Empty Quarter, a vast dark gap between the fifth and twelfth galaxies. In the Empty Quarter stars were rare and planets even rarer, and those that existed hung lonely and lonesome amidst the emptiness of the void. Stronti stood on the edge of that volume of space, sunless, one side tidally locked so that it was constantly bathed in the weak and distant light of the fifth galaxy, while it's other side, called Shonhi, was only bathed in the light of the twelfth galaxy. There was neither day nor night on the queer half worlds of Stronti and Shonhi, only a deep impenetrable night with the dim light of distant, miniscule galaxies to break the endless darkness.

When Zkauba had visited before the entry to Stronti had been a crowded, bustling port with vessels from dozens of worlds carrying visitors from across the known universe. Stronti had been like that, a crossroads for travelers both near and far. It didn't have much to offer in the way of natural beauty or high art, but the travelers still came. It was a waypoint between worlds, between galaxies, between where they had come from and where they were going, and that perhaps was enough. It had been enough to attract the On, a curious species not unlike the sea anemones one finds in tidal basins along the rocky New England coast. Unlike those strange little polyps, the On were neither shy nor cold, but rather quite gregarious. At least they had been, twenty years ago.

Now, two decades later, I approached the planet Stronti and found the space around it devoid of other ships. Approaching closer, I saw that some great planetary cataclysm had occurred. Almost the entire world had been enveloped in a planet-spanning ocean, not of water but rather of some black, viscous fluid. My sensors suggested it was made of organic molecules and was not unlike raw petroleum. There was still a city on the planet, and a port, but my attempts to contact some sort of authority went unanswered. Reluctantly, I drifted down through the atmosphere and following the memories held in Zkauba's brain manually landed my ship in the shattered aerodrome of what had once been a luxurious transportation hub.

It was a singular facility, once grandiose that had long since fallen into a state of disrepair and decay. The towering columns with their immense flourishes had long since crumbled into titanic shards of rusting steel and piles of dust. The semi-crystalline iris aerodrome had shattered, and proper environmental control was no longer possible. Thus, the great terminus provided no shelter from the storm that had enveloped the dying metropolis. The wind whipped and howled around my cloak and even though my armor was strong enough to protect me from the void itself, I still imagined the cold and wet being driven in through the joints and couplings. It wasn't until I forced my way through the tatters of a woven fabric door that I felt at ease enough to disengage my helmet and let my own senses take in an unfiltered view of the world.

Zkauba's seven eyes saw more than any man ever could, and as I walked those decrepit halls I could see the details of the craftsmanship, the quality of the work, and their flaws. I could also see the age, the eons of neglect and what toll they had wrought. What I could not see were any of the guards, agents, or petty bureaucrats that had been present when last Zkauba and I visited. Indeed, it seemed that the entire facility had been abandoned, and yet I had been contacted while in orbit and given very exacting and authoritative instructions for my approach and landing. It was odd, damnably odd.

The walk through those great concourses, which had once teemed with the sound of life and commerce but now were eerily empty, was disquieting. It wasn't just that they were abandoned, but rather that the abandonment seemed so complete. Even vermin and the feral descendants of pets were absent. It was as if centuries earlier all life had simply been wiped away. Except there was still power. The lights still glowed, though admittedly some had been shattered, and others flickered casting ominous shadows. It was enough to make me put my helmet back on and power up my armor and weapons.

It was just then, with my senses amplified that I heard the scream and the built in display indicated the direction of origin. Having no other options to pursue I turned in the proper direction, withdrew my chainsword, and let Zkauba's four legs carry me at nearly a full gallop. I left the concourse with its shattered glass, cracked planters, and crumbling frescoes behind and launched myself like Nessus assaulting Hercules, into a plaza of concrete and steel outside. But to my surprise and perhaps disappointment, there was no hulking brute to slay, there was no damsel in distress to rescue, but rather just a diminutive member of the On whose garb marked her as a sub-director for transportation and immigration. She was in essence, a customs official, and her cry was apparently in response to dropping what appeared to be a literal tower of documents, which had been caught in the wind of the storm and was now blowing about the plaza.

The native was like most of her species, not unlike an anemone in appearance, with a thick body supported by eight stubby legs arranged in a circle around the base. A pair of large manipulating appendages sprouted from just above the crown and were topped with three squat digits that seemed adequate to the tasks required of it. Finer manipulators sprouted from beneath the ring of eyes and above the mouth, and I presumed had originally evolved to aid in feeding. Along the midsection of the creature was a belt adorned with rings and colorful pieces of fabric that helped to identify her station. For some reason, it reminded me of the caterpillar from Alice in Wonderland, and I half expected it to pull out a pipe and began a solipsistic debate. Instead, she casual waved at me and then went about trying to gather the myriad of forms that she had lost control of.

As I walked toward her, she sighed, a strange bubbling sound, and greeted me respectfully. "Have you come to pay your respects? You are almost too late." She looked around at the derelict city. "All the other dignitaries have departed, as has most of the population. Only I, and my cohorts, remain puttering about, closing the doors and windows so to speak."

I bent and picked up a few pieces of paper. "Minister, I'm sorry I'm not sure I understand. I have come to consult the College of T'ssea, I have a conundrum they may be able to help solve."

She paused from her activity and seemed to regard me with those strange, unpupiled eyes. "Under Minister, but that doesn't matter anymore. My name is Gribfri en Trofs, call me Gribfri. As for the College of T'ssea they have disbanded, retired like the rest of the world." She looked at me again and I sensed a bit of sadness in her. "I doubt very much that they could help you a bastard child of the Q'Hrell."

I stood back in near shock at her words. "What did you say— the Q'Hrell?" She was speaking of the Progenitors, the strange and enigmatic creatures that hung at the edge of things. They were ancient and unfathomable, all but inaccessible. They drifted through space across vast distances. No one knew where they came from, only that they were amongst the most elder of species and should be approached with respect, and a modicum of caution.

She grabbed at some more documents and shoved them haphazardly into a pile beneath one arm. "You are of the Nug Soth, one of many spawn of Thaqqualah, on to which some bestow the honorific the Black Goat with a Thousand Young. Thaqqualah was once a Shoggoth, a simple slave of the Q'Hrell until they experimented on her, and made something more, something terrible—something even they were afraid of. You are their child, unplanned, unwanted, and abandoned, but still their child." She paused and seemed thoughtful. "Have you considered that such a position might be enviable?"

I gathered the last of her papers and handed them to her. "I'm not sure I understand."

Your progenitors, your forebears, have abandoned you, yes you suffer because of it, but have you considered that your suffering might be increased if they took more of an active interest? They aren't exactly known as benevolent. "She began walking away, and I with nothing else to do followed. "Imagine yourselves as servitors, would your cities be as grand, your art so emotive, and your education so enlightening? Or would all that be subverted in service to the Q'Hrell? It could be even worse; your very biology could betray you. There are some species who will forever be indebted to the creatures that spawned them."

Though theoretical, it was an interesting proposition, and one that I was not sure that I was qualified to ponder. After all, my identity as one of the Nug Soth was essentially a ruse. I looked like one of them, I spoke their language, I followed their customs and used their technology, but despite all of that, I was only doing my best to imitate them, my mind was that of a man and was wholly incapable of properly contextualizing the issue. Though I must admit there were analogs in human culture from which I could draw, but once again it seemed I was not qualified to ponder the question, I was a child of privilege and was unprepared to ponder servitude, save only in the most abstract sense. For a moment I regretted such limitations in my education, but then realized what that would entail and was grateful that by a simple quirk of fate I had been denied such experiences.

We walked down a great road, and once again I was struck by the deplorable state of things. The windows on either side of us were nearly all shattered, and the shards left on the streets and walkways to be weathered down into sand and dust. The thoroughfare itself was pockmarked by potholes and cracks that created a bleak landscape. In other places plants would take root in such crevices and slowly grow, breaking down the artificial landscape, but here in the dim light of distant galaxies there were only queer species of fungi. They were monstrous things in horrific colors. Mushrooms with purple veins and yellow gills bloomed next to blood red smuts and fields of velvety green morels. Inevitably, the conversation turned to the decay that surrounded us.

Gribfri made a non-committal sound. "There is a time for all things. We recognized centuries ago that a transition was approaching and that we would soon be no more. As we focused on that, we let the physical trappings of our great civilization fall to ruin." She harrumphed. "Ironic is it not, the very things we valued the most we simply abandoned, because we came to realize that in the face of the inevitable, they were simply worthless. If only … " She let the thought go unfinished.

It was then that I caught sight of another of her species had joined us in our journey, and then a moment later another. They poured out of alleyways and side streets until we had a small parade of her species following us, marching forward on their legs in a weird whirling fashion. All of them bore insignia of similar rank and I mentioned it to Gribfi.

"We minor bureaucrats were needed here to process the last of the forms and checklists. We are closing down our world, one must expect a bit of bureaucracy. Who better to handle it than us?" There was a murmuring sound of general agreement from the parade of looping administrators.

We marched on and in time reached what could only be described as a kind of great quay that jutted into the vast black ocean that had enveloped most of the world. As the rest of On marched forward Gribfi stopped and gently pulled me aside and performed a small ritual of departure.

"I am sorry we could not help you solve your problem Thaquallahan. Perhaps one day, we shall re-emerge and again grace the universe with our presence. Until then, I must bid you farewell. This is where we part company."

I watched as she joined the rest of her fellow bureaucrats as they waddled down the stone dock. I thought perhaps that a ship or some other sort of vessel would appear to transport them, and wondered what make of craft could make way in such filthy waters. It was then and only then that I took my first look at the vast inky waves that undulated beneath the howling winds. It was not water at all, but rather reminded me of some kind of thick gelatin that didn't flow at all, but rather quivered and quaked as the wind blew against it. It was semi-transparent and I could see inside of it vast complexes of radiating structures, small glistening orbs and masses of convoluted tissue that seemed to pulse and throb inside that awful translucent jelly.

I looked back toward where the On had walked just as something dark, swift and cyclopean rose up and in an instant seized one of the clumsy polyps and ripped its head off. The lower section quivered for a moment and then collapsed as the fluids that were both its blood and hydrostatic skeleton flooded out onto the stone. No sooner had one such tentacled monster retreated than another appeared and in swift and terrible action one of the other On was decapitated. Through it all, the On seemed unable to react, almost overwhelmed by the speed and ferocity of the attacks.

But I was not so entranced, and without thinking I drew my chainsword and leapt down the length of quay engaging the monsters that emerged from those corrupted pus-like waters. A single stroke of my weapon and three of the tendrils were dispatched, while a fourth impacted on a shield of extra-dimensional energy that I erected using the Sigil of Kilw. It took supreme effort for my upper arms to wield a weapon while my lower appendages crafted the spell, for my human mind had difficulty managing more than two arms, but here I was in luck for there was in Zkauba's body a bit of muscle memory, and it was well-practiced in the art of attacking and defending at the same time. As the obscene length of flash battered against my protections, I felt an overwhelming sense of confidence and struck out with my blade bisecting yet another monstrosity.

I was not prepared for the severed lengths of flesh to hit the surface of that corrupted ocean and merely dissolve into it. Nor was I ready for the two polypus bodies that struck me from behind screaming in anger. I fell to the ground, and it only took me a second to recover, but in that scant moment the two On that had attacked me were themselves destroyed. A single massive tentacle had reached out of the sea and cut them in two. I watched it happen, and as their soft bodies exploded it seemed to me that they had wanted it—that they were waiting for it. In the tiny fraction of time as the sweeping arm approached them, they seemed to take on a kind of universal reverence or piety.

Confused, I staggered to my feet and looked toward Gribfi stood. "You must not interfere; this is the way of things. Your species has its secrets, and we have ours." As she spoke another pair of her compatriots were slaughtered, and from the ocean a dozen more tentacles rose up and turned to menace me.

I assumed a battle stance and charged my shields to full. "It's like some damned Lernean Hydra!" I yelled.

I hadn't expected Gribfli to understand that, but she made a strange squealing sound and then spoke in excited tones. "Yesyesyes. That is a fair analogy!"

It was then that I remembered that both she and I were not speaking the same language, and it was not likely that we ever could speak the same language, but rather we were both dependent on active translators, mine in my armor, and hers somewhere in her vest. Either one had deemed it necessary to provide a kind of synopsis of the myth I had referenced, likely drawn from my very mind without me even knowing it.

"But we are not the monster, we are simply we. We are the Hydra, and it is us. We are like you Thaquallahan, our species has multiple states of being. For millions of years we have existed in our larval stage, accumulating mass and knowledge, preparing for the future, for this our transformation!"

"But it's killing you!" I shouted in frustration.

"No," whispered Gribfli, "it is simply adding our brains to its own. It's making us immortal!"

And then without any fanfare or discussion Under Minister Gribfri en Trofs, the last of the On, was engulfed by a tentacle, her internal fluid crushed out of her, and her head dragged down into that horrible, polluted ocean that wasn't an ocean at all, but rather some vast communal brain. It was as if the entire population of the planet had become one organism, on life form, one mind—a mind that was now speaking to me.

I fell to my knees in agony. I knew that it was whispering, but it was whispering with a billion voices and that was too much for my prosaic mind to handle. In a panic I summoned my ship to rescue me, knowing that I would never be able to outrun the thing that was now rising up around me. There were thousands upon thousands of tentacles rising up around me, and on each tentacle a whispering mouth that begged and pleaded and incessantly cajoled.

I don't know how I resisted. Perhaps it was the fact that I was already one mind inhabiting a body that was not my own. Perhaps it was because I was able to draw support from the entrenched mind of Zkauba himself, perhaps a human mind was simply too alien and too resistant to the demands of the On. Regardless, when my ship finally arrived, its gleaning body of hardened light was a welcomed sight, and I didn't so much as run inside, but rather stumbled, and collapsed, setting a dangerously blind course away from that terrible place at a velocity that was a hazard not only to myself and the ship, but to the very fabric of the universe.

It was only when I was safely beyond the reach of those voices that I allowed myself to relax and reflect back on the words that had been whispered to me, the promises made, the position offered. I had named them they said. Never before had they had a name, for they hadn't needed one, but I had named them "Hydra" and in exploring that myth they had become fascinated, not only with the name and the creature, but also with the very concept of alien influences. It had only taken moments, but in the vast collective mind that was now referring to itself as Hydra, a metonymic ideology if there ever was one, the concept had run rampant and had been embraced whole heartedly. Their biology had driven them to become something terrifying. The concentration of so many minds, so much knowledge, so much sentience into a single body had driven them mad, and with that madness had come something else. Space itself was warping beneath the weight of such a monstrosity. The On had become something akin to the Great Old Ones that stalked the stars, and I had provided to them a name which they had embraced. As a reward they wanted me to be as they were, and they whispered to me in a thousand voices.

"join us. join us. join us."

But I refused. I refused and with all the magics and science at my disposal I fled, employing eldritch wards and primordial sigils to guard my wake. Through space I fled, the titanic mass that called itself Hydra boiling out of the planet and literally clawing against the gravitic bonds exerted by the planet. They climbed out of the gravity well of Stronti, and with tentacles ripping through the fabric of space itself tried to reach me and drag me back. The fact that they couldn't, that my pitiful magics kept them at bay seemed to enrage them.

"We shall find you." Their voices hissed and burned, for they weren't voices at all, but some kind of telepathy, my mind embattled with the awful seething neural shrieks of countless individuals that spoke as one. "You cannot hide from us. Time and space are meaningless to us now. Millions of years, across the vastness of the universe we shall hunt you, we shall find you."

It was then that it uttered the phrase that caused me to recoil in terror and speed my light envelop back toward Yaddith, back where I was at least marginally safe amongst those who might still defend me. But the horror still clawed at my mind and the most dangerous of implications.

"Earth is no refuge for you Randolph Carter, we will come for you. We will come for you and yours and devour you all. You will be one with us!"

It knew my name! That alien abomination that festers in the deepest, darkest reaches of space between galaxies knew my name!

More importantly, it knew where I was from.

And it won't ever forget. I don't think it can ever forget.

The Hydra is coming, slowly but surely it will swim and crawl and climb through the darkness of the universe. It may take millions of years, but Hydra will come. I'm sure of it. It is inevitable. It is coming after me. It will come to Earth, and it will destroy everything it finds there. Millions of years before we have even evolved, and I've sealed our fate. I've doomed the entire human race.

I'm sorry, I'm so sorry.

By the Light of the Moon

The man in the Hawaiian shirt brushed the dreadlocks out of his face and caught a glimpse of the sun as it was setting behind the mainland. The dying rays cast ominous shadows across the sky. Behind him violent waves crashed against the beach and the ocean pier that jutted into it like some great concrete dagger. The sea was angry, churned wild from the storm that had dominated the weather all day. The sea was angry, but the sky was clear, almost serene. The moon was high in the sky, a full moon, like a titanic, yellow eye gazing down on the human world, and judge its sins. Sins that Malachi Chan had a habit of exposing.

It was Malachi Chan's job to pry into the affairs of other people; he worked for the Department of Justice and of late much of his time was spent on the east coast of Florida, from the wilds of Bone Key to the metropolis of Vizcaya, and on occasion the barrier island of Orchid Beach, where the old families, with old money cared to reside in their old houses. It was a bit of a drive for Chan, not that he minded. Being called out to Ocean Drive in exclusive Orchid Beach to investigate a double homicide at a beachfront mansion built out of white marble with mahogany accents was exactly why he had become a cop. He had double majored in Art History and Criminology, just like his grandfather, and just like his ancestor he specialized in art theft and fraud, something that had become rampant of late. The excesses of the late Nineties and early Naughts had created a boom in the art and antiques market, which had in turn created a thriving black market for stolen collectibles from comic books to the most ancient of relics. The Justice Department had created an entire division to deal with the illegal trade, and Chan was just one player in a very large game.

At the front door of the mansion a local cop gave him the stink-eye, but he had to flash his badge to gain entry and a gesture in the direction of the crime scene. The prejudices of the local residents had been passed down to the men who patrolled their palm-lined streets. It didn't matter that he had gone to Choate, or graduated from Lancaster College in Oxford, or that he had worked for two years at Christie's, some would always judge him simply by the color of his skin, and the way he wore his hair.

The interior of the house was just as opulent as the exterior, though Chan was surprised that the walls seemed rather bare. There was no artwork, no photographs, no paintings, not even an abstract post-modern wall hanging, just sheets of cool marble that lined the hallways that led to various rooms, including the mansion's private library where apparently the murders had taken place.

"Malachi Chan, DOJ." He said as he passed through the door. There were four men in the room, two were part of the investigation, the other two were quite dead. Between them was a massive book, something ancient and tattered.

The man closest to him had a jacket that said Sheriff and when he stood up, he took a deep, frustrated breath. "Lieutenant Tony Verona. That's Hastings from the Coroner's Office." He gestured to the other man who was dressed head to toe in a blue protective suit. Hastings was bent over the corpse of an infirm looking man. "Looks like a robbery gone bad. This was Kennedy Kincaid, 86 years old, and the owner of everything you can see. Old money. He's considered something of a recluse, not a regular in the social circuit. We called his doctor's office; they say he's been legally blind for the last decade. There are two slugs in his chest, he bled out in under a minute."

Verona pointed toward the other body on the floor, it had fallen at the base of a rather ornate pedestal case. The man was pale, almost white, as was his hair. There was a gun clenched in the dead man's hand. "This one is a local businessman by the name of Donald Fester, runs a shop down on Garden Avenue. Deals in rare books, movie posters, stuff like that. We have a file on him, a few investigations, a few suspicions, but we've never been able to prove anything." He paused. "The gun in his hand is his and properly registered. Hastings says it's been fired twice, we haven't had a chance to test for ballistics, but the size of the holes in Kincaid seem about right." Chan looked at the skin, it was pale, almost translucent, and his eyes, frozen open in death, were pink. "You don't see many albinos in Florida."

The coroner nodded. "By all accounts he didn't use to be, at least not the last time we had him in for questioning."

Chan reached into his coat pocket and took out a leather satchel and removed the fine gloves that were held within. They were as white as his own skin was black and they seemed a size too small as he slid his hands inside them, but they stretched and formed a kind of second skin that Chan could barely feel as his fingertips found their snug homes. His hands properly protected he reached out and gently took the book from between the dead men. It was heavier than he thought it would be. The binding was black goat skin, you could tell by the grain. It was old, maybe four hundred years, maybe more; the wrinkled and warped leathers spoke volumes to the trained eye. On the spine tooled letters in gold hinted at a title, but they had been rubbed away long ago and were illegible, even to Chan.

With care he lifted the book and carried it to a nearby table. As he did so he took note of the pedestal case and assumed that it had been made especially for the volume he now held in his hands. Of this he had no doubt. He set the book down on the velvet-lined table and ever so gently opened it to the title page. The paper was crisp and clean, and its condition bore no relation to that of the hoary leathers that encased it. The pages themselves were ivory and flawless, with no trace of a blemish or flaw. Chan examined the book, carefully turning its pages one by one, slowly at first, then as he progressed faster. In the end he was flipping through the book faster than he could read. Not that it mattered; the entire book was blank.

Verona screwed up his face. "A strange book. Why would you want to steal an old, blank book?"

Chan shook his head. "That is not even close to being the right question. In fact, we have a pair of questions we have to ask and answer." He closed the book and stared at its spine contemplatively. "Why would a man like Fester be willing to kill for this book?"

Verona nodded his agreement, "and the second question?"

Chan pointed at the second body lying just feet away. "Why would Kincaid be willing to die for it?"

Chan stood up and carried the book over to a queer marble pedestal that stood in the center of the room. There was an ornate bookstand on top of the pedestal, carved from ebony and lined with felt. It was the right size and shape for the book that Chan held in his hands. He set the book in what seemed to be its proper place, and indeed it fit there better than he could imagine. Resting on the felt-covered wood, Chan opened the queer volume to what should have been the title page, though he could not understand why one would choose that particular spot to display a book. The wall lamps were simply too weak to illuminate the pedestal. There was a small window in the ceiling to let in the light, but even that bothered Chan. Most collectors shunned the light of the sun; it acted as a kind of slow bleach causing the bindings and text to fade into dull shadows of their former selves. Why would Kincaid place a book directly beneath a window?

The problem made Chan's head ache, and he set the book down letting the thing fall back to the title page. He took in his surroundings. The library was octagonal in shape with no windows and only one door. There were hundreds, likely thousands of books on those shelves, and yet only this one, this unnamed book, was given a place of honor, and only this one had been removed from its place. To understand the value of a thing you had to put it in perspective, to place it in its surroundings, to put it in context. Even from a distance one could see that this library was something special, collected over decades, perhaps for an entire lifetime, perhaps even more. Yet two men had died for just one book out of the entire library, what made it so special? And just as importantly, what made all these others less so?

Each of the eight walls was easily twelve feet tall, and perhaps twenty feet long, and divided into sections by ornate, wrought-iron columns at each corner and another in the center. At first, he thought the columns mimicked stylized trees overgrown with vines, but as he drew closer, he saw that in actuality they bore a greater resemblance to some abyssal cephalopod or similar polypus monstrosity with curling tentacles adorned with primitive mouths like those of a hagfish. The shelves were thin pieces of grey slate, an extravagance to be sure, but one that created an illusion of invisibility. In the dim light the thin stone made it look like the books were simply hanging there in space, unsupported by anything but their owner's will.

If there was an organization to the collection, it wasn't immediately apparent, for books that appeared hundreds of years old were likely to be sitting next to titles that had been published in just the last few decades.

Nor was subject matter a discerning factor, and neither it seemed was quality. A leatherbound folio of *The Murder of Gonzago* was sandwiched between Hope's *Telemachus Sneezed* and Wanderly's *The Nightwatcher*. There was a battered copy of Wimsey's *Notes on Collecting Incunabula* that propped up de Vaillantcoeur's *Histoire d'Amour*, which in turn leaned against a WPA volume entitled *The Miskatonic River Valley*. Here someone had seemed to try something akin to organization for the next book was *The History of the Miskatonic Valley* by Pr. Everet Watkins. Something by Bottfolio entitled *Obscuri Libri* was wedged between two volumes of *The Collected Works of Robert Blake*, while Goddard's *The Rise of the Colored Empires* looked uncomfortable against Emerson's *History of Ancient Egypt*. After these there was a sudden run of vintage mysteries some of which were recognizable including Ariadne's *The Lotus Murder*, Rex West's *The Mystery of the Pink Crayfish*, and Klopstein's *Once More the Cicatrice*.

It was the next book that caught his eye, for he had himself been searching for a copy for the better part of a decade. There tucked beside something called the *Ethics of Ygor* was Edgar Allen Poe's *The Worm of Midnight*. The spine was a little shaken, and as he withdrew the book he saw strands of the cloth binding tear away, but it was a magnificently beautiful book, and he handled it with even more care than he had the other book. It was odd for sure, but while Kincaid and Fester had died over that odd book full of blank pages, to Chan this small hardcover was worth more. In Chan's mind this slim book by Poe was priceless. But as he flipped through the pages, his wonder turned to confusion. Every leaf inside that book was blank, devoid of words, of page numbers, of any ink at all. Just like the book on the pedestal.

As he gaped in awe, Chan thought briefly that the library had been robbed, that the original book had been surreptitiously changed with a blank book of similar shape and size. But no sooner had the thought crossed his mind he dismissed it; the binding was too well crafted, too well aged, the impressions that formed the titles and decorations of the actual cover were intact, and so any thought of theft was rejected. It was so odd that he took the book into the light and then flipped through it again, this time gaining evidence of an even weirder phenomenon. As the pages played through the light you could see impressions of where letters had once been. This book wasn't blank; it had somehow been erased, drained of all its content, made void of everything that had made it an actual book. He turned back to the shelves and pulled down another book, and then another, and another, and another, but the result was always the same. All the books on every shelf, from centuries old copies of Vallet's *Le Manuscript de Domm Adson Melk,* to ultra-modern editions of Vetch, were empty. The library had been corrupted, emptied, made meaningless by some force he didn't understand.

His head was spinning. He could feel his heart pounding in his chest. There had to be an explanation. He just didn't know what it was.

"This book isn't blank at all." Chan looked across the room. Verona was standing over the pedestal, but both the detective and the book weren't shrouded in shadow as he expected but were rather illuminated by a pale glow filtering in through the window above. In the time that Chan had been investigating the library the moon must have climbed higher into the sky, high enough to cast its weak, cold light through the glass portal above. Even from a distance Chan could see that the man was telling the truth, in the moonlight the title page of the book was suddenly no longer blank.

Chan crossed the room in great strides, closing the distance in seconds. He pushed Verona aside, nearly knocking them man to the floor. It was true the book was no longer blank, where there was once nothing, there was now something, something wonderful. The text was magnificently black, darker than the darkest ebony, and so well defined, so free of bleeding that it seemed almost an impossible task to set before any master printer of any age. In the center of the first page the book revealed itself,

The Oculus of Glyyth
Being Elias Ashmole's Translation
1654

That would make the book around four-hundred and fifty years old, something he just couldn't believe given the condition, style and skill. There was a decorative border at the bottom, an interweaving of loops and arcs that were generically Arabic in design; it was here he found the artisan's secret mark. The date was 1734, and the publisher appeared to be George Gamwell of Philadelphia. A reprint edition then, probably custom made, or at least very limited. With care he lifted a block of the text and took a look at a random page.

If anything, the interior reminded him of Trevisan's *The Lost Word*, for like that volume the one in his hand was a treatise on the occult. The text was doubled, on one page was the 18th century translation and on the other the original written in Early Modern English, the language of Marlowe, Shakespeare, Milton, Hobbes and the first King James Bible. Not that it made much difference, for Chan reading either text was difficult, more of a translation than anything else, and he only was able to understand the shortest of snippets, and the one he was looking at made little sense.

Glyyth is Their light and Their eye. Through Him They scour the world and cast Their light onto the works of men. Through Him and His They devour that which is touched and in devouring the very source becomes pale and lost. Glyyth is Their light and Their Eye, and men and the works of men are Their feast. What His works touch He devours. Only the sea may know and cleanse the vast wickedness of Glyyth that feeds as the flies on the cattle of mankind's knowledge and art. Only the sea can purify Their servants, Their artifacts and Their works. Only the sea can disperse the accumulated filth of ages. Nothing else is vast enough to swallow the accumulated poisons. Only the waters of the sea can drown them and only the purifying salts can bleach them clean.

Chan had of course heard of Elias Ashmole, an alchemist of sorts, and the namesake of the Ashmolean Museum at Oxford. However, he had never heard of him authoring such a book and had no clue as to what or who Glyyth was. It was a situation that filled him with dread, for as he stared at the queer book whose words only appeared in the moonlight, he realized how terrible a thing it must be. The only book in the entire room that was left with any content, with any trace of text, were the pristine pages of that queer grimoire in the center of the room, the one that looked like it had just been printed last week. It was a book two men had apparently died over, and one had been turned pale.

Through Him and His They devour that which is touched and in devouring the very source becomes pale and lost.

He looked over at where the old man's body lay, and even from a distance could see the pale, blank eyes that stared out of Kincaid's face, eyes that were empty, devoid of color, not unlike the pages of the library full of books behind him. Kincaid probably never even knew what had happened to his collection, he had started to go blind nearly a decade ago. A funny thought crept inside Chan's head. Something to do with the way the books had been emptied, the why of Kincaid going blind, and how Fester had been killed, but it was all too impossible to take seriously, and yet in Chan's mind it made a kind of sense.

The idea gnawed at him.

He could barely think that name, and he dared not say it.

The Oculus of Glyyth.

It lounged on the table like a beast waiting for unwary prey, and he knew now what prey that hungering book fed on to sustain its own horrid existence.

The Oculus of Glyyth.

The Oculus of Glyyth waited, its ivory pages hungry for more.

Something would have to be done.

Someone would have to do something.

He watched in a daze as Verona moved beside him and motioned toward where the book sat. Chan watched but he didn't understand, he was too distracted by his own thoughts. Verona's hand reached out, his fingers coming closer, ever closer to the thing that sat on the table. "Is this what all the trouble is about?"

Malachi Chan cried out, but he was too late.

Verona's fingers grazed the cover of *The Oculus of Glyyth,* and the book responded as Chan had expected. It lashed out, engulfing Verona's hand, forming an unbreakable bond with the flesh of the detective. "God!" Screamed Verona. "I can see. I can see it all. The truth, the monstrous apes of truth! The lurkers at the threshold that fumble at the gate! The flautists who pipe and reel in the abyss. The three-lobed eye that leers and laughs. And beyond it all, the festering, nuclear chaos that seethes and frets in the center of our galaxy." He was screaming. The color was draining from his skin, from his body, running down his arm and out his hands.

All the while, that evil book seemed to throb with hideous delight.

"He is Their light and Their eye ... He watches us for Them. The Moon-Beasts and Their God. He watches and He waits, and he learns. Ia, Ia, n'gaih mglaw-nagl nnn! Glyyth! Glyyth! Glyyth!"

Verona's screams drove Hastings from the room, but brought his colleagues running with weapons drawn, but there was nothing to shoot at. Verona was just standing there his hand engulfed by the book, his very life being sucked out of him. Before anybody could understand what was happening, before they could decide to do something, it was all over. When the book finally let him go, Verona had been turned white, his very life drained away. As he crumpled to the floor there was no doubt that he was quite dead.

In the confusion that followed it was easy for Malachi Chan to pick up the book and clutch it to his chest. Even through the gloves and his shirt he could feel the book trying to reach him, trying to show him the madness that Verona had seen, trying to drain the very life out of him. He ran from the library and then from the house itself, all the while enduring the pain as *The Oculus of Glyyth* clawed at his body and mind. It promised him things, terrible things, incredible things, wondrous things. It whispered secrets, dread and monstrous secrets. In an instant he knew more about the truth of the world, of the galaxy, of the universe than any other man alive. It drove him mad, but it didn't matter. Malachi Chan's course of action was set, and nothing could stop him.

Outside the house he passed Hastings and the man gasped as the book and Chan passed by. Hastings had seen something in the moonlight, a shadow of something unearthly, something inhuman. He watched as Chan ran across the street, towards the beach. Everything that Hastings new told him to run in the opposite direction, but he couldn't help himself. The little man from the Coroner's Office followed Malachi Chan, across the road, down onto the beach, and onto the Ocean Pier.

The waves encircled the pier, rising and falling like monstrous leviathans coming out of the darkness, coming out of the deep, coming out of the abyss. Chan reached the end of the pier in seconds, and Hastings watched as the man climbed up onto the railing and paused there. Chan was like a titan standing there on the edge, surrounded by the savage sea and bathed in moonlight, his forbidden prize clutched to his chest like some promethean boon.

He stood there just long enough for Hastings to catch up with him and issue a single desperate plea for the man to stop. But Malachi Chan couldn't hear him. Whether it was the wind or the surf or the madness Chan could no longer hear anything but the voice of *The Oculus of Glyyth* as it filled his very being with the eldritch knowledge of the audient void, or at least tried to. Even now the thin cloth of the gloves and his shirt served to protect him from the worst of it. Only the barest minimum of cosmic filth had seeped through, but that had been enough to drive poor Chan mad. He stood there on the edge screaming, and though Hastings could barely hear him, he somehow knew what the words leaving Chan's mouth were from the very book he held.

And then the sea took him.

Hastings couldn't tell the Coast Guard whether he jumped or fell. Not that it mattered. They searched for hours, their ships scouring the wine-colored waters beneath the cold pale light of the moon, but to no avail. They did find him eventually, not in the sea, but on the beach, just two miles down the coast. It was just before dawn and the beachcombers were out, but the light of the moon was enough to reveal the horror that stained the shoreline. The outgoing tide had left a monstrous sight. There had been a fish kill; an entire school of baitfish had been enveloped in something thick and black. It was almost like tar. A huge mass of viscous, black, filthy ink dotted with thousands of fish, and embedded there within a single human body, that of Malachi Chan, frozen in a tortuous pose.

It took a few hours to extract the remains from the tar, but after that was done the men in the protective suits burned what was left right there on the beach. They burned it with chemicals, and fire. They burned it until there was nothing but ash for the incoming tide to wash away. With each wave the remains were carried away bit by bit, until at last the sea swallowed it all.

Chan's death was ruled an accident, with the official cause of death being drowning. That is what the death certificate said, but Hastings knew better. The Coroner's Office could tell you the cause of death, but they could never explain why he had leapt into the sea. Nor could they explain why Malachi Chan's hair and skin had gone white, why his eyes were so pale, and why his hands were frozen in that horrible way.

They seemed to be clutching at something; something that the sea had washed away; something that thankfully no longer existed.

The Cat in the Pall

I t was a little more than two years ago, on June the 16th 1923 that I was brought to the restored house at Exham Priory. Prior to that I had resided in a small cottage on the outskirts of nearby Anchester dwelling with the man that I called Shakes. I had been with Shakes for most of my life and had lived with him in America in a town very different from Anchester, one filled with factories billowing dark smoke and the near constant sound of machines churning both night and day. In Anchester, Shakes had added eight others of my kind to our household, and these came with us to Exham Priory. They were, in no particular order, a Siamese who preferred to be called Mao; Lady Pyrr, of Persian descent; Katrina who was Siberian; the Manx Stubbins, and the queer Abyssinian Madame Cassandra. Finally, there were the siblings, two burly British shorthairs Johnnybull and Jackymac. These were not their birth names, nor were these the names used by the mans, but rather their day-to-day names.

As for me, these fellows called me Mr. Ginger, not because of my color, which back then was as black as moonless night, but because even amongst the tribes of cats I was light-footed. My steps were like a breeze through the grass, and when I ran, it was merely a rush of whispers. We were as most households of our type, a motley crew, friendly as cats go, but not without our moods and fights, but united when it came to defending our home and mates. Stubbins may have been a foul-mouthed bastard, but he was our foul-mouth bastard, and woe to the stranger who laid a claw upon him.

As eldest, and clearly Shakes favorite, it was I who dominated our new home. I say new, but that was both true and not true. Exham Priory tasted both old and fresh, and as I explored, I learned that new construction had been laid over old—ancient—foundations. The place reeked of freshly cut wood stained and painted with all matter of solvents and dyes, but also always lingering in the background was the ever-present odor of the aged stone itself, stone that had endured centuries of weathering and moss and lichen, and still held the scents of place that such age imbues. It was a large house though, large enough for several temperamental cats, with many high places with which to set up individual dominions and routines without too much conflict. I of course took control of the bedroom in the west tower, where Shakes slept, as well as the library which contained plenty of comfortable couches and chairs, as well as a rather massive fireplace that I knew would be needed to heat the place when winter finally came. Despite claiming these territories, I was a benevolent prince, and allowed the others to share the library with me, but the master bedroom was mine alone.

Shakes and our family was attended to by a pantheon of mans who each specialized in cleaning or cooking or tending the garden, and these were all strangers to us, and we spent the first few days learning their personalities and training them in their service to us. Also present in those first few days was a young man whom we called Tubby. I had known him from his many visits to the cottage, and knew from the years that Shakes would often go and visit the man in his own home, or in the village pub. They were good friends, and it pleased me that Shakes had such a person in his life. Once there had been others, but since his wife and son had died Shakes had become increasingly isolated, and at least Tubby was someone to speak with.

It was on the morning of the third day that the first hint of trouble was raised. Stubbins came to me with strange news. He had found his way out the kitchen door, and spent the night prowling, first around the walls of the great house and then later in the garden and woods beyond. But in all his explorations he had been able to catch no sign of any small animals of any kind. There were birds a plenty, but these kept to the treetops or to the edge of the cliff that overlooked the crashing sea. There were no signs of field mice, or voles or moles. There were no hedgehogs, no hares, no shrews, not even a dormouse.

"A bad sign," he muttered. Which was true, but as Stubbins was not the brightest of felines, I decided to have someone else look into the matter.

It was two days later that Madame Cassandra came to me with her report. All cats are by their nature sensitive to the preternatural, we are after all one of the few species able to move - albeit with some effort—between the waking world and that of Dream, but Madame Cassandra was particularly precocious when. She came to me in the way that she did, and I fully expected her to speak of something odd found in the stomach of a vole, or perhaps the colors of the intestines themselves were wrong. But there were no intestines to look at, no trichobezoars to marvel over, no deformed baby rabbits to excise from the wombs of their dead parents, no malformed toads with three eyes, indeed there was nothing to look at all.

Nothing tangible.

"There is something queer in the grounds." She mewled. "Some of the leaves on the trees and bushes are odd, grey and brittle, and not just the fallen ones. There are berries on the edge of the wood, but I don't know what species they are, but when I slice them open the juice is black and almost like a paste and the flesh is ashy. I've seen no trace of animal life, and yet ... " she trailed off. "The ground cover moves. The grass and litter on occasion shudders, as if mice were hiding within it." She arched her back a little. "I saw a whole field come to life, undulating and roiling as if it were full of vermin, and then it suddenly stopped. It became as still as it could possibly be. I crept in, but there was nothing there, nothing at all." She whined a little. "I don't like it Mr. Ginger, I don't like it one bit." She wandered off after that, as cats do, the issue unresolved.

I was intrigued, but after all my years I had become something of a house cat, and I took this to be a concern of the land outside our abode rather than within. It was early on that evening that I was proven wrong. With the sun setting over a calm ocean in a drift glass sky, that I myself began to detect something unusual. What it was I could not initially determine. It was a sound, a low annoying drone that set my whiskers to twitching, but the origin of the incessant rustling was unclear. Determined to locate the source of the minor discomfort I roamed from room to room, at ill-ease, constantly sniffing at the walls and columns that formed the outer structure of the edifice. Yet no matter how much I searched, or what I sniffed at, I could find no relief from the murmuring vibration that I could feel even in the very pads of my paws. It grew louder and it seemed to me that it was as if thousands of tiny feet were clawing their way up the outer walls of the building, climbing slowly from stone to stone, moving as a single mass up the towers and into the very sky above Exham Priory. The whole phenomenon lasted for about two or three minutes and toward the end the demonic marching tapered off at the bottom and then spiraled off into the towers and the sky above.

The mans had not reacted to the event, and as much as I wanted to simply ignore the phantasmal cacophony, I simply couldn't and after the mans had gone to sleep I called a convocation of my fellow cats and all reported sensing the same thing and being equally unable to discover its origin. At the suggestion of one of the younger cats, Katrina, the troop began to systematically explore the house from tower to ground. It was an exhaustive search of the upper levels and extended beyond the rising of the sun and into the early morning. The activity caught the eye of the mans who seemed both distressed and amused at the members of the home prowling about in search of what they knew not.

Our efforts were fruitless, we found nothing of any particular interest, though in the cellar we found a large door that none of us had ever been through, and we were all confused by the minute traces of scent that were both strange and repellant that were leaking out of the small gaps between door and frame. We also sensed a disturbance while we prowled the attic regions, though these were not in the attic itself, but seemed to be in the air above the house itself. It was something darkly electric, that clawed at the bases of our ancient feline brains and made us as uneasy as kittens in a room full of rocking chairs. It placed us all on edge, as if a great storm were churning into existence right above our heads. Still, the feeling was highly localized, and scampering down just one flight of stairs eliminated all ability to sense the psychic maelstrom.

That night, my normal routine upset, I retired quite exhausted. As usual, I was in the west tower, sleeping at the feet of the man Shakes, comfortable in my slumber. It was therefore surprising that quite unexpectedly I passed from the world and into Dream, rousing at the gates of Ulthar itself. Passage from one realm to another is not uncommon amongst cats, but I had made no effort to reach the virtual world that sat beside ours and was puzzled by the transition. The cat city was abuzz with activity though I could not say why, but as I prowled its streets, I caught sight of cats from around the world and beyond. On the temple road I fell in behind the trail of an otherworldly saturnine feline that stalked down the road and into the conjoined temples of Bast and that of Ulthar, for whom Bast is high priestess. It was a curious thing to see the iridescent hues of a distant cousin as it moved ethereally through our lower gravity and paid homage to our common maker the Q'Hrell quintet known as the Ulthar, but it was reassuring as well. To know that your species was favored by the makers, and that version of cats existed throughout the universe, more so than any other design, was somehow comforting, in an existential manner. The great candy-colored grimalkin kneeled before the altar of Ulthar and gave obeisance to our lord, and feeling a momentary pang of guilt I followed suit, bowing my head and closing my eyes in respectful devotion. Imagine my surprise when I looked up and found the mysteriously beautiful cat from Saturn standing over me, her mouth open wide and her eyes rolled back in her head. She was flehming, and I held still so that she could assess my status and confirm that I was neither a threat nor a worthy mate. Though I was puzzled why I should even merit her attention.

Imagine my surprise when she finally relaxed and spoke to me, her voice a deep melodic thing, like a dying star. "You have the stink of the Qabba upon you. Why do you reek of such pestilent things tiny one?"

I was deferential, she could have easily swallowed me whole. "Apologies my liege, but I am a simple terrestrial cat, I cannot even say what the Qabba are, let alone why I smell of them."

She sighed, "Do they not teach you the ways of the universe on your tiny little blue planet? On Cykranosh even the milkfed are taught of the Rats of Qybele, the thin lurkers of the void, children of the dark star-goddess Qybele."

I bowed my head in shame and being a crafty old cat made up an excuse. "My parents were killed while my eyes were still shut. I was raised by mans and only now have begun to educate myself in the ways of our lord Ulthar." I peeked and saw that she was exasperated with my ignorance, but also was poised to seize the opportunity to complete my education.

"No one knows where the Rats of Qybele originally come from, but they exist in the depths of space between systems, far from any stars, for the pure light of a sun may itself destroy them. They are vast bidimensional things that cross vast distances in instants and drive lesser minds mad with their touch. Only those of the feline variety are swift enough to catch and kill the cosmic vermin, though truth be told there are those sensitives amongst lesser species that might catch a glimpse, but here is where we differ from such creatures. We see them as pests, to be hunted and killed, where others see them as tremendous beasts, draconians of the void, to be feared and fled from."

"But I have never been to the depths of space, I've never even been off Earth, my most excellent of teachers."

"The Qabba lifecycle requires that their young be hatched on worlds with life upon which their enigmatically colored offspring can feed. Woe to those that dwell in the land infested by the Qabbalin, for the energy that binds their very molecules together shall be torn away, leaving nothing but dust behind." She paused and stretched her neck. "The worst of things is that even after the Qabbalin departs for space, it leaves in the land a festering presence, a corruption that effects even the most stalwart. It may linger for centuries, eventually spawning forth yet another child, one that must be nourished foully but which may grant terrible gifts to those who protect it and through it worship the dark mother Qybele. It is the charge of our creators to destroy such things, no matter where they may dwell." She paused and stared at me with those strange purple eyes. "Even now, the Qabbalin comes near to you!"

I woke with a start. Something was moving behind the tapestry, up the walls, through the walls themselves. The noise, it was not just a single noise, but a cacophony, an orchestral chaos of thousands of tiny claws scrapping against the wall. Enraged, I sprang from the bed and onto the vast cloth that concealed the masonry. It collapsed under my weight and fell, revealing nothing. At least nothing visible, but with all my senses I was confronted with the sensation of a horrid vista. It was not just one thing, but a horde of things, spectral memories of a terrifying event that had scarred the very foundations themselves. And then as soon as I resolved what it was, it was gone, vanished, as if it never was. I prowled up and down the floor where the cloth had fallen, but to no avail. I could find nothing, and after a few more minutes of poking and prodding I abandoned my searches and returned to the bed. We are nothing if not a practical species and it seemed that the only thing to do was to go back to sleep. I was even sure if Shakes had seen what I had seen, or he had just been disturbed by my antics. Thinking back to what the cat from Cykranosh said, I wondered if perhaps Shakes was a touch sensitive himself. I had never noticed it before. I tried to fall back to Dream, but that doorway had closed for the night.

Any doubt on what Shakes had seen was removed the next day when we all observed the men moving about the house deploying small circular wire traps filled with bait tinted with a small amount of powder of an unwholesome yellowish green in nature. The cats of the house tried to dissuade the deployment of such things, for it seemed a wasted effort, but mans are not known for their ability to perceive the preternatural, and thus the protestations of the household cats were ignored. Even the west tower bedroom was violated with one of the poisoned contraptions and though I made my distaste at the situation quite clear, nothing was done to change it.

That night I was once again roused from sleep by a spectral cacophony, but this time of such magnitude that even the great cloth that hung against the wall could be seen to be moving. I howled and hissed enough to wake Shakes who made the cool light shine so as to allow his weak eyes to better see the source of the maddening sounds. It was a fright to see the tapestry moving in that manner, as if it were a net full of fish struggling to escape. Almost immediately the haunting ceased, and the man poked and prodded the wall hanging in an attempt to elicit a response, but there was none. The wire trap that had been set in the room had been sprung, but no trace of what had triggered it remained visible.

Unable to return to sleep Shakes left the room and began to move to the ground level, and I as is my habit, followed. As we mounted the great terraced slope both of us heard the unmistakable sound of those ghostly rats behind the wooden panels of the great room. This time as the lights came on the action of that phantom army did not cease but rather continued their mad and maddening frenzy, I, with the help of the light and keen ears was able to discern that the great horde of spirit rats was engaged in a momentous migration from the upper levels of the house through the ground level, and into the depths beneath the restored domicile. I, and indeed all the cats of the house, careened down several flights of stairs and began yowling at the door to the sub-cellar, a door that had been closed ever since we had taken up residence. We crouched there at the bottom of the stairs for a minute or two, but then the storm of ghostly vermin ceased, and we settled our nerves and dispersed back amongst the upper floors and rooms of the house.

Late in the next day Tubby came to visit, and after a short conversation both he and Shakes descended through the door where they spent several hours out of the sight of I or any other cat. Then in the evening there was a great flurry of activity, and a number of couches were brought down the stairs and set up in a vault deep beneath the house. Shakes and I, along with Tubby all set forth to spend the night in the roughly built crypt. I took a moment or two to prowl about the place and in doing so caught sight of the human letters carved into the stone. I may not speak any human language, nor can I read the marks they make, but somehow, I knew that these dank scratches made reference to the dark mother Qybele and her human disciples. I shuddered with loathing at the thought that this place had been infected for so long that even the mans had forgotten about it. Frustrated I found my way back to our small encampment and it was not long before the Shakes was asleep, and I was curled up on his chest. His sleep was not sound, and Shakes tossed and turned before waking up screaming. Tubby laughed for a moment, but only for a moment, before both I and Shakes fell back to sleep.

It was hours later that the next wave of the phenomenon began. I woke to the sound of the cats in the upper part of the house howling at the door. The Qabba had returned, and I could hear them all around us, moving down the walls of the sub-cellars. I leapt from my place and began franticly running about trying to find the source of the spectral invasion, but to no avail. The rats were still moving down, deeper into the earth and I and Shakes could hear the scuttling claws as they clambered deeper and deeper, far deeper than the sub-cellar. It was then that I realized that what we were hearing were merely the spectral echoes of the monstrous void-spawn clambering in the spaces inbetween and that we would have to make a supreme effort to reach and destroy the monsters.

Then, all of the sudden, my comrades beyond the door ceased their screeching, but I was suddenly revitalized. I had found a small spot, a hole really, at the base of a stone block that sat in the center of the room. It was from this hole that the last echoes of the verminous horde could be heard, and I was determined to bring it to the attention of the mans. Finally, after nearly a minute of frenetic pawing and scraping Tubby brought his portable flame towards the crevice and discovered the slight draft emanating from the minuscule crack.

We spent the rest of the night on the brightly lit main floor. Shakes and Tubby talked incessantly well into the morning, and I listened intently trying to discern what they were saying, but to no avail. While cats may have made some progress in understanding the language of canines, even the greatest of cat philosophers has failed to make sense of the guttural sounds, that emanate from the mouths of the mans. Oh, we understand them plain enough, about as much as they understand us, but it is a crude sort of communication, and only the basics are ever conveyed. All I know is that later that day Shakes packed a large bag and left the house. Tubby was waiting for him in a car, and together they drove off into the setting sun.

The next day I called for a conclave and informed my colleagues of the situation and of my visit to Ulthar and the words of the Saturnine Feline. Mao was skeptical, but Cassandra simply nodded as if she had known these things for all her lives. Together we nine came up with a plan to deal with the terrors, the enemies of our Lords Ulthar. There was dissention. Lady Pyrr would at any opportunity, launch into discourse on the idea of moving, suggesting that we should abandon the man and the house he had built, in favor of one of the neighboring manors or farms. It was an interesting proposition, but I was too old to find a new master, and while Katrina, Stubbins and the twins might be able to earn their keep as working cats, Madame Cassandra had always been a house cat, and Lady Pyrr herself was not the most comfortable moving about the wilds or even the alleyways of a town or city.

It was two weeks after they had left that Shakes and Tubby returned, and they brought with them five of the strangest people I had ever seen. One was definitely sensitive for he seemed the meekest of all of them, and yet there exuded from him a kind of palpable fear, but also understanding. Johnnybull hissed at him, but Lady Cassandra approached him with reverence and would not leave his side for the entirety of that afternoon. Even at dinner she stayed by his feet. It was my fear that his presence and her infatuation with him might derail our plans. I confronted her later that night, but she assured me that all was well and that she merely sought to protect him from what she felt was an impending doom.

She was of course most prescient on that point.

Late in the morning of the next day Shakes and his cohorts gathered together a small quantity of equipment and began to gather at the cellar door. It was a surreal sight as the wooden gate was unlocked and the expedition to the lower level filed in. I was calm in the arms of Shakes even as the door was barred behind us and for the full hour it took for one of the party to pry up the altar stone and reveal the horror that lay beneath. There was a passage leading downward, steps worn so badly they were scarcely more than an inclined pathway, and lined as it were with all matter of bones. Most of these were easily recognizable as belonging to mans, though many were marked by the evidence of inbreeding and poor diet for they showed greatly diminished brain capacity and even queer alignments between the bones of the arms and legs that suggested the gait of a quadruped rather than an upright stance. Also present was a second shaft, this one was much smaller than the other, large enough for a cat or small dog to fit through, and it sloped upwards and from it issued a gentle breeze of cool air. With the air came a raft of odors all of which I recognized, and I immediately realized that this shaft must work its way through the very walls of the house, perhaps even up to the towers, acting as a kind of natural ventilator, but also as a passage for the Qabba to make their way from the upper levels into the catacombs below.

I will not bore you with the details of what the expedition found in the vast dimly lit caverns at the base of those stairs, but I will say that it not only sent Lady Cassandra's favorite into catatonia, but it drove Shakes into a violent rage. He attacked Tubby with his hands and teeth, frothing and raging in the most terrible way. I scratched him across the face, and the others had to pull him off his friend and restrain him. It took an hour for the party to make their way back to the wooden door in the sub-cellar, during which time Tubby whose throat had been torn open, slowly but inevitably bled to death. As the gate to the upper world opened Shakes began to struggle violently, screaming and frothing at the mouth. I think it was only he that caught sight of me and the others on the floor there, and he called my name. He screamed it actually, over and over and over again, but I was too busy. In all the madness it was only the madman that saw the household cats stream through the legs of the expedition and vanish down into the depths below. It was only the madman who saw our plan begin as the door to the netherworld was slammed shut behind us.

That was two years ago. Down we ran, down past the tumbled altar stone, down past misshapen skulls and tunnels of bone. Down past a twilight tableau of ageless horrors, of pens and abattoirs where mans and things that had once been mans were corralled and fed and slaughtered to feed those who once dwelt in this place, and the vermin that haunted the darkness beyond. Down we plunged into stygian darkness. Down into the abyss itself, warriors in pursuit of prey that itself crawled ever deeper into the unending caverns below.

Two years. We lost Mao first. She died the first time we caught up to them. They hadn't known we were in pursuit. But even with the advantage of surprise we were only able to destroy a hundred or so of them, and they killed Mao. She thought she could hide in the dark, that her color would protect her. But the natural place for the Rats of Qybele are the places between stars. The darkness only makes the Qabba stronger, and we, limited as we are to feeding on fungi, worms and grubs, have become weaker with time. Stubbins and Jackymac were killed in a rock fall, a year or so in. Johnnybull wandered off a week later, delirious with grief. I still hear him, or at least I think I do, howling in pain, out there in the dark.

Two years, and you my son are the firstborn of our first litter, and now old enough to lead our clan in pursuit of our quarry. Listen to your mother, Lady Pyrr may not be as perceptive as Madame Cassandra, but at least she hasn't been driven mad yet. I'm too old to go on, too old to keep the pace, to chase the draconian darklings that must be defeated. I was never much good at it anyway. You were born here, in the black, in the pall of the earth. You will lead, your mother and brothers and sisters, and the rest of the clan to victory. I know that for a fact. Madame Cassandra has foretold it. She may be mad, but she still can catch glimpses of the future, and of the world we left behind.

Go now, do what I could not. And if in your quest you hear caterwauling in the distance, if you hear a lost grimalkin calling out in the endless night, it may be Johnnybull, but it may also be me. Tired and slow, but still there, still in pursuit, still hunting in the darkness for the Qabbalin, the Rats of Qybele, a lone and lonely cat in the pall.

The Posthumous Recruitment
of Timothy Horne

Captain Timothy Horne of the 7th Hypnological Battalion was dead—or near enough to dead that other states of being didn't apply. That was what the recruitment packet had said. Normally, he would have asked his momma for her opinion of the deal, but he was dead, and she was still back in Belle Glade driving a bus in Palm Beach to make ends meet. If he agreed to participate, she would get a $10,000 signing bonus, disguised as a death benefit. If he passed the entrance exam, the bonus would translate into $3,000 a month for life—her life. What Horne got out of it was a second chance: he committed to ten years of service, and if he wanted to, he could then part company, no questions asked, no debts, with what appeared to be a hefty separation package.

For a black kid from the Glades well past the verge of death, it seemed a more than fair offer. It was better than the one he had taken when he joined up to fight the invaders. Of course, back then, everyone and their brother were joining ranks against the aliens. It was the human thing to do.

The one thing that the entire population of Earth could agree on was that the aliens had no business on the moon. The United Nations was still formulating a response when the deep space probes went offline. Then the Europa rover went silent.

In the course of three days, every piece of human technology outside the orbit of the moon went down. The ESA used the attitude thrusters on an old communications satellite to push it into a trajectory that crossed the 400,000-kilometer line marked by the moon—what would later be called simply the Boundary. The whole world watched as that immense piece of manufacturing and design trudged slowly past an imaginary boundary and was swarmed by half-visible creatures whose insectoid wings seemed to push against a medium we could not detect. They didn't tear it to pieces, but the result was the same.

A half hour later, the first communication came in. The Migou introduced themselves, and we learned that our world was subject to an interdiction. For some reason, one that was not explained to us, we had been quarantined. Nothing from earth would be let beyond the Boundary. Communications back were not responded to. Suddenly denied access to the final frontier, a frontier that only a few nations could afford to travel in, the world declared war on the Migou.

That war did not go well.

The Migou and their ships, great organic things that resembled the silica-based shells of microscopic algae, were not invulnerable, but it took a concentrated effort to bring them down. Afterward, they didn't last long. Whatever made them only half-visible also destabilized their very existence. It took hours, sometimes days, but in the end, the Migou and their vehicles dissolved into a plastic soup that burned the skin. The chemists and material engineers couldn't explain it, but the theoretical physicists could. Based on their studies of the alien bodies and artifacts, they had some startling news for the human race. The universe, our universe, wasn't particularly hospitable to life as we knew it.

Humans tend to think of the universe as having four dimensions: three spatial dimensions and time. The reality was that the universe was comprised of twenty-three dimensions, nineteen of which humans couldn't perceive, let alone take advantage of. The Migou could perceive some of those dimensions and were likely comprised not only of matter as we knew it but also of extradimensional equivalents. To our limited senses, that was why they were only partially visible and why they fell apart so quickly.

They moved and lived not only in the spaces we knew of but in those in between as well. If humans were going to fight and win a war with the Migou, the weapons employed would have to be radically different. The Gilman equations said this was possible, but every blade, every gun, every ship that incorporated the exotic extradimensional technology functioned only briefly before tearing itself and the user apart. Something about the human brain was anathema to the new tech, and the exotic machines responded a spectacularly violent way.

Horne had a vague memory that using alien tech was what led to his own death. He could remember the feel of something bizarre in his hands, something that fired bolts of blue, spiraling energy. The backwash had left waves of white scars across his coffee-colored arms. Even in death, those scars ached, reminding him of what had happened. He had wondered how it was that in death he could still feel pain. Was it a physical memory, or were those scars merely psychic, mere memories of the pain that had been inflicted? Then he had remembered his mother and her bus, and he stopped thinking about his own well-being and signed the papers.

That was three days ago.

It felt like they had been marching down the stairs ever since.

"Man, I thought the Nine Hundred Steps to Deeper Slumber was a metaphor." Horne mumbled to no one in particular.

Major Carter didn't break his pace but just kept up the steady downward march. "It is, Horne, that's why the number of steps varies from culture to culture. It's a test—a kind of endurance test. Making the transition from our world to the Dream Lands can't be easy, at least not at first. You have to want it, to work for it, to build a new set of bridges. What the psychophysicists call neural conduits. The steps are just a manifestation of that, mostly because that's what we've told you about during orientation. In other settings, it's other things: at the airbase in Wichita, they use a yellow brick road; in Britain, the imagery is of a wardrobe and a forest of coats. They're just symbols, obstacles to overcome in order to reach the Dream Lands."

Horne looked back at his companions in this weird effort.

An entire battalion had begun marching down those stairs: twelve-hundred men. Now he could barely see twenty. The rest were lost in the fog and darkness that seemed to seep out of the very air. There were no walls on the Steps to Deeper Slumber, no rails, no bannisters, no braces, or any other kind of architecture. There were just steps, endless runners and risers that just seemed to spiral downward into the mist. There were no lights either, and yet, still he could see—not far but far enough. The mist and the darkness beyond were ominous. If he looked too long, he could see things moving. He could hear things as well: the beating of great wings, screeching calls of titanic birds, whispering voices that said things he couldn't quite understand. Some of those voices sounded like his grandmother, others like his father. They called to him, implored him, and tried to draw him away from his downward progress. He wanted to go, but something in the back of his mind kept forcing him to keep marching.

"Is it true that the Dream Lands are ... you know ... the afterlife?" Horne didn't know who asked the question, and it didn't matter.

Carter answered it without even looking back. "It is true that we've documented individuals who have long since been declared legally dead on Earth, some hundreds of years ago. However, we think this is a very rare occurrence, that only one in maybe a thousand people are truly great dreamers, able to sustain themselves beyond death without help. Even with help, very few people are able to make the transition." Carter cast a backward glance and seemed to frown with disappointment. "You have to remember, boys," shouted Carter as he took a switchback on another flight, "the journey is worth it. Once you get to the Dream Lands, you'll be different, able to do things that you hadn't even believed possible before. This isn't Earth. It might look a lot like it and most of the physical laws are the same, but there are subtle differences and peculiarities."

Horne perked up and refocused on the back of Carter's helmet. "You're talking about magic."

Carter shook his head. "Not magic, metaphysics. The people who built this alternate reality tweaked it slightly, made it just a little more fantastic than our world. There are flying boats, non-human intelligences, artifacts that can be used to do things you couldn't otherwise. There are reports that in Kadath, there are beings of immense power who once ruled this world. They're called the Great Ones and just might be avatars of the Progenitors, or gods, or close enough to gods for our purposes." Carter glanced over his shoulder. "Oh, and before I forget, in Ulthar never kill a cat."

That was the seventh time Carter had told Horne the injunction about cats. It made him wonder what would happen if he did and if it applied only to Ulthar or to the whole of the Dream Lands? Did other places have similar but different rules? In Oriab, was it illegal to kill a dog?

Horne wiped his brow with the back of his glove. He was sweating; the forced march was getting to him. Out in the fog, in the darkness, a pattern was forming. At first, it looked like circles, a pattern of rings, but sometimes, it looked like a square or like a square and a triangle—but most of the time it looked like circles. It was as if the fog and the darkness beyond weren't there at all but were merely a complex of layered patterns; patterns that, as Horne went on, began to resolve into things that were not circles. The pattern was there in the steps, as well. It was the same shape iterated over and over again as if someone had printed the concept of stairs over a sheet of paper with a watermark embedded within. Not a circle but something geometric with angles. It took him a moment.

Horne squinted and widened his eyes to try and make it come into focus. It was five-sided with equal angles: a pentagon, like the one in Virginia.

Like the one he'd seen during training in Antarctica, the one that was made of grey stone and hummed and whistled as men walked past. You could tell how old it was just by looking at it; it felt ancient, and it told you so deep down in the base of your brain. The pentagon that was all liquid black inside, so black that even the targeting lasers vanished. The pentagon that they fed soldier after soldier after soldier into, forcing him to watch until it was his turn at last. No matter how hard he tried, he couldn't scream as that liquid black nothing swallowed him whole. That had been days ago, hours maybe; he wasn't sure. On the stairs, time meant little. As he continued forward, all he could think about was the pentagonal patterns forming around him and the number five.

He blurted out the number, and he wasn't alone. A whole chorus of his fellow soldiers had said it as well. He looked around and did a head count. There were only ten of them, not counting Carter.

Carter responded, "The builders, the Progenitors, or—in the old language—the Q'Hrell were pentaradially symmetrical in design. Their entire bodies and even their brains were divided into five sections. Not unexpectedly, they incorporated that number into much of their machinery, architecture, and art. The Dream Lands are no exception. The fundamental programming, which the psychophysicists call the quintessence, is five-dimensional in nature. Your brains might perceive this as random appearances of patterns involving the number five."

Carter's voice helped him to focus, to keep walking. Horne thought back to his classes in physics at Florida Tech. How Professor Benjamin Scapellati had discussed the theories of supra-asymmetry and how some dimensions acted as regulators on others. He tried to meld that half-remembered lecture with what Carter was telling them. If the Dream Lands were only based on five dimensions, the constraints would be different. Physical laws as dictated by the higher dimensions would be absent. The possibilities might be immensely terrifying but wondrous as well.

His scars ached, throbbed really. Something was happening. Was the fog thinner? Was the darkness less impenetrable? Were the stairs less steep?

Carter had picked up the pace, and without even noticing, Horne had followed suit. Carter hummed as he walked, almost too low to hear—a pre-millennial song by Inhouse. It still played on the classic rock stations. Horne couldn't remember the title, but as he caught the tune, he tried to remember the lyrics, something about James Taylor and an old coat and a box of photographs. It reminded him of nights on the Intracoastal eating guacamole and fresh fish tacos on the beach with live music washing down from the bars and clubs that lined the streets of Lake Worth. If he closed his eyes, he could almost smell the salt air and taste the cilantro and garlic. Somewhere in his memory, a bass guitar was pounding, but it wasn't any song that he could put a name to. He realized it wasn't his memory at all.

His scars beat out a tempo that echoed in his head. His eyes started to blur. His tongue felt fat, and he had that sensation in the back of his throat, the tightness just before the technicolor yawn occurs. All around him, the pentagonal pattern fell apart. Carter turned, and he had no face, just a huge Cheshire grin of ivory teeth staring back from an empty space. Horne's scalp itched. He brought his hands up to try to get his helmet off and run his fingers through his thick wiry hair, but his hands were different. They had become disconnected. The scars were empty spaces, and his hands had begun to drift apart in pieces. He could still move them, still flex his fingers and wrists, but they weren't entirely connected anymore. He could still feel them, but he could also feel the spaces in between.

Horne screamed.

The faceless thing that Carter had become was holding on to him, dragging him forward, that great terrifying headless mouth opening and words leaking out. Horne couldn't hear the words, but he could read them. "Hold on. It's just a little further. We're almost there!"

And then there was an arching gate, and the darkness was gone. So was the fog and so were all the other soldiers and so was Carter.

As he woke up, Horne realized that there had never been a 7th Hypnological Battalion. They had been an illusion, a way of making him feel part of something. There was safety in numbers, and the thousands of other soldiers were just echoes to help get him here, into the Dream Lands. Now, in this place, Horne felt different, inhuman. He could feel his body but also the particles of air and dust and pollen that moved around and through him. He looked at himself and realized that he perceived his surroundings through sensory apparatus that were more than just eyes and ears. He extended into a dimension that he didn't even understand. His body was no longer three dimensional but five, and he could see that, sense it, somehow.

A nonsense phrase came to his mind. He realized that he knew exactly what it meant. It had been years since he thought about that child's rhyme, but today, he finally understood what it meant to be a frumious bandersnatch.

He rose up on his twrils and, with his three multi-faceted subordinate eyes, took in his surroundings. There was a cat at his feet, purring and rubbing against him in a figure eight design. He was on a green hill overlooking a harbor. There was a vast ship, all steel and brass, larger than anything he had ever seen. Great towering stacks vented gouts of steam the size of storm clouds. On the decks of the Brobdingnagian construct, Horne could see fighter craft tethered like butterflies. Men and other things scurried about on the decks, in the rigging, on the hull, and on the huge wharfs and scaffolding. There were flying things, some with wings, some with great balloon-like organs, and some were like him, bandersnatch with twrils to climb through the ether.

"What do you think, Horne?" The voice came from the cat.

Horne played his sensors over its fur. It wasn't really a cat, though it looked like one. It was so much more.

"That's a warship." His voice was like wind being forced through a bellows, like a whale imitating human speech.

The Carter-Cat nodded, which was kind of an impressive action for a creature with limited anatomy. "Welcome to the Hlanith Naval Yard. That, my friend is the *Tars Tarkas*. She's almost ready to launch. She'll be your home for the next eight weeks while she steams to Phobos Base."

Horne tilted what was left of his head. "Phobos is a moon of Mars. We're steaming to Mars?"

"I told you; the rules are different here." Carter-Cat ran a paw over his head and face. "The human fleet is assembling around Phobos. Our allies are organizing around the other moon, Deimos."

"We have allies?"

"Grimalkin, alien cats. From Saturn mostly, though some are from Uranus. They aren't really cats, not as we know them, though there is something feline about them. Turns out that the Migou interdiction works both ways. Just as we aren't allowed off Earth, the grimalkin aren't allowed in. That has deprived them of some very prime hunting grounds."

What passed for Horne's ears pricked up. "What were alien cats hunting on Earth?"

Carter-Cat blinked. "Best you not worry about that. Just remember that the enemy of my enemy is my friend. And when in Ulthar … "

"Never kill a cat. You've told me. Rather self-serving, don't you think?"

"But nevertheless, true."

"What happens when the fleets are fully assembled?" Horne wondered.

"There's a gate on Mars, a big one. It's large enough to let the fleet through into real space. When that happens, the battle carriers will launch the fighters toward Earth. When melded with our own technology, the Saturnine grimalkin make particularly powerful drives. We can strike at the Migou from behind with a technology they won't expect."

"I was thinking more about me, about us. We aren't exactly human. What happens when we pass through the gate? I mean, aren't I dead?"

"You, Timothy Horne, are dead. But the gate on Mars isn't connected to Earth. It doesn't know that, doesn't even know we were ever human. When it spits us out back into real space, I'm still going to be a cat, and you are going to retain the form you have now."

"Which is what? What exactly am I?"

"You're something new, and you're not alone. The feedback from the energy weapon altered your template; you're a little Migou now. When you enter real space, you'll be able to access some of the higher dimensions. It's going to be weird."

Horne flexed his six arms and watched them spread out farther and farther until there was more empty space than solid. "Does this look human to you?"

The Carter-Cat used a hind leg to scratch behind his ear. "Nope, you don't look one bit human. It's a strange new world, Horne. Aliens have surrounded Earth, we've built virtual reality steamships to take us to Mars, our best friends are Saturnine grimalkin, and your commanding officer is a cat. I think we are going to have to redefine what it means to be human, don't you?"

Horne closed his eyes and looked at the Carter-Cat with his slin. If he mimsied just the right way, he could make him just be Carter again, mostly.

Together, they walked down the hill toward the titanic starship brimming with the various novel and multiform facets of humanity. Toward war, toward hope, toward the future.

The Eye of Cybele

You ask me why I will not come to Rome for the spring, why I will not attend the festivals, and throw alms to the fortune-telling, yellow garbed, castrated priests of Attis, or watch the mystery plays performed on the steps of the Temple of Cybele, beneath the eye of the goddess. As long as Rome is home to a temple dedicated to that terrible deity, I will not step foot upon her streets. You may call me foolish if you wish, but I know what terrible rites are performed in her name, and why no Roman citizen may join her priesthood.

It has been twenty years since I left the city in which I was born and raised, and still Rome suffers from what I did. Of course, my actions, as horrible as they were, were at the bidding of the Senate. I have always served Rome, and those days were not good and the portents ill. There had been a drought, and famine loomed in the west. The war with Hannibal in Carthage had dragged on longer than expected. Stones had fallen from the sky in unprecedented numbers. The populace had grown uneasy; the normal grumbles had become too loud for the Senate to ignore. The public needed to be assured that the gods still favored Rome.

The Decemviri Sacrorum, the ten men who curated the Sibylline Books of prophecy, were ordered to consult their pages. It took them two days, but finally the collegium found a passage that suggested that a foreign invader could be vanquished, if the goddess Cybele were brought to Rome. It was an outrageous proposal. There were other foreign temples in the city, but they were small things, funded by foreign dignitaries and traders who kept homes in Rome. The idea that the goddess of another nation might join the other gods in a state-sponsored temple was unheard off.

In the Senate speeches were made both for and against the proposal. The tone on the floor became so heated that threats of censure were made. After hours of discussion, it seemed that the motion would fail, when suddenly another messenger appeared. This one came from distant

Sibyl of Delphi and conveyed a similar message. If the troubles were to end, then the Matar Kubileya–the Mother of the Mountain—must be carried to Rome.

So, the delegation was created, and the five envoys, the Quinqueremes, were elected, a ship commissioned, staff assigned, and two dozen soldiers organized for the mission. It was simple really, first to Delphi to verify what the Oracle had said, then to Pergamon to petition King Attalus, and then on to Pessinus where we would retrieve the relics of Cybele—whatever was needed to symbolize her worship—and a handful of her priests to administer her temple. As long as King Attalus agreed, and Attalus had long been Rome's greatest ally and stood with her against Carthage.

I was a respected man back then, a former quaestor, I may have been the youngest member of the delegation, but all of Rome knew the name of Marcus Valerius Falto. The other delegates were just as renown; Marcus Valerius Laevinus, the former Consul of Sicily; Marcus Caecilius Metellus who had disgraced himself at Cannae, but then through hard work had somehow rehabilitated himself; Servius Sulpicius Galba, former Proconsul; and my fellow former quaestor, Gnaeus Tremelius Flaccus. We were known to each other as well, though not as familiar as we should have been. Rome has always been bigger than her citizens, and no one could know everyone. We may not have been friends, but we were committed to the saving of Rome.

It was during the first few days of the voyage that I familiarized myself with the worship of Cybele. It wasn't particularly necessary, but I thought perhaps it would be useful, and being that one of the slaves that accompanied our delegation was a Greek well-versed in the study of religious rites, I pursued it. First, he explained the myths of Cybele. The Greeks had conflated her with Rhea and a few other female deities, and as such her imagery was associated with eagles and lions, but these were not her original companions. To see her true origin, one needed only to look at her consort and son, the shepherd-god Attis. In the old country, amidst the black mountains of Phrygia she was the Mountain Mother, and she was attended by her flock of he-goats, who drew sustenance from her multitude of bountiful breasts.

What's more is that originally, Cybele was known as Agdistis, and was a child of Zeus. Agdistis was both male and female and its madness and strength was such that even Zeus was afraid. When Agdistis danced amidst the sacred mountains the earth itself shook, and the gods feared that she would spawn a new generation of Titans. To prevent this, they tricked Agdistis into self-castration. The piece of bloody flesh fell to earth and from it grew an almond tree. From this tree the water nymph Nana plucked a seed and held it to her breast, where it burrowed inside of her. Nana became pregnant and gave birth to Attis. Ashamed of the child, Nana left it in the woods to die, but Agdistis, now Cybele sent a he-goat to nurture it. Finally, a shepherd found the child, adopted him, and raised him as a shepherd. All the while Cybele watched him grow more and more beautiful, until inevitably she fell in love with him. On the day of his wedding Cybele fell from the sky as a black stone, landing on the slope of Mount Ida. From there she made her way to Attis and in front of the entire wedding party revealed her true self. The women in attendance went mad with fright, while the men cut off their manhood and offered it to her as sacrifice. Only Attis escaped and fled to the mountains. Alone, the memory of the true form of his mother slowly drove him insane, and he too castrated himself and then slit his own throat. But Attis was a demi-god and could not be killed in such a manner. His body would not lie still, it would not decay, the wounds healed, and he rose up. He was the mad shepherd god who accepted his fate and became companion to the goddess Cybele, who loved him despite the fact that he was a eunuch.

There were a variety of legends and lore surrounding Attis. A favorite parable of Panos, the Greek slave, was the story of Haita who learns that true happiness can only be achieved through ignorance. This was a fundamental teaching of the cult, that knowledge was a dangerous path to tread, for it led to dark places that men would be better off not seeing. Better to be a farmer, a shepherd or a hunter than a philosopher or a scholar. Amongst the backwater Greeks who had seen their own culture supplanted by that of Rome, it was an attractive philosophy. What could be better for a bunch of inbred goat herds than a religion that said that simplicity and farming was the way to salvation?

To me such nonsense, the pursuit of ignorance, a philosophy that failed to explore and understand the world around it was pure madness. It was our pursuit of knowledge that separated civilized men, whether they be from Rome or not, from the primitives like the Troglodyti and Icthyophagi. It would be a betrayal of the gods themselves to discard what you knew to be true in pursuit of a happy lie. Yet that was what the priests of Cybele and Attis seemed to teach. And now Rome herself was looking to embrace the cult.

The voyage from Rome to Delphi was uneventful. The soldiers had their training exercises, I had my studies, and the other Quinqueremes spent the voyage reading or singing. These distractions filled some of the time, but most of the days and evenings were spent watching the wine-dark sea with its bountiful schools of fish, playful dolphin, and mysterious, unknown shadows that seemed always to follow us at a distance. Birds followed us the entire way, and while some grew tired of their incessant screeching, I and other seasoned sailors knew that the presence of such creatures was a good omen. If they were ever to abandon us it would surely mean some doom was descending upon our small expedition.

It was at Kirra that I detected the first hint of trouble. There at the gateway port to Delphi waited a contingent of warriors, with shields bearing the symbol of Cybele herself. As we sailed closer, we could see that there were a half dozen of the armed worshippers of the goddess called the Korybantes. They waited for us on the dock, their swords drawn, their crested helmets swaying in the sea breeze, and a strange drumming coming from within their ranks. Behind them stood three men dressed in yellow, their faces and hair made up like garish women. Panos, the slave who had studied foreign religions, identified them as Galli, castrated priests of Attis who as the consort of Cybele, served her as well.

As we approached, our own soldiers prepared for battle, their swords were drawn and some assumed stances to repel boarders, while others readied themselves to leap onto the quay. But then, at the last second, as the ship slid into her berth the bellicose reception suddenly knelt down. They took a knee and saluted us, their swords crashing against their shields in a cacophonous display of bravado and allegiance. Even the Galli swooned before us dramatically. Panos laughed and told how some called the Galli the Non-Kings in Yellow, for in many places while they held positions of power and influence, they were not men nor women, and therefore could not bear the titles of King or Queen.

After our own guards confirmed that the welcoming party meant us no harm, we disembarked and began the trek up the mountains to

Delphi and the Oracle. There was some grumbling over this, as Metellus would have preferred waiting for the next morning, and therefore being able to partake of the local pleasantries. I admit that it would have been nice to sleep in a real bed, and eat fresh food, but the Oracle was waiting for us, she had an urgent message that all portents said must be delivered before the next day dawned, Accommodations had been made for us to spend the night in Delphi, and then set sail the next day.

So, we began the trek to Delphi, the Korybantes leading the way, the five emissaries on horseback, the Galli behind us, and the Roman guard in the rear. The climb was steep and followed a road well-worn from centuries of use. It was unpaved and surrounded on one side by large boulders and then the cliff wall, on the other side was a nearly sheer drop that overlooked a green and fertile valley full of small farms. Amongst the fields we could see what one would expect so far from any real metropolis. The scene was pastoral, with simple famers laboring behind yoked oxen. Goats and swine roamed along the banks of a small river that bisected the valley and led up the sloping mountain. The ribbon of silver led to a small cluster of buildings, just barely visible on the gray stone head overlooking the vale. That was our destination, the village of Delphi, and above it, the rocky crag that marked the entrance to the temple where Pythia spoke her prophecies and wisdom.

As we moved up that ancient track the Galli raised their voices in song. It started at first as a low hum, a kind of diffuse rhythmic droning that I could feel even inside my chest. Then the whistling began, a shrill foreign tune that pierced the stillness of the idyllic countryside and set us all on edge. Which apparently was the point, for soon after the Korybantes joined in, adding a rhythmic beating of their swords against their shields. It took me a moment, but I soon realized that the purpose of the tune was two-fold. For while the voices of the Galli were finally added to invoke their Attis and Cybele, the pace of our party had quickened, it was a marching tune that these strange priests sang, assuring that we reached our destination in a timely manner.

Even in the heat of the mid-day sun the warrior-priests maintained their pace, beating out a tune in time with their step. We must have been a magnificent sight: the armored Korybantes festooned in vibrant, green plumes; the Quinqueremes in their white and purple robes; the frenetic yellow Galli; and the guards in their red-tinged armor. We crawled up the mountain road like some kind of garish, giant worm which nothing, not even the eagles of the gods dared to molest. By the time we reached the pinnacle, marching past the small village of Delphi even we on horseback were filled with a kind of euphoria. We had been seduced by the elation of our escort, infected by their jubilation, and we smiled and laughed as the temple itself came in view.

Officially, Pythia, the Oracle at Delphi was a worshiper of the god Apollo, but it was not always so, and there amidst the white carved columns one could see the remnants of former divinities who had held sway there. There were images of Poseidon, Rhea, Themis and Phoebe, but the dominant image was that of Gaia. It was only then that I remembered the legend of Coretas, the goat-herder who saw his flock enter this very crack in the mountain and come out behaving in the strangest of ways. Following their lead, he himself entered the great chasm and found himself filled with the spirit of the divine Gaia. Like a god he could see not only the present, but the past and the future as well, and the threads that led from one to the next. Not only that, but he could even see outside, envisioning not only the threads, but the weave itself, the very fabric of the world that was, that had been, and would be. So, the oracle had been established, as first a Temple of the Earth Mother by a shepherd. It was only later that the women took on the role of seer.

But that was only legend, but a legend enshrined in the very stone of the temple. I stared at the great multi-horned goat heads emblazoned on the walls commemorating the memory of Coretas, and then looked at the small, stylized symbols that the Galli wore to honor their shepherd god Attis. I looked at these and could not help but wonder at the coincidence. Such speculation was short-lived, and I dismissed it completely. Along the rocky coast of the Mediterranean every tribe had their goat-herder legends, and one could barely throw a stick without hitting a devotee of some capran deity or another.

As we dismounted, we were greeted by hosioi—holy ones—whose fine robes bore the symbol of Apollo and wore kid gloves dyed with saffron. They welcomed us in the name of the oracle and offered to make our retinue comfortable while the Quinqueremes went for an audience. There was a moment of protest, but only a moment, for it was apparent that the words of the priestess were only for our ears. We were shown to a crack in the side of the mountain from which a terrible stench emanated. It was not unlike the smell of rotting flesh, or the smoking of meat, and I remembered that some of the legends told of how Apollo banished two great snakes, pythons, from the cavern, but the stink of their foulness still lingered, a cursed memory that would never fade.

Into the chamber we descended, our way lit by flickering torches embedded in the walls our sandaled feet uneasy on the rough-hewn steps. Down we went, and with each measure the light of the outside world faded, and we were left only with the regularly spaced but uneven flames of oil-soaked torches to keep the dark at bay. Even with those flames belching forth soot and smoke the rotted-flesh stink of the cavern grew ever stronger, until it permeated all of our senses and we could taste the filth on our tongues, and our eyes stung and wept in vain. Finally, when the air itself seemed to grow thick and waver in front of our eyes the steps ceased, and the chasm widened into a great chamber where sat a smoking cauldron upon a tripod of bronze, behind which sat the cloaked and veiled Pythia. She was an old woman, an honored mother, clad in the symbolic robes that bound her to the gods. To look at what sat there, huddled around the smoking brazier, I thought for sure she must have been at least five decades older than I, for she had the appearance of an ancient crone, bent and wrinkled with strings of gray hair laying in plaits across her face. Her eyes were large, like deep watery pools with flecks of light glinting back from the murky depths.

She lifted one claw-like hand and gestured for us to approach. The hosoi silently urged us forward. and with cautious steps we made our way into her presence, taking seats around her smoking brazier. She stared at us with those deep eyes, and I felt as if she were looking into my very soul and seeing all the good and all the evil that had been gathered over my years on Earth and knew where in Hades my soul would dwell. She smiled a wicked toothless grin, as if she could hear my thoughts and then threw back her shawl revealing the deep and ancient wrinkles that creased her face.

"Rome faces a foreign army from the south but marching from the north and west. I have seen the paths that lead from this point, and if Mother Rome is to survive, she must embrace a new faith. The Mountain Mother Cybele must be taken from her temple at the Mountain and transported to Rome. This must be done. I have seen all the threads laid out, only this one path holds any future for you and yours." She paused and let out a long sigh. "It will not be an easy path and precautions must be taken if you are to be successful."

It was Metellus that dared to speak a question, "What kind of precautions?"

The hag waved a hand through the smoke that poured from the brazier, as if seeing something through the haze and heat. "The priests in Pessinus are treacherous things you must not go to meet with them, and yet you must. Do you understand? The five of you must be there but to be there will mean your death. I can see that much. You must be present, but you must not be as you are now. The Priests are cunning and treacherous. you must be more so."

Metellus opened his mouth to speak again but she waved a crooked finger to silence him. "Afterwards, you will need the Korybantes and the Galli that accompanied you here. They can be trusted. They will fill a most needed role, after what is done is done. They will travel with you, but they must not journey with you to Pessinus." She rolled her head back. "That must be clear. Your Galli and Korybantes must not accompany you to Pessinus." With that, the priestess motioned and the prophetai came forward and gestured for us to follow. The old woman waved us away. "You must not go as you are Marcus Valerius Falto, not as you are!"

Even now I can remember that strange, cackling voice as it called after me to obey her pronouncements. Why I was singled out I could not say, but I was, and her words rang in my ears. Even as I lay in my bed at the guest house, I could not get her admonishment out of my head, and I stared at the ceiling trying to understand what the old seer had meant. Even during our trip back down the mountain and then that first day back on the ship, it was all I could think about.

It haunted me for days, even as we came before King Attalus at Pergamon and asked for his permission to take the goddess Cybele from her temple and carry her to Rome. Attalus was pleased to see us and acquiesced to our request almost immediately. Despite the fact that he ruled Phrygia he was in actuality of Greek descent and traced his lineage back to Alexander the Great. He ruled these people, but he was not one of them. He did not care if Cybele went to Rome. It was an honor of sorts, or so he said. We spent the night there in his modest palace, and for the first time in days, lulled by wine and fine food, sleep welcomed me into her arms.

It was the next morning that we began the last leg of our journey, and we left the Korybantes and Galli behind. If the horseback ride to Delphi was idyllic, the trek to Pessinus was grueling and unnerving. The road we traveled was surrounded by black shards of rock that had tumbled down off the shattered peaks that lined both sides. When I say road, I am being generous, it was little more than a trail littered with sand, pebbles and scraggly vegetation. How such flora could gain a foothold in the rocks that lined the way I could not understand, but it did, and those branches covered with black thorns attested to the harsh reality of living in such unforgiving terrain.

It was to combat that frigid wind that the soldiers brought out from their packs their heavy cloaks and offered the extras they had to the five envoys. Outfitted such I looked around and laughed out loud, for it was nearly impossible to tell one of us from another. The others joined in my mirth, for my observation was accurate, and even the senior officers cracked a smile. It was during this moment of frivolity that I suddenly understood the words of Pythia and I knew at once how we would meet with the priests of Cybele.

We marched into Pessinus on schedule and were greeted by representatives of the king that had been sent up the night before. It had all been arranged. We would meet with the priests after sundown and participate in a rite of transference. We would be on our way back down the mountain by morning. It was all very familiar, but I suspected that tonight's ceremony would not be as pleasant as that we had endured in Delphi. We were meant to be resting, and this we did, but we also prepared ourselves. Armors and weapons were concealed beneath cloaks. Soldiers were taught to speak as orators and given the details of what Rome expected. By the time sun set in the west we were prepared, or at least we hoped we were.

At the proscribed time we were led to the Temple of Cybele. There were ten of us in the party five soldiers disguised as the envoys, and five envoys dressed as soldiers. The remaining troops we left behind in the place provided for them. Our escorts were yellow-robed Galli their faces painted with rouge and indigo hues, and they whispered in a language I didn't recognize. We were led out of the village and to the temple. The low stone structure was lit by hundreds of torches and from the small hill overlooking it I could see that the place took the form of an open-air labyrinth built from stone. There was a flooded moat around the entire temple, and stairs that descended through a gate and into the waters. I assumed that this was part of the ceremony, with supplicants entering the waters, and presumably being made pure before making their way through the maze, and then into the presence of the Cybele herself.

Waiting for us at the entryway was one of the high priests, whom we were told was entitled Batakkes, and was the lesser of the two Archgalli. He danced around us in the most peculiar and flamboyant of ways, sprinkling us with sanctified oils and chanting prayers to both Attis and Cybele. It was a ridiculous ceremony but part of their ritual, and I was relieved when it ended with a thunderous clap. The Batakkes then pointed the way through the gate towards his brother Archgalli who used the title Attis to honor the god they served.

Into that cold and black water, we walked, single file, with pseudo-envoy, followed by pseudo-soldier until all ten of us were immersed in the sanctifying pool. It was then that the expected trap was sprung, for from hidden alcoves on both sides more than a dozen Galli stepped forward with spears of bronze and leveled them at our heads. We were ordered to disarm, and having no choice, fumbled underwater to loosen our belts and drop our still sheathed swords at the feet of our captors.

We were then marched forward at spear point, the Attis leading the way. We moved through that labyrinth at a dizzying pace and were given no opportunity to gain our bearings. Finally, we were forced, almost pushed, into the great central chamber where the Battakes was waiting for us. We were forced to kneel as the secondary high priest pulled back a curtain to reveal his goddess. Nothing could have prepared us for what we saw, for the image of Cybele was unlike any other I had ever seen. I had expected a great statue carved from white marble of some stern-faced woman, or failing that, a grotesque Madonna, a bloated mother with dozens of teats, but what sat there on the altar was neither of these. Instead, there was a rock, small enough to be carried by a single hand, but much larger than a fist. It was black and somewhat triangular in shape and covered in queer depressions and pockmarks. I had seen something like it before, amongst the prized possessions of philosophers who claimed they were fallen bits of the sky.

"Behold the goddess Cybele!" Announced the Attis with a flourish. "You Roman dogs wanted to see her, to take her from us, but we will never allow that. Tomorrow we shall leave this place and carry our Great Mother with us. We will go into the mountains, beyond the mountains and into the wilderness. We will go where Rome and her puppet kings cannot follow." His eyes were wide, and I could see that an ecstatic frenzy had seized him. "But first we shall show you the power of our Great Mother!"

He pulled out a knife and gestured at one of our number who was immediately seized by three Galli. There was a brief struggle, for the soldier dressed as a Quinqueremes knew that knives in the hands of madmen were never a good thing, but that struggle ended quickly with the flat of a spear to the back of the head. He fell forward but his captors jerked him backwards and threw him onto a stone table. The knife-wielding holy man strode forward and as he did the captive's tunic was raised up. The knife stabbed and slashed, the soldier screamed. The priest smiled and pulled. Blood poured out from between his legs and splattered across the floor. The victim shuddered and collapsed.

There was something bloody and horrible in the priest's hand, and the rest of us gasped in disgust as he showed the mass of flesh to those in the room. He marched back toward the altar. He was speaking, chanting, invoking Cybele and as he reached the object of his worship held out the thing in his hand and squeezed. There was blood, blood and something else that dripped out and covered the stone in the most vital of human fluids. They bubbled there, they bubbled, and the priest chanted, and his chanting grew louder and louder. The bubbling continued, and there formed a single great sphere, opaque and viscous. It swelled and pulsed in time with the chanting of the priest. It grew and grew and grew until it was bigger than a man's head, bigger even than the head of a cow. It was a horrid gelatinous thing that squirmed and bulged as it grew ever bigger. Then the priest howled and plunged his hands into the thing.

He tore into that veined and repulsive sack. Something squealed. His body blocked my line of sight, but when he turned, he held in his hand in infant, obviously a man-child, but one that had features no man ever had before. Instead of feet, it had hooves and legs of a goat. Its head was long and thin, and a wild mane of tentacles like those of a squid, encircled its face. It stared at us with cold, black eyes and I knew it was more than a man, and more than man could ever hope to understand.

The priest raised the tiny thing up over his head and spoke with pride. "Behold the Black Goat, the child of the Great Mother!"

And then the creature opened its mouth and spoke! I, and my compatriots covered our ears but even so that divine voice and those unknowable words, drilled into our brains and forced us to the ground. In contrast, the Galli fell to their knees in awe and raised up their voices in adoration. While we writhed in agony they reveled in ecstasy. While blood poured from our ears, light seemed to emanate from their eyes and mouths. I was sure we were about to die.

And then I saw the arrows.

Our rescuers were right on time, the guards we had left behind had stormed the temple. They had come to our salvation by running across the top of the maze rather than through it. As for how they were able to stand against that horrible voice, I could see that their ears were filled with globs off beeswax, a solution pioneered by Odysseus himself, though how they knew to do that left me bewildered. The attack of our men was a slaughter. The spears of the Galli were no match for Roman bows. Even the Battakes fell, a wooden shaft embedded in his throat. Gasping and pleading he drowned in his own blood.

The Attis, who somehow had survived the first volley of arrows, attempted to flee, cradling the newborn demi-god in his arms, but he hadn't gone more than a few steps when he froze in his tracks. Six Korybantes, their swords drawn, entered the fray and began to slaughter the remaining Galli. The Attis panicked and threw the swaddled child at his attackers. I thought they would catch the thing, after all it was the offspring of their goddess, but instead one of them simply batted it away with a shield. It plummeted to the ground and whimpered as it rolled to a stop. Another warrior priest stalked over to it and without a pause, crushed its head beneath a heavy, armored, boot. The Priest screamed and turned to run, but another soldier was waiting for him. A sword slipped into the priest's belly with a well-practiced thrust, and he died with a gasping breath, just as more Galli marched in.

I reached for a weapon, but a hand from one of my friends touched my shoulder. Like the Korybantes, these new Galli were those that we had brought with us from Delphi. We had left them behind in Pergamon so as to fulfill the warnings of the seer, but they had known better. They had not been barred from making the journey to Pessinus, only from traveling with us. It was then that I realized that this had been part of the plan all along. Our mission had been designed to wipe out the priests that resided here and replace them with those of Pythia's choosing. This was a religious conflict, one that Rome had just taken part in, and while just one of our men was gravely injured, a rival sect had been wiped away.

With minimal conversation the loyal Galli and Korybantes went about securing the area, gathering up the implements of worship and the artifacts needed to maintain a new Temple of Cybele. The stone itself was gently picked up with gloved hands and placed in a box of cedar decorated in yellow with the symbols of her faith. As we marched out of that unholy temple, our loot carried by priests, our wounded carried by a pair of Korybantes, we doused the bodies of the dead with oil and set them aflame.

We did not stay the night in Pessinus. We went down the mountain by torchlight the jackals and wolves howling as we marched with our swords drawn and our legs as heavy as lead. We reached Pergamon by dawn, and messengers implored us to meet with the king, but we did no such thing. We boarded our vessel and set sail for Rome. I half-expected royal soldiers to stop us, or a navy vessel to pursue us, but no such thing occurred. We left Phrygia without incident. A day out to sea and a small ship flying the symbol of the Pythian Oracle intercepted us. She took me to Rome to explain to the Decemviri Sacrorum what had happened to us, and what monstrosity my fellows would be bringing home. When I gave my report, they simply dismissed me without so much as a word of thanks or a note of trepidation. It was as if they knew what was coming.

When my fellow envoys came home, I watched from afar as the boat bearing the goddess Cybele entered the port and was hauled up the canal that leads to Rome. They filled her arrival with pomp and circumstance and made her entry into the city a spectacle. The Korybantes and Galli were greeted with adulation, but no mention was ever made that these priests were not from Phrygia. The completion of her temple was marked with a month-long festival. The artisans revealed a magnificent, seated statue of her, one not unlike that of Juno or Minerva. It was a massive thing of white stone, flanked with two great eagles, but instead of a face they installed that rock in its place, which stared out of her temple like some horrible triangular eye. Indeed, the stone gained the name the Eye of Cybele, and it watched like a cyclopean thing.

The Eye of Cybele

I could not stand the sight of it, and I moved to the countryside, where I could be alone, and the locals have worshipped the gods of Rome for millennia. But my sleep is still restless, and I find it wise that no Roman Citizen may become a priest of Cybele or Attis. Castration as an initiation rite cannot be allowed, for I have seen what terrible things result from such a sacrifice, and fear for Rome itself if it were to be allowed. After all these years, the populace still refers to that stone as the Eye of Cybele, but I know what that piece of rock truly is.

The eye of Cybele? No, my friend, that is not the eye of a goddess. It is her womb! And it waits patiently until once more it is made fertile and bears forth titans that men, and even the gods, might tremble before.

Aysaqendisa

Aysaqendisa ... the hungering womb ... I alone have survived her coming, though none may listen I will speak of our passing, our frenzied, fumbling, inevitable extinction ... and how we shall be remembered forever.

It was the twilight of our world. Our star had begun its collapse and was now little more than a sad remnant of its former brilliance. In response, our world had grown dark and cold, the polar caps had grown thick, the seas had retreated, rivers and lakes had gone shallow or dry. The skies were without clouds, but rather filled with smoke from the countless fires that burned unchecked in the dry woodlands and savannahs surrounding the cities. Those cities were all but deserted. The slow but inevitable decline of our world had led to a kind of ennui amongst our species. Millennia ago, procreation had been eliminated as a task assigned to the masses and instead had become a commodity like any other, taking its place as a commercial product alongside food and water, clothing and media. Like all other commercial products, dispassionate mechanicals, unseen and uncared for, produced, packaged and delivered these to waiting consumers. But such consumers had long since grown disdainful of the need or want of an infant, and like so much spoiled fruit, mewling newborns would rot on the shelves to be recycled back to the fields to provide nutrients to the increasingly infertile lands.

It had been decades since I had seen a child, and longer still since I had seen a woman. The cities as I have said were all but deserted. Vast residential towers that once teemed with life now held populations that could be counted on a single hand, and these were considered densely populated. Most places, most buildings, were empty, given over to haunting memories of populations that once were, caught it seemed, in automated loops of services for populations that no longer existed. I cannot speak of other megalopoli but of mine the population was—given the vastness of its urbanity—a near desert of humanity held together only by the mechanicals that maintained utilities and the etherlinks that on regular occasions vainly announced some occasion or another, again in a feeble rehearsal of what was once considered polite society.

It was on these twitching remnants of social media that the last vestiges of culture clung to life and pretended that humanity had a semblance of a future. But even here, the unavoidable descent into despair clawed at those who struggled to interact with one another. There were hints, rumors and whispers of some frightful danger lurking in the electroradiography messages. Not a physical danger, though that would have been something given the collapse of any and all semblance of law enforcement, but rather something spiritual or perhaps even psychic in nature. I recall seeing frantic, desperate reports made by pale and desperate faces which few seemed to acknowledge and yet seemed repeated over and over again. It was an unconscious acceptance that something was happening to the few of us that remained sitting alone in the dark shivering in fear, isolation and genuine cold. The fading sun and growing ice had set a chill about the world and there were so few of us left that we could not even rally to combat the creeping forces that seemed to conspire against us leading toward our inevitable doom.

It was in this clime that Aysaqendisa came out of the middle earth, the Mediterranean. None dared hazard where she had been decanted, but she spoke the old language—not Arabic or Latin or Greek, or Hebrew or even Assyrian, but the queerly lettered intonations of Kayblian which flowed from her tongue liked a song. The rabble of the wastelands, feral primitives that barely qualified as human, flocked to her and kissed her soft hands. Those who saw her speak, reported on the strange things she said concerning the unhurried eons she had waited in the earth to bring to those who would listen. Communications from voices not innate to this planet. She came from the wilderness, tall, olive-skinned and robust in hip and breast. She seemed to some, lascivious in nature as if the gods themselves had come forth and incarnated the very essence of the wanton. She came into the sprawling empty cities and perused the museums and galleries where the arts and sciences of mankind had once rendered works and instruments of the erotic and carnal. She spoke to the scholars that curated such things and listened as they explained their meaning or usage, laughing slightly when they finished and then politely correcting the half-truths that had been spoken. If necessary, she demonstrated the proper and immodest usage of such instruments on herself, her connubial followers or when possible willing volunteers. Such exhibitions of knowledge and base pleasures drove many witnesses away in stark moral terror, yet with each display her fame swelled. Those who had seen her shuddered when the name of Aysaqendisa was passed about the ether, but the fascination with her strangeness was undeniable. And where she went, the pervasive tranquility of our inevitable march toward mortality seemed to cease to exist. The days became filled with plagues of cacophonous terror, and the nights were filled with the weeping moans of loss and something else, something that could not be remembered but yet was not fully forgotten. On the streets, shadowy things were seen, limbs grasping torsos, bodies in tandem, a beast with two heads and a double spine clawing at the shattered moon as it climbed into the ashen sky illuminating the charcoal streets and ancient monoliths to heroes and events long since passed from memory.

After years bordering on decades Aysaqendisa came to my city—the vast, sprawling, ancient megalopolis where humanity had reached its pinnacle and then fallen into despair and disrepair. The ether had been electrostatic of her visit, and much was said of the lustfulness and unbidden desires that her revelations entailed, and I must admit that I ached to delve into the secrets that she kept hidden within her robes and to taste those queer painted lips for myself. I had a correspondent who lived up the line, he had seen her when she and her entourage had come to his city. Of Aysaqendisa, my friend spoke only in the most mysterious and haunting manner, suggesting the most outrageous, the most immoral, the most titillating possibilities that his diseased mind could muster the courage to transmit. He spoke of the darkened room where hands and mouths found succor, and long-suppressed appetites were finally whetted in manners that would make even the most jaded, bow their heads in shame. It was even hinted that those who knew Aysaqendisa personally looked on roiling vistas that threatened to drive them mad with desire. And so, it was one cool summer evening that I shook the dust off my finery and made my way through the vast empty streets, through subterranean transports, and elevated walkways. Shepherded on by the voices and illuminations of automatons built to serve billions and now merely going through the motions for the few of us clinging to a semblance of life. As I approached the theater, I caught glimpses of others who like myself had been drawn to Aysaqendisa, like moths to a flame. We shuffled out of the darkness, along the gray city avenues, shedding dust and detritus from our threadbare fancy, desperate for some semblance of spectacle and yet too inept to seek out true social interaction. One by one we came by the hundreds, drawn out from the vast disparate corners of the city. We were rich and poor, old and young, sick and healthy, male and female, black and white, and the multihued, multi-formed variations in between.

We came, and as in days of yore queued up to await the opening of the doors. We did not speak, and yet there was in the air that night, a miasma of sound, a meaningless hum, as if of electric insects calling to each other in the most primitive of intonations. I searched for the source of the cacophonous drone but to no avail. No one that I could see was speaking, and yet there it was, that numbing, meaningless murmuring that threatened to overwhelm my senses. It persisted until the doors opened, and her connubial ushers came for us. They were voluptuous things, graceful with heads of thick dark hair, clad in masks and gossamer veils that did more than hint at the curves beneath. They took each of us by the hands and led us through a dim lit hall to our seats. The air was thick with a heady incense and I being more indulgent than most, recognized the smoldering scent as that of black lotus, a soporific but in low doses a supposed aphrodisiac. I smiled at the clumsy but effective overture of seduction knowing full well that most of my companions would not recognize or be able to resist the narcotic.

There on the stage was Aysaqendisa, in all her terrible glory, surrounded by her prone followers in their ethereal robes. With a gesture, the lights fell and all around her, spawned out of a tomographic projector, we saw the manifold inhabitants of the universe rise up to join her. They stood with her in pure unadulterated nudity, their members raw and engorged and moist. At her direction these animate light sculptures fell on the waiting concubines and impossibly began to ravage them in the most lascivious of manners. Diaphanous gowns were shredded, and orifices were violated with pulsating organs of immense size and flexibility. There were moans of pain and ecstasy, and not just from the participants, but from other members of the audience who were witnessing the fabricated sexual conquest of humanity.

Disgusted, not just by what I saw, but also by the debauched reactions of my citizens, I rose up and voiced my displeasure only to be fallen upon by a bevy of bare attendants who pinned me back into my seat. Aysaqendisa strode through the theater and looked down from the stage upon my futile struggles. She said nothing, but somehow, I could still hear her thoughts as they wormed their way into my brain just as the hands of so many stripped me of my raiment's. This was the way of the universe, the way that life survived. Lesser species, those that had never reached their full potential, who had never made the leap into the vastness of interstellar space were the prey of those who had. But prey was not the proper word, for the greater did not devour the lesser, but rather took what it could from them, what they needed, the inherited uniqueness that had evolved over billions of years and added it to their own, to preserve the past and evolve forward into the future. It had been done millions of times on thousands of planets.

I closed my eyes in revulsion as she disrobed and revealed the pendulous multitude of breasts, phallic and yonic genitalia. She swarmed over the chairs and servitors and her toothless mouth fell upon my nether regions swallowing up what she found there. There was a terrible slurping sound and despite the revulsion I felt myself involuntarily respond. My skin flushed, and I felt my stomach churn as her tongue entwined around my flesh and the muscles of her throat squeezed and massaged me in a fashion that was both painful and pleasurable. I looked down and saw her eyes stare up and me and heard her voice in my head once more—*I want to taste your genetics* – It wasn't a request, it was a command and without choice my back arched and I spasmed into a shuddering release that tore through me as never before.

Aysaqendisa rose up from between my legs and her attendants released my arms. I thrashed away from them, crawling backwards over the row of seats. For a brief instant my eyes locked onto those of my unwanted partner, my rapist, the god-thing that called itself Aysaqendisa. In that look I could see the future that awaited all of mankind, and I ran, leaving the alien terrors to partake of their foul desires with my fellow citizens. I ran naked through the hallways, hot and humid with the scent of musk. I ran into the streets cold and dim, the dying sun rising to the east, the sickly pale moon still lingering in the sky like the dead eye of god watching the final death spasms of his creation. I ran down stairs and into waiting subway cars and huddled in fear beneath the windows. I ran all the way home and sealed the door with long forgotten locks and bolts and pins. Shattered I crawled into my bed and stayed there until night fell once more. It was then and only then that I limped into the shower and washed away the bloody remnants of ejaculate and the thick streamers of dried saliva that still clung to my flesh. I gathered up my bed linens and bundled them into an old burlap sack. With great effort I dragged the befouled packet down the stairs and into the basement, stuffing it into the incinerator where I watched with glee as the fires reduce it to ash and smoke.

Hours later, back in my rooms, I sat staring at the terminal, the connection to the etherlink calling to me, begging me, taunting me. I don't know why I finally gave in, but I did. And against my will I wrote to those who lived down the line, to cities where the entourage was yet to visit. I told them what marvels I had seen, what dark wonders she would show, and I told those with whom I corresponded that when Aysaqendisa comes they must attend her visit. I wrote these things under duress, with my every thought in rebellion, with my very body yearning to escape from the seat where I typed. In the end I tore myself away, the messages sent, my hands cramped from being unable to resist the need to tell untruths for the monster that had taken that which I had not wanted to give. Once more I fell into my bed, curling up into a ball and lying there in near catatonia.

It was only days later that I awoke with a start. You would think that hunger or thirst or some other routine organic function would have stirred me from my self-induced coma, but instead it was the dream, the terrible dream, and what came with it. I dreamt of Aysaqendisa, of her eyes, her dark unendingly deep eyes, her cruel mouth and rough tongue. I dreamt of her flesh encircling mine, swallowing me up, devouring me. I dreamt she ate me up piece by piece, limb by limb, bite by bite until I was nothing but masticated remnants of flesh and bone floating in a sea of acidic digestive fluids. I dreamt all this, and it was this that woke me, this horrific dream and the gift it brought with it. Never before had I been so turgid, so engorged, my own flesh was stabbing me in the abdomen, begging for release. It had been decades since I had experienced such a response and with it came the aching desire to be satisfied. Desperate for release I used my hand to pleasure myself rhythmically pumping the stiff shaft of flesh that had risen up from between my legs. I pumped and pumped and pumped until I began to chaff and burn. I tried to spit in my hand to provide some lubrication but that only lasted for a few moments before the chaffing began again. It was hours later that I sat on the ground turned raw by the roughness of my hand, blood leaking from the tip of my glans. I had ejaculated blood. My testicles were empty. I had ejaculated blood because that was all I had left to give, Aysaqendisa had taken everything else from me, she had drained me dry.

I applied a topical ointment to ease the pain, dressed and then left my home. I didn't bother to lock the door; I didn't even bother to shut it. I wander into the open city, and slowly, inevitably made my way back to the theater. I wander up the stairs assaulted by the stink of dry meat—the stench of death. No one else had ever made it out of the room. The bodies were still there, dry ashen things drained of their fluids, all their fluids. Aysaqendisa had taken my people from me, had taken the city from me. All that was left were the dried husks, turning to ash in the cool dying air of a dying world.

I spent weeks on the line trying to catch up with Aysaqendisa and her servants, but to no avail. She left me a clear trail to follow, but I never could catch up. I followed for a year, followed the trail of dead bodies, followed the trail of dead cities, followed the trail of dead cultures. I would like to think that it was because she was a swift, monstrous god, but the truth was that I slept more now than I ever had before, and when I slept, I dreamed, and when I dreamed, I had no choice but to masturbate for hours upon hours. Wearing what flesh I had into a desensitized leathery knob, burned and callused. After a year it fell off, or perhaps I ripped it off. I can't remember. It doesn't matter. I didn't need it anymore.

Aysaqendisa had taken everything else from me, she might as well have taken that too.

I tried the Ethernet once more, a general call, but no one answered. The mechanicals had stopped, there was no one left for them to serve. On the fifth day of my fifteenth month, I found the place where she had turned on her servitors, where she had split them from stem to sternum and eaten their ovaries and drunk their blood. Vermin had infected what remained and the rotting flesh had been given over to maggots that crawled in and out of it, humping along in a twisted parody of life.

I don't know why I was allowed to live.

Aysaqendisa

Perhaps it was to see her leave, to ascend, to transform into something that I cannot describe, something that was human but hot human, humane but inhumane, a vessel for what was left of us, the sad lonely dregs of humanity entombed inside the ravenous flesh of an alien whore. I called her a whore, I suppose it is fitting, after all she fucked us into oblivion and left us—left me with nothing, not even a cock to jerk off with.

Our star is dying, our world is barren, and so is my flesh.

Our genetics belong to Aysaqendisa now, perhaps someday in the future she will remember us and pause to birth our species once more. Perhaps, I doubt it, but I can still hope. As the sun goes down, I touch myself and try to draw forth some last sense of frission.

The Last Days of Ulthar

t had been five hundred years since the burgesses of Ulthar had forbade the killing of cats. Five hundred years and Ulthar had grown from a hamlet to a metropolis that would rival any other. And yet it had grown in ways that only dreams can. It had spread its cobbled streets and low walls and reached sturdy towers into the sky. It had new wharves along the River Skai, but at the same time it had preserved those features that had made it most famous not only in Nir but in Hatheg and even in far Celephais, mainly that Ulthar had been, was and would forever be the city of cats.

It was not an easy thing to be a city of cats. It is one thing to pass a law forbidding the killing of a cat in a hamlet or village, it is quite another to enforce such a law in a city such as Ulthar had become. There were, by some counts, a cat for every man, woman and child who lived in Ulthar. Other accountings suggested that this was not true, that there were in fact two cats for every such resident. The true numbers did not matter, the simple fact was that they lounged about the city in such numbers that any wagons and carts driven through the city did so in a controlled and cautious manner so as to protect the feline inhabitants that wandered there. This was such a concern, that the great markets and the warehouses that were needed to supply such a city were kept at the very outskirts of its borders, where farmers, artisans, artificers, and merchant caravans could ply their trade without traversing the majority of its streets. There were still cats in these markets and stores, but the wheels that ground through the streets had less to fear here than in the depths of the urban landscape.

There were other concerns of course. The city was in one manner very clean, being free of rats, mice, lizards, snakes, and any other such vermin that might attract the attention of the felines that stalked its streets. In another manner, the city was quite filthy, being the depository for the daily droppings of a legion of animals most of which that could not be trained to use the plumbing. To solve this issue, the burgesses had ordered a proliferation of sand parks be strategically placed throughout the city, and a small corps of men that served to clean these parks on a daily basis.

The feeding of such a multitude of cats was in itself no small task, and a veritable fraternity had sprung up to shoulder it. The Maukin had begun as a kind of charitable organization, gathering up bits off scrap from the butcher, the fishmonger, and the dairyman. These varietals were then made into a kind of dried kibble, which made it both easy to store and transport for distribution about the city. Over the decades the society had evolved and taken up an almost priestly role, conflating the name of the city Ulthar, with that of the Elder God Uldar whose task it was to keep vigilance over the loathsome things that had filtered down from the outer void to drowse in the haunted and lonely places of the Earth, in the wastelands of the desert and ice, the pits and folds of the darkest caverns, and of course the depths of the abyssal ocean. Legend, or at least those promulgated by the Maukin, held that the God Ulthar was, in its way, possessed of certain feline traits, as were its offspring, the various feline monstrosities that had come to be seen in the waking world as either demons or gods, the most prominent being Bastet. Thus, the Maukin came to be not only the caretakers of the cats of Ulthar, but also the priesthood of a minor Elder God.

Despite its charitable and theological tenets, the Maukin Fraternity was undeniably a firm hand in the operation of the city itself, drawing from its coffers a significant sum. This was never done directly, but rather in the form of boons, grants and services. The temples of the society were maintained at city expense, and a holiday celebrating the good works of the Maukin and encouraging donations to their cause, was held annually. The festivities and décor for this merrymaking were paid for out of the city purse.

It was therefore inevitable that an ideology opposing both the Maukin, and their furry charges would arise, albeit in secret, amongst the shadows of the Ultharian alleyways. It was a particularly venomous organization, led by none other than Esnick, the banker who also served as treasurer for the city and had grown tired of being servile to men and creatures he thought of as less than himself, and therefore less deserving. In his view, the city of Ulthar could be so much more if it simply weren't for those damned cats. He and his like-minded fellows set a task before them, one that seemed outrageous, perhaps even impossible, they would rid themselves of the vermin that infested their city and assume their rightful place in its streets.

For years they worked, meeting furtively in out of the way taverns outside the city, in glades near the Enchanted Wood, and even in caravans organized and hired for that very reason. A multitude of ideas had been proposed and evaluated to accomplish their goals. Poisoning the various foodstuffs was considered, but it was soon learned that the Maukin themselves partook of the mixture they fed to their charges, and therefore any such toxin would be revealed by their deaths long before the feed could be distributed. The use of zoogs, a natural foe of catkind, was considered, and a small number were taken from the Enchanted Wood. Unfortunately, at least for the conspirators, the violent tendencies of the zoogs could not be harnessed for the task at hand. The zoogs were quite adept at killing, but refused to focus on their feline adversaries, finding the killing of their trainers and caretakers equally as fulfilling.

In wicked desperation, Esnick had dispatched emissaries to meet with the men of Leng to broach the subject with their masters who dwelt on the far side of the moon. Of the three men sent, only one returned and he, without his tongue or fingers, had the most difficult of tasks reminding his employers that the moon-beasts and the saturnine cats had been allied for more years than Ulthar itself had been on the maps of the realms. With all their own ideas exhausted Esnick and his friends sent abroad a small cadre of agents to make discrete inquiries in pursuit of their diabolical pursuit.

Thus, it was that Chinthe came to Ulthar. She was a dark woman, from the Southern Isles, with her hair worn in braids festooned with ebonite beads carved from shells found only on the shores of the Lake of Yath. She had studied with the priesthood in Celephais, and with another in Serranian, and a third in Kadatheron. She had served as a priestess at the base of the mountain Hatheg-Kla and as a sibyl in a cave in the cliffs near Ilek-Vad. In all of these roles she had fulfilled her duties with an unmatched fervor, and in the process raised the ire of those others with which she ministered for the Gods of Earth and those who sought their favor. She was it seemed, too fervent in her devotions, and too curious for her own good. She delved too deep into parchments and other texts held in the various libraries and collections of these diverse ministries, learning from them a multitude of secrets, enigmas, mysteries and yes even heresies that made her quite dangerous and therefore quite despised. It is one thing to make an enemy of a man, it is quite another to make an enemy of a religion. And so Chinthe, the student, the priestess, the soothsayer became known as Chinthe the Heretic.

She walked into the city on the Day of the Fifth Whisker and took in the city, traversing its streets and taking the measure of the people who lived there. She let the aroma of the city envelope her, let its sounds fill her head, and made sure to sample the great varietals of foodstuffs that made themselves available. She wandered thoroughfares and across byways and bridges, and down alleyways and avenues and flowered cul de sacs. She did these things with a sense of wonder, and with a sense of respect, and in doing so learned secrets of the city that its own residents did not know, for how could they, they had been born and raised in those walls and roadways. They took what they saw for granted, and never suspected what the curved and meandering architecture truly meant.

Chinthe met that first night with Esnick and his counselors. Chinthe bore a letter that carried the seal of one of Esnick's agents. The missive suggested that Chinthe might present a novel solution to the problem that plagued Ulthar. Esnick welcomed the woman with a bottle of wine from orchards that bordered the River Skai. When all had finished their portion, the corpulent baker finally raised the question about how she planned to solve their problem.

Chinthe smiled a vicious little smile that made some of the men in the room draw back in fear while others felt themselves tinged with a forbidden lust. "You seek to eliminate the pestilence that infects Ulthar, I seek to aid you in your task."

"And how would you do such a thing?" Asked Esnick stroking his moustache.

"I would seek to do what you cannot bring yourself to do, usurp the role of the Maukin, and draw from them their powers both sacred and secular."

"And how would you suppose we do that?"

Chinthe shook her head. "I am not a fool Sir. If I were to tell you my clever plans, and they are clever, how then would I be paid for my cleverness?"

"What do you seek in return for your cleverness?"

Chinthe paused for a moment to think and then took up the empty wine bottle and turned it over in her hand. "The vineyard that produces this vintage, you own it?" Esnick conceded that he did. "If I accomplish my task, I will take this vineyard as my payment." From her robes Chinthe the Heretic brought forth a small scroll and handed it to Esnick's own advisor. The two read it over and then conferred in hushed tones, then finally Esnick took up a quill and put his mark upon the bottom of the page.

"Now, tell us of your plan."

Chinthe sat back in her chair and put her fingertips together in front of her face, her dark almond eyes glinting in the lamplight. "Our first task gentlemen, is to poison the Maukin Fraternity."

. . .

It was two days later that the first act in Chinthe's plan was put into motion. Several barrels of smoked eels were tainted with an extraction of venom from the purple spiders of Leng. Then in the dark of the night the barrels were left at the gate to the main chapter house of the fraternity where they were whisked inside and added to the larder. It was barely a day later that the entire order, even the smallest of chapters, fell ill. The chirugeons of the city fearful that some fever had taken root in the metropolis ordered the Maukin quarantined, and the distribution of kibble suspended.

This created a void in the ordered society of Ulthar, one that Chinthe recommended as a religious advisor to the burgess council chose to fill. With the Maukin's unable to feed the cats of Ulthar the poor creatures were in danger of going hungry and in a city of so many, the thousands of mouths of even small predators might become dangerous. Under Chinthe's orders the entire production of milk from the surrounding farms was requisitioned. To this a small amount of soporific was added, not much but enough. The tainted milk was set about the city in barrels that were split open and allowed to drain into the streets where the cats of the city were allowed to drink their fill, lapping it up gleefully. No cornerstone of the city was left untouched, and five tuns were taken up the spiraled tower at the center of the city and opened up and allowed to flow unbridled down the path that they had been hauled up. Citizens at the base of the spire waited for the inevitable flood that would envelope the lower portions of the area, but to their surprise it never came. Indeed, save for a few saucers full here and there the entirety of the milk that had been hauled up had inexplicably vanished. The spectators searched and searched but they could not find a grate or pipe by which the volume could have been sluiced away. The only one who seemed unsurprised by the whole matter was Chinthe the Heretic, who simply nodded as if the whole affair was entirely expected.

That night as the intoxicated cats slept, the city guard was roused to investigate a most strange occurrence. There was about the streets reports of strange noises, most curious and upsetting. Old women reported a rustling in the trees and through the bushes and gardens. In the quarter by the docks retired seaman recorded a sound that they swore was like a gale wind whipping through the sheets of their sails. Fearful, they drew the shudders of their windows tight, cinched up their curtains, and retired to their beds in hope that the noise would subside, and they would be passed by unharmed. Responding to such reports, the watch found nothing. Though this was not always to the preference of those that had summoned them. Yards that had once been full of furniture and furnishings were now empty. Streets once cluttered with the necessities of life were now bare, and alleyways that had been home to rubbish bins and unclaimed detritus were likewise scoured of their contents. The city woke the next morning the victim of an impossible act, somehow vast portions—entire quarters had been scoured clean, as if by the hand of some fastidious demon horde that took the valuable and the worthless just the same.

And still Chinthe the Heretic just nodded as if all of this was going to plan. Esnick and his compatriots voice concerns, but Chinthe dismissed them. No one had been harmed she reminded them, and the fact that strange things had happened only played into their hands. The plan would continue she told them and there would be no deviations.

The application of soporific milk continued the next day, and that evening the citizenry of Ulthar braced themselves for another night of unseen and inexplicable rustlings and thefts. The more thoughtful of residents gathered their belongings off of stoops, and porches, and balconies, and out of yards and alleys and secured them inside sheds and closets and entryways. Houses that had once been immaculate found themselves cluttered in the hope of deterring the theft.

But that night there was no rusting in the trees or any other vegetation, and there were no thefts or disappearances of property. There was instead a low and terrible humming that seemed to resonate from the very walls and roadways of Ulthar. It was a rhythmic thing that came in most curious cycles. The woodwrights of the city thought it akin to a rasp working out a plan with occasional pauses to assess progress, an assessment that the farriers wholeheartedly agreed with. It should be noted that although the sound was pervasive, it was not necessarily injurious. Indeed, many suggested that on that night their repose was perhaps one of the most restful of their entire lives.

On the third day the citizens of Ulthar went about the day with a kind of restful happiness in their hearts, and they greeted the tiny felines that shared the city with them in a most joyous manner, sharing with them their morning sausages and kippers and eggs. That is most of them, the likes of Esnick the Banker and his cohorts still scorned the four-legged beasts and soured at the joviality that had spread about their city.

That morning in the midst of all this cheerfulness, Chinthe the Heretic urgently called on Esnick and put the question to him one final time. This was the crux she informed the man who lounged about in his tub, from here on forward there was no turning back. Esnick just nodded and told her to get on with it. Chinthe seemed almost melancholy as she left the banker's manse that sat at the top of the lane known as the Curl of the Tail.

After they had dispensed the day's milk, Chinthe ordered the barrels carted out of the city and delivered to a small encampment to the north of the city, just beyond the hills but not yet within the boundaries of the Enchanted Wood. There, far from the prying eyes of the city Chinthe ordered the huntsmen into the wood and instructed the gathered woodwrights in her design. When all was understood and all were about their task, Chinthe took her leave and returned to the city of Ulthar a frown upon her face.

The wind blew cool that evening, and the citizenry of Ulthar took the opportunity to go out into their streets and yards and with a bottle of wine or port celebrate the passing of the day. All about them, the cats of Ulthar lay fat and torpid from the narcotic laced milk they had spent three days consuming. Again, their came that curious vibration, the one that seemed to come from the walls and roadbeds of the city itself. The one that neither the city elders nor city watch could explain. Again, there were those that thought it familiar, but the only people who could have identified it with any certainty were too ill to speak. Chinthe could have told them, for she knew, but nobody asked her, and it was too late anyway.

The next morning the residents of Ulthar, both human and feline, woke well rested and amiable. The sun seemed to take on a rather cheerful glow and more than one resident was caught whistling a happy tune as they went about their work. Indeed, even the cats seemed overzealous in their affections, rubbing against legs and demanding to be stroked and provided the comfortable lap to curl up in. It was not until late morning that the pursuit of affection turned into a more forceful demand for attention. Which was then quickly escalated into a frenzy of seemingly unprovoked scratches and the vicious bite. It was then, and only then that the men, women and children of Ulthar realized that the daily supply of milk had not been delivered.

Runners were dispatched and inquiries made at various municipal offices, but all of these were met with the same lack of information. No agency or ministry would admit responsibility for the delivery of the milk over the last few days, and furthermore none would act to undertake the task and organize an immediate delivery. The citizenry for the first time in memory was left to act for themselves and feed the now annoyed and hissing cats on their own. Larders were quickly investigated for whatever tasty and meaty morsels could be found. These were normally reserved for housecats, those furry companions that were quite different in temper than the outdoor cat, but these were desperate times and those called for desperate measures. Larders, butcheries and fish houses were ransacked, and the streets strewn with whatever could be found to distract the feline horde and assure that its belly was appeased.

That night the women of Ulthar listened to the howling and screeching that bellowed from the streets and made sure that their children were locked up behind strong doors and shuttered windows. In the meanwhile, the men of Ulthar armed themselves with whatever they could find that they thought would be helpful against the legion of moggy demons that seemed to prowl outside.

With the sunrise the fears of the men and women of the city were found to be justified. Four members of the night watch had been attacked, slashed multiple times by some edged weapon. None had been killed, but all had suffered grievous bodily harm, one had even lost an eye, while another would likely never walk again. While the doctors attended to the wounded the remaining members of the guard called for action. A delegation of senior officers marched to the great temple and demanded consultation with the High Priest Atal. But Atal, who served the Gods of Earth, and had done so for centuries had grown feeble in his senescence, and could barely move let alone speak, was of no use to the men who entreated him to act.

The delegation left dejected and clambering for aid. Chinthe the Heretic was there, waiting for them, and she offered a solution to their problem. It was a terrible thing that she offered, but they listened to her as she spoke of this and that and the other thing. She spoke, and they listened, and it didn't take much to convince them to do as she said.

And so, five men mounted on zebras that were both stout and fleet of foot made their way out of the city and headed north along the road that led over the hills toward the Enchanted Wood. But it was not the wood toward which they were heading; it was to the glade where the hunters and woodwrights had finished their work.

It took hours for the guard to make their way back to Ulthar for they brought with them a huge tarpaulin covered wagon that took all four of their mounts to pull. It came plodding along down the road leaving behind it two thick ruts. Even from a distance it could be seen that the structure underneath the cloth had been built from empty barrels of milk that had been used to placate the cats of Ulthar, but they had been turned into something much, much larger. It was still barrel shaped, that much could be told from the look of it, but what was beneath was hidden from view. But the sounds, the cacophonous, chattering, whistling sounds that came from beneath hinted at what was beneath. As it passed through the main gates a great pall came over the city. Religious men made the sign of Koth and invoked the name of Lobon, fiercest of the Gods of Earth. Mothers grabbed their children from the streets and hurried on home. Shopkeepers closed their doors and barred them from the inside. And in the chapter houses of the Maukin Fraternity, the brothers stumbled from their beds and to their doors and windows and wailed in despair at what they knew was to come.

The covered wagon was marched through the city in the most systematic of ways, spiraling as it were, sunwise from the outer walls to the very center of the labyrinth that was the streets of Ulthar. It made its way, and as it did the cats who are the most curious of creatures took notice and fell in behind forming what could only be described as a great retinue of the feline persuasion. And all the while that terrible chattering from underneath the tarpaulin continued, now joined by the incessant meowing from those that followed.

Once the center of the old quarter had been reached the drivers paused and several attendants then loosened the ties and the canvas cover fell away revealing the source of the terrible cacophony. The barrel staves had been repurposed to build an immense wooden cage the full length of the oversized cart and half as tall again. Inside were dozens upon dozens of screeching lemurian zoogs, their eyes wide with fear, the tendrils about their mouths whipping about in rage. With the unveiling of their natural enemy the cats of Ulthar developed an immense rancor and arched up their backs in the curious way that cats do and begin hissing and spitting in the most venomous of ways. The closer ones tried to leap onto the cart, but between the driver and the designer of the cage a foothold could not be gained, and the unorganized feline masses had to content themselves with chasing the monstrous construct through the streets and out the gates into the fields and beyond.

It was only when the last cluster of the cats had followed out of that the gates were closed and locked. This left only a handful of the species, those too old or too young to follow the captive zoogs, inside the city walls. The majority of the cats paid no notice to the slamming of the door behind them, and continued to follow the cart as it crested the high hill to the west, where the setting sun illuminated the scene and the thousands of cats that swarmed the landscape.

It was at this time that the Maukin Fraternity appeared at the gates, they came laden with bags and chests, whatever valuables they could carry, and demanded that they be allowed to depart. At first the guard refused, noting that that if they wanted, they could leave in a day or two, once the horde of felines had dispersed. If the Maukin wished to join their charges they could do so then. But there came a curious rumbling, and the great tower that had stood for as long as any could remember, swayed and then came crashing down, scattering dust and debris over the old quarter. To the west one of the great walls bowed up and seemed to tumble over, then to the east the same thing occurred. Panicked, the guards opened up the gates and the Maukin fled through them. They were only the first.

Great upheavals wracked the city, toppling fortifications and buildings as if they were the children's playthings. In moments the Maukin were not the only residents of Ulthar that had fled to the surrounding countryside. In time, as structure after structure fell, the whole of the city was evacuated and marched southwest down the road that ran along the River Skai, a despondent mob clutching to the meager things that they had fled with. Even Esnick had escaped, though now bereft of his vaults and hirelings, he walked slow and defeated like everyone else.

It was only as the last of them crossed the great hill of Alamondar that a saddened few cast a backward glance and witnessed the most curious of occurrences. There, in the fullness of the moonlight they saw the barrel shaped cart still yoked to the quartet of zebras, as it darted desperately about on the plain, as if it were attempting to escape some unseen predator. At first, they thought it was merely an attempt to flee from the ravenous horde of cats, but then a sudden movement caught their eyes. Whatever calamity had befallen the city of Ulthar, the maelstrom of dust had long since dispersed, either settled or blown away by the winds that blew down from the north. But where the city had once been the observers could see nothing, no ruins, no debris, and no devastated structures. There was nothing to see, because there was nothing there.

But still there was something down there on the plain, something moving, pursuing the oblong cart full of screeching and terrified zoogs. It was titanic in size and had about it a darkness akin to the void, and it moved in a sleek manner. It was, despite its size, a terribly silent thing, terribly silent as it moved across that plain, at least until its one appendage made contact with the cart and a horrific caterwauling filled the landscape. Another appendage came down and crushed the pinned cart, the draft animals that pulled it, and presumably all the zoogs that were trapped inside.

From the back of her mother, one small child who bore witness dared to speak. "Look momma," she said, "a kitty."

The Last Days of Ulthar

And not far away, Chinthe the Heretic laughed as Ulthar the cat city played with the toy she had used to rouse it from centuries of slumber.

The Island of the Gathoga

The sun was low on the horizon when we first spotted the island, and it took us another hour to find a cove that we could make landfall on. It was like many others that filled the sea that divided Britannia from Hibernia, high, craggy cliffs with thin forests of low, wind-swept trees. The beach itself was rocky and filled with boulders that could have shattered our small boat into pieces, but it was a risk we had to take. We had hoped to have made it all the way to Hibernia, but the winter winds had shifted blowing us off course. There were storm clouds to the north, black, bilious things that did not bode well. We took the beach, cursing the lack of a quay as we plunged our boots into the churning waves and pulled ashore. We complained, but we were grateful to be off that cold, black sea. I longed for the clear blue waters of the Mediterranean where the dolphin frolicked, and fish schooled, and massive flocks of seabirds dotted the shores. Here, there was barely even a beach, and the fish were as dark as the water. Even the birds hung in the sky like portents of doom.

"Hail Caesar!" The voice came from the ridge above and though it was a welcome sentiment and tongue it set us all on guard. Our hands went to our swords as the broken figure came out of the mist that draped the wood beyond the shoreline. He came shuffling down the bank. His face was tattooed with a stylized bird that embraced his right check and eye. He was dressed in the way we would have expected, in the roughly made woolen fabric that all the locals wore, but what surprised us was the buckle that he wore in the middle of his chest to secure the crude cloak to his person. It bore the eagle insignia of the Legio IX Hispania, our own regiment!

Lucius, our commander returned his hail and while he and I went to meet with this stranger the rest of the crew dragged the boat further ashore. There were thirty of us, a full complement with tents, armaments and enough food for two weeks, assuming we didn't forage off the land or from allied farmsteads. Lucius introduced both I and himself, and then demanded the same from the stranger.

"Once I was Quintus Petreius Quietus, Petri to my friends. I served under Agricola when he reached the River Taus and later when he explored Hibernia." His voice was rough with years and his beard had gone gray. The skin on his hands had turned the dull bronze that comes from tanning leather.

"Agricola's expedition to Hibernia is more than twenty-five years past," noted Lucius. "What are you doing here centurion?" He gave him respect even though he might not have deserved it.

"I haven't been a centurion in a long time," he sounded a little sad. "Come with me, I'll explain all, and why you must leave here as soon as possible." Lucius looked at me and sought silent confirmation that I had heard the dire tone in the man's voice. Of course, I had, even the men on the ship had heard it. I suspected that the rest of the legion in their barracks on the far shore may have pricked up their ears and wondered why they suddenly had such an ominous feeling.

The path we followed was well-worn and it led us over a small rise and through the wood. The trail was wide enough for a cart, and to the side we spied a clearing where several small roughly hewn fishing boats were stored along with several dozen large fishing nets. Beyond this we reached the crest of the ridge and the sound of waves, and the wind died down. There was a clearing below, maybe a centuria in size, and filled as it were with what one would have expected of a village so far from civilization. There were no streets, only dirt trails some wider than others that ran between what I generously would categorize as buildings that radiated out from a central hall. To one side a pen held a large flock of sheep, and between the buildings goats roamed freely, as did brightly colored chickens. Scattered throughout were several large firepits, all of which were in the process of being lit.

We thought we would go down further and take stock of the locals, but Petri didn't take the trail down into the village. Instead, we followed the ridge and came upon a small hut and an even smaller fire surrounded with benches cut from the trunks of trees. He bade us to sit and then offered us fresh water which we gladly accepted.

"You will forgive the Kallakberii, it is not their intent to be rude, they simply cannot afford to be hospitable, it is not in their nature." He pulled out a small clay jug, "Mead?" We declined but he took a long swig of his own. "Whatever you need of this place, you will ask it of me. I have all authority to deal with ... visitors."

"I would not consider us visitors," Lucius snorted. "The new governor wishes to expand his territory. The north seems too barren and too filled with Picts and other barbarians. Agricola himself said that Hibernia could be taken easily. We are here as scouts for the legion, to find allies and establish fortifications from which to conquer."

Petri shook his head. "The Kallakberii are unsuitable as allies. They are farmers and fishermen, not soldiers. You'll have to sail on in the morning. The mainland is only a day away if the wind is right."

Again, Lucius snorted. "I'm not so sure of that. This is a good-sized island, and the beach may be rocky but could easily be made suitable to receive war galleys. If the people are—as you say—then they will make excellent auxiliaries. There is no shame in supplying the legions of Rome with food, comfort and skilled labor." He laughed boisterously and playfully slapped me on my thigh. I smiled back but kept an eye on our host who seemed dejected by such talk.

"You will not find this to be a suitable place for your base Commander Lucius. Nor will it be one that you can barter with or raid. The people will not serve you, not at sword point, not for coin, not even as slaves." He took another mouthful of mead from the jug. "If you do not heed my warning, if you do not leave as soon as possible the only thing you will find here is death."

There was an uncomfortable silence that lasted longer than it should have. It was only broken when Lucius scowled, "And who is it that will kill us? You old man? The villagers below? They're savages. What are their numbers? What could this island possible support, two maybe three hundred? We may be only thirty, but we are Roman legionnaires. We could conquer this entire island in two days, maybe less."

Petri lowered his eyed and stared into the fire. "I will not argue with you. I served, I know the tactics and strengths you hold. I have no doubt that you could force yourselves on these people, take their lands and crops and livestock. You could enslave them easily and build your port and fort. But none of that would matter, you will all fall to the beast that stalks this land in the dead of winter."

Lucius shook his head with a smile. "Another day, another monster. Do you know how many times I have heard about a monster that haunts the land and defends the local tribe? Do you know how many priests dressed in cloaks and skulls I have killed?"

"You mock me, and with good cause. I and my fellow centurions were much like you, we were warned, and we scoffed as well. But they are all dead, killed by the beast ten years past, and only I have survived. Survived to tell my tale and warn others so that they would leave the Kallakberii in peace."

Lucius grabbed the jug from our reluctant host and took a long drink from it, the excess running down his chin. "Fine, tell us your story old man, but be warned, we've heard too many tales of giant wolves and cave bears to be easily amused."

I nodded my agreement and this time when I was offered the jug, I took my own draught from its thick and heady brew. What good is a campfire story without a drink to go with it?

Petri took a deep breath and spoke solemnly. "It was during the return from Agrippa's exploratory campaign to Hibernia that a summer storm came up and the fleet struggled to stay together. The mast of our ship was shattered and the section that fell killed three centurions almost immediately as it shattered the hull. We took on water fast. A few of us made it to other vessels, but I saw many others dragged beneath the waters by their armor. Only I and four others survived by clinging to wreckage, to make it here to this island."

"The locals nurtured us back to health, but that took us into autumn and by the time our quartet was well enough to set about building a boat to rejoin our comrades the air was already growing cold, and our time had to be spent working with the Kallakberii laying in supplies for the winter. We smoked fish, brined vegetables and reinforced the pens for the sheep. Marius used stones to build a pen for rabbits. The winter wasn't particularly mild, nor was it harsh. We made it through, and no man woman or child starved, and the Gathoga never came out of the cave. That is what they call the beast that stalks this place, Gathoga. According to legend it only appears during times of severe stress such as winter famine."

"I warned you not to waste my time Petri," snapped Lucius, "I've killed too many druids, and their grove gods too listen to this nonsense."

"The Kallakberii do not worship Gathoga, indeed they dread his coming. The locals claim to be descendart from the goddess Kallak, from whom their tribal name derives. I myself can make no claim to the patronage of Kallak, but my fellow Marcus, who was more educated in the ways of the gods and their worship, suggested that she was one of the three-thousand children of Oceanus and Tethys. Kallak is not a kind deity, she may not be cruel, she may not be demanding, but she is not kind. Her children—her worshippers—are not blessed with great size, or strength, or beauty, or intelligence. They are a mediocre race, with few heroes. Only Gathoga defends them, and only when things are desperate."

"And you've seen this daemon?" Snorted Lucius.

Petri nodded solemnly. "I wish I hadn't. It was in our seventeenth year here. We had all taken wives and they had born children. This marking on my face, it identifies me not only as a member of this tribe, but of a particular family. I, my wife and my child all bore the same design. It was the winter after my daughter turned sixteen, after her face was tattooed, two years after my wife had drowned, that Gathoga appeared. That year the harvest had been poor and the fishing bad and the winter had lasted longer than normal. Spring had not come, and food was short. We had taken to boiling bark and grass into a thin soup to fill our bellies, it didn't help much. Have you ever eaten seabird? It is a foul, oily meat, and the first few times we ate it we vomited violently. Later, we learned how to dry it and then add it to the soup. We even ate the bones, boiled and crushed up, for all the good that did. After weeks of this, even the seabirds were gone. To feed our family—to feed our village—Seda, that is my daughter's name, and I set out daily, hunting the small game and feral livestock that might have survived the winter. To bring home a squirrel or two, or even a rabbit was considered a good day's hunt. One morning, we came across the tracks of a large deer and after hours of tracking it I caught a tawny glimpse through the snow-laden boughs of a tree. It was a magnificent creature, one that any hunter would have been proud to take as a trophy so as to mount the ten-pointed skull above his door. I was so hungry I didn't care about the glory, only about the meat that would fill my belly and that of my daughter and the rest of the village.

Careful, slow and patient I aimed and easily put an arrow in its rump. It didn't even make a sound it just ran leaving a trail of hot, thick blood. Exhilarated I ran after it, almost blind in my pursuit. I followed the beast for more than half the day, finding it blood out and panting beneath a fallen beech tree. I slit its throat and let the blood run over my hands to warm them. Then I gutted it, and it was only after I had eaten half the liver that I noticed Seda wasn't with me, and then I realized that she hadn't been with me for a long time. I dressed the animal and hauled it back to the village. I had expected her to be there, but she wasn't, and none had seen her.

We ate some and then I and my fellow legionnaires marched back into the forest, with night falling, in search of my warrior daughter. We found her weapons not far from where I had first shot the buck. We followed her trail, and oddly enough it led to where I had gutted the beast and left the entrails. Much of what I had left behind had been eaten by crows, but something larger had been at the offal as well. Two trails of blood led away from the slaughter site, one was mine, the other seemed to be that of an animal dragging what it could away, and the trail of Seda seemed to follow this second blood line. It was an hour later that we reached the shoreline and lost the trail. We found her boots and her clothes, tattered and bloody as if they had been torn off her by something large and predatory. We brought them back to the village and asked about bears or wolves, but the Kallakberii just shook their heads and said she was with Gathoga now. As if that explained everything, as if my child had meant nothing. The locals even refused to mourn her passing, I was left to suffer comforted only by my fellow legionnaires, but not for long."

"It was a week later that we lost Marcus. He had been out hunting, his wife had asked him not to go. To go fishing instead, to take the boat and head toward the coast for a week or two. He refused, and his wife cried as he walked into the forest. We did find his body, torn to shreds, the ravens pecking at his eyes and entrails. The villagers cried as they buried what was left of him, but when I called for warriors to stand with me and hunt down the beast Gathoga none of the locals would stand with me. Instead, they invoked Kallak and said that Gathoga was her will, her way of protecting them. It didn't make any sense, at least not then."

"Sulla was taken two days later. The beast came into his own house and took him while we all slept. It knew how to get in. It knew our defenses, the layout of our homes, the bed that Sulla slept in. It came and went, and we never saw it, only the bits that it left behind, and the blood that led into the forest. Callus went after it. He donned his armor, his galea with its faded red crest, and took up his aged scutum, strapped on his pugio and marched down the trail, a pilium in one hand and his gladius in the other. He wanted me to go with him, but in my grief, I refused. I never saw Callus again, not him, not his armor, not his weapons. It was as if he had been swallowed up by the ground, as if Pluto had come up and taken him, wiped him off the face of the earth itself."

"Quintus went mad with fear, he fled into the hills, into the caves, he thought that would protect him, that the caves would be a defensible position. He never once considered that they might actually be home to the beast he was trying to hide from. The villagers found him spread thin across the hills, an ear here, an eye there, his intestines wrapped through the forest like twine. We gathered what we could and set it to burn on a funeral pyre."

"The next morning the weather broke. Spring came and the waters around the island were suddenly thick with fish. We caught more than we could eat and reveled in our sudden good fortune. We had survived the winter where others had not. But the losses I had suffered through that winter had broken me. Things were never the same between myself and the Kallakberii. I became an outsider living among them, obsessed with only one thing—the creature called Gathoga."

"You learned its secrets, its weaknesses. You learned enough how to kill it!" Lucius was suddenly ecstatic.

Petri shook his head, "I learned enough that I didn't need to, that I didn't want to. After the winter passed the creature became more docile— or at least less aggressive—it stayed well away from the village. It built a den, multiple dens actually, and rarely used the same one once a week. It took to hibernating for long periods of time, through summer and winter, it emerged only to feed. I learned it wasn't strictly a carnivore. It only killed on rare occasions. It prefers fish. It can run faster than anything else I've ever seen, and swim like a porpoise. It is larger than a bear, but its skin is like that of a rhinoceros or elephant. The claws on its feet are as long as daggers. It has a tail, spiked along its length, its primarily used for swimming, but it can be a formidable weapon on its own. And it's smart, incredibly smart. Smarter than a dog, smarter than a cat. Smarter than some legionnaires. It may be the deadliest thing I've ever seen."

He paused then, and Lucius took the opportunity to laugh heartily, "A good tale old man, a very good tale, but my men and I aren't afraid of legends and tall tales. Don't worry, we don't intend on being here that long, and if we do decide to come back it'll be to build a fort and house a garrison. That means money and food and civilization for these savages. It'll be the best thing that ever happened to them."

Petri shook his head and opened his mouth to speak, but Lucius wouldn't let him say a word. "You'll show us where we can camp for the night, and then in the morning you'll go over our charts with us, show us where the settlements on the mainland are. You do this, and we'll be gone in a few days, and I'll try to forget that this place ever existed."

I couldn't tell if Lucius was telling the truth or just telling Petri what he wanted to hear. Not that it mattered, things didn't exactly work out the way he had planned.

The winter storm that had blown us of course and forced us to take shelter finally overtook us. It lashed us with freezing winds and icy torrents with a ferocious strength that our tents were no match for. The villagers took pity on us and allowed us to occupy their halls and homes. It might be worth saying that when Lucius asked for this favor his hand was on his sword. On the third day the storm finally blew itself out and legionnaires and villagers alike crawled out like worms soaked and desperate for the sun. It didn't take long for us to learn that our ship had been destroyed by fallen trees, and that much of our foodstuffs which had been stored within or in our tents, had been lost to the rain. In short, we were suddenly low on supplies and stranded on an island where we were not at all welcome.

It was Petri who took stock of our situation, though I think Lucius was aware of it instinctually. The village had not been well-provisioned for the winter. There was enough food to get them through, but not enough for the thirty mouths who had suddenly joined them, not for thirty extra mouths that belonged to hungry legionnaires. Petri immediately set us all to half rations and set the best hunters and fishers to their tasks. He also set himself and a few others to the job of repairing our ship. It would never be a warship again, but it could be made seaworthy, at least somewhat. If Gathoga came, this might be our only way to escape its wrath.

Lucius had a different perspective. He refused to let the men work on the ship, and instead seized control of the largest and most well-built lodge and set his men to work inside. I as a mere scribe, was not allowed access, and the men would not speak of what they were doing. But, from the vast quantities of stone and dirt that were being moved and the number of thin branches and stout poles that were being harvested and shaped, I began to have an inkling of what was going on. They worked for more than a week, and afterward Lucius moved himself and all the other legionnaires into their new barracks. It had been reinforced both inside and out, and the entrances had been reduced to a single large gate at the front. This was comprised of two doors built from logs a foot wide each and barred in place by similarly large pieces of timber. The whole enterprise had made the Kallakberii moody. We should have been helping lay in supplies, but instead we had become an occupying force consuming more than our fair share of resources, driving the whole community towards lean times far sooner than they expected.

It was by my count, the ninety-seventh day after our arrival on the island that the first soldier, a man named Valen, turned up missing. They found his helmet on the trail to village midden. There was a trail of blood that went on for a hundred yards, and then it stopped. Lucius had the men search for hours, but to no avail. Gathoga had finally come for those who did not belong on the island, and Valen was just the beginning. Over the next two days we would lose three more comrades, all without anyone seeing anything, without any screams, with little to no evidence that they ever even existed. Lucius demanded explanations from the Kallakberii, but they didn't speak our language. They couldn't understand us, let alone answer any of our questions. No matter how badly we beat them or threatened their children. Only Petri was responsive to our demands, but he just kept telling us the same thing, that Gathoga had come, and he would kill us all.

He said this as he hung from the center of the barracks hall, strung up by a rope, his mouth little more than a bruise, the skin around his eye beaten until it was nearly the same color as his tattoo. His blood had pooled up on the roughly hewn wooden floor. Lucius spit in his face, "Let it come." He walked away a look of anger masking the fear that seethed in his breast. "Let your monster come for us, we are legionnaires of Rome, and we fear nothing." A low cheer went up around the great room, but I could see the older more experienced soldiers, and in their eyes was worry and trepidation.

The Island of the Galthoga

It was hours later that the attack came. It came by night, when all but the sentries were asleep. The guard outside screamed, and we all bolted upright from our blankets grabbing our weapons. Even I, who was not trained as much as would have liked to be, grabbed my dagger and assumed a defensive position. As I did there came from the other side of the gate a terrible clattering sound. This was followed by a muffled scream and then the easily recognizable sound of an armored body being thrown against the front gate. The creature roared, and it was a sound unlike any I had ever heard before. There was something of a lion about it, but also the screeching calls of a carrion bird, and the low grumble of a bear. It snuffled at the gate and then pushed on it.

The doors flexed slightly, and Lucius ordered six men to reinforce it with extra poles. As they did this he turned to the rest of the men and ordered them into position. I expected them to form up in the center of the room, but instead they took up stations along the walls. Their shields up, their spears raised. Seconds later the primary bar to the door snapped and threw splinters across the room. The only thing holding the door shut were the extra poles and the six men that held them. Even from across the room I could see the terror in their eyes. They had dug their boots into the ground and found footing where the dirt floor had been replaced with hewn logs. A piece of the gate broke away and from out of the dark a massive paw reached in and tried to claw at whatever was keeping it out. Lucius nodded to a nearby soldier and his spear was suddenly in the air and then instantly buried in the flesh of the creature's arm. It screamed in rage and its flailing tore the door open wider. Lucius ordered the men to ready themselves and then with an almost serene sense of calm he ordered the gatekeepers to let the beast in.

The six dropped their beams and dashed for cover but the beast burst in with an explosive rage. The one side of the gate came free of its hinges and caught half of the fleeing men in the back. They stumbled and disappeared beneath its weight as the beast came in. It was larger than I had thought possible. Larger than a rhino, but smaller than an elephant. It crushed the fallen gate and the men beneath it with its weight, snapping beam and bone and weapon as if they were twigs. With its undamaged claw it swung out at one of the gatekeepers that had managed to avoid the debris and with a single swipe it took half his head off. He fell, blood gurgling from what was left of his mouth, his brains spilling across the floor.

I had expected our forces to attack, but Lucius ordered them to hold their positions and they listened to him, almost hugging the wall. They stood there cowering behind their shields, but the spears at the ready. The only person that wasn't along the edge was Petri. He was still hanging there in the center of the room, beaten and bleeding, but even in his daze he could see the creature as it took cautious steps into the lodge. "Get out," he whispered through shattered teeth. The beast paused and snorted angrily but then took another step. Petri struggled against his bonds. "Stop," he yelled, "don't come any closer," there was desperation in his voice. But the beast wasn't having any of it. Cautiously, angrily, it padded into the center of the room ignoring Petri's pleas.

It was only when the creature was mere feet away from the hanging figure that Lucius found voice and gave the order "NOW!"

All around the room the shields dropped, and spears were turned and plunged down into the floor. I could hear ropes and bindings snapping as a hidden network of supports and cabling was suddenly cut. In an instant the supports for the floor fell away and the thin wooden façade fell away, and with it the creature as well. It did not go down without fighting. It swung out as its rear feet dropped away. With its one paw, the spear still sticking out of it, it swatted at Petri and tore him and the ropes that bound him down from the ceiling. Together they fell into the pit, the pit Lucius had dug over the course of weeks and filled with wooden spikes. Gathoga screamed in agony as it was pierced in a dozen places by spikes as thick as my arm. Blood spurted in great founts as the thing flailed in agony.

I could see Lucius smile as his plan came to fruition and he gave the order for his soldiers to attack. The legionnaires marched forward and with practiced precision launched their spears into the suffering monstrosity. It was a slaughter. In moments the thing was covered in blood and gore. In a great heave it collapsed, and its breast ceased to heave with breath. We stood there surrounding the pit watching the blood pool around the dead demon and the man who had warned us about it. I don't know where it began but from somewhere a cheer of success welled up and filled the room and echoed out into the night.

An hour later we were outside. Great bonfires had been lit, and the Kallakberii had been roused and gathered. From inside the hall Lucius came and with him he carried the head of Gathoga. There in the light, we could see the horns and the tusks, the fangs and the terrible black eyes surrounded by scales. It was the first good look at the thing I had gotten, and I saw something, something that I doubt Lucius had seen. It was there under the blood and gore, a splash of color. That I dashed forward to see more of, but before I could Lucius roared and threw his trophy into the roaring flames.

"Your demon is dead," he pronounced as if they could understand him, "you are free now, and safe!"

But all around us the Kallakberii simply lowered their tattooed faces and shuffled home in a kind of despair. That didn't matter, Lucius had defeated the beast, and that was cause for joy. The wine flowed, and the formerly meager rations were turned into a celebratory feast. For the first time in long months the legionnaires were happy.

It didn't last. I knew it wouldn't, for no one else had seen what I had seen.

A week later three villagers failed to return from the forest. Their clothes and boots were found in bloody tatters scattered in various places around the island. We demanded explanations from our hosts, but they still couldn't understand our language, and we couldn't understand theirs, but we could make out one word, a word that Lucius could do nothing but deny.

"Gathoga is dead," screamed the maddened commander, "I killed him myself, I showed you his head!"

But the locals just shook their heads and muttered that sad chant that seemed to doom us all "Gathoga! Gathoga! Gathoga!"

That was five days ago. Lucius fell this morning. He was standing by the bonfire watching the sun rise. A shape, Gathoga swam out of the dying darkness of the forest and cut him across the middle. He clutched his belly and then fell to the ground, his innards spilling out in loops thick with blood. I wish I could say he died instantly, but he didn't. In fact, he died slowly. He lingered in agony for a very long time.

We took the ship, the six of us who were left, and rowed as best we could away from the island, away from the Kallakberii and their damned guardian demons. They watched as we drifted away—not the Kallakberii—the Gathoga, all three of them. They climbed the rocks around the beach and roared as we put more and more distance between us and them. We raised our swords in false bravado and cursed at them, those terrible monsters. They roared back at us and then did the unthinkable. One by one, sleek and silent they slipped into the water and began swimming toward us, faster than any animal I had ever seen.

We rowed, we put our backs into it, and strain our legs and arms. We screamed at each other and urged each other on to row for our lives. The first one leapt out of the water like a fish, like a shark or whale, and it took one of our number with it when it went back into the water. They came at us like that for an hour. Flying out of the black waters and tearing at us like raptors after vermin in a field. They whittled away at us one by one, taking us down into the sea, and leaving nothing behind.

I'm all alone now and I set this our story, the story of our death to paper so that whoever finds this ship and this record will know the truth. Of the Goddess Kallak, I can tell you nothing, but of her children—the Kallakberii—and the Gathoga, their guardians, I can tell you this. For only I know the truth, only I saw it there in the firelight—the markings across the face of the monster—the Gathoga. The same kind of markings borne by those three monstrosities that have slaughtered the last of my friends. They aren't just markings though.

That thing that Lucius killed, the first Gathoga, it had the same tattoo that old Petri had on his face. Gods help us, it was his own daughter, that monstrous chimera was Petri's own daughter. And we slaughtered her right in front of her own father.

They've crawled aboard the ship. The planks creak under their weight. They're coming for me. Pawing at the door, scratching at it. Looking for a way in. I suppose it's what I deserve, it's what we all deserved.

The Collection of Gibson Flynn

G ibson Flynn came to the city of Vizcaya for the books. His job teaching Comparative Literature at Miskatonic University was only a job, and only a means to an end. His passion in life was his collection of books, first editions, preferably signed. A college town like Arkham had a plethora of used bookstores catering to students and professors alike, and even had a small annual literary festival, but Vizcaya was a metropolis and in Flynn's opinion had some of the best book shopping in America. Flynn thought it was because of the demographics; the old came to Florida to die, they came from the Northeast, the Midwest, Canada and even Europe. They came for the sun and the heat, and brought with them all their precious things, including books.

Then of course there was the annual festival. Few cities could compete with the Vizcaya International Literary Expo, it flooded the town with dealers from across the country for three days, filling five city blocks with more pages of literature than could ever have been read. Not quite as large as the National Book Fair or similar shows in Los Angeles and Chicago, VILE still drew hundreds of authors from all over the world, based on two synergistic factors: timing and location. Vizcaya in November brought in authors from North America and Europe looking for a last brief vacation before the dying summer gave way to impending winter. It was also a time when publishers had a desire to showcase their new books in advance of the holiday shopping season. The two forces combined to bring some of the best names in the literary world to a crossroads of the world, where North met South, and Anglo met Hispanic. With the presence of big-name authors came serious book collectors and some serious book dealers.

For Gibson, whose hobby of collecting had begun to border on mania, it was three days of pure joy, seeking out signatures and rare books to add to his collection, hopefully at bargain prices. It was an annual pilgrimage, and Gibson not only longed for the event, but the afterglow as well. Whatever he found over the next few days would become part of his collection, and he would sit in his study and bask in the beauty of his ever-expanding shelves. They were part of him, he cared for his books, cleaned them, categorized them, insured them, made sure they were safe. He belonged to them as much as they belonged to him, and everybody knew it. There had been offers from other collectors, all refused of course, the Collection of Gibson Flynn wasn't a thing that could be bought or sold, once he made something part of his collection, it was almost impossible for him to let anything go, even if he found a better, more desirable copy.

Weaving his way through the Friday morning crowds, Gibson dodged the rows of delusional self-published authors with cover art by three-year olds, dodged chiropractors and clinical psychologists and their free informational booklets, turned a deaf ear to the pale college student in dreadlocks who wanted to tell him all about the government's vaccine conspiracy, and skillfully danced through a boisterous retinue of Hare Krishnas, before pausing at the first actual book stall. He gave most booths little more than a cursory investigation. For the most part, the books he was looking for, the things that he would pay for weren't to be found amongst the tents hawking remainders and cheap reprints of Austen and Melville. Not to say that he hadn't had some success in such venues in the past. In 2002 a little shop bearing the name Paper Cuts, had thrilled him by having a complete three-volume set of The Collected Works of Robert Blake. Gibson had gladly paid the $30 asking price and never bothered to show the proprietor the inside of the back cover, where the last page announced that this set was #6 of 300 just above where a cancelled check signed by Blake had been tipped in. Similarly in 2006 he had come across The Miskatonic River Valley, part of the WPA's documentation of American rivers, not something he was particularly interested in, but he bought it for $2.00 flat and then was able to trade it for a $75 volume of poetry Burrowers Beneath signed by the author Georg Reuter Fischer.

Gibson was proud of finding these books; they were excellent additions to his collection, but the core of his library were pieces by British writers in the Weird Tradition; Arthur Machen, Gerard Kersh, and of course Errol Undercliffe. Flynn had a signed first edition of *The*

Man Who Feared to Sleep, and the revised corrected editions edited by renowned scholar Mick Neumann. These sat proudly on his shelves next to the collected five volumes of Undercliffe's pseudonymous novelizations of early British horror films, *The House of Hammer*. He also had the Miskatonic University Press edition of Undercliffe's newspaper columns on life in Brichester The Inhabitant at the Lake. By far however, his proudest piece was an original postcard crammed with Undercliffe's distinctively miniscule and somewhat indecipherable handwriting sent to pulp writer Randolph Carter's publisher, Undercliffe would have been ten at the time. Gibson had always been pleased with finding this particular missive as its contents were not included in any of the five volumes of The Collected Letters to Randolph Carter. This was what drove Gibson to the book fair; it's why he haunted bookshops and flea markets, and why he was always on the hunt for more books by Undercliffe and his disciples. Not that he found much, but he found enough to keep him happy, and if you didn't look you definitely wouldn't find anything.

A banner caught his eye, a booth simply named Fine Bindings, it held shelf after shelf of books bound in leather and trimmed in gold. Gibson wandered in and systematically scanned the titles for anything of interest. Most of the titles were in Spanish, some in Latin, a few in French, nothing in English, and therefore nothing he was interested in. He politely nodded to the owner and ducked back into the crowd. He made two more stops, one place called Papyrus another The Tattered Paige, both proved fruitless. Thankfully he had some success at his third stop, Cover to Cover where he found a handsome copy of Edward Pickman Derby's Azathoth and Others. It took him a few minutes, but he was able to convince the proprietor to drop the price from seventy dollars to fifty.

Around the corner Gibson was overjoyed to see that one of his favorite dealers was back in their usual spot. Dead Ink Books occupied two hundred square feet of tent space at the juncture of the two main thoroughfares of the show near the entrance to the Antiquarian Annex. Originally specializing in out-of-print weird fiction; the little shop had over the years expanded into carrying affordable classics as well as hypermodern first editions by the best-selling authors of the year. The owner was a stout fellow with an olive complexion and a thick beard, whom everyone called Font. Whether Font was his first name, his last name, or some sort of nickname, Gibson wasn't sure. What he did know was that Dead Ink Books was one of the finest dealers at the fair, and maintained a reputation for excellent selection, acceptable pricing, and customer service. Gibson was also unavoidably attracted by the shop's name being derived from Randolph Carter's last novel *The Silverfish Plague*. The relevant quote was posted on a huge piece of poster board at the entrance to the tent.

Writing, whether it be fact or fiction, poetry or prose, is a fundamental act of procreation. As with all such acts, most do not bear fruit, and others are thankfully aborted or stillborn. Of those literary offspring that are midwived through birth to publication, too many are malformed perversions of literature, and too few are euthanized. Of those that go into the world, only a minority will achieve success and only a rare handful will achieve the immortality so often dreamt of by their creators. Most books have ephemerally short lives. Some may drag their allotted spans through multiple printings, and even rejuvenate themselves through desperate but degenerative reissues. Yet, though some must be mercifully smothered and still others must be viciously snuffed out, the vast majority of books go quietly, peacefully, out-of-print. If publication of a book is birth, then out-of-print must surely be a literary death. Yet strangely, these books persist, dead yet not dead, haunting secondhand shops and libraries like forgotten ghosts, dreaming of past lives and future resurrections. It is not unheard of; some books do come back into print. Yet most will wait forever, undead books with tattered jackets, broken spines, moldy and half-chewed pages, once so full of life, now nothing more than ... dead ink.

Under the tent, and out of the sun, Gibson took off his glasses and made for a set of shelves marked Collectibles. He passed over signed copies of Sex in the City and The Da Vinci Code, paused briefly at the leather and gold bound copy of Dune with a bookplate signed by Frank Herbert, and then moved on. A first edition of Cold Mountain didn't even rate a pause, and Gibson snorted at a mis-shelved copy of Morrell's First Blood. Next to the Morrell, Gibson paused and suppressed a sudden gasp. The book was thin, less than a hundred pages and bound in a cream-colored cloth that had seen better days, but the name on the spine was still clear and as he gently tugged the volume off the shelf his eyes grew wide, and he smiled slightly.

In his hand Gibson held a handsome copy of Zorad Ethan Hoag's only book Dreams From R'lyeh. Gibson had only ever seen one other copy before, in the Special Collections room at Arkham State College. Hoag had published the thing himself in a run of apparently only a hundred copies, each one signed. When they didn't sell the author began giving them out as gifts to friends and family, most of whom were so distraught by the contents that they either returned it or destroyed the volume outright. When Hoag died, his distant cousins sold the remaining copies with the rest of Hoag's books to a junk man who eventually passed the lot on to the local library. What had happened after that was unknown, but it was always assumed that the vast majority had been lost during a fire in the library warehouse.

Gibson took care, handling the book gently and slowly opened the cover, he confirmed the presence of Hoag's signature and noted the neatly penciled in price of $200. He sighed; for such a rare find he would have paid double that. As he examined the book, he suddenly stalled, for in the lower corner of the first front end page there was a circular embossed stamp from a previous owner. Gibson cursed at the idiot who dared to mar such a lovely item with evidence of his own fleeting ownership, but then did a quick double take as the text of the embossment resolved itself. He blinked and read the tiny, raised curve of letters again. Then he straightened up and with a look of wonder and joy on his face caught the eye of Font the proprietor.

The man was smirking and gently nodding his head. Causally he took a few steps and joined Gibson. "Nice, isn't it?"

Gibson made a gesture of disbelief. "Where did you find it?"

Font pondered for a moment and then as if it was nothing, as if it were the most common of occurrences said, "I picked it up a few days ago in a shop a few blocks away, a seedy place, mostly filled with tattered junk and loose pages. Nothing really worth looking at, I don't even know why I went in there myself."

Gibson digested these words, chewed on them, let them roll around and work their way into his brain. He was holding a book that had once belonged to Errol Undercliffe, a book that bore his stamp, which had once been touched, perhaps even read by the man. It was too much to take in. Suddenly Gibson Flynn felt weak in the knees, his throat closed up and with great effort he stammered out "Can you tell me exactly where?"

A few moments later he was moving back through the crowds, the small volume of poetry wrapped in plastic and his wallet two hundred dollars lighter. He was following Font like a puppy on a leash. Where Gibson had weaved through the crowds Font barreled, cutting a path like a linebacker in front of a quarterback. They traversed city blocks, moving further and further from the center of the festival, down past the point of respectability, where even poor college students didn't bother to go. Font stopped at a street corner and gestured at a dilapidated storefront that sat at the edge of an empty field. He pointed and then hustled back down the street leaving Flynn alone.

He made his way across the street; there was a line of homeless men sitting on the side of the building. They all wore that same ubiquitous outfit that marked them not only as destitute but mentally ill as well. They wore faded hoodies and track paints, with their arms bandaged from where they had presumably picked at their scabs, or injection points. They were rocking back and forth, each to his own beat, mumbling nonsense words that no one, not even they, could understand.

Flynn gave them a wide berth and walked through the open door. The first thing he noticed was the smell. Old books have a distinct odor, a woody, dry scent like a house with termites. Then there was the sign, nothing fancy just a piece of canvas with hand painted letters that said Ephemerrata. There were piles of paper everywhere. One table was covered with books with broken bindings, another had stacks of sheet music. There was a long box of comics sitting next to tomato cases filled with vintage paperbacks. In a corner an oversized pile of clothes hid a pudgy little man with round glasses and a shock of grey hair.

The proprietor sucked down on his lower lip and stood up. "My name is Pike. I own this place. You looking for something special?" He slurred a little as he spoke.

"Gibson, Gibson Flynn. Another dealer said he found this here." Flynn unwrapped the book and showed it to the odd little man. "I was hoping you had similar pieces?"

The man nodded and sidled over to one of the many unmarked shelves and pulled down a thick folio sized volume wrapped in tanned leather with gilt trim and embossed letters down the side. Wear had taken its toll on the piece and whatever had once been written down the spine was now illegible. He laid it down on a table and slowly opened it up.

"The Qanoon-e-Islam, not to be confused with Jaffur Surreef's book of the same name, is attributed to the 10th century Persian philosopher and scientist Ibn e Sina, though this is likely apocryphal. Printed in Madrid and dated 1622, bound in goat skin with gold trim and superb craftsmanship, only eight copies documented to exist." The man said these words as if Gibson Flynn should know them, should care. "The Spanish text is printed in Carolingian. Richly illustrated it appears to be a catalog of pre-Islamic myths and monsters found amongst the peoples of the Middle East." He flipped the pages slowly and repeatedly paused to display several illustrations of macabre creatures. "The last page bears the marks of several previous owners including one in Spanish two in French and four in English. Most notable are the wax stamp of renowned colonialist Joseph Curwen one of the founders of Miskatonic University. There's another stamp I can't identify."

Gibson Flynn shook his head. "I was looking for something more modern."

The man turned reached under a table and pulled out a wooden crate. It was piled high with the shattered remains of old leatherbound books that had seen better days. Some of these Flynn recognized. There was a bug-eaten copy of Pent and Serenade's auction catalog for the Church of the Starry Wisdom library, and then a folio that looked like a copy of the Jarrow and Marshall translation of The Pnakotic Manuscripts. There was even a small pamphlet, a photocopy of Dunnes' dictionary of the Tamsiqueg language. There was a sudden sound of exclamation and the bookseller wrenched free a bent and battered volume, the cover of which had long since faded.

"This was in the same lot." Hissed the man.

Flynn took the book. It was dirty, grimy, and unpleasant to the touch. It stank of mildew. There had been words on the cover once, but they had been worn away long ago. He opened it carefully and at the first page gasped uncontrollably in joy. The page was water stained and torn, dented just as the book had been bent. And yet, despite these flaws, despite the fact that he would have to spend a small fortune restoring it, he knew he had to have it. The first page bore the library stamp of Brichester University, below that was the hand-written name of the infamous cult leader Roland Franklyn, and next to these was the blind stamp of Errol Undercliffe, above all these in the center of the page was the title and the publisher.

In his hands Gibson Flynn was holding a copy of The Revelations of Glaaki, Volume 7: Of the Symbols the Universe Shows, edited, organized and corrected by Percy Smallbeam. Published by The Matterhorn Press. There was no date given. He flipped through the pages and found that there were penciled notes throughout, in a cramped hand he quickly recognized, they were in Undercliffe's own crabbed little script.

From what he had read Undercliffe had vanished researching Franklyn and his cult. There was something else, something about this book that was important, something that tugged at the back of Flynn's brain and made his mouth go dry. But he shrugged it off and read a passage that had been underlined on one of the pages.

> *Those who would know the unknowable truths of the universe, those who would attain the unattainable, must sacrifice all human vestments so that they may be reborn and perceive not only the unveiled nature of the universe, but of himself as well.*

It took a moment, maybe more than a moment, but Gibson Flynn knew that he had to have it, would pay anything, but he couldn't let Pike know that. His mind was racing, plotting, trying to figure out how to negotiate with the man. Finally, he stuttered out "How much?"

The queer bookseller puffed up to full height and with a voice full of pride announced, "I'm sorry, it's not for sale."

Flynn's eyes grew wide, "If it's a matter of money … "

Pike waved his hand. "I'll be glad to let you have it, but my price has nothing to do with money. I need you to do something for me, things actually. I need you to run some errands." He handed Flynn a list. "Visit these addresses, get what they have waiting for me. The shop closes at six, but I'll be here waiting for you till midnight." Flynn looked at the list. "Can you do this?" He rested his hand on the book. "Can you do this, for this book?"

He nodded.

It took thirty minutes for Flynn to walk the ten blocks to one of the shadier sides of Vizcaya, and he dodged street people begging for change the whole way. From the outside his destination appeared to be a crumbling warehouse that even a fresh coat of paint couldn't hide. The interior matched the exterior and was dimly light by flickering lights high up in the rafters. Row after row of shelves held video tapes, DVDs, and blue ray discs, while an acre of tables was filled with boxes of magazines. Along the walls books of all sizes lined makeshift shelves. The Discrete Man billed itself as the largest purveyor of gently used adult material in the state, and Gibson had no reason to doubt the claim, though he could not think of any other store exactly like it. He noted the gangly cashier with grey skin and sunken eyes reading a trashy paperback and casting occasional glances at the quiet, furtive men who roamed the aisles. He took a moment to get his bearings and then made for the cashier.

"I'm supposed to pick up a package."

The man with grey skin gestured toward an office marked Manager. "She's waiting for you."

Flynn didn't like the way the floor felt beneath his feet, he didn't like the way the air smelled, and he hesitated as he turned the handle and went through the door. She was waiting there for him, sitting on the gunmetal desk that occupied most of the room. She was the largest single person Flynn had ever seen, and she wore nothing but a thin silk dressing gown that hid nothing. Fat rolls on her arms ballooned and deflated as she waved him in. Her four chins shook with each breath. It was heard to tell where breast ended, and fat began.

"You've come for these," she offered him a brown paper bag a few inches thick. He balked at it. "Go ahead honey, take it, have a look inside. You should know what you've come for."

He slid the contents out and found himself looking at a stack of porn magazines from the early seventies. Nothing fancy, a publication called Knight. A memory flashed inside his mind. He checked the dates of the issues and realized what he was holding. Six issues of the 1972 run of Knight each contained an early story by now infamous, hardboiled crime writer Georg Starch. Most copies went for a hundred dollars or more, and Flynn was holding a complete set. He slid them back inside the paper bag.

"Thank you." He went to leave but her gravelly voice called him back.

"You've got to pay for those." She said.

"I'm sorry?"

"I told you," she dropped to her knees before him, the floor creaked beneath her weight, "you should know what you've come for."

As she worked to arouse him, he tried but failed to control himself.

The acrid taste of vomit filled his throat and nose and spilled out all over the floor. She didn't seem to care. In fact, it only made her work harder.

It was noon when he finally stumbled down the street, found a coffee shop with a restroom and tried to clean up. It burned as he relieved himself. He sat on the toilet in the handicapped stall and wiped himself down. There were marks, small ones, on his shaft and on the inside of both thighs. They were dark, and under the skin, like bruises, small curves and loops. They must have been from her teeth he supposed. He didn't remember, didn't want to remember, all that she had done. He scrubbed himself clean, or at least tried to.

Lunch was a tasteless slice of meatloaf covered in a thick glob of brown gravy that tasted exactly like nothing, in an entirely different way. He washed it down with a glass of bitter iced tea seasoned with some sort of artificial sweetener that made it taste like industrial cleanser. It didn't matter. He didn't even wait for the bill. He just threw a twenty on the table and left.

All that mattered was completing the errands laid out for him.

All that mattered was the next address.

All that mattered was the book.

He needed the book.

He would do anything for the book.

How much worse could the next address be?

It was a private home, in a nice neighborhood. The lawn was well kept, as were the roses. The man who answered the door was small, thin, and old, he didn't speak, he just let Flynn inside. It wasn't until the door shut that Flynn realized the man was wearing a spiked dog collar. The inside of the house was dark, but clean and well furnished, if a bit out of date. It was too clean, too tidy, and too perfect. Flynn realized it was only a stage, a front for something else.

The stairs in the basement were lit by a string of white holiday lights. There was plastic sheeting hanging on the walls and coating the floors. There was a house hanging on the wall. In the center of the room was a plastic kiddie pool. In the pool there was a woman, naked, young, bound and gagged. There was a stench, a stink that made Flynn choke. It wasn't water in the pool.

The man handed Flynn a stack of paperbacks, six trashy science fiction novels the Chronus Triumphant series, written by Michael Diamond. He had heard of these, they were space opera in the vein of Burroughs, ER not Bill, with a heavy dose of bondage and sado-masochism. The subtext supposedly promoted a philosophy of voluntary servitude for women. Flynn took them.

"Susan's pool needs to be topped off." The man smiled. "You need a drink?"

Flynn walked over to the pool. The smell of urine burned his eyes. He undid his fly and closed his eyes. He concentrated on the sound of his stream as it splashed into the pool. He tried to ignore the moans of ecstasy that emanated from the woman at his feet. The man watched and laughed.

The burning sensation was gone, but the marks had spread, expanded. They were forming patterns now, lines, straight lines, spreading out from his groin, down his legs, on to his belly. They ached, but Flynn didn't care. He needed the book. He would do anything for that book. It didn't matter what was happening to him. Whatever it was could be taken care of on Monday with a shot of antibiotics. Right now, all he wanted was the book. Nothing else mattered.

An hour later he was at a bondage club, standing there in the center of a room in his Hawaiian shirt and jeans, surrounded by men and women in leather and latex, all of whom were watching him. There was a whip in his hand, and a naked eighteen-year-old girl before him. With each lash a welt appeared and blossomed into bloody lines that dripped down the small of her back and between her cheeks. He whipped her again and again and again until those drips became a stream. He crawled between her legs and let the blood pool in his mouth. It was warm and salty and as it trickled down his throat the people watching applauded. He walked out with an inscribed copy of the novel Hung by Leonard Chris.

His next stop was a restaurant that catered to coprophages where he was given a three-course meal. Afterwards as he sipped Greek coffee from English bone china his host handed him a copy of Dwyer's guide to underground lifestyles. Before he left, he paused to use the restroom. The marks had grown clearer and more discernable, and they had spread. Lines moved out of his groin in chains of queer loops and lines. Some of them almost looked like letters.

It was half past nine when he entered the last address. It was a butcher shop. He was taken into the back. They undressed him. They cut his clothes from him with surgical scissors. They washed him, gently. Scrubbing the flecks of vomit and piss and shit from his skin. There was a bowl of warm oil, and they anointed him with it. Coating him from head to toe. It smelled of myrrh and sandalwood.

In the candlelight the marks nearly glowed beneath his skin, long strands of them. They were letters, and words, and sentences. If he stared at them long enough, he could almost read them. But whatever they said didn't make any sense.

But it didn't matter.

The butchers bound his hands and from these bonds hung him from a hook. They slid a basin beneath his feet. They shoved a gag in his mouth and tied it behind his head. He felt a pinprick, a needle in his arm. And then his arm went numb, and his legs went numb, and then he couldn't feel anything at all.

But he could watch.

He watched the knives slice into his flesh, and peel it back. He watched the long lines of nonsense words be sliced off of him like a master chef might trim some fat. He watched as the butchers held the thin membranes that had once belonged to him up to the candlelight. He saw the shadows cast upon the wall and suddenly the nonsense words made sense. They had been inverted before. Now free from his body they could be read, understood even. It took more than an hour to flay the skin off of him, but in the end, it didn't matter, whatever they had given him, he didn't care anymore.

This was the final task. The book was almost his.

They wrapped him in bandages and salve and then gave him a hoodie and a pair of cotton track pants. He wasn't completely skinless, far from it. They had only taken thirty or forty percent of him. He would live. They handed him his own skin, laid out on stretchers so that it could be read. They had scraped the fat off of it, and quick cured it. In some ways it looked like a page from a book that had been sent through a shredder and then reassembled using bacon grease for glue.

He put it in his backpack along with all the other things he had gathered and limped away. Each step was filled with agony, but he didn't care, his tasks were complete, the book was his.

It was just before midnight when he finally made it back to the shop. The book dealer was waiting for him, smiling. It was a crooked smile, almost evil. As Flynn handed over each item, he made a queer little sound of glee that made Flynn think of a pig. When the last item was exchanged the man drew in his breath as if he was gasping for air.

"Well done my friend, well done." He handed him a brown paper bag. Flynn knew that what was inside. He had done it. "The seventh volume of The Revelations of Glaaki was his. "A deal is a deal. You certainly earned this."

Flynn clutched the book to his chest and smiled. "A deal is a deal." He turned and took a step or two toward the door.

"Don't you want to know?" Called the bookseller.

Flynn stopped and slowly turned. "Know what?"

The dirty little man waved the skein of skin at him. "What this is? What it's for?"

Flynn closed his eyes and moaned in frustration and agony. He wanted to say no. He needed to say no. But he couldn't. "Of course, I want to know!"

So, then the man showed him.

It was in the backroom. The pages hung from the walls and the ceiling, some were like his and still in skeins holding them together, others were more cohesive and no longer needed any supporting framework.

"He speaks to us through the book. It's one of the few copies left in the world, and he needs it restored. He needs all nine volumes rewritten; he needs the world to know the truth."

"Who?" sputtered Flynn through his aching lips.

The man stared at him as if he had said the stupidest thing ever. "Our God of course, Glaaki." He stared a little harder. "You can hear him, can't you?"

And of course, Gibson Flynn could. He could hear that whispering, hissing voice that spoke not to his ears or his mind, but to his very cellular structure. Those whispers, those words, they were changing him, they had already changed his skin, produced the words and sentences that had been flayed away from his body.

"You have a choice now Mister Flynn. You can take that book, as I've said you've earned it. You can take that book and add it to your collection, and in a few days that voice you hear will fade, and eventually you'll heal, and forget all about what happened this day. You'll have your collection; you'll always have your collection."

"Or?"

"Stay here, listen to the voice, amplify it, help it help us. Be part of something bigger than your own collection."

Flynn looked at the page that hung before him and read the words that had been grown there on what had once been human skin.

The Revelations of Glaaki
Reconstituted and Harvested
by Walter Pike

He read those words and thought about what they meant, and what the queer little man's offer really entailed. It's not like he had much choice in the matter. The proprietor, Pike led him outside and sat him on the side of the shop with all the other disciples. He could hear them all now, make out their words, understand what they were saying, and how soon the spoken words of each one would manifest on their flesh. When the time came, they would go to the butcher and have the pages harvested.

Flynn found a spot. It took a few moments but finally he heard the whispering voice clearly. He heard the words, found their rhythm and began amplifying them. He thought back to the pages that had hung in the back room. Rocking back and forth he counted the moments, waiting for his body to bring forth the word of God, of Glaaki. It was good to be part of something. It was truly a beautiful work, a fine collection, and more so than ever before it was his, and he was it. He closed his eyes and strained to hear the whispering that permeated his body.

Soon he would be an even greater part of the collection.

A *Man of Letters*

by Marcus Theodore Page

Arkham: Witch Hill Press, 20**. $49.95, Hardcover, 400 Pages
Reviewed by E. P. Fyte

It should be obvious to regular readers of my reviews that I am not a fan of the fiction written by Marcus Page. I found his novel <u>Dark of Night</u> pretentious and derivative of the worst parts of Robert Blake and Ward Phillips. I called Page's <u>A Mourning Shadow</u> "a solemn letter from a love-stricken teen with an Oedipal complex". His short story collection <u>Whispering Shades</u> was a juvenile exercise in literary hero worship and imitation, that despite its immaturity, likely garnished the kind of toxic attention he so obviously was in pursuit. In my mind Marcus Page had been set on the shelf with Chalmers, Denbrough, Undercliffe and others who have afflicted the public with their overly dramatic and self-indulgent prose.

So, it came as some surprise when editor Kate Lynn sent me <u>A Man of Letters</u> Page's posthumously published account of his last days at Carter House. When I asked why she would send a copy of the manuscript to me, Lynn bluntly informed me that the cover letter to the manuscript conveyed Page's request that I be the first and only critic to review his final literary work. Written as a reluctant journal, <u>A Man of Letters</u> provides sufficient evidence to suggest Page was slowly descending into what can only be described as type clinical depression. Exacerbated by a diagnosed neurological disorder, the associated medication, alcohol abuse, creative process issues and financial concerns, it is clear the isolation of the Carter House and the events that occurred, or were at least presented by Page to have occurred, were responsible for his being crushed under a fallen bookcase. Lynn's introduction makes it clear that Page's death was ruled an accident, but I have my doubts. That the manuscript was posted on the day of his death, makes me think that Page had come to realize that his end in some manner or other was inevitable.

Technically authorship of A Man of Letters, should be shared by both Page and the scholar Jo Shea. Shea spent considerable time at the estate while writing her biography of Randolph Carter, and apparently amassed a history of the Carter House, including a record of odd events associated with the property spanning nearly four centuries. Page incorporated a significant number of these events into his journal, counter playing them against his own odd experiences while staying at the estate. That A Man of Letters may be classified as fiction, non-fiction, memoir, or history may be meaningful to critics and scholars, many of which will attempt to pigeonhole it as a Carterian weird tale, or a Snellian paranormal apologetic, but in my humble opinion Page has created a new classic for fans of the weird to marvel at.

Much of this book is about writing and the act of writing, it is also about the limits of the first-person narrative as it relates to the truth. Page reminds us that "Tales in the first-person narrative are told from memory, and therefore by definition are unreliable." Such is the relationship between the reader and the narrative in A Man of Letters. It is plain that Page, given his mental state is far from a reliable narrator. Moreover, Page through his actions makes us doubt him and all his statements; he refuses to discuss certain past events; he drinks heavily, and he abuses his medication. Most telling, he claims to be unable to produce any fiction while staying at Carter House, but when his partner the artist Clive Bayer confronts him with a new story "Hollow Words", written in Page's own hand, Page insists that he has no memory of writing it.

It is in a state of complete distrust of Page, that readers are presented with a series of events which may be interpreted as evidence of preternatural forces at work in the house or more importantly the estate as a whole. The first of these is an attempt by Page and Clive to walk from the house to a nearby store, which is just a mile away. That the two men are unable to accomplish this task, a task Page was previously able to accomplish alone, results in a passage reminiscent of Blake's The Labyrinth of Naught or Lindsay's Picnic at Hanging Rock. Such tales in which a simple mundane task is made fantastic by the apparent intervention of some malignant force that prevents its completion, has become a common literary trope, but Page's reliance on it here can be excused by the significant discussion that occurs between Page and Bayer acknowledging the existence of these other works and suggest they may actually have influenced how they interpreted what was happening. Interestingly, when Page offers a plausible explanation for this implausible event, the reader has by this point learned that the author's point of view is simply not to be trusted and is therefore ironically forced to side with Clive and accept that something preternatural has occurred. The reader has therefore been gently tricked into suspending disbelief.

Mirroring several themes from Koji Suzuki's Ring Trilogy, the conflict between Clive's belief that something supernaturally malevolent is occurring, and Page's unwillingness to accept such a proposition, provides the conflict that drives the majority of the narrative, and allows Page to incorporate Shea's accounts of murder, madness, and strange phenomena associated with the estate. That Page borrows heavily from events related by Shea about famed mystic Etienne-Laurent de Marigny who in his papers tells of receiving a letter from the Carter House in 1922, and then being continually plagued by letters that would turn up unopened and unread, throughout his home in the most impossible of places for the next five years, —is forgiven by the skill in which he describes how Clive's studio succumbs to the forces apparently at work in the house:

> The room was empty, except for me, and the bed and the art deco dresser, and the letters. They were everywhere, inches thick, like a blanket of moss on a forest floor. They were identical to the packet I found in my room the month before, and identical to the ones I had found in the desk in the study prior to that. They were not the least bit yellowed or brittle with age. The return address, the address of the Carter House, was handwritten in ink fresh, and crisp. The same was true of the delivery address: Mr. Marcus Page, General Delivery, Arkham, Massachusetts. Were it not for the fact that each one bore a postmark from Arkham dated in the first quarter of the Twentieth Century, they could have been written yesterday and delivered that morning. I wanted

to scream, but I didn't, I didn't make a single sound. I had been expecting this, well not this exactly, but something. After all that had happened to us, after all that I had read in Shea's manuscript, about the things that happened here in this house, something like this, it was inevitable. I shut the door, went downstairs and poured myself a drink and then another. It was hours before I realized I had lost Clive, that the house had taken him away from me, consumed him, and erased him from my life, as if he had never existed.

Some will complain that this is yet another example of a writer writing about the angst of writing, but this is only a superficial analysis of the text. Indeed, Page is talking about writing, but he is talking about a form of writing that rarely exists in these days of word processors, spell checking programs and on-line encyclopedias. Page is actually putting words on a page, putting pen to paper, and the process is very different than using electronic media, and indeed the results are different as well. The handwritten journal page serves to preserve the raw unedited and unexpurgated train of thought that flows from a writer, which in formal fiction would then be rewritten in a later draft. This manner also preserves the unexpected errors that creep and seep in, such as when Page begins to slowly succumb to a seizure and the text written during this slow failure of his faculties shows its signs. In a novel the author would describe such events and it would be made plain to the reader what was happening through heavy-handed exposition. In the journalistic style, the breakdown in spelling and syntax invokes a range of emotions in the reader—most notably a growing sense of frustration that echoes Page's own, until that is, the narrative comes to an unintelligible halt, as in Page's recollection of one of his dreams:

"Bleeding," he said, as if he had never heard the word before, as if it were from a foreign language.

"You're bleeding Clive. There's blood on your arms and legs, soaking through your clothes. You're bleeding. Why are you bleeding?"

And knowing that this was a dream, and that this conversation was nothing more than part of that dream, I can still remember what he said to me. Letting the letters fall from his fingers, letting them fall to the floor and settle around his blood-soaked feat, Clive Bayer said, "He cut me Mark, the Prince, the Sepia Prints cut me, and took my flesh, made me his."

I try to speak; I open my mouth, to ask him to explain, to tell me what he was trying to say. Thass when I feldt it, the knive inn betwen my shoulders, cutttin, takin mi flesh. Ntil, i cloud knot stann ...

If Marcus Page had written his fiction like this, perhaps he would have achieved some better notice amongst the literati.

In A Man of Letters Marcus Page has written a masterpiece. If there are to be any negative criticisms, it is perhaps one that I have complained about before. Page's characters are often indistinguishable from one another, even when they are speaking; I have found it difficult to discern one actor from another, finding instead that they often meld together into a literary gestalt not unlike the characters in a David Lynch film. However, while that is an issue in his novels, it is not so much a concern in this narrative as Page clearly acknowledges he cannot ever hope to do more than translate the other characters through memory. Consequently, while Page, Bayer, and the other characters all seem to speak with the same voice; it is because Page is speaking for them. Similarly, just as Randolph Carter's fiction was mostly devoid of any significant female presence, so is Page's final work. The only contemporaneous female figure is that of Lara Sing, the owner of Carter House, who only ever intrudes by telephone. There is of course Doctor Shea, but she is consigned to the past and we only know what little Page tells us of her. I suspect that Page's interactions with any members of the female persuasion are significantly edited, not because they are unimportant or unpleasant, but rather because Page himself is incapable of finding their voice. Thankfully, the tale we are presented does not suffer for the lack of too few women.

My only other complaint, and mind you this has nothing to do with Page's writing, but rather with the systematic and even malicious manner in which I have been the subject of an abusive viral marketing campaign. It was amusing at first, and I don't know how they do it, but I really must protest. These things are in my mail, my office, my home, even my bed.

A *Man of Letters* by Marcus Theodore Page

This constant influx of letters from the Carter House, it simply must cease.

Editor's Note: E. P. Fyte completed this review on March 12, 2008. Three days later, his home in Kingsport Massachusetts was consumed by a fire, fueled by his vast collection of books and papers. Fyte's body was completely burnt beyond recognition and identification was based on the recovery of medical implants. On August 20, 2008, Kate Lynn left her office in Arkham for lunch and was never seen again. The following spring, Lynn's Volkswagen Beetle was recovered by workers dredging the Manuxet River. While her body was not inside, her purse and identification were intact, surrounded and preserved by the mass of water-logged papers that had swollen to fill the interior of the vehicle. Clive Bayer is a successful commercial artist residing in Partridgeville, where he has been happily married since 1992. He has no recollection of ever meeting Marcus Page. Despite frequent inquiries to the publisher, Marcus Page's <u>A Man of Letters</u> has yet to be released.

Dedicated to Cailin Kiernan who inspired it.

The Battle of Arkham

The Miskatonic was burning. Something had been done to the water, not to the river, but to the water itself. Blue flames were moving across the shallows, swirling like leaves in the autumn wind. Cain didn't know what it meant, but he knew it couldn't be good, if anything, it probably meant that things were going to get worse. Probably much worse, reinforcements had been delayed, air support had been stalled because of a communication snafu and command had lost contact with the amphibious forces coming up the river. His squad was passing over the Peabody Avenue Bridge and the eerie illumination cast a strange dance of light and shadows about the ruins of the city. It was just the impetus Cain needed to reassess … well everything really.

The most merciful thing in the universe is the inability of the human mind to correlate all its contents.

Thurston's Paradigm, Cain had learned it in a class on modern philosophy, back before the war started, before thousands of years of human progress was devoured by the ravening hordes of alien hybrids. He had been a student then, an environmental engineering major, but to Cain that was a lifetime ago, and luxuries like philosophy and constructed wetlands had been replaced with energized assault weapons and radiation ablative armor.

Command had designated the area south of the river as contested territory. Truth was the University had been an enemy beachhead since day one. Intel suggested that along with similar sites in California, Oregon, Florida, London, Moscow and Tokyo, Miskatonic University had been ground zero for the invasion. Problem being that no one really recognized it as an invasion. It wasn't until the CDC and WHO had failed to contain the outbreaks that the military was called in, but by then it was too late. What had begun as a strange genetic anomaly affecting only a handful of people worldwide, had become infectious and then exploded into a battle to save not just nations, not just humans, but all life on the planet, and to hear the brains talk, maybe even the universe.

On the south side of the bridge the team moved two blocks south through the burned-out merchant district and took up defensive positions in the old Arkham Graveyard at the top of French Hill. The target, the university library, was two blocks due west, it didn't sound far, a ten-minute walk on a normal day. But normal days were long gone, and all the reports said that the area was crawling with Whateleys and worse, at least two Vugg-Shoggog. It was going to be a street fight, building to building, progress measured in the death of things that used to be human, things that used to be people, normal everyday people that had succumbed to Morgan's Syndrome. Energized assault weapons versus ten-foot-long tentacles with jaws filled with snapping teeth and weird drill like claws. Cain was in charge of a blood bath waiting to happen, all to rescue a few books from the library.

The street fight was a diversion. Despite their monstrous size, unnatural weaponry, and inhuman reasoning, the enemy had a serious weakness; their thinking was two-dimensional. The things simple couldn't rationalize fighting in multiple elevations simultaneously. Come at them from the ground alone and they would fight you to a standstill. Come at them from the sky, and the damned things would start hurling makeshift artillery forcing anything airborne to withdraw. Do both, attack with ground and air support, or even with just elevated snipers, and the Whateleys just froze, they couldn't focus their attention. They would swing wildly from one direction to another. It was as if the very concept of attacks coming from multiple elevations was completely alien to them, they just couldn't comprehend that things happening in multiple planes could be impacting them at the same instant. The brains said it had to do with how they perceived space, they thought in angular terms rather than curves. This was why their movements were always linear with sharp ninety-degree turns, like the eponymous target in the classic video game Centipede. This weakness formed the tactics for the mission at hand. Cain and his squad would assume positions on top of the hill east of the campus and initiate an assault that would draw the enemy away from the library. Amphibious forces would lend support from the river, while Special Forces were dropped from the air directly into the campus. Once the Special Forces had secured the objective they would rendezvous with the infantry on French Hill and be evacuated from there.

Static crackled from the plug in Cain's ear, a shrieking *szzzzzk*. Instinctively he reached for the spot on his back where the cable from his helmet plugged into the cylinder strapped to his back. A sudden but mild shock made his hand jerk back as the static resolved into something resembling a voice.

"Cain you have been instructed not to interfere with the communications interface."

Cain nodded slightly. "Sorry, reflex action. With radio equipment, static can indicate a loose connection."

Another spurt of static spurted into his ear and then the voice again, "We are not radios Cain, and the static is a byproduct of the translation process. There are concepts, protocols, words that have no counterpart in human languages, the translator and your brain interpret these as static, but they are not. You have been told this before. If you cannot understand that perhaps I should find another host."

"That won't be necessary Phillips. I apologize and I'll keep my hands to myself."

"You must learn Cain, *shannnntttt*." Cain winced. "Contact has been re-established with both *skrreeee* and *shrammmk*. They are in position. Romero Squad is go for engagement."

Cain signaled Romero Squad, and without a word he and the five soldiers under his command rose up to take positions and find targets with their scopes. The weapon felt good as it settled in against his shoulder and the scope engaged with his helmet display. At 200X magnification the occupants of the university grounds jumped into horrific detail.

They swarmed the campus; Cain counted more than five dozen Whateleys in the central quad alone. It was hard to believe these things were once human or at least mistaken for human. The invaders had hidden themselves in plain sight. It wasn't until the sun started tossing high energy solar flares, and the light had shifted toward indigo, that anybody started to notice that there were monsters in our midst, not even the monsters themselves had known.

Morgan's Inherited Dismorphism Syndrome, MIDS for short, had been first diagnosed amongst newborns in western Massachusetts in the late twenties and early thirties of the twentieth century. Children were born with severe teratological defects that would make thalidomide babies look comparatively normal. Doctor Morgan found dozens of kids with the most monstrous of mutations including tails, gills, hooves, tentacles, even functional mouths and eyes in places other than the kids' faces. All the kids had been born to mothers who had been raped, and Morgan theorized that the rapist had been linked to the Dunwich Event, a supposedly natural nuclear explosion that had devastated the landscape for nearly a hundred square miles. Paranormal researchers called it the American Tunguska and liked to suggest that the explosion of a flying saucer had caused the disaster. Morgan took his report to the authorities but between cleaning up the Dunwich Event, occupying the town of Innsmouth and a deadly hurricane in Florida, the Federal Government had apparently been overwhelmed. By the time action was taken most of the children and their mothers were gone, vanished into the wilderness that was depression era America.

Cain watched through the scope as a particularly large Whateley reared up its head and lashed a tentacle into the air. They were called Whateleys because that was the name Morgan gave to the man from Dunwich to whom he attributed all the rapes. Though calling Wilbur Whateley a man may have been overly generous. From the reports Cain had read Wilbur had died when a dog ripped out his throat down in the very university they were preparing to assault. Examination of the body had revealed similar teratologies, tentacles, eyes, hooves, to those found on the children. Attempts to preserve the body failed, in a matter of hours Wilbur had dissolved into nothingness. It was another trait shared by his descendants.

There was something goatish about the creatures. The eyes, the fur, the horned growths on the head reminded Cain of paintings he had seen of devils and demons. But nothing he had ever seen had ever suggested the fusion of monstrosities that formed the rest of the body. Arms and legs ending in massive elephantine hooves, tentacles springing from a body the size of a small car, tentacles ending in eyes or mouths, or spikes, or claws. No two Whateleys were ever identical, but they seemed uniform in their desire to breed and feed on anything that moved.

Cain took a deep cleansing breath and gave Romero Company the go code. He flipped the safety off and gently almost lovingly pulled the trigger of his weapon. The Tillinghast rail gun, the weapon his squad was armed with, used superconducting magnetic coils to accelerate explosive shells to supersonic velocities. The Whateleys were resistant to most small arms fire, but at supersonic velocities coupled with explosive impacts, the shells were able to penetrate armor and deliver their contents into the bodies of the enemy.

Lead was the poison of choice, and if someone had discovered that early on things might not have gotten as bad as they had after Morgan's reappeared in 2012. When the sun shifted the emergency rooms had been flooded with crazies who feared the worst was upon us. It wasn't and most of their symptoms were psychosomatic. But there was a small minority who were generally affected. Humans can't see into the ultra-violet, but dozens of people were suddenly showing up screaming that the sun had gone black. These people were the first hint of what was going on. Their eyes had the ability to detect wavelengths beyond those in the normal range of human vision. At first researchers thought this condition was the result of a genetic mutation, something linked to the mother's X-chromosome, or something in the mitochondrial DNA: Wrong on both counts. Surprisingly they found something entirely new, something they called a gammaplast, an unknown organelle that had characteristics in common with both mitochondria and plant chloroplasts, the places where energy was produced for cells. The gammaplast functioned much like a chloroplast, but instead of turning light into cellular energy, it used gamma radiation, something the sun was now emitting in significantly higher quantities.

By design, the Tillinghast shell arced through the air, if you tried to fire in a straight line the Whateleys simply moved out of the way. They were monstrously fast. Fire in arcs and they couldn't see the shell until it was too late. Cain lost count as he fired round after round into the maddening hordes that occupied the college grounds.

The gammaplast also contained a massive amount of DNA. Human chromosomal DNA is linear; with 46 chromosomes the stuff in the gammaplast is hexagonal and contains more than 300 chromosomes. This was the source of the ability to see ultra-violet. It was also the source of the changes to come; it turned men and women into Whateleys and then as they grew larger into the composite things called ...

VUGG-SHUGGOG!

DAMN IT! How had he missed that? There was a goddamned Vugg coming down the street right towards him! If Whateleys were the size of cars, then Vuggs were bigger than a city bus. The things made Whateleys look like kittens. Hell, if a Whateley got in a Vuggs way, it would tear it apart as soon as go around it. Fifty feet of living nightmare was swarming up the hill. It was a quarter mile away and moving fast. The shells were penetrating but they weren't slowing it down, the thing was too big, the lead too slow to interfere with the gammaplast and shut the thing down. In a half a minute, maybe less they would be overrun.

"Phillips, we have a Vugg. Where is that support?"

"*Shhhtnk* is inbound."

Cain took aim and fired into the primary head of the thing as it moved out of the college and made its way across Garrison Street. A heartbeat later a cluster of facial tentacles exploded in smear of green and black smoke. But in that time the thing had crossed Garrison and was now weaving up Lich Street towards his position. Less than half a block and the thing would be on them. The squad was concentrating fire but to little avail. God that thing was fast. Where was the support?

He heard it before he saw it. A buzzing sound, like a swarm of bees, it droned out all the other noises, the screams of the Whateleys, the recoil of the guns, the roar of the Vugg, all were lost as the sky filled with dozens of airborne Special Forces. No larger than a man, seven Mi-Go warriors came at the Vugg from above and behind. Cain knew that their fungoid allies repulsed some people, but to his mind they were beautiful. An oblong egg-shaped exoskeleton seemingly woven from some sort of resin, extruded a dozen crustacean-like appendages and multiple pairs of translucent wings. The head reminded Cain of a coral, or a mold, or perhaps even an exposed brain, folded and creased with a half dozen stalked sensors craning about tasting the world more than seeing it.

As the Vugg reared up to strike at the Mi-Go, Cain saw three more of the flying creatures dart into the clouds, heading away from the city, and he knew that sometime during the opening of the firefight Special Forces had been delivered safely. A sudden movement drew his attention back to the ground. The Mi-Go had distracted the Vugg caused it to focus its attention sky ward, and that was all that was needed to allow the Marines to come in. Cain watched as a lone soldier with three hundred pounds of heavy armor on, darted into the street using what amounted to an immense steel syringe, speared the Vugg just below the neck and pumped the beast full of a lead-based toxin. The harpoon still lodged in the Vugg's neck; the marine rolled away as the worm thing began to thrash about in agony.

Cain's team held their fire, giving the Marine a chance to find cover, and time for the poison to do its job. The Vugg is a composite creature; its strength comes from its ability to decentralize some functions, but to combine others. Separate the monster into its component parts and those individuals become just as vulnerable as any other Whateley. The poison that the marine had delivered was also chock-full of DMSO, a solvent with such a high transmissivity that it had spread the lead compounds right into the central nervous system. In response the Vugg was tearing itself apart, trying to separate contaminated pieces from those that were uncontaminated. It was like watching a child shake apart a stack of legos. The individual parts became easy targets for Romero Squad.

The Vugg was down but it had been only the first assault on their position. Cain ordered suppressing fire as the Whateleys began to swarm up after their fallen brethren. Cain personally covered the Marine as he dashed straight up the road and took shelter behind a low rock wall about twenty feet away. The wall did little to hide the bulk of the amphibious soldier; he was easily seven feet tall and more than three feet wide. Even at this distance Cain could smell the Marine, they all smelled the same, like the sea at low tide. It was pheromonal, something emitted by their gills. Cain called over "What's your name soldier?"

The armor clad Deep One made his way over to Cain's position in a fluid grace that reminded Cain less of running and more of a cross between gymnastics and ballet. "Howard, sir. Ricou Squad. Or what's left of it. It has been one Hell of a day. Intel said there were only Whateleys and two Vugg. They failed to mention the polyp that ambushed us as we came out of the river."

Cain nodded as he fired at another Whateley that had crossed the imaginary line that his mind had drawn down the center of Garrison Street. "Typical. I'm Cain, the brain in the backpack is Phillips."

Cain's earpiece roared to life. "*Shtthnkk*. Cain, I don't appreciate the humor. *Zanhkkk*, The target has been secured and the courier is en route to your position."

"Howard you still armed?"

Howard shook his head. "Only thing I have left is a grenade, and you don't want me to use that until we are ready to leave."

Cain had seen a grenade go off before, and he had no desire to see this one do its work until he was well on his way out. Cain stared down at the swarm of Whateleys. They had reached the nearside of Garrison and were working inevitably forward. Cain and his team were slowing them down, but the horde was going to reach them and when that happened the Tillinghast rail guns would be useless.

"The package is on its way in. I was kind of counting on Ricou Squad to help us defend this position, but it looks like we're going to have to go on the offensive, any objections to going in for a pick up?"

Howard's lidless eyes grew large, and his gills flexed nervously. "Begging your pardon sir, but those Special Forces types give me the creeps."

"I'm with you brother, but we both know that you're a hell of a lot faster than he is, and frankly the sooner we get out of here the better."

Howard figured this out just seconds after Cain. "You have a plan?"

Cain did have a plan, one that just might get them out alive.

With care Cain repositioned his men onto Lich Street. Cover had ceased to matter once the Vugg had started toward them, and as long as he kept out of striking range of the tentacles the squad should remain intact. Evenly spaced, the five men under Cain's command began slowly moving down the avenue, rail guns blazing, Cain and Howard right behind them. When they reached Parsonage Street, he ordered one of the men straight down the center while the other four split into two teams and took up crossfire positions on top of abandoned cars. From a slightly safer position Cain fired into the maddened horde of monsters as Howard searched for any sign of the courier.

To the south, halfway down the block a small figure broke from the shadows and in an instant Howard was dancing down the street like a deranged frog. Cain smiled and tried to stay focused. The boy had guts.

"*Stnzzzzz*, Cain, were running low on ammo. At the current rate of consumption, the team will be out in two minutes."

DAMN IT. Cain ordered the team to a more controlled rate of fire. The Whateleys surged forward, closing the gap in a mere instant.

"HOWARD WE HAVE TO GO! Phillips, send the evac signal." Cain took a step back from the front line.

"*Tsssz*, do we have the package?"

An alarm sounded in Cain's helmet. The man walking down the

centerline was out of ammo. "HOWARD WE HAVE TO GO NOW! Phillips send the evac signal." A second alarm sounded. The things crept closer.

"*Tsssz*, do we have the package?"

A third alarm. "SEND THE GOD DAMNED SIGNAL! HOWARD WHERE THE HELL ARE YOU?!" A fourth alarm, a dam broke, and the wave crashed over into Parsonage Street. Five more alarms went off notifying Cain that the soldiers he had been commanding were gone, the re-animated bodies of Romero Squad had ceased to function.

Suddenly he was in the air, tucked under the left arm of Howard as he made a mad dash toward the graveyard like a deranged quarterback.

"PHILLIPS WE NEED EVAC NOW!"

"*Tsssz*, do we have the package?"

Cain glanced over to the figure tucked under Howard's right arm. It was a hideous thing, as if a rabid jackal had been fused with a man. It reeked of death and decay, of decomposing flesh and sewage, the odors not of its own making, but rather of its food. Ghouls preferred the contents of their meals to be at the minimum several weeks old. Cain gagged at the stench but swallowed the rising wave of vomit as he saw the case being held by the corpse-eater.

"We have the package. WE HAVE THE PACKAGE! NOW GET US THE HELL OUT OF HERE!"

"*ZNNT*, evacuation signal sent."

There was something vaguely comical about all this. Cain and a ghoul tucked underneath the arms of a Deep One running through a graveyard being chased by slobbering hordes of mutant hybrids. Comical in the sense that such a thing would have seemed impossible just a few years ago. War makes strange bedfellows. When the Whateleys attacked, man thought he was alone, the general populace didn't know about the Deep Ones, Ghouls, the Mi-Go or the human brains the Mi-Go had been stealing for millennia. They didn't know they shared the world, the solar system, with things that seemed horrifying, but compared to the Whateleys were just distant cousins. The Mi-Go weren't the worst of course; there were others more alien. But at least they weren't extra-dimensional. The Yith and the Q'Hrell were enigmatic but at least they could be reasoned with. The Deep Ones could even control Shoggoths ...

Cain stared at the phalanx of Whateleys, they were faster than Howard, and it was plain that they weren't going to make it, plain and simple. Something had to be done, and Cain knew what that something was. "Phillips I am sorry." He reached around and ripped the cylindrical brain case off his back. The electric shock came but Cain fought through it and shoved the metallic casing into one of the loops on Howard's belt. Then, without missing a beat he grabbed the last of Howard's grenades and with a swift but well targeted motion, pounded on Howard's elbow with his free hand.

Reflex kicked in and Howard's arm opened sending Cain tumbling to the ground. As he rolled Cain saw the kid pause, he barked an order "KEEP MOVING HOWARD! DELIVER THAT GODDAMN PACKAGE!"

The Whateleys were just yards behind him now, he could hear them pounding, crawling, slithering up the hill. Without hesitation he pulled the pin on the grenade and tossed it in the direction of the Whateleys. In his head he counted

ONE

TWO

THREE

There was an audible click, Cain heard a goddamn click. And then the world exploded, filled with proto-shoggoth matter and pain. Cain never heard the buzzing sound that filled the skies. He never saw the protoplasmic shoggoth swallow up the Whateleys, never saw the Mi-Go swoop down and pluck Howard and the courier out of the graveyard.

Cain never saw these things, never heard them because the proto-shoggoth swallowed him up, blew him out, and sent him flying like so many pieces of meat. He only learned about these things later when they brought him back. Not his body of course, that was gone. But they found his head, and the Mi-Go carefully sealed his brain into a metallic cylinder and set Cain to work.

He works with Phillips and all the other brains; they work on the package, trying to pry loose its secrets. Every once in a while, someone, usually someone with a body, will ask him if it was worth it. He pauses for a moment; he stares through artificial eyes at the ancient pages. Somewhere in this book is the key to freedom, not just for humans, but for all the peoples of the world, maybe the universe.

Was it worth it?

Deep within the last city of men, in the forgotten recesses of Kadath in the Cold Wastes, Cain thinks, "Yes" and goes back to his task of translating the Necronomicon.

The Mania of the Unforgotten

It was three months after I left home that I finally began my journey back. A week to find my way from the forgotten and obscure backwoods village to the edge of what modern men call civilization and then to the hospital where my friend had been interred for his illness. He had been there for years, incarcerated for unspecified crimes, or at least crimes he would not speak of. Not that it mattered. His imprisonment had little to no impact on his life. He had always been a recluse, and this coupled with his outrageous behavior and appearance had garnered him a reputation amongst his fellow artists. He was in all senses a drama queen, but a highly respected one whose artistic sense could not be confined by the walls and chemical treatments of the institution that had attempted to restrain him. His imagination knew no boundaries, some suspected that not even the physical laws of our meager realm could contain it. He was a great dreamer and while his imprisonment had done nothing to diminish his fancy, when his letters to me grew increasingly morbid, recounting the various physical ailments with which he was afflicted I knew it was time for me to visit him.

And so, I journeyed to that place, that blanched institution where he had been installed, with the full intent of bringing him home. Imagine my disillusionment when I discovered the extent of his degenerative condition and that the doctors who tended for him refused to release him to my care. Frustrated beyond all reason I foolishly made threats and intimidations, acts that under the circumstances should have been more carefully considered. With little fanfare and even less due process I found myself constrained to the very same institute my friend had been obligated to.

My incarceration caused little change to my daily routine; indeed, I was able to spend more time with my aging comrade than when I was free. Thus, it was that I came to the most disheartening of conclusions.

The Mania of the Unforgotten

My friend was dying, and there was nothing to be done about it. Perhaps the most maddening consideration was that my friend was well aware of his situation and of the dire consequences that his passing would entail. It was through his conspiratorial advice that I pursued a plan to leave the facility and return to the shadowed valley that I called home. As forlorn as it made me, I left the bed of my beloved friend and resigned myself to never seeing him again. Indeed, I avoided him as much as possible, going so far as to even suggesting that I had never known the man in the first place.

It was a month of lies before the doctors said I could travel. A month incarcerated behind sterile walls, walking down guarded halls, listening to the sobbing wails of those whose melancholy had overwhelmed them, and to the shrieking howls of shackled lunatics the law had deemed criminally insane. A month to let my wounds heal, a month to let smooth-faced interns and hoary senior physicians poke and prod and probe me—not just physically, but psychically as well. My doctors specialized more in the mind than the body, though I suffered through interminable examinations of both kinds. A month of their introspective gaze and they finally deemed me fit to travel. Not cured mind you, not well, merely fit enough to leave their care and venture forth into the world. And specifically, not alone, that simply would not do.

Dr. J, an alienist of few years, spry enough to travel and not valued enough to be missed from service, would come with. It was his duty to assure my behavior was acceptable while I was shepherded home, and then once we were there, find a suitable guardian to whom my care could be allocated to. Of course, we would both be escorted by Mr. B, a hospital orderly whose iron-grey hair betrayed the passage of years that his face had somehow avoided. The hospital had graciously provided transport. We would be conveyed in an official vehicle, a black sedan registered for official travel. I was just thankful it wasn't an ambulance or even a police car. Could you imagine my shame at being driven around in such a vehicle? I would have died from the embarrassment. We were an incongruous trio—the doctor, an orderly and their tamed hysteric tethered by a regiment of properly administered pharmaceuticals. I was fit alright, as long as Dr. J fed me my medication in the proper dosages and at the appropriate times.

It was on the morning that we were to leave that word came concerning my friend's condition. Details were limited but from the whispered rumors it was clear that he was no longer conscious, and his breathing was labored. I considered my options. There was some value, at least from a caring perspective to my staying and looking after my friend, but there was also a risk. My friend and I had discussed such things and we had decided on a course of action. It was not my place to change those tactics when he was no longer able to communicate.

So, we drove. From the manicured gardens of the hospital and on to black asphalt ribbons daubed with streaks of titanium white where death by velocity and momentum or sudden changes thereof seemed to be imminent. It was only through the skill of Mr. B that we survived at all, and I was surprised that I had not fallen victim to a bout of apoplexy. I suppose that was why Dr. J was there, to comfort me, and to administer the pills.

From the highway we found our way up worn stone byways wrapped round tortuous hills, and down into verdant vales choked with misshapen trees and an undergrowth of impenetrable brambles. Inevitably, the primitive road crossed a region of fetid creeks where gluttonous frogs watched our passing with glistening black eyes. They called to us—to me—in their fat, croaking voices. The chorus of their obscene grunting were words that burned into my brain. *Hurry,* they called in a cacophonous refrain, *you must hurry.*

I turned to see what my physician thought of the things that were being said as the sedan rushed passed, but Dr. J took no notice. I dared not say a word of such things lest he take out the thin black leather journal that was hidden in his coat. I feared he would use a small pencil and make a note, all the time his head shaking ever so slightly, and his tongue pressed up against his teeth issuing forth a disapproving *TskTskTsk.* Or perhaps he might take it upon himself to change my medication—to increase both the frequency and amount that I had to suffer under, my brain already swam in a fog, I could not risk making that worse. There was of course another risk, he could consult with Mr. B and then they would both decide that the other doctors had been wrong and that I was not well enough to travel. My journey would be cut short, and the captain would turn our conveyance around and I would have to endure the trip home in silent frustrated rage—lest my rights and privileges be even further curtailed. So, I said nothing. The frogs croaked, and I listened to their words that urged me on in a language only I could understand, and I said nothing.

But within my breast a dread anxiety grew, and it was only through the extreme force of will that I kept it in check. But all the time I wanted to scream, to rage against the dawdling pace at which we voyaged. *Faster*, I wanted to demand, *go faster you obtuse dullard. I must get home before it is too late.* But I said nothing. I held my tongue and let my keepers proceed at their own pace. No matter how damnably slow it was. I thought back to when I was detained, there was in my apprehension no sense of lingering sluggishness. Indeed, my seizure had been carried out with surprising haste, one might even say it had been a whirlwind of judicial process. Now that I was on the verge of liberty there seemed to be an undue amount of hindrance. It had only taken a few men and a handful of papers to imprison me, release apparently required an entire bureaucracy. And whereas my initial intake was handled with raised voices and ear-piercing claxons, my return was almost lackadaisical, an exemplar of tranquility, a condition I found almost intolerable.

It was near dusk, the sun setting behind the mountains to the west when the scenery began to look familiar and take on that strange ethereal quality that my home is known for. Dr. J was looking at the map, but we had left documented thoroughfares behind long ago, and it was up to me to provide direction to Mr. B, though there wasn't much in the way of direction to provide. The road was the road, it twisted and turned, sinistral in its own way. Working its way through the landscape with nary a turn or crossroad to ignore. All around us the groves grew denser and gloomier as the road angled upward over the meager bones of a mountain worn-down by time into little more than a hillock. There was a turn there, hidden in the shadows of a copse of ancient willows their branches wafting in the wind like the shrouds of mourners.

At my direction Mr. B took the secreted byway, just as Dr. J's cellphone chirped alive. We passed through the trees and the shadows they cast made the whole world disappear. I recited a small prayer to the gods for safe passage. Mr. B gripped the wheel tightly. Dr. J shouted into his phone as if the contraption would carry his voice back to civilization if he just spoke loud enough. There was a weak flash of light as we passed through an opening in the canopy, but then it was gone, and we plunged back into darkness. I held my breath. I counted to three. And then just like that we were through to the other side, and I smiled a wicked smile, happy to be home.

My delight was short lived, Dr. J tapped Mr. B on the shoulder, the phone still pressed up against his ear. "Pull over here," he ordered. Then his attention turned back to the phone. "Yes, yes I can hear you now." He went on talking, but my attention was drawn elsewhere. As the car stopped, I opened the door and cautiously stepped out into the world, my first step of true freedom in such a very long time.

It should have been a joyous occasion. There should have been a small village, little more than a cluster of a few buildings with a few more aging homes along the road in the distance. From where I stood, I should have been able to see the roof of a tower poking through the trees on the slope of the mountain to the west, and there at its crest a double peak and the hint of a Brobdingnag face in the crags on the northside. I should have been able to hear the wind rushing through the forest carrying with it an eerie almost outré melody whistled perhaps by some dark spawn of an elder goddess who had once touched the earth in this eldritch spot. There should be residents, townsfolk come out to greet us—not men exactly, but close enough to fool the casual eye. There should have been something, anything really, but there was nothing. The whole area was a barren wasteland, a mire of sand broken only by windswept debris. Even the mountain was gone. To the west as far as I could see the village, the valley, the wood, and the mountain that it rested under were gone. As if they had never existed.

Behind me, a car door slammed. Dr. J was speaking to someone on the phone. "No, we are here now. No, just as we suspected, there's nothing here. Hold on." His eyes met mine. "You should know, your friend at the hospital he's ... "

"Dead," I said cutting him off.

Dr. J shrugged and went back to his phone. "We won't be here long. We'll be back late tonight."

I fell to my knees. I felt tears well up in my eyes. I was too late. My friend—our friend—was dead, and with him the dream that sustained our home. I picked up a handful of earth, but it wasn't earth, not as I knew it. It was little more than ash, the legacy of something that once was but wasn't any longer. Touching it left me feeling empty, I couldn't even mourn properly.

Out of the corner of my eye I watched Dr. J put his phone in his pocket. "Mr. B would you please help our patient back to the car?"

I bowed my head as Mr. B took a step forward and then another. If I could not mourn for my friend, or the world he had created and that I had lived in, then at least I could take pity on my own self, destined it seemed to be entombed in a state psychiatric hospital for the rest of my life, or until the memory of wonder and magicks faded and I could be integrated into society. For this torment, this torture, this sentence, this I could weep for.

But Mr. B's hand never came for me. There was instead a strange wet piercing sound, and then a gasp of breath, followed by a dripping that beat out a strange tattoo on the ground. I turned to look at as Dr. J fell to his knees—a stain of crimson on his white shirt. Mr. B circled round him a flash of steel in his hand. It was so fast. One moment the good doctor's head was attached to his body, and then in the next it wasn't. The blood ran crimson over the body and down into the ashes that pretended to be earth, and those sad cinders soaked it up hungrily.

Mr. B knelt down next to the body and his eyes caught mine as he drew the ancient sigils and signs and encircled his sacrifice with the proper wardings. "I believe," he said as the last glyph was cast in blood and dust, "I have always believed."

We rose up together as the air between us shimmered, and the sky melted, and the skein of the world parted. I could see what was inside, on the other side. I could see the mountain, and the valley and the village that nestled in the shadows. I could see a figure its hand beckoning.

I walked over to Mr. B, "How?"

He shook his head. "I was his caretaker for years, decades. I read the things he wrote, the things he dreamt about, the things he loved. I fell in love with his world, and I suppose with him as well. When he got sick, we made plans. Your arrival complicated things but nothing really changed. He taught me what had to be done." He looked at the body and the magickal circle and the rent in the fabric or reality he had coaxed into being. "Wasn't really sure it would work."

I looked back at the figure that waved at me, was it me, or was it Mr. B that was being summoned? "You should go," I said.

He shook his head. "It's not my time yet. You need a dreamer to anchor the village to the world. I can do that for you. Not today, not tomorrow, but soon. I'll master the art of dreaming and then I'll bring you back. I'll bring you all back."

I opened my mouth to speak but he raised a bloody finger and pressed it against my lips. "It won't stay open for long; you need to go."

I pulled his hand away. "At least tell me your name."

He pulled me close, and I felt his breath against my cheek as he spoke his name into my ear. As he pulled away, I wrapped my hand around his neck and pulled his face toward mine. I kissed him, the blood and sweat rushed into my mouth. And then I stepped back and fell into the dream, the dream my friend had fashioned from years of terror and joy and mania.

We are still there, we zanies of dark mania, waiting. We know we won't be forgotten, at least not for long.

In memory of Wilum Hopfrog Pugmire

Author's Afterword

I have always told stories, my friend Joe Pulver use to joke that I needed to tell stories, not as an occupation or to entertain, but to quiet the voices in my head. He wasn't wrong. I suffer from insomnia, driven mostly by an overactive imagination that won't let me stop thinking. When I was younger, before I started to write, I would be up into the wee hours reading or watching old movies on UHF channels. It instilled in me a love of Abbot and Costello, Charlie Chan, The Thin Man, Godzilla, and B-Grade horror movies, mostly because these were the things that kept me distracted.

Learning to write changed everything, but to start off things weren't very good. I binned most of my juvenilia, but there's still a whole trunk full of hand-written stories under the bed, including a Robert E. Howard Kathulos pastiche on an old legal pad. Thankfully I've never outgrown pastiche. I don't think there is anything wrong with it, plus I try to be just a bit subversive with it.

The Cthulhu Heresy and Other Lovecraftian Sins highlights about fifteen years of fevered writing, some of which was hard to sell. The fundamental idea behind the Heresy Quartet is a rejection of nearly a century of Cthulhu Mythos canon – the idea that Cthulhu fthagn – that Cthulhu still sleeps. There are a whole stable of editors who simply refused to accept my rejection of that idea, and my offering of an alternative. I am not the first to suggest this; John Brunner's *The Atlantic Abomination*, and Larry Niven's *World of Ptavvs* are essentially mythos stories in which Cthulhu wakes up and begins to ravage humanity. Robert Bloch does something subtly similar with *Strange Eons*, while Charles Stross shoves it in our face with *A Colder War*. But all of these rely on the fundamental conflict of man versus the mythos, the Cthulhu Heresy postulates that Cthulhu doesn't care at all about Earth, or mankind, or the other creatures that dwell on it that might serve him, and just moves on, without even a wave goodbye, and that has a devastating impact on those that worship him or are artistically sensitive to his cosmic psyche. A bunch of editors rejected the idea out right, or demanded I do severe rewrites to bring it in line with the rest of the genre. They didn't want to shake things up.

But the Cthulhu Mythos needs to be shaken up. It constantly needs new voices, new perspectives, new ideas, new characters, new tropes and new ground to push it new directions. For example, back in 1996 *The Call of Cthulhu* roleplaying adventure *Masks of Nyarlathotep* introduced The God of the Bloody Tongue avatar, at the time it was an incredible new representation of the monstrous god, now nearly thirty years on, its rather commonplace (I even think there is a plushy). Thankfully, because its mostly in the public domain, someone is always writing mythos fiction. Admittedly, most of what gets labelled as mythos fiction simply isn't, or maybe it is, but it's simply a rehash or terribly written. The editor David Hartwell used to talk about pieces of fiction that help to move the genre forward. And every so often a piece appears that does that, that is simply brilliant, daring, dangerous. A piece that bucks the norm and because of that it stands out, and you may not like it, but its needed.

I like to think that one or two of my stories do this, that they stand out, stand above, stand the test of time. I hope that decades from now this book sits on some collector's shelf and is treasured for a selection, some small fraction of the words within. I can't imagine a better legacy for what I am trying to do here.

Pete Rawlik
The Devil's Garden, Florida

Publication History

"Here Be Monsters" first published in *Dead but Dreaming 2*, Miskatonic River Press, 2011.

"The Innsmouth Revelation" first published in *Fungi #21*, edited by Pierre Comtois, 2013.

"Down Through Black Abysses" first published in *A Lonely and Curious Country*, edited by Matthew Carpenter, Ulthar Press, 2015.

"Notes for a Life of Nightmares: A Retrospective on the Work of Henry Anthony Wilcox" first published in *Cthulhu Lies Dreaming*, edited by Salome Jones, Ghostwood Books, 2016.

"The Ghost Stones of Mthura" first published in *Skelos #4*, 2020.

"Arkham Arts Review: Alienation" first published in *Fossil Lake* edited by Christine Morgan, Davearna Enterprises, 2014; second publication in *Fossil Lake* edited by Christine Morgan, Sable Drake, 2014.

"The Angels of Pestilence" first published online in Shoggoth.net, Dec. 2022.

"The Best Laid Plans" first published online in Shoggoth.net, Dec 2022.

"The Calliope Comes Back" first published in *Caravans Awry* (2018) edited by Duane Pesice.

"The Spaces Between" first publisehd in *Lovecraft Ezine #38*, September 2016, edited by Mike Davis; second publication in *The Black Stone*, curated by Raffaelle Pezzella, Eighth Tower Publications, 2021

"The Guilt of Nikki Cotton" first published in *Heroes of Red Hook*, 2016, edited by Oscar Rios.

"By the Light of the Moon" first published in *Between Twilight and Dawn*, 2020, edited by Oscar Rios.

"The Cats in the Pall" first published in *Tails of Terror* 2018, edited by Brian Sammons.

"The Posthumous Recruitment of Timothy Horne" first published in *Tomorrow's Cthulhu*, edited by Scott Gable, Broken Eye Books, 2016.

"The Eye of Cybele" first published in *Further Tales of Cthulhu Invictus*, 2017, edited by Oscar Rios and Brian Sammons.

"Aysaqendisia" first published in *Lustcraftian Horrors*, 2021, Hydra M. Starr.

"The Last Days of Ulthar" first published in *Weird Tails*, 2020, edited by Robert Poynton.

"Island of Gathogtha" first published in *Tales of Cthulhu Invictus, Britannia*, 2020, edited by Oscar Rios.

"The Collection of Gibson Flynn" first published in *The Children of Glaaki*, 2017, edited by Sammons and Barrass.

"A Man of Letters" first published in *Innsmouth Magazine*, February 2012.

"The Battle of Arkham" first published in *Eldritch Chrome*, edited by Brian Sammons and Glynn Owen Barrass, Chaosium, 2013.

"The Mania of the Unforgotten" first published in *Vasterian*, Spring 2020, Vol 3 Issue 1.

About the Author

PETE RAWLIK is a long-time collector of Lovecraftian fiction, and in 1985 stole a car to go see the film *Reanimator*. He successfully defended himself by explaining that his father had regularly read him *The Rats in the Wall* as a bedtime story. His first professional sale was in 1997 but he didn't begin to write seriously until 2010. Since then, he has authored more than fifty short stories and the Cthulhu Mythos novels *Reanimators*, *The Weird Company*, *Reanimatrix*, and *The Eldritch Equations*. In 2014 his short story "Revenge of the Reanimator" was nominated for a New Pulp Award. In 2015 he co-edited *The Legacy of the Reanimator* for Chaosium. Somewhere along the line he became known as the Reanimator guy, but he fervently denies being obsessed with the character. He lives in southern Florida where he works on Everglades issues and in his spare time tries to go fishing.

About the Artist

DAN SAUER is a graphic designer and artist living in Salem, Oregon. In 2016, he co-founded (with editor/publisher Obadiah Baird) The Audient Void: A Journal of Weird Fiction and Dark Fantasy, which features his design and illustration work. Since 2017, he has worked extensively on book covers, interior art, and custom typography and other graphics for Hippocampus Press, Centipede Press and other publishers. His art often takes the form of surreal collage and photomontage, as pioneered by artists such as Max Ernst, Wilfried Sätty, J. K. Potter and Harry O. Morris. In 2020, he launched his own publishing imprint, Jackanapes Press, which is devoted to publishing weird fiction, poetry and other strange things.

www.JackanapesPress.com
www.DanSauerDesign.com